I0772614

THE SMELL OF TELESCOPES

A Collection

by

Rhys Hughes

Eibonvale Press
www.eibonvalepress.co.uk

'The Smell of Telescopes'

This edition published in 2007 by Eibonvale Press
www.eibonvalepress.co.uk

Copyright: Rhys Hughes 2006

Cover art and design and interior illustration by David Rix,
copyright 2007

Author Photograph by Hannah Lawson

Printed by Lightning Source
www.lightningsource.com

Originally published by Tartarus Press, 2000.

CIP - Kataložni zapis o publikaciji
Narodna in univerzitetna knjižnica, Ljubljana

821.111-32

HUGHES, Rhys
The Smell of Telescopes / a collection by Rhys Hughes. -
Ljubljana : Eibonvale, 2006

ISBN 961-91652-1-7

224396032

THE SMELL OF TELESCOPES

A Collection

by

Rhys Hughes

Eibonvale Press
www.eibonvalepress.co.uk

'The Smell of Telescopes'

This edition published in 2007 by Eibonvale Press
www.eibonvalepress.co.uk

Copyright: Rhys Hughes 2006

Cover art and design and interior illustration by David Rix,
copyright 2007

Author Photograph by Hannah Lawson

Printed by Lightning Source
www.lightningsource.com

Originally published by Tartarus Press, 2000.

CIP - Kataložni zapis o publikaciji
Narodna in univerzitetna knjižnica, Ljubljana

821.111-32

HUGHES, Rhys
The Smell of Telescopes / a collection by Rhys Hughes. -
Ljubljana : Eibonvale, 2006

ISBN 961-91652-1-7

224396032

To
Sarita Sikka

*tantrinada kabitta rasa, sarasa raga rati ranga
anabure bure, tire, je bure saba anga*
——Bihari

Contents

9   The Banker of Ingolstadt

21   Ten Grim Bottles

35   Spermaceti Whiskers

49   The Blue Dwarf

59   The Purloined Liver

71   The Squonk Laughed

81   Telegram Ma'am

93   Depressurised Ghost Story

113   Thanatology Spleen

127   The Tell-Tale Nose

139   A Girl Like a Doric Column

147   The Orange Goat

157   Nothing More Common

177   Muscovado Lashes

195   A Person Not in the Story

225   Bridge Over Troubled Blood

Contents

245   Burke and Rabbit

259   The Yellow Imp

275   Lanolin Brows

295   The Haunted Womb

313   Mister Humphrey's Clock's Inheritance

335   There was a Ghoul Dwelt by a Mosque

343   The Purple Pastor

371   The Hush of Falling Houses

395   The Sickness of Satan

421   Omophagia Ankles

THE BANKER
OF
INGOLSTADT

"I wish to open a student account."

The clerk removed his tinted spectacles and wiped them with a dirty cloth. The figure seated across the desk had the hungry appearance of the usual undergraduate, the pale skin and sunken eyes, but was plainly a lunatic. He considered ringing the bell for assistance, but a quick glance around the chamber confirmed that most of the staff had finished work early. So he cleared his throat and muttered:

"You are registered at the university?"

"That's correct. I'm studying *Sociology and Reanimation* with Doctor Waldman. Is there a problem? I was told that your bank offers discounts on carriage travel and tickets for the multistage opera, not to mention a 200 florin bonus for freshers, and a 1000 shilling overdraft facility subject to prior arrangement. Have I made an embarrassing error? Shall I deposit my grant cheque elsewhere?"

"Let us not be hasty. The Bank of Bavaria is indeed rather generous with its terms for customers entering Higher Education. But I'm afraid we have to be completely open with each other and you have already tried to deceive me. Perhaps you would consider a Golden Oven account instead? To put a crust on your funds! How about a Double Mangle? That one limits withdrawals to 10 doubloons a week, but is index linked to the number of fatalities in wars with Prussia or France. Every type of account is open to you – except the one tailored for students. You can't possibly have enrolled at Ingolstadt university."

"Why not? I judge that a gross insult!"

The clerk toyed with a quill resting on a vast ledger. "Because, Fräulein Radcliffe, you are a woman!"

"Absolutely! The first female to register with Doctor Waldman on the *Sociology and Reanimation* modules."

She added darkly: "It's a Rancid Sandwich Course!"

Curling his lower lip around a clubbed finger, the clerk moistened the tip with an inky spittle, opened the ledger and proceeded to flick through the sheets. His prints crowded each other out on every page, as if he derived pleasure from smudging the names scratched in neat rows, in lieu of blotting the identities of the owners. Finally, he reached the last page and slammed the book shut.

"These are the financial records of every student who has opened an account here since the founding of the college in 1250. Not a single one has ever been a woman. Indeed, there's not enough space in the margins to write 'Fräulein' instead of 'Herr'. And suppose you did deposit your grant cheque with us? We could hardly mix your funds with the male money in the student vault – that would be unseemly. A new vault would have to be constructed just for you, and painted pink, with lace hanging from the combination dial on the lock. Do you truly want to put us to so much bother? I'm sorry, Fräulein Radcliffe."

"Call me Mina." She brushed back her auburn hair and undid the top button of her bodice. "If I open a Double Mangle account, my money will also have to be stored with that of men."

The clerk clucked his tongue disapprovingly. "You sound excited by the concept. No, that's an account for feeble pensioners, which is why I'm amenable to extending its terms to you. There will be a surcharge, of course, to pay for a chaperone. Now then, do you have any proof of identification?"

Mina placed her handbag on the desk. The clerk frowned. It appeared to be sewn from many different types of leather, but the skins had been badly cured, and had not originated on any domestic animal. Parts of the bag sprouted hairs, dark and fair, while other patches were studded with nipples or navels – cameo and intaglio designs which suggested motherhood rather than a fashion accessory, with something embryonic in its womb, a sextet of mysteries, if one might pardon the expression. Then she pulled apart the enamel clasp – a tooth in a gum – and rummaged around for a minute, finally producing a square card which held a miniature portrait in oils of her likeness, and an official stamp.

"Oh dear, Fräulein!" muttered the clerk. "That is a Students' Union Card, and as we have already established, there is no such thing as a female undergraduate. I don't know how you came by it, though I suspect theft or forgery, but I am not willing to be duped by such tricks." He indicated the ledger. "As I said, there has never been a woman with a student account in our business history."

"May I see?" Mina drew the ledger toward her with two delicate but strong hands. The clerk averted his eyes as her wrists slipped out from her sleeves. A dim urge vaulted the security barrier which separated his id from his ego, a desire to lean across the desk and touch her knee. He repressed it and gasped. Did he know *how* to touch a woman's knee? The answer was negative, but a disturbing memory came loose from the spike where it had been impaled, ready for filing and obfuscation. It flapped around inside his cranium. The palm rests on the kneecap, the fingers close around it, the hand slides gradually up... No, it was a fraudster! An impostor memory!

He was rescued by a squeal of delight from Mina, who had found an entry which excited her. For a moment, he was worried, fearing she had discovered a name to challenge his assertion, but he knew the ledger like the back of his pituitary gland. What was she saying now? He rubbed his ears, feeling a little dizzy, twiddling the moles on his neck.

"Look, it's his signature! I can't believe he really sat here and signed this!" Mina pressed her lips to the name in faded ink. "Victor Frankenstein!"

"Who? Oh, that wastrel! Yes, I remember him well. He defaulted on a loan. Said he wanted funds to insulate the attic of his lodgings and then spent the money on electric eels! You're not related to him, are you?"

"Heavens, no! Victor was by birth a Genevese, and his family was one of the most distinguished of that republic. I am from Montevideo, but my father was English. Have you really nothing better to say about this incredible genius? It was Victor who first succeeded in imparting life to the limbs and organs of corpses. Without his pioneering work, the university of Ingolstadt would not now be running its *Reanimation* courses. He was my hero when I was growing up on the outskirts of my home town. I remember attempting to galvanise a dead horse when all my friends wanted to do was arrange flowers or tie ribbons in their hair – at least I thought it was dead! And when my mother expired of cholera, I insisted on attaching two electrodes to her temples and flying a kite in a storm. It didn't work, but I still recall the detonation inside her coffin. I keep the ashes in this locket. Would you care to see?"

"Those ashes are coloured, Fräulein!"

"Well, my mother was a mulatto. Originally from Senegal."

The clerk flicked his dirty cloth over his perspiring face. He felt that his tongue had swollen at the back of his throat. "Then you are part black?"

"Indeed. Is there a difficulty with that?"

For a brief instant, he started to rise to his feet, but the cold air which rushed to ventilate his stale buttocks was so original and alarming a sensation that he reversed the direction of force and pushed himself down as firmly as possible. But his voice had the shriek of one who has stood to shake a finger.

"And you still insist you have enrolled at the university, here in Ingolstadt, with its white steeple and civilised cobbles? A Hottentot floosie!"

Mina narrowed her eyes and the icy beams which stabbed from their green depths chilled the marrow in six of the clerk's ribs.

"It is a great privilege for me," she said quietly, "to study with Doctor Waldman, the same scholar who taught chemistry to Victor Frankenstein. I will now trouble you no further, but take my money to an alternative bank."

Quick as a pig's tail in a mincer, the clerk shot out his arm and seized Mina's elbow. He made a valiant attempt to smile. "I assure you, Fräulein Radcliffe, that no other bank will be interested in dealing with a tainted female. Not only that, but there are, in fact, no other banks in Ingolstadt. However, the Bank of Bavaria is more tolerant and generous than most. So let us consider our little problem. You wish to open a student account, but it is impossible for you to be a student. When I suggest a more suitable type of account, you grow surly. We are getting nowhere. Thus I suggest a private arrangement, just between you and me. I will hold the money for you, mingled with my own savings. If you wish to make a withdrawal, you may visit me after closing hours."

"Mingle my money? Where is your prudishness now?"

He shuddered away her objections. "My savings have no interest in physical contact, I assure you. They prefer to reproduce through sheer fiscal discipline. Naturally, there will be a hefty charge for this favour – I will have to falsify documents."

Mina's voice quavered slightly. "How can I be sure you will not try to cheat me?" She watched for any betrayal of compassion in his answer, the merest flicker of humanity, but there was none.

"Ah, but I *will* cheat you, Fräulein! You shall have to come to my lodgings whenever you require a few coins. There will be a strict limit on how much you may withdraw at one time. You will be compelled to visit me often. My rooms are very secluded. They have never known a female presence. Even the fleas are exclusively male. It is strange, but when I consider my history, I find a number of anomalies... Different memories, many of which do not belong to me. As if once I was married... Please excuse me, I am rambling. Your astonishing implication that women are somehow equal to men has quite disordered my senses."

"Very well. You leave me no choice. My grant cheque is worthless unless it is cashed. I have rent to pay, books and equipment to buy. I have a glittering career ahead, and I do not wish to spoil it by dying in the gutter."

"Your mind almost has a grasp of algorithmic reasoning, Fräulein. I applaud you. Every phenomenon is prone to the occasional incongruity. Supernovae in distant galaxies, irregularities in chasing up debtors, and now a girl who thinks like a man!" He lowered his tone to a clipped snarl. "Sign the back of the cheque and write a short contractual statement declaring that you hereby entrust the entire amount to my keeping."

Mina took the quill, dipped it in a pot of ink near her elbow and scratched the required marks on the cheque. She dried her signature by flapping the piece of paper before passing it to the clerk, who folded it and slipped it into his top pocket. Then she asked: "May I have my first instalment now? Just a shilling or two."

With a nonchalance which had something of the madhouse about it, in the same way that even a kind smile can suggest the final closing of a dungeon door, the clerk replaced his tinted spectacles. Now he was isolated from her, filtered out from his own humanity, which still seemed to consist of many parts. He rested his elbows on the desk, cradled his chin in his hands and sniffed. "Do I know you, Fräulein?"

"I demand the return of my money!"

"What is all this fuss? I have no idea what you are talking about. Do you suppose you can just burst in here and threaten a member of staff? The Bank of Bavaria always takes very good care of its employees. A single shake of this silver bell will summon guards who will hurl you into the street! And why have you unbuttoned your bodice? This is most unwelcome. Remove yourself from my restricted sight!"

A thousand expressions crossed Mina's face. At last her visage settled on a single aspect, a clench of jaw and

smouldering of eyes which was poised midway between impotent fury and – here the clerk felt a vague discomfort – languid amusement. His throat uttered an injunction of its own, tinged with too much panic, a croak scarred and notched with a rasp.

"Begone! Take your provocative bosom and radical egalitarianism away!"

Mina's tears were perhaps just a little strained. She clutched at the lapels of his coat, sending clouds of dust toward the panelled ceiling.

"I have a family to support! My fiancé is a poor tailor!"

His lips trembled, at different velocities, as if they attended rival funerals. He struggled to maintain his heartlessness, but now there were two organs pumping congealed blood inside his chest – hers as well as his own, or so it felt. He ached, and his fingers probed for the button of a secret compartment in the desk. The hidden drawer slid open and he plucked a coin from a mound, pushed it across to her and hissed: "Here, Fräulein. I can hardly keep up this charade. I want to be callous, I really do, but somehow you have touched me in places I had no idea I possessed. My sympathy – ah, how I shiver to use such a word! – has been roused. Please take this guinea."

She almost seemed disappointed. "Are you sure?"

He nodded and sat back, awaiting her gratitude, but she sighed and lifted her peculiar handbag onto the desk, obscuring the golden coin. Then she dipped inside and produced a selection of blades, scissors and little picks, tiny saws and screwdrivers.

"A sewing-kit, Fräulein? Really, this is hardly the time to start mending socks!"

The last item to emerge was a hammer. Mina weighed it carefully in one hand for a moment, nodded to herself and arched over the desk to deliver a single blow to the forehead of the clerk. He felt the shape of the wound, a hexagonal dent with impact lines radiating across his skull, like a multifaceted third eye or mystic sunburst in the centre of his brow. He was much too astonished to collapse or emit a scream. But the assault had also dislodged his sense of time. He realised that Mina was now standing next to him, a screwdriver inserted into one of the moles on his neck, twisting the tool furiously.

"What is this? Are you murdering me?"

"You have failed the test. You must be dismantled."

And then he did shriek, but it was a short-lived example of the form, for when he opened his mouth, Mina used the opportunity to insert her scissors and snip off his tongue.

Mumbling thickly as the oedematous blood filled his throat, he remembered the bell and reached out to ring it, but again she anticipated his intention and lopped his fingers and thumb off with a miniature cleaver, so that they tumbled over the edge of the desk and bounced on the mosaic floor. Her hands and implements seemed to be all over him, prodding, jabbing, cutting, wrenching. Now she was on her knees beneath him, slicing between his thighs. He bent forward and vomited blood, which spattered onto the upper curve of her partly exposed breasts and gushed in torrents between her cleavage. Constricted at the waist by a belt, the bodice positively bulged with his gore until it frothed back out of her bosom, and, as her breasts wobbled with the work, the red juice spurted in thin jets.

This was hardly the climax to his career he had been expecting. Half a century of plodding toil in the security of his position, inconspicuous but lurking, like a glass spider, before retirement to a small villa in the Böhmer Wald, done up to resemble an office. He had always believed himself to be suspended between two unknown worlds: that of his managers, who inhabited a cubic empire of interlocking conference chambers, awash with the odours of walnut, wine and bathchair lacquer, and that of his clients, which resembled a straight line, a street in a poor suburb, packed with terraced houses without a chink between, leading from one infinite smoky horizon to another. But now both worlds were growing dim, and tears were hatching from under his lids, as Mina struggled to lever his eyeballs out of their sockets with spoons. Both suddenly came free, with a horrible slurping sound, and as they dropped onto his cheeks, they swung like the pendulums of a cuckoo death, the optic nerves of one entangling with those of the other, braiding his visionary sense into that of a Siamese cyclops.

For the first time in his life, one eye was able to directly stare at its twin. It was a different shape, feminine – for the lashes high above were fluttering. Many parts he; now they were leaving him, returning home, and he almost recollected an earlier dissolution, numerous accidents. Mina, he realised, had returned to the mole on his neck. It was not a mole after all, but a bolt, with a screw-thread which passed through his throat. It held his head to his shoulders and she was loosening it with an adjustable spanner. It came out with an inner screech, and his skull began to wobble alarmingly. He attempted to stand, but he lacked knees: they lay under the desk. And every cell of his body rejoiced to be liberated from an unnatural fusion.

There was still time to ring for assistance. Limbless, voiceless, there was only one course of action available. He nodded at the bell and his head fell from his torso, rolling on the polished surface of the desk and knocking the bell over the edge. It tinkled once as it landed. Then before utter blackness blew into every corner of his mind, he became aware of the wall splitting from ceiling to floor. It was a concealed door, and through it came an ancient figure, thin and menacing, with a shock of white hair and a peculiar limp. Was this the manager of the bank? His hopes fell with his blood pressure as the figure cried:

"Tough luck, Mina. The practical is always the hardest part."

"Sorry, Doctor Waldman. I tried my best."

"I know you did."

"It was nearly right. After my theory exam I was so confident. But there was a trace of compassion buried in its subconscious. It had to be destroyed. A single flaw and the creature is useless."

"This is a discipline for perfectionists, Mina. I believe you will do better in the resits."

"I hope so, Doctor Waldman. I certainly intend to use these limbs again. They performed very well. But the head is not right. Back to the morgue, I think!"

"Let me help you cram all the pieces in your handbag. You are my favourite student, Mina, and I know you will go far. I feel it in my selection of hearts."

"My only wish is to emulate Victor Frankenstein."

"Oh, you will surpass his achievements. Your aptitude is as staggering as your originality. What a remarkable project for your finals! The Utterly Evil Banker!"

Together they passed through the door, locking it behind them. The props would remain until the examination room could be booked for a resit.

In a corridor of the university, Mina stopped and clutched at Doctor Waldman's sleeve. Her eyes were like icecaps awaiting a mysterious sledge.

"I must succeed," she said, "for the sake of the human race. The centuries to come will be characterised by unrestrained progress. Science will give us weapons of which we cannot conceive. Motorised guns which can spray thousands of bullets every minute, flying machines which can level whole cities with explosives, armoured wagons and undersea boats, rockets capable of sending germs or poisons to distant countries in a matter of hours, unimagined sources of destructive power borrowed from the sun, mystic rays to blind or carve up crowds, electric gadgets able to monitor and punish citizens. In short, everything necessary for autocrats to stamp their psychoses over the nations of the world! And who will create these devastating tools? Graduates, that's who! What better way to limit their excesses than to nip them in the grant?"

"You always grasp the big picture, Mina."

"We must ensure that as many students as possible are discouraged from graduating. They must be mercilessly hassled at the fresher stage until they drop out. Naturally, there will be those who refuse to abandon their studies, but I can't be expected to cure the problem, merely alleviate it. If my Utterly Evil Banker proves a success, and if I can get it to breed, the banks of the future might be staffed by callous sadists, working tirelessly to oppose students. Such is my dream, Doctor Waldman. I am banking on monsters!"

He patted her shoulder admiringly. "That is what *Sociology and Reanimation* is all about."

Arm in arm, they strolled to the morgue. But they kept their own arms folded.

TEN GRIM BOTTLES

I want to tell a story about the cannibal who lives under our old stone bridge but first I need some characters and a pot – I mean a plot. Not much is known about him. It is almost certain that he has lived there since the beginning of time and answers to the name Toby. Aside from that, he is often feared for his bad breath. He never cleans his teeth between travellers.

Lladloh village is just that sort of place. There are too many wonders to get worked up over one little cannibal. The uncanny is a part of everyday life; if you can't digest the odd over breakfast, it is best you leave quickly or do not come in the first place. Having said that, the village is impossible to find unless your arrival is absolutely essential for some anecdote or other.

There was a gaunt fellow who came to visit us last summer. I remember him as a flapping crow of a man, all dressed in faded black, with a tall hat and a nose. This nose was so prominent, so remarkable, that nothing more need be said about it. But his dark cloak rose high in the wind as he roared in on his old motorcycle and he cut quite an impressive figure. Glum as the devil's dentist, I said to myself.

In his battered sidecar, poorly concealed by a dusty tarpaulin, a box of tall blue bottles jumped. The stranger stopped his motorcycle in front of the public house and made his way inside. In the gloomy interior, he tipped his hat at all and ordered a whisky. "For my tongue is as dry as an ancient flatworm," he remarked. To which Emyr, the landlord, replied, "Merely as dry as that?"

The stranger regarded him with pinpoint eyes. "Oh, drier than that by far," he added. He rolled the whisky in his mouth and let loose a chuckle as sinister as a finger in a pie. But Emyr was not going to let him go so easily. "How far exactly?" he pressed. "As far as the furthest star in the Milky

Way," the stranger whispered. "As far as Judgment Day from the Day of Creation." He finished his whisky at a gulp and ordered another.

"Quite far then?" said Emyr. He placed the little glass down onto the bar, making two wet rings like eyes. "Further than Aberystwyth, for example?" And this time, the stranger toyed with his drink, swirling the contents around, watching the sediment rise and fall. "I think so," he agreed. "Oh yes, much further. So far that by the time you get there, you have quite forgotten the reason why you went." But few people present in the bar that day could see how this differed from going to Aberystwyth, and so the poetry was lost.

I was one of those who happened to be there. It was obvious that a battle of dark wills was in progress. Emyr is not overly keen on serving locals, let alone visitors, and indeed he resents all attempts to make small talk. So when the stranger turned his head to take in all the patrons and said, "Does anyone here have an ache in their soul?" we knew that trouble was brewing. It was at this point that Hywel the Baker spoke up from the shadows. "I have an ache in my hands," he said thickly. "And how do they ache?" the stranger asked, with a leer. "Not how, but what sort," Hywel replied. "What sort then?" the stranger returned, knitting his brows. "A fruit ache," said Hywel, spluttering crumbs. "But there's none for you."

The stranger hissed and it seemed that he was grinding his teeth together. But eventually he turned back to his whisky and this went the way of the first. I was able to take the opportunity of studying him more closely as he stood there, elbows on the bar, tall hat tipped at an angle over one of his disturbing eyes. Later I was learn that these eyes were like tiny obsidian mirrors, although it did not seem so to me at the time. But you know how folks will have things; the eyes of a stranger are always like tiny obsidian mirrors in the same way that a ghost is not a real spectre unless it is trailing a bloody winding sheet behind it and talking with a voice tuned to the pitch of the autumn wind.

"Perhaps I have an ache in my soul," said someone from another corner. And now my knees knocked together and everyone else in the bar looked to their cups. For this was the voice of Elizabeth Morgan, the fiery witch of Cobweb Cottage, who rarely spoke except to augur some crisis and whose nettle jam was an inarguable reason for living one's life in a state of quiet desperation. But when my curiosity finally overcame my better judgment and I glanced up, I saw that she was talking to herself and staring at the bottom of one of her shoes.

At last the stranger stretched himself and once more addressed those gathered. "I am looking for the local poet. All these villages have one. I see no reason why yours should be any different. Lladloh is it? Well then, my fine fellows, where can I find the Bard of Lladloh?" And suddenly I bit my lip, for this personage was none other than my good self, or so I liked to think. "Why do you seek him?" I ventured, not entirely sure that I wanted to hear the answer. The stranger turned those mysterious eyes upon me and a faint smile cracked the stiff parchment of his face. "I have a service to offer," he said slowly, bowing a menacing bow and doffing his dusty hat.

I felt a sudden, absurd urge to throw myself at his feet, grasp his ankles and cry, "It is me, sir," in a vain attempt to solicit mercy. But as I did not even know what he had planned, I managed to restrain myself. My hand shook as I raised my drink to my mouth and took a long draught to steady my nerves. "What sort of service?" I managed to gargle into my beer, the bubbles exploding around the lip of the glass and sloshing over the floorboards.

The stranger moved a pace closer and his left eyebrow arched ever so slightly. "I am an extractor of egos," he announced with a hint of a chuckle. "I travel the land seeking out poets whose ambition is greater than their talent and I remove the source of irritation that is making their lives a misery. In short, I cut out their egos. I perform an egoectomy! I have the tools, such tools you have never seen before in all your dreams. I made them myself. Out pours the ego like blood from a broken nose and I collect it in a blue glass bottle. The operation is almost painless. My fees are reasonable, but I make a good living. My services are always in great demand, if not from the poet himself then certainly from his friends and family!"

I glanced around the bar at my companions. Would they betray me? Despite their public endorsement of my verse, what did they really think? I noticed that they were all frowning. There was indecision etched on every face. The stranger stepped forward another pace and stroked his pale chin. All eyes in the bar were now turned upon me. The very air bristled with some horribly subtle meaning.

I guessed that my drinking companions would not be able to resist the temptation to give me away for much longer. This was a profoundly depressing insight. I had no wish to lose my ego. After all, it was only a very small one. I had spent the last five years attempting to build an extension to it, but had repeatedly been denied planning permission for the project. In other words, I was an unpublished poet. A failure. But I liked to think that I had preserved at least some measure of pride, of hubris, throughout all my rejections. I did not want to lose this small crumb of what I still hoped my identity might one day evolve into.

I had produced reams and reams of verse in my thankless capacity as self-styled Laureate of the locality. My untitled magnum opus, in twelve handwritten volumes, told the sombre story of a young man who wandered cemeteries at night in a state of lyrical angst but who fell in love with the reanimated corpse of a drowned girl who rose from her grave before him during a freak thunderstorm. Her name was Gwyneth Bellows and she had been dead for just a month, so she was still quite maggoty as well as bloated, but this minor objection aside, he found her rather fetching. Indeed, he eventually summoned up the courage to propose to her and she accepted.

They spent many secret nights arranging their

elopement. Finally, on a predetermined hour, he came for her and they slipped away, hand in hand. They raced through the deserted streets of the village, laughing silently, her worm-gnawed feet clattering on the cobbles like the hooves of the devil himself. The man felt delirious with joy, as if he had just imbibed large quantities of black wine. Once beyond the village, he paused to kiss his prospective bride and found that her decaying lips tasted of sweet nepenthe. Everything seemed perfect. They would escape to some distant land, they would swim among the wrecks and coral reefs of an exotic shoreline and lurk among dank forests where voodoo drums pounded a hole in sanity. They would consummate their unholy marriage and conceive an eldritch child. It would be a phantom pregnancy.

These were the thoughts entertained by the man when he suddenly realised he had forgotten his pet raven. A true romantic never goes anywhere without a pet raven. So, stroking his true love's matted hair, he left her alone on one of the fields behind Iolo Machen's farmhouse and hastened back to his garret to fetch it. However, when he returned, she was nowhere to be seen. But Iolo's sheepdog was standing in her place, wagging his tail and extracting the vestiges of marrow from a splintered thighbone. Needless to say, the young man was inconsolable. He vowed that he would never love again. But despair had a perverse effect on him. As well as wandering cemeteries of an evening, he also began to saunter down to the local pub. This might have been perceived as bad form for a romantic, whose purpose in life is to seek out the phantasmagoric. But what better place to dabble with frightful spirits?

This then was the theme and development of my major poem. I had seen the manuscript of this masterpiece bounced around more publishing houses than there were eyelids in Emyr's meat pies. I had also been more than a little confused by the reaction of editors to the work. They generally replied that my poem stretched credulity and suggested that in future I should only ever write from personal experience. But that is precisely what I had been doing.

Anyway, unpublished or not, I was still the closest equivalent to a Bard that existed in Lladloh. And now the stranger had satisfied himself that I was indeed the one he sought. "Well," he hissed, as he regarded my trembling frame, "I think that there is little need for modesty here. Come now, my fellow, why not admit your profession? You will not regret it, I assure you. As I said earlier, there is only a little pain. Just a few incisions and a little blow with an iron hammer and all will be over! You'll probably be on your feet again within a couple of days, if nothing goes wrong."

I stammered and sweat poured from my brow. "There must be some mistake sir!" I gasped. "I am not a poet. Oh no indeed! I can't even read the stuff, let alone write it! Besides, poets all have curly hair. How can I possibly be a poet with hair like this?" And with a desperate look, I appealed to all those gathered to confirm the truth of my words. But they merely continued to frown ambiguously.

The stranger was now so close to me that I could smell his fetid breath and see the phosphorescent veins that glowed faintly under his skin. He jabbed a finger at my chest and icy chills ran along my breastbone. "Good poets have curly hair," he pointed out, "as you say. But bad poets have hair that... dangles." He raised his hand and brushed my greasy fringe. Another fit of trembling seized my body. I shivered and dropped my glass, which shattered into a thousand sharp fragments at my feet. "Look!" the stranger cried and pulled open his coat. All along the inside, held in place by black ribbons, strange steel instruments glittered. He toyed with a selection of hooks and miniature saws and then drew out a twisted scalpel. "Ten egos I have collected this season. Ten hideous egos in ten grim bottles! You shall be the eleventh. Do not fret! The operation takes little more than a couple of hours."

I lost all control of my legs and collapsed to the floor

among the rivulets of spilt beer. I clasped hold of his bony knees and closed my eyes. It is said that when a man loses his life, he sees the whole of his past rush before him. I wondered if this also happened when a man lost his ego. I sincerely hoped that it did not. I had no desire to relive all my mistakes, all my dashed dreams. The shock alone would probably finish me off.

It was Emyr who saved me. With haughty contempt, he growled at the stranger: "What is all this nonsense? Do you mistake this man for the local poet? Any fool can see that this is not he. I am insulted by your insinuation that I would let a poet drink in my establishment! What sort of place do you think this is? This is not Swansea! Do you believe that we have no pride? Of course this man is not the local poet. You'll find the local poet where any genuine rhymester would choose to spend his time. Down by the river, under the old stone bridge. His name is Toby."

The stranger curled his mouth in a sneer and angled his head to one side. Suddenly, he pulled away and departed with a nod at Emyr. "If he refuses to pay me, I shall be back to claim my fee," he said. Emyr proceeded to wash and wipe the stranger's glass. "Don't worry about that," he remarked. "Toby is a very generous soul. You won't be back." We watched through the open door as the stranger mounted his ancient motorcycle and started the engine, roaring away in a cloud of oily smoke. Clambering back to my feet, I made for the bar and ordered another beer. Unusually, Emyr insisted I have one on the house.

We never saw the stranger again. We found his broken motorcycle lying in the centre of the road that leads over the bridge. And we also found the box that had held the blue glass bottles. Only one of these bottles was intact and I brought it back and set it up behind the bar. What happened to the contents of the other nine can only be guessed at. However, poetry has started to appear on the walls of the bridge, awful poetry, written in what appears to be dried blood. It is said that this blood glows faintly at night. It is also said that Toby has recently taken to wearing a tall hat and picking his teeth clean of travellers with a curiously twisted toothpick.

Even more disturbing than this is the fact that someone has been taking sly drinks from the bottle behind the bar. I suspect that it is Emyr. It seems I will soon have a rival. This is the last thing I need at my stage in life. Had I submitted to the operation, my own ego might now be the one which is being consumed and I wouldn't have to worry about competition. I sometimes stare out of the grimy windows of my garret, hoping that the stranger, or one like him, will return. It is a forlorn hope. More often, I take myself out to my favourite cemetery and lay myself down in that opened grave which I refuse to see refilled. Ah Gwyneth! She alone understood my essential nature. How I yearn for her puffed face close to mine, her wormy embrace! There is another poem somewhere in this, I am sure. Who knows? If I persist, I may yet attain the status of creative genius.

SPERMACETI WHISKERS

He sharpened dawn on a strop and shaved the ice from his windows. When the sun weaved its way through the alleys to his shop, he sat it in his chair and trimmed the beams. Motes danced between the blades of antique scissors. Even in July it was cold in the depths of the labyrinth; the town was as mysterious as a hand beneath a table. He enjoyed comparing its secrets with those still wandering lost in his past. His mind, crewed with desperate memories, mirrored his environment perfectly, as if the maze of streets, achingly cramped with nibbled life, had been reflected from the polished dome of his head.

Aware of this symbolism, he stitched shards of a broken mirror into his hat. The glass had smashed while he was soaping the chin of a loaded pistol. It was a convex mirror, the one reserved for customers who liked to observe their own necks, ready to catch an itch in the act. Owning a frown too wide for his head, he did not mourn the loss. He preferred to spend money with his left hand; his right was saved for gestures. Trying to splice the loose threads of his existence into a cable of meaning, he hung his identity. He spoke only bad Italian, though the aftertaste of a dozen languages coated his tongue.

He had come to Pirano a month before, deeming its position right at the top of the Adriatic a snug embrace for a simpler career. A childhood with the buccaneers, cutting the locks of rogues and romantics, had made his fingers nimble as peppers. Having worked with the most notorious and hirsute sea-rovers, an urge to settle down overwhelmed him. While others wasted their booty in bordellos and theatres, he saved enough to start a small business. He wished to legitimise his skills, to license his blade and deal with honest stubble. He now tolerated only innocent cut-throats, those which can be folded in half.

Not that he was able to entirely shrug off history. It clung to him like a damp sail. His jars of lacquer smelled of typhoons and cannibals; his combs, toothless with scurvy, tasted of knives. He had forgotten his real name during the sack of Panama, but his habit of waxing moustaches with whale oil saved him from total anonymity. He used his nickname like a compass: a pointer to inner peace. His dreams, which he could hear but not see, were filled with contradictory orders shouted by l'Olonnais and Morgan. His shipmates, likewise afflicted in the siege, raided his stock of hair restorer to regrow their egos.

Two of these ruffians became his best friends. A carpenter, Lanolin Brows, and a cook, Muscovado Lashes, sometimes helped him with his work, grinding apricot stones for shampoo. 'Lin was a Swede, with a nose sharper than a chisel and a frosted eye. 'Vado was a Malagasy, tall as a spoon and cunning as a whisk. Both fought fanatically on land and sea. 'Lin wore a suit of armour carved from teak and wielded a saw. 'Vado fought with pot and ladle, dishing his victims a gourmet doom. Both had pleaded with him not to retire; the seas, they claimed, would grow lank and unkempt if he packed away his heated tongs.

His customers, however bloodthirsty on deck, were always polite and diffident in the presence of his towels. Even Morgan, most successful of the buccaneers, refused to jump the queue but quietly took a seat behind cabin boys and prisoners. He would rifle through the pamphlets scattered on the low table, the improbable stories about the slack morals of Cuban missionaries, and listen to the percussive rhythms of the shears. He was always nervous; the odours of cropped hair and aftershave disturbed him. Barber shops, he used to say, were torture chambers for his lice. But in the chair he was confident.

"Well now, 'Ceti, did I ever tell you about my village? Marshy and poor, absurd crime rate. Llanrumney."

"Yes, sir, lean forward. Keep quite still."

"Not too much off the back. Local girls would die for

my curls. But what would they do in your home town?"

This question had irritated him ever since. He learned hairdressing from Exquemelin, the most stylish barber-surgeon on the Spanish Main. He recalled talking to him effortlessly, debating the rival merits of combs made from turtles and tortoises. Perhaps he was Dutch? But there were no windmills or cheeses in his dreams to confirm the supposition. Each time he crossed borders, his thoughts were adopted by the surrounding culture like orphans in baskets. In Pirano he mislaid the flavour of the sea and picked splinters of limestone from his teeth. The karst landscape to the north was barren as a pickled mermaid.

Sometimes he did glimpse water between gaps in red-tiled buildings. A stroll down to the lighthouse, tiny flame dancing above what seemed to be a nameless church, could have been enough to convince him that Pirano was still a port, that the link with his youth was intact. But he never managed to find his way on to the Punta, the promontory. The lanes were complex and risible, they led him in ellipses away from his destination. In the Jewish square, the vaulted passages and arcaded courtyards filled up with exotic scents, provoking him into a misplaced nostalgia for the present. Beards wove a symbolic net.

He sharpened dusk on a strop and closed his shop for the night. The business was failing already, he could tell. As he secured the shutters, replaced the unused scissors on the shelf and swept a clean floor, black silence suffused the room; the shop bulged. All over the town, hair grew from angry or serene heads, its texture denied to him by an inexplicable process. What kept customers away? He had mounted a striped pole outside his door, his windows were made from Venetian glass. It could not simply be a question of appearances. Did the citizens mistrust his instruments? Did they lack suitable banter?

In his rickety kitchen, he set a kettle to boil and dipped his last yam into the liquid. Soon he would be reduced to stewing belts, shoes or empty wallets. This happened when he worked for l'Olonnais in Nicaragua, shortly before that pirate's violent death at the hands and teeth of the Darien Indians. Hunger was nothing new to him, though back then it was a nomadic emptiness, which moved from gut to throat as he hunted for food. Hunger in one place is worse than in many; while the kettle whistled the flavours on board, he counted the coins in his hidden purse. Money grows inward, like a fringe in reverse.

Previous hungers were bearable because he was generally full in his warped mirror. Sometimes periods of famine were switched so rapidly with periods of plenty that food took on the glowering appearance of a storm. Once, just off the coast of Mayaguana, they were hemmed in by a flotilla of coconuts. Each globe was ripe and matted as a starving stomach. Sweet milk slicked the deck, as 'Lin and 'Vado cracked the spheres with drills and cleavers. Since then, he regarded coconuts as guardian angels, solid as hymns and coarse as martyrs. If he asked in tastes rather than words, they always turned up to help him.

His profession was so linked with his survival that he could hardly imagine another way of staying whole. His ointments and powders, for the dusting of nicked lobes, saved the lives of many in Jamaica, where death was schooled not in wounds but their infections. He tended l'Olonnais on the rigging of a sinking caraval, smearing an unguent mashed from Havana chillies over his bleeding limbs. Barbering had never let him down while he floated on brine; only now, on a stable surface, was it acting like a whore. How much longer did he have to wait before his first customer entered his shop? Would the bell over the door never speak?

Another time, becalmed in the Lesser Antilles, he wove a durable rope from snipped hair. This was when he sailed with Pierre le Grand, an eccentric and reckless captain. Dice were cast and it was decided to use the cord, heady with a myriad colours, as a cable for the anchor. It was gnawed by a shark, that evening, and in the ensuing cyclone their barque was blown the whole way back to Tortuga. On this voyage he perfected the perm, but realised it would have to be reinvented at a later date. At least hunger was blunted by hope at sea; in the depths of a shop it mimicked plumbing and flooded the mouth with despair.

He imagined the building torn loose from its foundations and pushed along the alleys by a freak wind. Would it finally burst out of the maze and tumble into the silent sea? He clung to this febrile idea as the yam rose and fell. He dished the thin broth and lifted it to his lips with a fork, to save some for the following day. He felt the meal was digesting him, rather than the opposite. He wrestled his way into his old sailor's coat and opened the back door, stepping out into an invisible bustle. On balconies higher than his gaze, unseen neighbours lounged. Shrill curses swooped on his shoulders like gulls.

"It's old 'Ceti Whiskers! Bet he shaves throats like rope and turns customers into overpriced pies."

"Never ask a corsair for a singe."

"Combs with a rum bottle, I say, and dries with a cannon. Better to sweep the streets with a beard."

He hurried past, through the oldest of old squares, where the giant cistern spoke riddles to itself, and up a cobbled hill in the shadows of the Church of St George. The bell tower, set as far apart from the main edifice as a debate from an argument, loomed with an ironic sort of wit, a tongue poking forever upward. Although unable to find his way right up to the town walls, for a clear view of the Adriatic, he had discovered a reasonable alternative. Here was a house with a room at eye level and no shutters. Inside, a family ate spherical bread: with a corrugated crust, a loaf played the role of a coconut.

Kissing his tongue with his teeth, he crouched and watched the wife and children chew slowly, like squid, in the splendid chamber. The burly husband, who poked every dish with his finger before tasting, sat with a deflated sack between his legs, as if to catch his stomach. The interior was so brightly illuminated with candles that friars could burn monks on the window. The family dipped into the display with lassitude, regarding each dish as a visit to an obscure relative. Not that they were ignorant of the importance of nourishment; merely that food for them had acquired abstract edges and aloof textures.

Returning to his shop, he thought he detected footsteps behind him. It was the sound of a man who favours his left leg: perhaps a government agent was tailing him? The Italian republics did not like former pirates settling in their towns. He turned and wove in his usual random fashion, hoping to confuse his pursuer. The starlight blew darts at the shards in his hat and he glittered as he ran. Pirano was small enough, despite its cryptic heart, and he soon found himself passing the cistern, one of the few familiar landmarks among the tangle. Here he paused to drink ripples from the surface of the water.

Hunched over the side, still and stony, he waited for the hunter to pass. There was a flapping noise, a slack mouth kissing departing cakes, and then the silence of a town where echoes are caught in washing lines. Turning the final corner, he encountered one of these cords blocking his path. Heavy with patchwork washing, the vestments of a giant family, the line bent from a lofty window, brushed the pavement with buttoned hooves and curved to a window even higher, giving the arrangement a squint. The distance from one balcony to the other was only three feet, but the line was long enough to choke an island.

Too stiff and huge to brush aside, sheets, shirts and skirts formed an impenetrable barrier against his homecoming. He sought an alternative approach. Up a sweep of steps, down another backstreet, through a midget courtyard: there was no entry this way. Washing lines netted the dark. A dressing gown punched him in the eye. He pretended to be a cat, climbing a low roof and picking a path over broken tiles. He had the whiskers but not the balance; he was forced to jump down, defeated, feeling he was no more than a shirt himself, pegged by the assumptions of brutal citizens. Voices warbled from high above:

"Bet 'Ceti doesn't wash his clothes in hot water. Bet he cleans his socks with an abrasive tongue."

"He uses sapphires instead of soap!"

"Gives a despicable blue rinse. The usual camouflage for an oceanic rogue. He wears tidal fashion!"

Lurching away from the insults, he considered his remaining option. He must find the facade of his shop and enter like a customer. He tugged at his hair, acting the part of a scruff. Only by adopting the mentality of a client would the building call out and reel him in. But even at the end of the sick alley which led to his front, ropes had been strung. Now they were empty; the linen which would throttle on their narrow strength was still being worn by disobedient sons. So it was necessary for him to duck and weave, as if avoiding petrified traces of cutlass strokes. When they were full, he would be caught.

The bell chimed as he opened the door and he leapt in anticipation, lunging for the comb. Then he remembered he had no money to pay himself. He coughed apologetically and lowered his head as he passed the chair. A hook accepted his hat. This was a bigger fright for him than the time he was shipwrecked with Betrand d'Ogeron near the Guadanillas islands. Only embarrassment was to be feared more than octopuses. Those who called the buccaneers unmannered and boorish had no idea of the social graces which governed their every act. A corsair's etiquette is that of a vicar; only the quality of china is different.

He was finished on his own. It was time to apply for help, before a barber became a fish, hauled to a spluttering doom in a knot of washing. He mixed dyes and carved a pen from a stick of soap. On a napkin's back, he wrote his first letter, addressed to his old comrades. 'Lin and 'Vado would come for him, blowing away the laundry with a zumbooruk or cutting it to bandages with pikes. They would rescue him from this arid Sargasso where he was stuck fast and he would embrace the real sea again, sailing with Captain Rock or Bartolomeo el Portugues, trimming the beards of the whole of Maracaibo and Cartagena.

Sealing the letter in a bottle, he crept out once more. Sea was his only method of sending messages, but it remained more elusive than ever. At last, after a fruitless search, he recalled the cistern. Large enough to mimic the briny deep, it accepted his epistle with a sigh. Quickly he hurried back. Already a pair of trousers had been added to the cord. Too exhausted to veer, he squeezed between the legs. Once in his kitchen, he curled up in the oven, his makeshift bed, without brushing his teeth. No need: the sugar content of life was not high enough to rot his icy gums. They had ossified into crossbones.

When he finally achieved sleep, a cast-iron dream entered his guts, filling him like a sail soaked in wine. It was a blind dream, but voices vibrated in a vast room. At first he thought they belonged to mutineers, plotting on the lowest deck of a galleon. But they were gentler than the harsh whispers of floating killers. It was the family he regularly spied on; they were breaking bread, straining thick beer between their lips. A face leered at the window: it was the barber. For an instant, he did not recognise himself and he was appalled by the apparition. The family were aware of his presence and digested it.

Once the face moved away, the husband rose quickly and followed him through the labyrinth. This fellow was a postman: his sack trailed after him like a musical note squeezed in a mangle. At the cistern, he noticed the barber hiding his head in the water. He passed by and squatted in an open doorway, as if delivering a parcel to a dwarf. When the barber came up for air and continued his escape, the husband stepped in his shadow's footprints, which were deeper than his shoes. He waited outside the shop until the barber re-emerged. Later, he fished the bottle out of the dark cistern and lowered it into his sack.

Waking in the oven, the pirate rubbed his sooty eyes and considered the meaning of the dream. Was it symbolic of anything other than itself? He hoped not. He crawled out, sharpened dawn on a strop and hovered over the empty chair. The delivery of his letter in this fashion was too neat to be true, like a perfectly shaved chin. Closing for an early lunch, he decided to check the cistern for his bottle. But the nets were woven too finely; he could not penetrate the washing. He returned to dusty silence and chewed his tongue like a pie. Dusk arrived; a new morning climbed up behind and time molested his life.

The weeks passed. One night there was a sound of tearing: his front door rattled. He cowered in the oven and strained his eyes. The lock was blown apart and the door opened, letting in a cloud of sulphurous smoke. Two figures stood on the threshold. When the bell sounded, one patiently reloaded his carbine and took careful aim. The second eruption peppered the wall with shot, leaving the bell unscathed. While this figure cursed and stamped the carbine to splinters, his companion pulled out a cutlass and severed the cord holding the device. It tinkled to its doom. Nodding at each other, the beings advanced.

"It's darker than the attack on Porto Bello. 'Ceti always preferred glow-worms to lamps. His eyes are anchors."

"I can stir a pot with his halo."

"Pride comes before a trim. We'll leave before he finds us. Mustn't belittle the stubborn soak. Wondrous fool."

He felt numb as he observed them. Were these his first customers? A minute more disabused him of this notion. They lowered something down on the chair and patted it on the head: this was the real client. Then they gave the shop a cursory pillage. Reaching for a tall jar of whale oil on the shelf, they smeared wax on their faces: one on his lashes, the other on his brows. They vanished like eels, leaving the taste of saltpetre on the floorboards. Baked with emotion, he paddled from the kitchen toward the chair and looked at the object. He was saved: resting on the cracked red leather was boundless sustenance.

At the end of the year, when the washing lines were raised to cheat the rain of a soft landing, a postman took a short cut down the passage. The lock was still smashed, so he pushed into the shop. Slumped over the chair, the corpse seemed to be smiling. Perhaps it was the decay. On the seat, an enormous coconut with elaborate curls rotted in sunlight. There was a comb tangled in its hair. When the news spread, neighbours came to dispose of the bones. Some say Morgan bought them for his flag. All lies are true after a rinse and cut. And now dawn looks like a rebel and even smooth dusk is going through a phase.

THE BLUE DWARF

"All I require" the blue dwarf cried, as he placed his hand on my knee, "are your trousers and your soul."

"Oh, little man," said I, "this is a foolish request! They are both too large for you. They would flap in the wind and set up a commotion. Who would want to be your friend then? You would have to shout above the noise: *'Blueberry pie at my house.'* Even so, no-one would come to visit. You would have to sit alone, absurdly attired.

"But let me tell you of the time I bartered both. The world was a younger place then; we did not value so highly such things as trousers and souls. The former were objects merely to be worn; the latter were baubles brought out over dinner to amuse guests. Neither had pride of place in the wardrobe, as they do now."

"I do not wish to hear this," replied the blue dwarf, and he turned to go. But I soon had him by the scruff and he was forced to amend his statement: "Perhaps I will listen after all."

"Very good," I agreed. "It is possible you will learn a truth here, though I doubt it. The amoral fable suits my tongue rather better than the moral kind. Attend then, unclouded fellow.

"The region of which I speak is a dreary region in Gwent, by the borders of the river Severn. And there is no quiet there, nor silence. The waters have a saffron and sickly hue; and they do a fair bit of palpitating beneath the red eye of the sun..."

The blue dwarf sighed: "Bugger!"

Actually, I exchanged my trousers for a clock and a carrot, and lost my soul as I was doing so. Do you know Monmouth?

The market there is notorious for pickpockets; I knew this before I set out, yet took no precautions. I was intent on driving a hard bargain for my trousers. The imps who run the stalls are good at offering low prices for items that come their way. They can talk the meanest miser into parting with his silver for a length of old rope. It is essential to be on your guard at all times.

Nor are they too particular about where their goods come from. I suspect the clock I received fell off the back of a steeple, and the carrot had been uprooted from an allotment. But I was desperate; and the imps and their customers are protected by the market-overt law. This states that goods sold at such markets, whether stolen or not, cannot be returned to the original owner (with the clock came an irate pastor).

Anyway, after I had spent an hour or so talking one stall-owner into giving me the clock and carrot, and had divested myself of my baggy britches, I made my way back to my house. Halfway home, I realised my soul was missing. Nimble fingers had filched it. Doubtless it could now be found on a soul stall. But I had nothing on me with which to barter it back. I decided it would keep until the following morning, when I would return with an umbrella and a parrot.

In my kitchen, I made a thin soup with the carrot and set the clock above my hearth (the pastor grumbled about the fire and claimed it was singeing his heels.) At last there was a knock on the door and Myfanwy stood on the threshold. I invited her in, showed her the clock, poured the soup and gazed into her large brown eyes. The combination of broth and timepiece so impressed her she consented to marry me at once – the effect I had been aiming for. "Hurrah!" cried I.

We finished the meal and listened to the clock striking the hour. She suggested we go out for a walk. I declined, of course – I had no trousers. I made some excuse about wishing to stay at the table to hear the clock strike another hour. She thought this an excellent idea and suggested we pass the time by playing dice with our souls. Again I made my excuses; I told her my soul had caught a cold and had to be kept inside. She saw through this deception at once.

"And to think I nearly kissed a man without a soul!" she growled. She stood up to leave and I rushed to restrain her. She glanced down at my bare legs. "What's more, without trousers too!" she added. It was all I could do not to fall on the floor and burst into tears. I fell into an easy chair and burst into tears instead.

Myfanwy had left me, and my efforts at seducing her with pendulum and root vegetable had come to nothing. She was the greatest baker of blueberry pie in the region and men of all kinds came flocking to her oven; she could afford to be choosy. She had picked off the crust of my amorous overtures to expose the lack of filling beneath. I had lost her for good. Let this be a lesson to all young lovers, especially in these days, when inflation and curry has pushed up the price of both trousers and souls. Wear the former and 'ware the latter.

The following morning, I took my umbrella and parrot to the market in an effort to retrieve my soul. But it had been sold. I was much put out by this. The imp who owned the stall offered to do me a very nice soul in maroon-and-black, but there is nothing quite like having your own soul; it fits you like a favourite overcoat, or like an idea in a single word. The imp would not reveal to whom he had sold it. I decided to cut my losses and buy back my trousers.

Incredibly, my trousers had also been purchased. I was so stupefied that I relaxed my guard and ended up exchanging my umbrella and parrot for a pair of tinted spectacles. I wore the spectacles – they turned everything as blue as my funk – as a reminder to myself never to be so foolish again. Indeed, I have never taken them off.

I sat on the side of Monnow bridge (if you do not know Monmouth, this is quite close to Agincourt Square, behind the giant waterwheel) and dangled my legs above the fetid river. As I was grumbling there to myself, Owain ap Iorwerth came up to me. "What's the matter, Gruffydd?" he chortled, pleased to find me in a state of despair. I told him. "Oh well!" he grinned and slapped me on the back. I think he meant for me to fall into the ravine, but I merely coughed loose a tooth.

Owain ap Iorwerth, you see, was my greatest rival for the hand of fair Myfanwy. I made my way home and, too depressed even to finish off the soup I had so lovingly prepared the day before, took to my bed. I was startled by a knock on the door. When I opened it, I was overjoyed to find Myfanwy there, holding my trousers and soul.

It seemed I had misjudged her. She loved me, to be sure, and after storming out of my house had made her way to the market. There she had searched for the items and bought them for me. My clock and carrot, she quickly confessed, were so utterly remarkable, both as singular objects and also as a sum greater than the parts, that she had seen the error of her ways. She begged my forgiveness.

Naturally, I told her it was I who needed to apologise. After some thought she agreed; I did so and we fell into each other's arms. But, unfortunately, this is the real world; life is a sour cream poured on stones. It soon became apparent she had sold her own trousers and soul to purchase mine. A hatstand and three harpoons had been thrown in.

I was in a quandary. How could I marry a woman without trousers or soul? Neighbours would gossip; I should be ashamed to show myself in public. I did not mention this to her, of course; I am a sensitive sort of man. The sort of man who does not despise pink socks because of their colour, but because of their hue.

In the days that followed, I did my best to act as if nothing was amiss. But her blueberry pie lost its flavour, and her lithe limbs lost their ability to slide against mine without friction. More to the point, when we went out with each other, people stared at us. They suspected she was lacking trousers and a soul; you could see it in their eyebrows, which jumped alarmingly whenever we approached. Some even made jokes in our presence. "That's the spirit!" they would cry, or, "What a turn up for the books!" Pedestrians can be very cruel.

Owain ap Iorwerth noticed as well, because one day she left me for him. He had done the noble thing, buying back her trousers and soul and returning them to her. This showed me up as a thoughtless lover. The irony was that he bartered his own soul and trousers to obtain hers. I gritted my teeth and, in order to impress Myfanwy with my sacrifice, re-exchanged my trousers and soul for Owain's. This had the desired effect, but only for a while.

The long and the inside leg of it is that all three of us ended up exchanging and re-exchanging our trousers and souls a great many times. It was a ludicrous and vain episode of my life. Eventually, after a year of this fabric-and-phantom farce, the trousers and souls were jumbled up and we did not know which was which. It is an unbearable sensation, not knowing if your trousers and your soul are the ones you were born with, and we all rushed off in opposite directions, taking up residence in the three corners of the scalene world.

Before I left Monmouth, I made sure I took a blueberry pie with me, to remember Myfanwy by. And it still remains uneaten in my pocket. The day I meet her again will be the day I take a bite; the day I encounter Owain ap Iorwerth will be the day I beat him to death with it. It is tasty and solid enough for either eventuality.

"And that tale is absolutely true," I told the blue dwarf, "which is why you shall never succeed in removing my trousers or my soul. I suggest you run along and torment someone your own size. I spy a woodlouse down there; it has a waist more your size."

"You fool!" The blue dwarf wriggled out of my grasp. I saw now he was not really a dwarf; he was standing on his knees. When he arose, he was almost my own height. He pulled off his wig and his coat and stood there before me with a wide blue grin.

"Myfanwy!" cried I.

"Yes, you fool!" she returned. She reached into her pocket and took out a blueberry pie. "At last we meet again! I have been searching for so many years. Our trousers and souls were indeed jumbled; you have mine and I have yours. That is why I asked you to remove them. Now we can be married and live in near bliss for months!"

I shook my head. "A disguise, eh? I suspected this all along." I pulled off my own wig and removed my own coat. "I am not Gruffydd after all; I am Owain ap Iorwerth. And I have come to take you away with me, to claim your love and your baking talents!"

Myfanwy threw back her head and laughed. "Exactly as I planned! You have fallen into my trap!" She removed her new wig and took off her new coat and it was Gruffydd himself who now glared at me. He shifted the blueberry pie in his hand and prepared to lunge. "At last I shall be avenged! I have waited long ages for this."

"Ha!" I screamed. I followed his example; I pulled off my new wig and discarded my new coat. And then I jumped off my stilts and snatched the blueberry pie from his trembling fingers. "A blue dwarf!" he cried. "What is the meaning of this?"

I reached forward and pulled the tinted spectacles from his nose. At once he understood. He bellowed: "You are not a blue dwarf at all. You are a yellow imp!" I nodded and raced back to the market.

The bottom has dropped out of the trouser market; there is no longer life in souls. Blueberry pie is the new thing. Sometimes we resort to devious tactics to get it.

THE
PURLOINED
LIVER

"Purloin My Liver," said Edgar.

"I beg your pardon?" Annabel frowned and steered around the carcass of a sheep. Flies rose in a dark cloud.

"The village." Edgar folded the map and gestured at the collection of thatched cottages. "Purloin My Liver. An old market town. Stop in that pub and I'll buy you a drink."

Annabel assented and parked off the road. As she stepped out into bright sunshine, she gazed at the signpost that hung from the side of the building. "Odd name for a pub!"

Edgar shook his head. "We're in the sticks now. This is rural heritage." He followed her gaze upwards. "The Plucked Eyeball? Sounds rather quaint to me. I like it."

Annabel shrugged and followed him inside. The bar was deserted and gloomy. The warped beams of the low ceiling forced them to crouch down to avoid striking their heads. "Anyone home?" Edgar cried.

The barman appeared from the cellar. "What'll it be?" He was a grotesque figure, obese and hunched, a meerschaum pipe in the shape of a screaming skull protruding from his mouth. His dirty moustaches drooped like dying vines. A single, bulging, working eye rolled endlessly in its socket; the other dangled loose on his cheek.

"What do you have on cask?" Edgar inquired mildly.

The barman rested his gnarled hands on the unlabelled pump handles. "Leprous Pustule, Purple Haemorrhage, Garrotted Baby, Witch Burn, Eat My Cousin and Twisted Ear." He turned to another part of the bar. "This is Severed Torso, a sour cider. Bloodless Zombie is a pale ale."

"A pint of Twisted Ear please," said Edgar.

"Half a Severed Torso for me," added Annabel.

The barman drew the pints. "Travellers eh? Off to the Fair at Grind My Bones? Should be good this year. A wicker man stuffed with virgins. Reverend Cleaver grew them himself:

real virgins!"

Edgar remained nonchalant. "Sounds fine." He knocked back his pint. "We'll give it a try." He seized Annabel's glass, drained that one as well and handed money over the counter. "Have one yourself."

"Very kind of you sir, don't mind if I do!" The barman poured a foul green mixture. "Crucified Toad. I brew this one myself." Instead of placing the glass to his lips, he held it under his cheek and lowered his prolapsed orbit into the murky depths. Once immersed, the eyeball took on a life of its own; it rose and fell in slow circles, refracted to hideous dimensions by the viscous fluid.

Outside again, Annabel smirked. "What an odd fellow!"

"Not at all; we're in Shropshire now," Edgar reminded her. "Look, sorry for hurrying you on. But I'd hate to miss that wicker man. These are real country ways! Cream teas and brutal prejudices!"

Annabel started the engine and pulled out onto the road. "What's so special about burning virgins? Why not teetotallers or bank managers or poets? Why not travellers for that matter?"

Edgar chuckled softly. "It's just that virgins are flammable. Most other people aren't. It's like pebbles and coal." He consulted the map. "Grind My Bones is the next village along. Left at the fork."

"I see." Annabel turned a sharp left and followed the road between towering hedge-rows. Conditions grew steadily worse; the car began to bounce and shudder. She cleared her throat. "What did your pint taste like? Mine tasted like squeezed abdomen."

"I know." Edgar nodded to himself. "Mine was sort of waxy. Real ale, you see. None of that fizzy rubbish we get in the city." He leaned out of the window. "I can't see any wicker man. I can't hear any virgins screaming either. They do scream, don't they?"

"Perhaps they just whimper." Annabel cursed as the road became a mud track. They reached a dilapidated farm house and saw it was a dead end. "We must have come the wrong way."

"That's impossible. Stop the car and I'll ask directions." Edgar waited for Annabel to pull up and then jumped out of his seat. The front door of the farmhouse was covered in human hands nailed to the rotting wood. Edgar prised one of these hands loose and rapped on the door with it. Bolts slid back and a thin man peered out.

"Yes?" The man blinked at Edgar. His eyelids worked upwards; his eyes had obviously been put on upside down.

"Is this Grind My Bones, or anywhere near it?" Edgar asked. "We're off to see virgins burn and smoulder."

The man sighed sympathetically. "This is Applaud My Death. You must have taken the wrong turning on the road." He squinted at the map Edgar offered him. "Oh no, you don't want to be trusting them old things. The men who draw them are liars."

"Really?" Edgar rubbed his jaw.

"Besides," the thin man continued, "you'll be lucky to see anything roast today. The wicker man's been cancelled. Reverend Cleaver's virgins all caught the pox and died. He hasn't been able to rustle up any more. Why do you think I'm at home?"

A sudden idea struck Edgar. He whispered something to the thin man. The emaciated fellow chuckled and rubbed his palms together. "In that case you'd better come in and have a bite to eat. I've got some Minced Grandmother in the pantry, or you can have Basted Forehead."

"What the traditional local dish?" Edgar asked.

"Shepherd's Pie with vegetables. Real shepherds: crook, smock and dog. Watch the splinters. The vegetables are brain-dead poachers. Or you can have Poacher's Pie with brain-dead shepherds."

Edgar walked to the car and returned with Annabel. They followed the thin man into the interior of the farm house. They sat down at a table in the kitchen while their host rattled pots and pans over the stove. "This is real living!" Edgar enthused. "Honest food and honest folk. They really know how to force agricultural labourers between pastry here! No corners cut; the whole labourer, with a cheese topping!"

"Sounds grand." Annabel licked her lips. She picked up the knife and fork before her. The knife was fully twelve inches long, a vicious blade encrusted with blood. The fork had a tongue impaled on each of its cruel tines. She tentatively licked one; it was a male tongue. Edgar glared at her and she blushed bright red.

"Hussy!"

The meal was astonishingly filling. It was washed down with glasses of Adam's Apple Cider. While they were eating it, the thin man disappeared for some minutes to make a phone call. Edgar and Annabel could hear him mumbling something in the hallway. Edgar covered his smile with a grimace picked from the pie. Annabel shook hands with her meal. "Stop playing with your food!" Edgar roared. He belched a red belch. "Yum!"

Eventually, the fellow rejoined them. "Well that's settled then. Are you ready for dessert?"

Annabel shook her head. "We'd better be off, really. We're just passing through, you see; on our way to Stafford to visit relatives. We thought it would be nice to make a detour through Shropshire, rather than taking the motorway."

"Nice?" The thin man seemed confused. He pulled at his forelock, the one strand of hair that remained on his head. "Is that a foreign word?" He brightened. "The road between Impale My Dog and Heretic On Pyre is blocked. You won't reach the border by nightfall."

Edgar reached out and placed a hand on her arm. "We don't want to cause offence. Let's just stay a little longer."

Annabel shrugged and assented to dessert. It

turned out to be a type of Spotted Dick – though the thin man insisted it was called Diseased Tom. As she ate, she could not fail to notice the way Edgar and her host kept glancing anxiously at the clock on the mantelpiece.

Edgar made a small cough. "Have some more, my dear."

"No thank you," she replied, but the thin man had already ladled more of the crusty pudding onto her plate. He held up a jug within which something quite foul stirred sluggishly.

"Clotted?" he inquired.

She shook her head. After she had devoured this second helping, they sat in silence for a while. She rapped her fingers impatiently on the table. Edgar and her host cleared their throats and kept looking at the time. The thin man stood over by the window and peered through the grimy glass. "He should be here by now."

"Who?" Annabel demanded. She frowned at Edgar, who affected not to notice and pretended to be suddenly interested in the condition of his fingernails. "What's going on?"

"Perhaps he's had an accident. Reverend Cleaver is a poor driver at the best of times. I told him not to fit those scythes on the wheels of his tractor. Won't fit down the lanes, I said. Would he listen? Not on your life! I bet he's mangled a cow."

"What's going on?" Annabel repeated in a firm voice. She rose from her chair and moved towards the door. Without thinking, she kept the long blood-encrusted knife in her hand.

"Sit down." There was desperation in Edgar's voice. "Please don't spoil things! We may never get another chance like this one. This sort of life is dying out. Heritage!"

Annabel snorted. "Well you can stay if you want. I'm off." She reached into her pocket for her car keys and dangled them in front of him. His eyes grew wide with a sudden panic.

"Wait for me!" he cried.

As they left, the thin man turned his face towards them and nodded courteously. But there was bitter disappointment in his strange eyes. "Pleased to meet you. Come again some time. Visitors are always welcome at Applaud My Death. Well farewell! Unsafe journey!"

Annabel climbed into her car, watched in mordant amusement as Edgar scurried in beside her, and roared off. She placed the long knife on the dashboard. They bounced back down the lanes they had driven up. "What's going on?" she demanded.

"Nothing!" Edgar squirmed uneasily on the seat. Before long, they came across a tractor lying on its side in a ditch. A broad man dressed in a black cassock, with a dog collar, was kicking the exposed engine. Blades and bovine flesh lay tangled together.

Annabel slowed the car and wound the window down. "Can we help you Reverend?" She was astonished when the huge figure turned round with a mouth full of highly imaginative oaths.

"I was off to Applaud My Death," he said, when he had recovered his composure, "but ran into this ridiculous creature. Harry Spleen rang me earlier to tell me that a travelling couple were sitting in his kitchen. The woman is a virgin, apparently."

"I see. Well we can't help you there, I'm afraid. We don't know any virgins." She stepped on the accelerator and screeched away. Back on the main road, she pulled into a lay-by and turned to face Edgar. "You told that thin man I was a virgin! How could you?"

Edgar was apologetic. "I'm sorry. It's just that I've never seen a wicker man before. The chance was too good to miss."

"But it's a lie; I'm not a virgin!" Annabel shook her fist at him. "I might not even have burned properly. What would you have done then? Siphoned some petrol from my car?"

Edgar laughed. "They wouldn't really have set you on fire. All that is just a metaphor. Country-speak. You don't really believe that they burn virgins round here? You'll be telling me next that you think all these place names actually mean what they say."

"Don't they?"

"Of course not!" Edgar wiped tears of mirth from his cheeks. "What? Purloin My Liver and Grind My Bones and Applaud My Death? They're just colourful similes. Like the names of the drinks and the food. It's all an elaborate act. Tradition, you see."

"Well the landlord of the Plucked Eyeball had obviously had his eyeball plucked. And that Shepherd's Pie really did taste of smock and crook. How do you account for that?"

"Coincidence. Anyway what about Purloin My Liver and Applaud My Death? Nothing happened in any of those places that could possibly be linked to their names."

"Well your liver was stolen for a start." Annabel blinked and clucked her tongue. "I saw it happen."

"What?" The shadow of a doubt crossed Edgar's face. His fingers prodded his side. A sudden horror enveloped his features. He gazed at Annabel with terrified eyes. "Where?"

"In the pub. A dwarf stole it. I thought you knew." She picked up the knife from the dashboard, held it up to the sunlight for a moment, and then thrust it deep into Edgar's side. She worked it backwards and forwards and then pulled it out. No blood followed. She pointed at the gaping wound and the empty space beyond. "See?"

"It's true!" Edgar was incredulous. He pulled the wound open and thrust his fingers in. After some minutes of groping around within, he gulped and clutched at Annabel. "But without a liver I'll die!"

"Of course." Annabel returned the knife to the dashboard and once again started the ignition. "Perhaps I can sell your body to a local brewery." This time she made no attempt to avoid the carcass of a sheep that lay in the path of her car.

Edgar went into convulsions and began moaning. A little while later he fell silent. Reaching over, Annabel checked his pulse and smiled. Then she took both hands off the steering wheel for an instant and burst into spontaneous applause.

THE
SQUONK
LAUGHED

The title of this story should also be its final sentence. Let me set the scene and tell you how it happened.

A blunderbuss above an unlit hearth; a stack of pterosaur bones within it. And I, glass of sherry in hand, ragged slippers on a low stool, reclining at my unease in starched shirt and ruff.

The turrets were crumbling. A slate slid into the gulf below.

"Alack," mused I, shifting my weight on the antique cushions, each stuffed with a thousand rare moths. "Heavy is my lymph, for I am alone. There is nobody to share my gloomy abode, or help me repair the leaking roof. Solitude and hollowness are my lot."

A rattling at the window; a feeble pressure on the pane which had naught to do with wind or rain. I adjusted my green cap, set down my drink and stood with a nervous jerk. The bare boards supported me from chair to latch, though they had been carved by my traditional enemy.

"What is this? A visitor? Enter, I beg you! There are soft furnishings inside, an iron chandelier and the memory of warmth."

Throwing open the casement to admit my guest, I was astonished by his melancholy expression. There was more woe contained in the circumference of his visage than in all the dungeons of Asturias. A constant stream of tears from two enormous eyes had worn deep furrows in his cheeks; his lower lip curled down to his feet, which protruded directly from his neck, as if the rest of his body had fled this source of misery. His spherical form did not suggest harmony – he was studded with warts which seemed not to belong to him.

"I believe I know what manner of being you are," quothed I, in a suitably formal tone. "You, sir, are a squonk. There is no sadder entity in the whole mistaken cosmos. But the natural habitat of your species, *Lacrimacorpus dissolvens*, is deep in the hemlock forests of Pennsylvania. How came you to my mountainous retreat?”

It was unfair to delay the creature on the sill. I bowed and beckoned and it hopped across the chamber to the grate. While it shivered and sneezed over the cold ashes, I retrieved the cushions, which had taken flight, attracted by the guttering tallows in the iron chandelier.

“Sit here, Señor Squonk, and render yourself comfortable. That is a curious medallion you have slung around your ears. I am Humberto von Gibbon, an exiled poet, formerly of Mogrovejo, now of the doldrums, in both senses of the word, for my island has been set adrift on that briny latitude, and my soul vainly drops like an anchor to lodge a halt, a sinking which entails it dragging along the bed of despair.”

My guest rolled its eyes at me, sneezed again and proceeded to lick its patchy fur, spattering raindrops, tears and dribble in all directions.

“Ah, so you misunderstand my motives? No matter, weepy one, I shall reassure you with a glass of *Oloroso*. There is comfort in wine, is there not? Observe the décor of my apartments. This castle on its giddy perch, to whose stone portals you have wandered, is the only habitation on this dramatic island. It was built by my worst foe, Ugolino Cadiz, for my unbearable confinement.

“Yet I am free to stroll the balconies and scheme a method of climbing into yonder gulf. Then I might construct a raft from trees and sail off to the horizon. Whether I perished or no, it would be of little matter. A gesture of resistance, at the very least. Here, I am marooned in a sequence of dismal chambers, each a slightly different shade of grey. Bells connected to pressure points on the floor chime whenever I walk through the labyrinth, seeking an exit.”

I poured a large measure for my new friend, but he seemed overawed by the vintage, easing his nose delicately into the bouquet and then recoiling.

"A little early for the fire of the grape, perhaps?" I queried. "That is understandable, though here the conventional hours are no longer observed. There is only one route through the interlocking cells of my dwelling, and the varying degrees of steely colour which greet my eye as I pace the route are cleverly arranged to form a distinct monochrome impression of my tormentor's face, as if he designed the order and contents of the rooms on a grid-plan of his sneering countenance.

"So too the bells, when activated, sound a lilting syllable identical to the intolerably dulcet tones of his own throat. Thus I am condemned to be always haunted by his presence, indeed to *live* within an abstraction of his likeness, his mocking voice calling out to me, 'Humberto, you are an oaf', in a constant cycle of trudging through nested grief. But I persist because Ugolino hinted that a secret door might lead to freedom. I search in vain; a cruel jest."

The visitor puffed his cheeks at the hearth, frowning as the dead embers refused to burst into new life. I stooped to pat his misshapen head and he shivered at my touch. Stroking a squonk is an action not so very far removed from brushing the cheek of a distraught cloud.

"You wonder why there are no flames in my grate? Another prank! He has stacked firewood in the cellar, but the moment I drag it up here, I see it is merely painted pterosaur bones. Only the food retains its character; indeed it improves with conveyance, possibly to accord with the law of cosmic balance. For every disappointment there is a small joy. But how callous of me to speak of joy in your presence! Also too many joys combine into one irregular lump which has much in common with wretchedness. I despise such joys!

"My wife does little to comfort me. Ugolino turned her into a blunderbuss and mounted her on the mantle, in both senses of the verb. She may be discharged once, and after that her life is gone. By blowing out my brains with her, I also commit murder and doom myself to Hell. I have had enough of earthly torments and care not to substitute them for those of a supernatural character. Now allow me to show you my extensive library; it is my major ease. Here is a bestiary bound in the sloughed skin of a tazelwurm. It contains a chapter on your kind. Permit me to read aloud its fustian descriptions.

"Ah, you are too modest to entertain such a notion. That is why you are so reticent. Very well! I shall satisfy myself with a single observation: *the squonk may never be caught, for the moment it is bagged it dissolves entirely into a puddle of tears.* If this be true, Señor, then we are polar opposites, for here I am always snared, but my endless lamentations do not result in such a reprieve. Indeed they seem to leave a desiccated wedge of indestructible dejection behind, totally arid and dry, who yet manages to drip another tear down his overlong nose."

A shadow passed across the window, a large globe which dropped out of a cloud and began to drift toward my castle. I saw a rudder and propeller, eager faces peering over the side of a basket. My guest rubbed his hands and nodded to himself. Then he reached for his curious medallion and lifted it to his eye. I now saw that it was a miniature form of *camera obscura*, such as are employed by certain painters in the Spanish Netherlands.

Before I could inspect this marvellous apparatus – which is what I assumed was expected of me – a blinding flash disordered my vision and I fell back, clutching my head. The squonk lowered the machine, cast a glance at the sky and hopped back across the boards. In a moment he had turned the latch and was standing on the sill, waving to the aerial sphere, whose occupants duplicated his communication with considerable vigour.

"Have I offended you, Señor?" I cried, aghast. Another slate fell into the void. It occurred to me that I had been a complete boor, offering *Oloroso* instead of *Rias Baixas*. I turned to dash the despicable bottle on the stones of the hearth, but a harrowing absence grated on my consciousness. The blunderbuss was gone! Then I understood the nature of the trick that had been played on me.

My wife had been abducted for a souvenir!

I rushed to the window, but it was too late. The flying orb had drawn level with the chamber and the squonk jumped into space to meet it. My outstretched fingers brushed the warts on the back of his head, and then he had landed in the basket, the blunderbuss tucked under one arm. Ballast was discarded; the globe rose above the turret. The men who steered the device were Pennsylvanian farmers – I noted the missing teeth, the straw hats. But they also had something of the dastardly Iberian about them – the pointed beards, the golden earrings. I surmised that they were emigrant Cadizites, cousins and agents of Ugolino.

Tottering on the sill, I called up: "Please kill me! Without my wife I am nothing!"

The squonk rested the gun on the tiller of the rudder and aimed at my chest. I opened my arms to receive the shot. To be released from my desolation and fly with my wife to paradise! I was ecstatic. But the explosion never came: a spot of turbulence rocked the craft – there are pterosaurs on the island, though I never see them – and by the time it had settled, I was out of range. The chance was gone.

As a believer, I am not permitted to finish myself. I must escape or die of old age. Ugolino is not a simple monster: before he uprooted the whole *Picos de Europa*, he took care to evacuate or metamorphose all the inhabitants of the range, except me. It does not serve his purpose to tyrannise everybody. I was a poet; I wrote a song for him. He did not like it. This is my punishment. And now the original mountains are regrowing, or so I speculate – the bears, *Ursus ibericus*, and the goats, *Capra hircus*, are returning.

There was a single consolation in this latest sleight: my mistress could now come out of hiding. She had been locked in a wardrobe with my waistcoats ever since my wife returned home early from her flamenco class. I strode to the piece of furniture in question, unbolted the door and helped her out – a duelling pistol. Then I hung her in my wife's place, on a hook above the hearth. A poor substitute really; a flintlock floosie, always powdering her pan.

If I do not leave before the castle falls down, I will be turned into a pair of shears. That is the prophecy.

I wonder if there is a parallel between the visit of this squonk and the other two who came last month. They also arrived in balloons and stole a teak hatstand and grandfather clock – my valet and cook respectively. One might almost suspect that package holidays are being arranged by the Pennsylvanians. But why?

The hemlock forests are jealously guarded by the squonks. Is Ugolino trying to win them over to his side for commercial purposes? But why does he need so much of the plant? The last I heard, he was assembling a college of philosophers in Valencia. What use have they for hemlock? And does he really think a vacation on my unlikely isle can cheer up a squonk, the saddest of all beasts?

The answer is obviously that he does. For when I set up a tripod by the window and fixed my younger brother to the screws, placing my eye to the lens and adjusting the focus, I was able to study the balloon from afar. I saw the passengers in great detail, and they were fighting over my wife. Then a peculiar expression came over the spherical face of my visitor, and something happened which had never previously been deemed possible in the history of cryptozoology.

100 TELEGRAPHS
TO
TELEGRAM
MA'AM

The Queen sits on her throne, writing telegrams. There is a knock on the door. It is Perry, the inventor. "What do you have for me this time, Mr Perry?" He holds up a slim object, dripping like a snake fang. The Queen frowns. "Well what is it?"

"A fountain pen, your majesty."

"Is it faster than a quill, Mr Perry?"

"Much faster, ma'am."

The Queen discards the quill, which tickles the floor.

Many more things have just reached their hundredth birthday. There is a frayed glove in the second drawer of a maple desk in a forgotten room in a cheap hotel in Brighton. There is an octahedral ruby cut from a flawed stone by a myopic jeweller with a blunt chisel in Winchester. There is a saying among the folk of Bideford, Devon, which declares, "Better to dip an organ in cider than a piano in rum," and another in Folkestone, Kent, not recorded – they have both turned one hundred. And a vast telescope in the roof garden of Sir William Herschel. And the silver ring used by Prince Albert to restrain his erections, hidden in a rococo box when not in use, and the box itself, or rather its lock, and in the pocket of the locksmith's grandson, a farthing. There is a bicycle lying under a gorse bush on the North York Moors, where Joan Bailey lost it after her lover struck her on the head with a mallet, and she went wandering without her memory to Coventry, eventually becoming the manager of a puppet theatre, while the bush grew to help the lover avoid suspicion. There is a plough nailed to a wall in an Oxford tavern.

These have existed for exactly a century, and telegrams must be sent out to all of them.

The Queen is still sitting on her throne. Throughout the palace, the clocks are striking midnight. She covers a yawn with a hand. "Oh why must I congratulate *everything*?"

The people are growing agitated, politely. Agents ride out beyond them, disdaining the clamour. "Our monarch has abandoned us!" The agents say nothing, except the younger ones, who reply, "No she hasn't!" But the people will not listen. There is discontent in Dover. There is a hubbub in Huddersfield. There are murmurings in Manchester. The agents gallop faster. There is a gnashing in Grantham, not of teeth, which are rare there, but of groceries, pears gnashed against plums. "The monarch is neglecting us!" "No she isn't!"

An agitator mounts a soap box in Leeds. He has a speech prepared. A republican agenda. He opens his mouth, but an agent rides up to him and delivers a slip of paper.

"What's this? A telegram?"

The lowest button on his shirt must celebrate.

Prince Albert sits with the Queen in the bedchamber, holding hands. There is an aspidistra in a vase. The vase has recently received its telegram, the aspidistra has not.

"I can't take much more of this!"

She strokes his moustache. "Our duties must be fulfilled, dear. It's the constitution, you know. A secret part of modern government, vital to the integrity of the state."

"I am a man. I have desires. You are never being here, in my arms, like a wife. What shall happen when my erection restraint wears out? It was forged over ten decades ago."

"We will order another, from the Sheffield Kama Sutra Co."

"I am sure to die of frustration!"

The Queen sits on her throne, writing telegrams. The fountain pen is faster than the quill, but the workload does not lessen. There are more things in the world now, more objects to grow old. And as the Empire continues to expand, it gets worse. A gold mine in Natal. A brewery in Australia. A religion in Rajasthan. There is a knock on the door. It is Stephenson, the inventor.

"What do you have for me this time, Mr Stephenson?"

"A locomotive, your majesty."

"Is it faster than a horse?"

"Much faster, ma'am."

"Kindly demonstrate, Mr Stephenson."

"It is too large to bring indoors."

The Queen cocks an ear and hears a distant whistle and the scrape of a shovel on coal. The years chug past.

The Prime Minister is arguing with the Lord Chancellor.

"But the tradition is doing wonders for our economy. Think of the technological offshoots it has created!"

"The Queen is exhausted. Remember what happened to George III. He went mad. And William IV took to drink."

"Nonetheless, the tradition must continue. Too much time and effort has been invested to cancel it now. I have personally meddled with the archives of the Patent Office, altering dates and names, so that future historians will not perceive a link between progress and the tradition. You know which tradition I mean."

"The tradition which is kept secret from the people?"

"Yes, precisely that tradition."

"The tradition which has been indirectly responsible for numerous inventions, including the cantilever bridge, tarmac, the dynamo, sewing machines, the gyroscope, the compression refrigerator, corrugated iron, dirigibles, and the first class stamp?"

"That's the one! Strike this from the record!"

Agents sit in the buffet cars of locomotives. Behind them, they tow nine carriages full of telegrams. At various points along the route, they open the doors and leap into the night, clutching a message. One has a trowel concealed under his hat. He lands awkwardly, shuffling toward a nameless village. The locomotive turns a bend and leaves him alone. He enters a churchyard, searching mossy headstones for the correct name. Here it is! He crouches and hacks at the fog-drenched earth with the trowel. At last the coffin is revealed. Pausing for breath, he glances around. An owl in a blasted yew returns his look. The agent jumps onto the coffin and inserts the edge of his tool under the lid. Rusty nails yawn from crumbling wood. Spiders flee. He throws back the lid like the cover of a Penny Dreadful and gags as a moonbeam, challenging a cloud to a duel and running it through, impales a madly grinning skeleton, bones jutting from mouldy suit! Hurriedly, the agent pins the telegram to the collar of the skeleton's shirt, replaces the lid and soil and dances the plot flat, with a lame leg.

Prince Albert has sickened and died, of frustration, or typhoid, it is not clear which, possibly both. "Now I will have more time to devote to the writing of telegrams!" sobs the Queen.

The agitator squats in the hold of a prison ship. A warder approaches, checking cells with a lantern. Something is wrapped around the glass, casting a stream of words over beams and bulwarks. At regular intervals, for no discernible reason, the warder lashes at his captives with a cat o' nine tails. The agitator counts ten stripes on his legs when it is his turn. He notes that the extra tail is a length of paper, dangling from the handle of the antique whip.

The Queen sits on her throne, writing telegrams. There is a knock on the door. It is Littledale, the inventor.

"What do you call that thing, Mr Littledale?"

"A typewriter, your majesty."

"Is it quieter than a locomotive, Mr Littledale?"

"Slightly, ma'am. It is powered by ribbons."

"Can it do the writing for me?"

"Not at this stage. In a century or two."

"It must write a telegram to itself when that happens."

The French President is worrying his Chief of Police.

"What are the English playing at, *mon cher*?"

"I don't know, Monsieur President."

"They are cutting down trees at a furious rate. Obviously to make paper. But paper for what?"

"English novels, perhaps?"

"Ah yes! Do you like English novels, *mon cher*? I ordered one from London last week. A Defoe. The seventh word in the twelfth line of the sixty third paragraph of the ninety fifth chapter had a telegram glued to it. With noxious fish glue!"

"An extraordinary coincidence, Monsieur President! I also ordered a Defoe from London last week. At the centre was a compressed oak leaf and stapled to the leaf was a telegram."

"Rosbif! Barbarians! Louts! We must consider forging an alliance, *mon cher*, to discover the meaning of this."

A gold tooth under a pillow in a Padstow cottage, still waiting, without an owner, for a fairy. A wig in a box at the rear of a kennel in Durham, guarded by a dog with the morals of a cat. The belief that some cherries contain real stones, probably flints, held by the farmers of Thetford. A picture of a summer day in the Cotswolds, painted with clotted cream and magenta jam, in an unhygienic bakery in Winchcombe. A pistol in the hand of the very last man to fight a legal duel in Breckland, eating cherries to ignite the charge. A rotten hymn.

The Queen sits on her throne. Telegrams, knock on the door. A figure who wears his sideburns like camshafts.

"Who are you? I have no inventor called Babbage!"

"With respect, ma'am, I have been seeking an audience with you for thirty years. Allow me to demonstrate this analytical engine here. It is an early type of computer and can be programmed to perform a large body of functions, such as writing telegrams."

"How dare you talk of body functions in my presence?"

"No ruler can afford to be without one."

"I am busy! Take it away!"

Tears in the palace. A silver ring taken from a box, lovingly pressed to lips. "Once I was your barrel of sauerkraut. You whispered to me, '*Liebe Kleine. Ich habe dich so lieb, ich kann nicht sagen wie*', and I presumed you were asking to visit the bathroom. But now you are gone. And my life has become a telegram without news."

"You sent for me, your majesty?"

"Yes, Prime Minister. We have a problem. The tradition of sending telegrams to everything is one hundred years old."

"Then you must send a telegram to the tradition."

"But how? How can one send a telegram to a tradition? Who can carry it? Where will they go? I am bewildered."

"You must try, ma'am! You must try!"

The Queen tries:

> *Dear Tradition,*
> *Congratulations on reaching the centenary of*
> *being yourself.*
>
> > *Best wishes,*
> > *The Queen.*

No, it is too absurd. Something must be done. The law will have to be altered, so that only old people receive telegrams, not everything. A secret bill must be passed.

The Prime Minister weeps at the thought of change.

A dream: a world where inanimate objects can rest in peace. Unemployed agents race nowhere in automobiles. Paradise! But a cloud looms on the horizon, cooling the idyll. There will still be much work to do. Wines, books, spoons, piers, guitars, floods, hearths, stables, gutters, pots, vendettas, crotchets, cuffs, doors, accidents, comets – these and many other items have been set free, but the population is increasing at an exponential rate. What if people come to outnumber things? How can this be avoided? Only a war, the like of which has never been imagined. That will stall the trend. But with whom?

On nights when the silver ring was kept in its box, Prince Albert gave her children. And these children have also produced children. One is named Wilhelm. Machine guns, gas.

We are not amused.

DEPRESSURISED
GHOST STORY

My soul lives on a ledge. I have always been a climber: my first conquest was the north face of our family home in Colchester. Alarmed by the sight of her only child scrabbling among the ivy, my mother rushed out and held her apron to catch me. But I succeeded in gaining the highest chimney and remained there until starvation compelled me to descend to my punishment, which turned out to be more hunger – I was exiled to bed. Always prudent, my father nailed my window shut, but I spent an intrepid night clambering over the precipitous furniture.

Later, in Eton, I forsook lessons to begin a passionate relationship with the gables and turrets of the college buildings. At this time, I was introduced to the telling of ghost tales, courtesy of our Provost. Though untroubled by his morbid fables and anecdotes, I never became a confirmed sceptic of the paranormal. My fellow pupils exchanged his tombic romances like farthings, but I was simply uninterested in anything which could not be scaled and it seemed unlikely a spectre would afford a grip for boots, even those fitted with crampons.

After my wholly inadequate schooling, I attended university to study engineering. I excelled at mathematics whenever a quantity had to rise up the gradient of a steep formula; the rest of the time my failures were as immense and unlikely as a glacier. My tutor chided me one afternoon: "You have the loftiest intentions, but they reside in your feet." Over my door I fixed an ice axe, a symbol of reality cooler than any abstract logic. I was not alone; other acrophiliac students joined me in expeditions around the dour peaks and chalk cliffs.

I graduated with a poor degree and immediately started out on a life above the clouds. I wandered over the Alps, rolling down one peak only to ascend another, like a snowball which has gathered infinite momentum.[1] My allowance was soon cut, but I did not return to face my father. I applied for a job in East Africa as a technical consultant. I found time to climb a number of equatorial mountains, though I was mauled by a leopard on the summit of Kilimanjaro and forced to rest on a plantation. One of my close neighbours turned out to be an explorer by the name of Shipton. Within an hour of meeting we were planning an ambitious expedition to Central Asia to explore the unknown G— N— Range.

We shared a philosophy of light travel. He was a more lyrical fellow than I, the sort of climber who writes up his adventures in books. I have an idea he did actually publish his memoirs in several volumes. I have no reason to suppose he remembers me; our collaboration was rather brief. We argued over the exact location of the forbidden Q—— valley, mentioned in a Tibetan folktale, one of those translated by X. D. Laocoön. A scuffle broke out; we exchanged blows with a map of the area. He threw me off his premises. Now I was fired with a determination to reach the valley before he did. I staggered away, silently vowing: "You have beaten me to a pulp, but I shall beat you to fame..."[2]

I spent five years saving money for the mission, collecting climbers and equipment, getting myself in shape for the arduous task. Eventually I was fit and rich enough to feel reasonably confident. Crossing the horrid peaks of the G— N— Range would cost a fortune in leather soles: I hired a Polish cobbler to accompany me. Other hopefuls applied from England and continental Europe. We arranged to meet in

---

[1] This is untrue. Had I really gathered infinite momentum, my mass would also have been infinite. The immense gravitational field set up around my body in such circumstances would have made me the centre of the universe. Obviously this did not happen.

[2] Then I returned to his villa and shouted the words through his window. He attacked me with a globe. At this point, I discovered that small scale maps inflict more painful bruises.

Calcutta. Arriving there after a rough sea voyage, I was pleasantly surprised to discover all but one of my recruits had turned up. The missing chap was our radio operator. Later in the Hotel D——, fiddling with a short-wave wireless, we picked up his attenuated signals, drowning beneath the civilised accents and restrained static of the BBC World Service.

We set off on August 5th, 19-, after a hearty breakfast of rice and lentils, heading north on the 09:05 express. We had an entire carriage to ourselves, for since my disagreement with Shipton I intended to do all my exploring in the opposite way to him – if he planned to take little on an ascent, I was determined to carry up as much as possible. It chaffed with my real principles, of course, but my pride outweighs my sense. And while my story is rattling along the rails, let me introduce you to the prosaic souls who formed the core of my party. Because I am quite modest, I shall refrain from saying which of the following names belongs to me, though it has the sweetest ring to it: C. Bowman, J. Tolkien-Twigge, O. Eckenstein, R. Darktree, M.A. Zimara, C. Weasel, H. Melmoth, E.S. Abbott, A.G. Woden, B. Cadiz, D. Delves, I. Evans... (The remainder of the list has just been obscured by smoke from the train).

I can hardly see the paragraphs in this fog. The quality of our coal must have been very poor. Having studied Hindoo ceremonies, I made a joke which raised blisters but no smiles – the stoker had died at his post and his wife jumped into the furnace. I repeat it here because I know readers have a darker sense of humour than climbers. Actually you are a very good audience: I wish you had come with me instead of those miserable fellows. But you would have grumbled about the cold in S—— , where we disembarked and hired ponies to take us over the B—— Hills. Right to the borders of M—— we rode. (I know you are trying to reconstruct my route. You are bored with the pace of my document and want to make a dash for the end. I do not advise this. The narrow passes of L—— are infested with bandits. Please stay close to my prose).

Months of hardship and weak tea sapped the energies of my followers. We stopped in the shadow of R— D—— and bathed in the thermal springs. Some of my team, rather less educated than the others, had never heard of X.D. Laocoön and the forbidden valley of Q——, nor were they overeager to learn the mythology of this region. I taught them anyway. Every valley in Tibet is filled to the brim with ruined cities, sorcerous treasure and immortal lamas. Q—— was the only empty one. It was remarkable because of the things it did not contain. I suppose you might say that the places of magic which surrounded it gave it a lustrous presence and outlined the mystery: like depicting a tree by painting the sky which lies between its branches. According to Laocoön, it was the only place on the planet never trampled by any kind of feet, not even when there was only one continent and all the mountains were flat.

I was not entirely convinced by this, for I knew there were areas of Colchester equally untrodden, though these were generally very small. Yet the allure of Q—— was excessive. I reserved for myself the first step onto its soil. Ringed and supported by a circle of jagged mountains, like a bowl of soup guarded by a dozen grumpy waiters, the valley was surveyed many centuries ago by a levitating monk. That, at any rate, was the tale related by Laocoön. I was too suspicious to query the word of one who has been criticised by doubters. Closer to our objective we lurched, pressing our destination into a corner. We traversed the Y— R— Glacier, losing our supply of teapots down crevasses while I cut spiral steps in the ice. At the end of this stage it was apparent we needed to employ porters from local settlements. There were caves in the bottom of the Glacier: muffled troglodytes played dice with frozen tears. They shouldered our cases with a stoicism exhausting to behold.

The porters were fine chaps, but they were difficult to address. The leaders of our initial group were Tsongkhapa and Dromtönpa. We soon added Langdharama and

Shantarikshita to the ranks. Entering a remote village on the Z-— P—— Plateau,[3] I was extremely grateful to hire Bertie. He was old and frail, but the simplicity of his appellation was a crucial factor in our offer of employment. Besides, feeble porters totter most carefully and are ideal for carrying scientific equipment. After two or three weeks of his dedication, I asked him how he came by such a name. It emerged his father was a Scottish engineer working in Bengal who decided to construct a bamboo bicycle and pedal home. This eccentric resolution carried him no further than the Himalayas.

"What happened there?" I inquired.

"He lost his way after turning left at Lhasa," Bertie explained. "He wobbled into our village with a puncture and a fever. After we tended him and restored his health, he became a shamanic figure, devising all manner of apparatus for our convenience."

These, Bertie went on to expound, included attaching electric motors to temple prayer wheels to accelerate local devotion. The engineer had an idea that the efficacy of these devices corresponded to the rate of spin. There was a threshold of so many millions of revolutions per minute above which a prayer would actually work. Unfortunately his career was finished when his sporran was caught in an axle. He was pulled in and rotated to a pious demise, leaving unfinished his dream of converting the entire world into a prayer wheel by rearranging the mountains to spell out a mantra. I insisted that a single rotation a day would scarcely be enough to satisfy the highest Heaven. Bertie agreed.

---

[3] For anyone who mistrusts my geography or believes I am being coy about cartographical detail, let me add that the Z—— P—— Plateau lies between the R—— and J—— Rivers. It is —— miles long and —— miles broad and contains the villages of B—— and O—— . In the latter village lives a chap named A—— M—— who distils a brandy from the W——————— plant. I suggest you try it some time, it may do you good.

"I did not say he was sane, merely my father."

There is no time for more extracts from the conversations we enjoyed along the way. They were wholly of this quality. But I am already exactly 1669 words into my account and at this point it is good manners to reward my readers with some action (with this bracket the total has increased to 1708 words – dash it! I am overwriting. Better edit the next line.) As we approached the serrated peaks... lucky to be alive. I have never seen any sunset to compare with that one. The slopes shimmered like enormous fires put to bed in clean sheets but rolling around. I was overawed. One of the English climbers fell to his knees and started muttering that these peaks were impenetrable. I wanted to shoot him like a mad yak, but mastered the impulse before dusk. We set up camp.

Before retiring, I made a speech: "We have braved many dangers since leaving the luxuries of home. But the peace of mind afforded by good food and wine will shortly be eclipsed. For on the far side of these mountains the serenity of Q—— is waiting."

Bertie came to my tent after midnight. "The men are frightened. They have no problem with serenity, but ghosts might also be waiting. There is no lonelier or remoter spot on the surface of the Earth. Where better for evil phantoms to take up residence?"

I laughed. "That is a common misconception of mountaineers. Actually the opposite is the case. This is probably the only valley in Tibet which is not crowded with the wispy dead."

"How can you be sure? No-one has been here before."

"Exactly! Ghosts tend to hover near the place where they originated. In lonely and remote areas, where there are few beings to expire, hardly any can exist. Here there are none."

Pointing out the relevant passage in Laocoön, I sent

him away with a relieved smile on his weathered face. My Polish cobbler, I decided, would be able to use Bertie's skin as leather if anything happened to the tough old McSherpa. As I lay in the fresh dark, I thought about my own logic. A valley without people is a valley without spectres. It seemed too obvious for comfort. Something was wrong. Unable to sleep, I lit a lamp and tired myself anew by catching up with my diary. Wonders avoided Q—— with an unnatural consistency. Its ordinariness was miraculous. This is a paradox also true, I am told, of charladies.

The following morning I was shattered, but I insisted on leading the final push up the sheer wall of soft snow and slippery rock. More ancient than a stupa, Bertie bulged with exertion. Halfway up, he admitted he was not a Buddhist but a follower of the original Tibetan religion, Bon, with special protection from one of its obscure demons. I was pleased with his confession, as it released me from a moral obligation to assist him. When a devil watches over you, a more spectacular descent is usually reserved. It may be of interest to record that I was first to the top, though I did not boast of my achievement aloud, contenting myself with a little dance. The consequences of this action were... (yes, an avalanche has swept away the rest of this paragraph. It has taken one of my readers with it. There he goes! Him with the beard).

I was also first to descend into the valley proper. The inner slopes were gentler than the outer. (While you dig your way out, let me reassure you that none of the team lost our balance in the accident. We were above the fracture, whereas readers tend to lurk at the base of a story. I pity you. But it is your own fault for coming this far. Next time you must try to be more careful.) I planted the flag of my nation in the frost and sat in the slash of its shadow, trying to ignite a portable stove. There were no teapots so I brewed coffee while my colleagues joined me. Bertie, last of all, delivered the precision instruments to my feet. I set up a number of regulation experiments with the barometer and manometer, measuring the pressure differentials. There was a roaring pain in my head and the edges of my vision were indistinct.

I ignored my ailments. "Well, this is it!" I announced. "The last of all solitudes; the hymen of the planet. Now we are here, the world really has lost its virginity. Look around. Apart from a floating sage, no human has ever seen this fastness."

"I feel a trifle dizzy," answered Bertie.

"Altitude sickness," I replied. "The pressure is quite low.[4] If the feeling persists you must open a vein. Now then, I suggest we rush around like lunatics, to trample most of the unblemished spots before tiffin. An expedition must be thorough in its desecration. Otherwise our claim to be first will be open to doubt."

I exempted Bertie from the task. He sprawled on the snow, reading my copy of Laocoön. The valley was roughly the same size as Colchester, flat and completely barren of animal or plant life.[5] I made a total circuit, in the opposite direction to my companions, which was a decision they had arrived at. I felt agitated, but there was a force inside me which bawled with delight, as if my subconscious was enjoying a holiday. For a strange reason, I was reminded of my old Provost at Eton. After a hearty stamp of the valley, the other climbers joined me for a light meal. I said nothing about my experience, though they were equally disturbed. We fidgeted away the majority of the afternoon.

In the evening, I watched the stars wheel in the sky. They had never been observed from this region and I waited to

---

4 I am disgusted with the way you always complain about the pressures of work. Try to remember what a lack of pressure entails: nausea, confusion, haemorrhaging. Reconsider before asking your boss for extra leave. Do you want to bleed from the ears and eyes.

5 This region is almost as devoid of life as the following 32 paragraphs are devoid of notes.

catch them doing something different. Disappointed, I crawled inside my tent. I fell asleep rapidly, as if prompted to do so. My dream was remarkably coherent but pedestrian. I saw myself stand and leave the tent. My comrades were also emerging; we seemed pleased just to stretch our arms at full length. Then we got up to all manner of silly games: prancing, skipping and waltzing. We felt as if we were prisoners released from long captivity, ecstatic simply to have a space in which to exercise. Suddenly I woke in a cold sweat. Somebody was clawing at my tent. I cried aloud: "Who is there? Bertie, is that you?" I fumbled for my ice axe. There was a mocking laugh. I gripped the tool and thrust the spike upwards. It punctured the fabric but did not penetrate a fleshy body beyond. I frowned.

Crawling out, I was amazed to notice that the tents of my companions were also shaking. There had been a fresh snowfall, but no footprints led away from my site. Like an economical cactus, each tent poked out a spike from an ice axe. Then the occupants emerged and stood in confusion, while exchanging terrified glances. Nightcap askew on his head, Bertie began to chant a mantra, calling on his patron demon to guard his life. I insisted he refrain from his diabolism.

"But we are being attacked by ghosts!" he wailed.

I raised a hand. "Nonsense! I have already explained that no wraiths exist in the valley. No-one has ever died in this location. Therefore our ordeal must be due to some natural phenomenon. A practical joker perhaps? I suspect our radio operator has finally caught us up. His silly sense of humour was well documented."

"If that is the case, where is he now?"

I scanned the horizon. There were no hiding places in the chilly dip and the starlight reflecting from the shallow walls illuminated the scene cheaply and efficiently. "I do not care to argue with a Sherpa. As leader of this party I order everyone back to bed. I will have an answer to your insidious question by morning."

Reluctantly, the explorers returned to their tents.

Bertie wanted to curl up with me for safety but I warned him that the men might talk. With ninety six little shudders, he pulled his nightcap down over his eyes and left me alone. I pondered. Quite plainly, the radio operator was not with us. His aerial would be visible even had he hidden under a snowdrift. The remaining explanations were a freak wind in the shape of a body or else a levitating monk come to take revenge for our violation of his territory. I gazed up, but the stars were all where they should be, no constellation blotted by a serene silhouette.

I said nothing about the matter over breakfast, though Bertie huffed and agitated to bring it up. My colleagues were keen to begin the journey home, but I was too curious to depart now. I stalled them with scientific blather about the need to conduct a week's worth of experiments. Furious haggling was set in motion and we settled on a stay of three days. Bertie moaned at this news and retired to study Laocoön's anti-phantom remedies. Unfortunately, this section, at the back of the volume, had been eaten by a goat on the train to S— .

That night my dream came back, with a changed choreography. I danced a tango rather than a waltz. Each time I passed my berth, I heard fretful snoring coming from within. The others strutted with me, icicles clenched between their teeth. I woke to a staccato tapping of heels on the side of my tent. I sat up and placed my eye to the hole I had jabbed the previous night. There was nobody outside, but I saw the pale irises of my comrades peering from their own gashes.

Bertie was inconsolable. He gibbered in an embarrassing fashion from the security of his sleeping bag. I crawled out and shook him free. To my extreme dismay, he repeated our dance, stark naked. He whipped up snow in a swirl which seemed momentarily to congeal into the shape of my Provost. Wagging a glacial finger, the illusion crumbled with a horrid jollity and I brushed academic flakes from my shoulders. Bertie fell to his knees and clutched at my swollen ankles.

"You promised an answer! Tell it to me!"

"Get a grip on yourself. Perhaps we are all suffering from delusions occasioned by extreme altitude. Or maybe we should stop cooking with yeti dung. The problem is medical."

Bertie shook his head. "It was a ghost."

I snubbed his hysteria and returned to bed, sleeping soundly until a beam of early sunlight poked through the rent, buying my brow with a coin of light. The climbers were in mutinous mood, refusing to cook breakfast. They lazed and shared Laocoön, alternately chuckling and yawning over his syntax. I persisted with my measuring and classifying, though there was a severe lack of things to which these processes might be applied. I worked without a break, eventually filling my notebooks with observations before packing away my instruments for the descent. I watched the moon pour over the horizon, licking my toasted face with its butter tongue. I decided to spend my last night in the open.

I perched on a folding stool and did my best to remain awake. But my bones were too heavy, knocking against each other beneath my skin. At the same time my spirit broke free from the rigging of my nerves, like a sail fleeing a mast in a storm. I was standing in front of myself, roaring and giggling, waving my arms in triumph. Soon I was joined by my comrades and we held an impromptu party. Bertie was present, looking less worried than in the daytime. I kicked and jabbed at my body, seated on its stool. Then there was a cry and another Bertie rose up from his sleeping bag, shaking a fist as he raced past us in his slippers. He continued towards the edge of the valley, vanishing over the rim. Obviously his body was leaving his spirit behind. We did our best to console the soul, which seemed a trifle glum, like a yolk without a shell.

Once more harassing my sleeping torso, I was startled when it jerked and I was sucked back inside. I opened my eyes to see the others emerging from their tents. They demanded: "Were you making that noise?" They began to accuse me of being the joker responsible for disturbing their sleep on the previous nights, but I protested vehemently. It was better to seal my lips about what I had witnessed – I did not want them thinking I was mad. I merely related the barest facts.

"Bertie has deserted us. The barometer will have to be abandoned. He fled in his nightcap and pyjamas."

There was nothing we could do. Had he been British... As it was, the sensible course of action was to forget about him. At first light we left the Q— valley forever, heading back towards the Z— P— Plateau. A week later we reached the Y— R— Glacier. It was faster going down. We dropped off Shantarikshita, Langdharama, Dromtönpa and Tsongkhapa, useful workers but taxing on the grammar. We failed to rescue our teapots from a crevasse but brewed tea in the thermal springs near R— D——. Somewhere beyond M——, after crossing the L— passes into the B—Hills, we were astonished to notice a ragged figure coming closer. It was Bertie, a man so broken his decrepitude had turned full circle back to health. Only his toothless smile betrayed his identity. He screamed: "Out of my way! I must get back to Q—— at once!"

I gripped his arm. "What happened, Bertie?"

His eyes were blank. "I ran all the way to S—— , where I milked the local goats, hoping to bottle Laocoön's missing pages. I soon trapped the one who had devoured his anti-phantom advice. I drank the milk and became aware of my true predicament."

"Are you returning to collect your spirit?"

He nodded, struggling out of my clutch. "Laocoön knew the dangers of the valley all along. This is why the levitating monk did not attempt to land there. The human race has been around for a long time, and before us there were demons and ogres with souls. The surface of the planet must be crowded with ghosts. Trillions of spooks all competing for the same piece of land. Think how uncomfortable it must be! Layers of wraiths struggling for space, like ashes in an oven.

Even in the polar regions there will be troll spectres crowding the icebergs!"

Plainly he had lost his sanity, but I decided to humour him. "Ghosts everywhere except in Q——? Without population it also lacks revenants. Doubtless a paradise for apparitions?"

"Absolutely. Land is now at a premium for phantasms. When we entered the valley, our souls were overjoyed to see so much open space. They were determined to stay there, rather than return to the crowded outside. They formulated a plot to ensure we remained. Every night they came out of our bodies and attempted to frighten us to death. Spectres must linger in the vicinity of their passing away."

"Come now, Bertie, this is claptrap. Spirits cannot depart bodies at will. They are strapped to the bones."

Leaning forward, the Sherpa tapped his nose. "That is normally true. But the low pressure caused our souls to expand and the ectoplasmic knots worked loose. Unfortunately our ghosts were not terrible enough to induce heart attacks in our bodies. Every time we awoke, they had to take refuge back in the mortal shell. But on the third night, I ran away in my sleep. My soul was unable to stop me and I have been a hollow man ever since. It is essential I reclaim my spook!"

I shuddered. "What will happen otherwise?"

"Without a spirit I am a zombie. I can decay but not die. My phantom will thus never be registered as legitimate. This means suspension of all afterlife privileges. No free chains or walking through solids. I know it wants to leave the valley to look for me but it has no idea where I might be. I hope it has enough sense to stay put until I return. Now I must go. I am unravelling at the navel."

The climbers chortled as Bertie trotted off. They did not credit his story and maintained that even if it was true they would rather socialise with other ghosts when they expired, rather than occupy a valley alone. I was less confident and felt a peculiar need to follow the Sherpa. Instead I contented myself with calling:

"How will you reabsorb your soul, Bertie?"

He turned briefly and replied: "My religion has a ritual for such an event. I will devour the ghost."

"Bon appetit!" I watched him recede in the distance, a torn particle in a cosmos of unblemished snow.

Still joking over this encounter, my colleagues reached S—— before me. I dragged my feet, resentful of their company. The shadow of a flying sage passed over the ground... I looked up at a rogue cloud... Everything I do ends in disappointment. I rejoined my expedition in the station. Its members were playing football with my Laocoön. Pages were strewn over the track. We boarded the 05:09 express to Calcutta, but I sat on the roof. I booked a passage back to East Africa when we reached the city. The others retired to the Hotel D—— , a prime location for picking up the BBC World Service.[6] I had nothing to say to them; they did not even wave me off as my ship left port. Cold rascals.

Arriving at my plantation, I was dismayed to find it had been burned down. Witnesses claimed to have seen a man throwing burning maps onto the crops. I wondered who he might be. There was nothing for it but to visit my parents in Colchester, where I had left them so many years previously. I stopped in the Pyrenees on my way, but climbing had lost its savour. In a decayed cathedral town, I happened to bump into my old Provost, who was searching for rare books. He might have bought my Laocoön had it remained intact. I was desperately short of money. As it was, he asked me to share a bottle of wine (Vin de Limoux, not to be recommended... Dash it! I have spilled some over the next sentence.) We fell into

---

[6] The BBC World Service had not even started at this time, but I hope to obtain employment with the organisation and am thus determined to make as many references to it as possible.

conversation... but he insisted that when I set my experiences down on paper I should avoid dots as much as possible... He had no love for them. My confession was a purge and I left him feeling stronger.

When I reached my childhood home, I found it empty and boarded up. A neighbour peeped at me through her curtains and came out to relate a glum story: my father was dead and my mother had been locked in a madhouse. It seems they never gave up waiting for me to return. One night they heard a noise on the stairs. Rushing out to embrace me, they were shocked to find a pale Scotsman mounted on a bicycle. He required directions to Aberdeen. My father collapsed and his own ghost jumped onto the contraption: with a most ungentlemanly yell, the pair pedalled off into the aether. My mother grew depressed; she knocked on the door of the local asylum and asked to be admitted. Fortunately my father made a will before his demise, leaving the estate to me. I was thus ensured a reasonable degree of luxury in my troubles. It was a great help...

Now I sit in my room, planning a return expedition to Tibet. But the difficulties are insurmountable; I have lost my nerve. Besides, I hear on the radio that Shipton is already there, mapping the region with accuracy and panache. I search the bookshops and market stalls for another copy of Laocoön[7] but there are none to be had. I decide to make use of my skill as an engineer. I will knock down the house and rebuild it in the form of a mantra, a global prayer wheel which may bring me even more solace. Only my Provost can really help me understand my predicament, but I am wary of him. I must stay away from Eton.

---

[7] X.D. Laocoön's ethnographic books have largely been discredited, but a first edition of his masterwork, Fables From The World's Attic, can fetch upwards of $1000 (enquiries to Gamma-Ray Russell, Coverley House, Carlton-in-Coverdale, Leyburn, North Yorkshire). Laocoön – "the translator without a conscience" – probably never ventured further than his own attic.

There is something on my roof again. Every night this happens. It is driving me to distraction: the tiles are scraped by unseen feet. At first I thought it was a levitating monk. Then I believed it was the wraith of my dead reader, the one crushed in the avalanche. But yesterday I levered open my window, thrust out my head and saw my own ghost scuttling behind the highest chimney. It is puncturing the eaves with intangible crampons. How did it get there? I have a theory. In the low pressure of the valley it swelled too big to fit in my body properly and was detached on the way to Colchester. Yes, my soul lives on a ledge. But the rest of me prefers the comforts of a furnished room.

Thanatology

Spleen

He wore a cork leg and people said he kept puppets in its hollow. He was unable to prove them wrong. Fixed to his stump by rusty screws, it could not be removed; he had not peered inside for decades. While he slept, it kicked to be free of the blankets; he wondered what else was known about him. To reckon his age he carved numbers in his foot, and his sole ached like a goblet which has never held wine. He was too slow to be a dashing heel: he was a gradual rogue. His memories had turned damp and unruly, a crew of desperate images tossed into a chaotic sea from rigging which is unravelling in a storm. He creaked.

Careful to avoid scurvy, he lacquered his knees with pressed limes. On the slopes of Sassolungo, he collected small stones for buttons. What better way for a vista to fasten a spirit as striped as a shirt? Worn at the edges, his breath nudged the frosty air like an elbow; he darned his lungs with liquorice. The eternal thimble of night roofed him with songs and bells, but let in stars. His attic was the mountains, always full of revellers dancing on ice. The yodelling proved inaccessible in the dark. Once he limped up, lost the path and tripped over an alpenhorn. Hammered flat, it became his longest needle.

In the ripples of the limestone peaks, he saw the petrified surf of Jamaican bays. He was stuck like a mother who is afraid of milk. Sixteen tattoos sailed his neck; the veins beneath were unfamiliar currents. Why had he chosen Wolkenstein for his retirement? Salt was unnatural here; a man was expected to flavour broth with edelweiss. Even the pretzels were sequined awkwardly with imported sodium. But he knew the oceans had once licked the valley; there were ancient shells lodged in the rocks. On the tumbled battlements of a precipitous castle which buckled a stout range, he measured a lobster's waistline.

This ruin was the antique home of the most

notorious local, Oswald, the winking troubadour. The majority of it had sheered away into a gorge of untuned trees. What remained was a lute without strings; marmots made merry on the shattered steps until chamois appropriated them for serious business. The view, wide as a sail, relaxed his regrets. In the walls of the crumbled kitchen, he discovered a stave of fossilised limpets, fixed in the strata like chords. He played the melody on his false limb with a pair of scissors, treble blade a little sharp. Bats took flight, whipped his ear in leathery rhythm, a malign choir.

He preferred the flap of rags to that of wings. So fine a sailmaker had he been that Morgan asked him to sew his coats. During the siege of Panama, he trailed behind his comrades, picking up shreds of purple wool which had once been blue. The fighting was incredibly vicious, but there was a deeper quality to the havoc, an ineffable wiping of belief. Though he wore his name like a sealed pocket, it was picked when he passed into the Cup of Gold, city of burnished lips. A quick replacement came with a blast from a zumbooruk mounted on a donkey: the grapeshot riddled spleen and eloped with his leg to the pit.

Why had Morgan, alone among the rovers, preserved his identity? His stocky, entrepreneurial character never changed, or changed like keys in an astronomical clock. The crew nurtured rumour, declaring that love for La Santa Roja, a female, had solidified his name in a house right at the base of the Cup, a theory backed by the ship's carpenter, Lanolin Brows, who spied her on a balcony through a wooden telescope with lenses ground from pearls. She was wine, the reason for the attack. But Morgan refused to recognise love; he was Welsh, he insisted, and the grease of his diet had pasted his ego to his arteries.

"Do you think I value a girl over jewels? In my village, compassion comes from diamonds; women are harder."

"You have torn your britches, sir. A knife."

"Make me a new pair, green and crimson. And why not replay the raid with rag dolls? Entertain the sailors."

The opportunity was too good to waste, though it meant intruding on 'Lin's territory. The carpenter whittled automata in his spare time from driftwood and guano. His shiny figures, animated by little fires burning in their abdomens, were a delight to behold on the deck of long voyages. The men who could not read learned all about former campaigns and future barbarities from these shows: the capture of Puerto del Principe and the invasion of Maracaibo. Competing with 'Lin would not be easy, though the navigator, Omophagia Ankles, assisted him with yards of silk, tubs of rich buttons and perforated doubloons.

Now he descended the peaks with a sigh. He felt he had coins in his gums but nowhere else. Oswald's castle cooled rapidly at dusk; in a long field beyond the tiny church of San Silvester, a goat and rabbit nibbled nettles, facing each other like virgin duellists. Never properly cut for a violent career, his sympathies went out to them; killing and rape hung on him poorly, billowing around the waist of his conscience. Jabbing his stomach, he sounded the hull of his pseudonym. The insertion of a puppet there to steer his blood was one of the navigator's ideas. 'Phagia never joked, so a cloth spleen must work.

He reached Wolkenstein and entered his shop. A self reliant culture smothered his gables; the Ladini and Austrians were superstitious, quiet but rarely thirsty. They did not ignore him; he was too buoyant to drown in espresso neglect. Words came as infrequently as savours. From the far end of the varnished valley, where the lathes of Ortisèi span improbable camels for seasonal pilgrims, to the roughly hewn limits of Oswald's own estate, he was liked in silence. Do pirates ever stop laying tables with cutlasses instead of spoons? He was doubted and welcomed for the wave in his hair. But no friendship sailed.

"Who is the foreigner in the toyshop? He waits in

the doorway as if to greet customers. One thigh is vintage."

"'Tology Spleen. A lateen soul who tacks images."

"Does he hope for Sassolungo to settle? The odds are rigged against his sales. He will shift no figures here."

The Ladini carvers were an equal to anyone at sea, however Swedish, and could fashion a pine-cone into a nativity scene with a toenail. This extreme skill with wood was the origin of their careful fascination with cloth. His own products, stuffed with napkins, were regarded as too wise for chisels, too soft for vices. His hands were slow with pins, and they chided his thumbs for not leaving home. They did not buy his work, which filled his shelves too well to be removed, but bludgeoned it with bread. They were looking for something horrid when they entered his shop, as if pumpernickel was a test for ghosts.

He had stitched a thousand puppets in his career and was determined to shipwreck his blisters. He had never gazed deeply into water or glass and his possible age scared him; retirement is a time to dilute ambition with rum. He remembered the aftermath of the Panama massacre, recovering from his wounds in a monastery, blessed by 'Phagia, who had the breath of a monkey. Not all helped him. 'Lin, whose teeth were serrated, rasped at Morgan's delegation of entertainment duties, and challenged his rival to a public cabaret. Both toiled to reconstruct a cast of raiders from a surfeit of requisitioned materials.

Kissed by tapers, the rival shows were judged by Morgan, whose left eye was more cultured than his right. 'Lin raced ahead, his puppets bold as fuses, slick as decks. Controlling the strings with his ears, 'Tology dragged through the plot like an anchor and was proclaimed the winner by an audience bored with battles which are quicker in the telling. Mindful of his crew's needs, Morgan agreed. Leaving Panama after three weeks of looting, mules overflowing with gold coin, so burdened there was no room for names, they halted in a field, within spilling range of the Cup, to crown 'Tology with a knotted napkin.

From that moment, as official puppeteer, he was persuaded to forget sails and collars. Concentrating on melodrama left him with pale cheeks and eyes broad as astrolabes. The cork leg came from a hop's worth of sherry bottles. His cleverest performance turned a ship into a marionette and thus the crew into men who work on toys. Aided by the barber, who weaved hair into cable, he fixed two cords from the rudder to goblets of sherry on the captain's table. Whenever Morgan raised a cup, he would steer the ship with taste; the darker sip to starboard, the tawny to port. In this fashion, destinations became drunk.

Things fell apart after Panama; there was no more need to live like buttons. The crew parted company, many wasting their share on chocolate. The greater part of the loot returned with Morgan to Wales; some said it was secreted in a cave unmarked on any chart. Others went into business and failed spectacularly, an error he avoided by declining to follow his profession beyond its horizon. In Wolkenstein, he bought a store already full of completed marionettes for a low price. The former owner had fled in unmentionable circumstances. In a local restaurant, diners mocked his decision and all his ensuing ideas.

"Now here's a funny one! 'Tology Spleen thinks that Oswald borrowed tunes from fossils. Plays a clam a day."

"But he doesn't give a patch for vampires."

"All the wrong superstitions, if you ask me. Lock your window, spit on a dog, stuff garlic cloves in cuffs."

Desperate to escape, he rushed his meal, though to others it seemed he was chewing weeks and months rather than knödel. At the musty rear of his shop, the most enigmatic stock lurked: teething sculptures and fake spines. Stitching the present into a shroud for the past had scuffed his fingers like slippers. To reclaim the whorls of each digit, he exchanged sewing for unpicking; he hoped his blisters would emigrate back into the needle. The shapeless flaps of cloth which had once been characters were placed in the window. He also pulped the wooden figures left in the room into linen, as if sacking a forest.

The smashed castle had no other visitors; he came to think of it as his own. Even the boy who was employed to sweep the entire valley with a broom neglected it. What was the secret which surrounded Oswald? Who was he winking at from his picture, which adorned the labels of Ladini wine? On the sill of an almost inaccessible oriel, a symphony of shells hushed in anticipation of his baton. Tapping his leg with his scissors, letting the melody thin out toward the temples, something brushed his throat; a falling mouse. If the undead had to support themselves with honest work, would music or dentistry hold sway?

He had learned about vampires from Morgan's cook, a shining man who set tales like supper. To his home island, traders from the east brought the hair of penanggalans, bodiless parasites which fly about the country at dusk looking for victims. The creatures are fuelled by vinegar, cough often and can be thwarted with pepper and thorns. 'Lin and 'Phagia added a vaultsworth of advice to these declarations. Occidental vampires waste less energy in defying gravity: they transmute into aristocrats, who are lighter than air. Oswald might have strummed himself into a corner where refrains and anaemia were inflated.

The sun is the enemy of musicians, who enjoy the company of candles and glinting earrings. Working through the high petrified cycle of songs was akin to climbing ladders without eyes. So the disease scraped off on him, like resin from a diseased bow. Playing the music of vampires might be a hazardous venture, when the arpeggios stretch like membranes over a performer. Tunes concealed vast power; a flat truth, a sharp fact. There were precedents: a drum in Bermuda turned a bosun into a shark. This was not a sailor's tale, but a fish's, and he stood at the rail when it told itself. Never underestimate minims.

At the hem of his first year at altitude, his work came

so close to completion he toasted his pins, dunking them in grappa. Every rag puppet he brought with him was reborn as a napkin or bandana, and the inherited wooden figures had been crushed into tablecloths. All that now separated retirement from rest was a single box. The previous owner had been eager to protect its contents, with a lock carved from garlic. He picked that with a sprig of parsley and groped inside, pulling out an exact likeness of himself, a puppet double. Even his cork leg sealed the same dry white panic, judging from the way it jerked.

Why would anyone want to carve a replica of such a mediocre pirate? A toy of Morgan, certainly; also of Montbars, or William de Marisco. But of a lame sailmaker? There was an omen here, a prefiguration of doom. In the sombre light which filtered through the window, he turned his double over in his hands. He shook it; a rattle. He probed the spleen, and felt another puppet beneath. It had purpose, he knew that with all his heart, which was still real, not worked with cords. But he could barely imagine what it was. Then he reflected. In the restaurant, he confided the event in spaghetti, which was later read.

"'Tology Spleen is a dunce. Oswald was a mongrel rather than a full bat. His mother wedded an octopus."

"She had no gills; the sea was up in arms!"

"Her blood fell to his right side, gave him half a face in mirrors. He looked for the other in melody."

The waiters who washed the pasta plates were experts at deciphering messages in the uneaten whips; all diners write diaries in the dish. And it is difficult to lie in oregano sauce. He heard them chatting over the sinks and fled without paying; beer is cheaper at home, so he was forced to pay himself when drinking away his fear in bed. His false leg kicked sleep to death; he rose and fretted over the implications. Now there was no mystery to Oswald's wink: one side of his gaze was simply rejected by reflection, which refuses to employ fables. The rays which hasten out of vampires are too brittle to bounce.

Again, he picked up the puppet and studied it carefully. There were only two anomalies apparent: size and life. Other details were flawless, including the numbered sole and gleaming knee. If a vampire is unable to use a mirror, how does it dress or shave? There must be other methods of grooming in the evening. Else they would be no better than werewolves, a deplorably scruffy subset of monsters. Would they not create mannequins, jointed dolls in their own image, which might be manipulated to mimic an act of dressing or washing? Yes, this was the answer; puppets were evil. Measuring silk was silvering fangs.

The existence of this replica meant he was also a vampire. Somehow, Oswald's music had nipped him on the fringe. But a life on the six seas, repairing sails soaked in the gore of innocents with his own nerves, and the gore of Spaniards with monkey's, had lent him a degree of balance in judging the ludicrous. Unusually, he pledged to confirm his undead status before flying around the house. How had his predecessor guessed his appearance? That was another problem requiring a barrel of thought. It was necessary to catch a mirror first, to see if his face broke on the glass or jumped up into itself like human ugliness.

There were no reflecting surfaces in Wolkenstein. The valley was so clean all shallow images had long since been scrubbed away. Chalets with wooden cheeks and baskets of red blooms for ears make poor heads for the stuttering eye. The ship's barber kept a mirror; perhaps he could borrow it for the crucial look? Sassolungo is not the only wild peak in the Süd Tirol; there is the glimpse which collects wings. He had no idea where a pirate with combs might hide after singeing a city, but 'Lin would know. He prepared an appeal for the carpenter, chipping out the stomach of his puppet double into a greedy hearth.

A fire supplied the doll with motion. He allowed it to stagger away from the village, toward the high northern passes. The messenger and the message were one and the same; 'Lin would understand. A carpenter should bevel anxieties as well as cabinets. Meanwhile, there was little more he could do to determine his species. From sailmaker to tailor to puppeteer to vampire; life is an odd collection of stitchings. Had he picked up an infection after losing his spleen? No, the petrified music was the virus and Oswald had calculated precisely its effect on the generations who scaled his castle for melodic inspiration.

A mulish combination of leech and squid, the winking troubadour was unable to create heirs in the conventional manner. Using his connections with the denizens of the deep, he persuaded limpets and lobsters to rise up, and set early on his wall. A normal man casts seed on a wife; Oswald was compelled to scatter shells on a stave. Anyone who sounded the notes would become pregnant with vampirism, and to escape the curse would have to seek new performers. The previous owner of the shop waited patiently for the sailmaker, hiding in the rafters, chiselling a puppet from life, a mannequin as a substitute mirror.

The pirate had one regret. Why had he not snapped off the false leg before sending it on a journey? He might have seen whether other puppets were stored inside or not. Too late now; he had to assume there were and that they resembled his successors. The chance it was a fantasy, a story hoisted up the mast of reality like a pair of trousers, closed with each passing collar. He was ready for failure; he designed a patchwork coffin from the coloured scraps in his window. From sails to puppets to napkins to sarcophagus; the hems of existence are stranger than its cuffs. Quite a comfortable fit: he snored there.

Days were digested like scales. At last there was a thumping on his door. A sextant was demanding admittance; he was astonished to encounter Omophagia Ankles on the threshold. The navigator lifted a glittering hat for his inspection. It was not a mirror but the fragments of one, soaped along the brim, as if a shaved pistol had smashed it.

Taking it from his visitor with due reverence, he offered a bottle of cognac in exchange. A man who mends purses is aware of the price of favours; other pirates may fritter boons like cannonballs on the Main, but sailmakers fold them up. With a sigh, 'Phagia chastised him.

"'Lin received your appeal. He'd already planned to see the barber, so you owe him nothing. He gave it to me."

"No problem. I just need to upset its looks."

"Morgan is reforming the crew for our last voyage. You are slow and thus have a whole year to meet us in Sardinia."

He swallowed his tongue as the navigator departed. It tasted of ice and mountain petals, rather than shoe and salt. Joining the splinters of the mirror together was work as arduous as patching a cathedral's wounds with silk. He was so tardy finishing it, even sluggishness died from old age. He knew what to do if the news was poor; he would end Oswald's line with an improvised stake. When he finally gazed into the mirror, fingers reached for his spleen and the contours of the puppet inside. It was not another victim in there, but a shape of death. What would his neighbours say to this overthrow of tradition?

The boldest yodellers found him with an impaled body; they stumbled into his shop and over the longest needle in the world, which darned his spleen to the floor. He was buried in his rag coffin, under the altar of San Silvester. Strings were attached to his arms and legs and whenever a pilgrim entered the chapel, an unseen jig was danced six feet below. The coffin is no longer there: by all accounts, Morgan himself seized it for a sail. However, shards of the barber's mirror can still be found on the hats of the locals, each carrying a reflection which arrived too late to convince a corsair of his humanity.

THE
TELL-TALE
NOSE

Atchoo! – runny – very, very dreadfully runny it had been and is; but why *will* you say that it is sore? The cold had numbed my nose – not pained – not tormented it. Above all was the sense of smell diminished. I sniffed nothing in the pantry or in the oven. I quivered no nostril at the laundry basket. No wonder the young man nearly caught me unawares, despite the condition of his socks! He has told you his version of the affair – it is time to hearken to mine.

I knew he wanted to kill me, on account of my eye. It bothered him, my blue iris, the eye of a vulture. Though myopic, it noted his anxiety, his increasing panic, observed all his little preparations with a cool, albeit hazy, detachment. He shuddered when I turned it upon him, as if the orb was a supernatural window into some forbidden realm: the tinted, bulging pane of a beaked god's bathroom.

He had never been so kind as the week before the murder. He cooked my meals, brushed the pale locks of hair which crawled on my shoulders, wound the ebony clock in the hallway, secured the house against robbers by nailing the shutters. He even dressed up in my late wife's underwear and plucked a mandolin, as she had done, so many years before. He cared nothing for my gold, but expressed an interest in a box of wicks I kept on the mantelpiece – spare wicks for a dark lantern I used for fishing the fetid lagoons which ringed the city.

I gave him the box and busied myself in the construction of a giant puppet from a spare nightgown and candle·wax. I stuffed its false torso with my previous week's catch and fashioned a crystal eye to fit in the single central socket of its lopsided skull. This bauble was covered by a leather eyelid, on a spring, and the entire mannequin was operated by cords. Then I arranged the puppet between the sheets of my bed, crawled under the frame and waited. It also had a heart: the mechanism of the ebony clock, fully wound and secreted in a suitable cavity.

For seven nights I lingered in my cramped confines, on the frozen bare boards, while the young man looked into my room, taking an hour to open the door and thrust his head through the gap, but each time he did so, I lost my nerve and felt unable to pull the cords which would cause the mannequin to sit up and open its eye. My arm was paralysed as if by a mystic stiffness. I think it was the dark lantern! Yes, it was this! Its hinges creaked, ever so quietly, and this almost imperceptible sound filled me with anguish, as do all the quietest noises in the world – cell division in lambs, an execution with a guillotine made from cheese, an illicit affair between a barometer and a balloonist.

Naturally, spending a whole week out of bed impaired my resistance to germs and I developed this horrid cold. The sixth and seventh nights passed in unbearable suspense, my mouth set in a rictus grin as I tried to prevent myself sneezing. I welcomed each morning, for at the first note of birdsong the young man would withdraw his head and allow me the freedom to slither out of my confinement and give vent to the meteorological pressures within me. Listen to my nose as it expels the emerald typhoon! Does it not sound like a second voice?

On the eighth night I succumbed. A sinusoidal wave of phlegm rushed along my sinuses. In desperation, I covered my nostrils with my generous tongue; a useless precaution. Might as well attempt to cap a geyser with a mouldy rug! The detonation echoed off the underside of the bed like a carbine shot. "Atchoo's there?" my nose cried, and with the spasm which racked my body, my arm jerked involuntarily, tugging the cords which crossed the floor, climbed the wall, ran back along the ceiling, tripped over a pulley and speared down to hook the mannequin.

The puppet abruptly sat erect, and the young man kept quite still and said nothing. For a whole hour, he remained thus, and I guessed the single eye had sprung open, but that it was too dark to glimmer, and presently I heard a groan, a slight noise which may have been the wind in the chimney, a mouse crossing the floor or a cricket which has made a single chirp, but it was clear the young man would interpret it to be an expression of mortal terror from his intended victim.

When he had waited a long time, very patiently, he resolved to open a crevice in the lantern. I imputed this not from a change in the level of illumination in the room, for I knew he would contrive to permit only a single ray, the slenderest possible, to flee the apparatus – one incapable of diffusing from its rigid path – but by an extremely subtle odour from the oily wick, as well as the unbearably quiet grinding of those glacial hinges.

I then heard an intake of breath – an intake sharper than a peeled bell. The ray had connected with the puppet's vulture eye. How could it miss? The blue crystal I had selected was immense; it dominated a full half of the face. And the leather eyelid quivered on its spring. Yes, it must have been like this! With the clockwork heart pounding within the wax breast! Pounding like a plum ready to burst in an excess of anguish! The young man would not tolerate this; he would be compelled to silence it.

With a loud yell, he threw open the lantern fully and leapt across the room and onto the puppet. In an instant he dragged it to the floor and toppled the heavy bed over it. Now I was exposed and aghast at the possibility of discovery, but the young man was so intent upon finishing his grisly task that he paid no note to anything outside the diameter of that azure eye. I fled, unseen, scuttling along the boards and out of the door. Now it was necessary to hide away. But where?

I have already alluded to my evisceration of the hallway clock. So too have I related how the young man was wont to wind it every day of that fateful week. Too deluded was he to realise he was winding nothing which might be construed as a *precision* instrument. No, no! I had replaced the mechanism with an orange! Thus there was quite enough room to conceal my body within its sable depths, and accordingly I slipped inside and closed the door.

Here my knees knocked and my teeth ached, with trepidation, no doubt; but my occupation of a timepiece did not suggest to my mind the gradual yet unstoppable progress of decay and death. For there was no pendulum or escapement to count the twists on my mortal coil. Betwixt chronometer and orange there are few points of similarity – only the pips are the same. I gained courage as I listened to the young man pulling up the planks in my chamber. The rasp of a saw, the sloshing of a tub, confirmed his wise precautions.

He was dismembering the puppet, carefully so as to collect every drop of blood. And blood there would be in plenty; for the figure's hollow limbs were filled with fish from the fetid lagoons, or what I assumed to be fish, and I rubbed my hands in glee, believing that my revenge on the young man was nearly complete. He was never a real son to me. He had turned up at the house uninvited on my wedding night and refused to leave. Somehow my wife and I came to regard him as a piece of furniture. We regularly adopted chairs and tables. Why not a man?

By the time he completed his labours – about four o'clock, though I could not be sure, for an orange does not strike the hours, though a puppet's heart under floorboards does – there came a knocking at the street door. He descended with a light step, confident he had nothing to fear. There entered three men, who introduced themselves, with perfect suavity, as officers of the police. A shriek had been heard by a neighbour during the night; suspicion of foul play had been aroused. At this, I chuckled softly to myself. The neighbour in question has hearing almost as sensitive as my own; it is a trait common to the inhabitants of our street.

The young man led them about the house. He bade them search – search *well*. He was more confident of escaping detection than a chameleon in a hall of mirrors. And so was I, for the ebony clock, with its warped and twisted frame, did not seem a feasible hiding place for any object, but luckily my own bent limbs and mutated body slotted exactly into its bonebreaking curves. As I expected, in his mania to be of assistance, he even carried chairs into my bedroom and insisted the officers rest from their fatigues there, directly above the grave of the puppet. Satisfied, the officers chatted together, all very amiable, of trifles, and other confections.

Now I knew that the clock would be ticking beneath the young man's feet and that he would gradually find this fact unbearable. He had lived too long in the neighbourhood not to have developed acute hearing. I listened to him arguing with the officers – *trifles were inferior to profiteroles!* – in a high key and with violent gesticulations, and I knew I would soon be rid of the fool. He gasped for breath, paced the floor with heavy strides, foamed, raved, swore! He swung his chair and grated it upon the boards – custard slices were the lowest class of cake! – but then betrayed himself with a scream.

"Villains!" he shrieked, "dissemble no more! I admit the deed! – tear up the planks! – here, here! – it is the beating of his hideous heart!"

Immediately there was the sound of stressed wood, popping nails, a triple gasp of amazement, a creak of knees bending. I ground my molars in repressed delight. This was the culmination of my plan! The police officers were certain to judge the young man insane when they reached down to retrieve mere hunks of wax, cogs and fish scales dusting a great glass eye! Confessing to the murder of a puppet! They would have no choice but to arrest him and carry him off to a madhouse.

Such was my hope. But all too soon was it to prove forlorn. For one of the officers announced hoarsely: "Yes, it is a heart! And here are the kidneys! And there the lights, folded around the tongue!" And he called for a handkerchief to wrap up these items as evidence for the prosecution. I was much too stupefied by these revelations to account them a jest. Then, as

I uncreased my deformed brow in an inverse frown more conducive to profound thought than the standard kind, an abominable fear came upon me, a feeling that my past was catching up with me, like a skeleton on a unicycle – unsteadily, clankingly, ludicrously, bone shakingly...

I have mentioned my late wife and her mandolin. Also her underwear. However, I have neglected to offer an account of how her plucking drove me to distraction. From our wedding night, when the young man first turned up, right through all the early years of our marriage, she kept me awake between midnight and dawn with the infernal silences of her melodies. Truly, she was the *quietest* mandolin player on the globe, and as I have already intimated, it is the *barest* sounds which I cannot *bear*.

In the middle of a dull and fitful slumber in the autumn of one year, I was roused by an even more excessive silence than usual. I opened my single central eye and beheld her sitting on the edge of the bed. Either from deliberation or impulse, she had neglected to string her mandolin. Consequently, the airs she sounded were no more than that – the rustle of fingers on the stale vapours of the chamber. I rose in a passion and wrested the instrument from her grasp. How many blows were sufficient is unknown. Perhaps it required a dozen – who shall tell?

I cut her up into very tiny pieces and flushed her down the toilet. Doubtless the young man observed me from some hidden recess. He was fond of lurking in corners; I dare say the genesis of *his* crime was in this scene. As the cistern refilled, I presumed the matter was at an end. But now, so many years later, I was forced to reconsider the matter. Not all the municipal sewers flowed to the sea; a few older ones, twisted by a geological upheaval, deposited their effluvia in the fetid lagoons which ringed the city. Why had I forgotten this?

It was more than possible that her remains were channelled into the lagoons, partly preserved by the formaldehyde discharged by the chemical works and mortuary establishments on those clammy shores. For more than a decade, her viscera might have risen and fallen with the secret sluggish currents, drawn not by the moon but the mass of the city, to lap the crumbling jetties and rotting boardwalks where the oddest fishers sat, rods in hand, hooks catching on the corrugated surface of the infinitesimal wavelets and straining up, to lift the lid of scum from the deeps, the toxic fathoms.

Yes, this was it! And what if I had caught her pieces on my last expedition? No use berating myself for not noticing the coincidence at the time; I never actually *look* at the results of my catches. Oh no! The dark lantern I carry through the hollow streets and beyond the deserted suburbs is merely for the sake of appearance. I wish to fit in with my nameless colleagues on the quays. I do not open the device, for the reason I have already elucidated – the hinges, the excruciatingly *quiet* hinges.

Now I discerned the sounds of a brief scuffle. The officers were grappling with the young man. The rattle of handcuffs, the echo of a truncheon. It occurred to me that I was still safe. In those days, forensic medicine was a primitive art; the officers would never know that the recovered heart, kidneys, lights and tongue were not mine! Who was clever enough to open the handkerchief where they nestled and tell the gender of their owner? Nobody, not then! So all I had to do was remain hidden a few more minutes, while they left the house. The young man would be locked away, as I originally hoped, but for a different reason.

They came down the stairs and passed the ebony clock in the hallway. A little longer and I would be free! But now I felt a twitch in the nostrils and a momentous pressure building up within my lungs. My head ached, and I fancied a rushing in my ears; but still they lingered at the door. Why *would* they not be gone? I pinched my nose between callused thumb and finger, but the pressure increased. Was it possible they felt my presence inside the clock? No, it was the partial vacuum occasioned by my voluminous intake of breath which kept them here, tugging them toward my place of concealment. They fought this force, they strained against it.

At last, I could stifle the eruption no longer. I must let it loose or die! Then it came, a miniature hurricane! – Atchoo! – With the release of pressure, the clock shattered. The door blew open, a backward slam, and the orange rained juicy segments on my head. I stood exposed, my twisted frame shivering before the three officers. I saw that they carried one enormous handkerchief between them and that they had faces sewn up the wise way – one without eyes, another without ears, the third without a mouth. So here was the end of my chances for peace. I would be carried off with the young man, possibly to occupy the same cell, while the old house was locked up and auctioned off for its construction materials. But something had to be said.

"Germs!" I shrieked, "spread no more! I admit the deed! – tear up the handkerchief! – snot, snot! – it is the sneezing of my hideous nose!"

A

GIRL

LIKE A

DORIC

COLUMN

1....."Excuse me, is your girlfriend feeling unwell?"

"I don't think so. Why do you ask?"

"Stop me if it's none of my business, but she seems to have a... It appears that her... I mean to say..."

"Dribble it out man. What's wrong with her?"

"Her head is made from blue marble."

"What? Nonsense! Wait a moment, so it is. Somebody must have stolen the original and substituted this lifelike replica. Who would do a thing like that? Why didn't I notice anything?"

"Gangs of pickfaces roam the subways. They target a victim and make a replica head from whatever materials they feel comfortable with. Heads which are already loose can be swapped in seconds. I bet your girlfriend had a heavy skull on a slender neck?"

"Yes, but it wasn't particularly valuable."

"To the right people it might be..."

"That sounds rather ominous. Please explain."

"The gangs export them to China. I read about it in the paper. Huge demand for heads over there. They use them for ornamental purposes. It's just not safe to take a lady out."

"Good job I didn't like her very much. But I promised her father to get her home in one piece before midnight."

"Will he notice that her head isn't real?"

"Absolutely. He's obsessed with details. Besides, she sings for him in the parlour after supper. It's a family tradition. I'd better confess and face the music, or lack of it."

"Rather you than me. What will he do?"

"I shudder to think. He's very protective. He works in the foundry. Perhaps he'll boil my ankles over a red-hot girder. Why do relationships always have to be so complicated?"

"I asked myself the same question when my wife left me. The ceiling was falling down and she was fed up with getting plaster in her hair, so she just walked out. Packed a suitcase and went, without saying goodbye. She was run over by a steamroller."

"That's life, I guess. But what shall I do?"

"Maybe I can help. I'm used to dealing with vengeful fathers. It'll cost you, though. I'm not a charity."

"I'm willing to pay. What's the price?"

"The girl. I collect females like her."

"I'm not sure. She might not want to go with you. She's very choosy with her affections. You are bald and ugly."

"With a blue marble head how will she tell the difference? Come on, it's either that or facing the father alone. If you're worried about how I'll treat her, put your mind at rest."

"Well I'd like to know. It's only natural."

"Of course. She will be assisting my religious studies. I'm turning my house into a temple. It's a sacred task I have lined up, nothing odd. Think of her as a foundation of spirituality."

"I can't argue with that. Let's shake hands on the deal."

"That's more like it. You won't regret this. I'm a professional and always guarantee my work. Wait and see. I bet if you have trouble with a father in the future you'll seek me out."

"I don't intend losing another girlfriend's head!"

"I think you'll find most women have loose ones these days. Perhaps you'll get lucky and meet a divorcee. They tend to use glue. But nothing is really secure on the subway any more."

"The next stop is mine. You'd better follow."

"The stop belongs to the railway, but I know what you mean. Shall I take your girlfriend's arm to help her down?"

"She's not yours yet. Come on, let's jump off here."

"We're right behind you... Not that way, dear... You have a complex and exquisite network of veins, like a map of an antediluvian city ruled by intelligent reptiles... Mind the gap..."

2...."Well that was a cheap trick to play on me!"

"Not at all. I fulfilled my side of the bargain. You have little to fear from that father now. A successful mission."

"You replaced his head with a mahogany one!"

"Some people are never satisfied. I'm a pickface, but I work alone. You should have realised that when I talked so knowledgeably about China and the export market. But I'm only able to carve heads from hardwood. A marble head is quite beyond my ability."

"Do you make a habit of this? How many commuters have you deceived? I ought to inform the transport police."

"Don't be churlish. Just give me your girl."

"I guess you deserve her. But I feel nervous. Why do business deals always have to be so complicated?"

"I often ask myself that question when I'm sitting at home, burning incense to the deity who lives in my broom cupboard. He lurks behind the buckets and refuses to come out."

"Heavens! I thought dry-rot was bad enough. What sort of god is he? Does he answer prayers or hurl lightning?"

"Neither, I'm afraid. I think he might be one of the *Old Ones*, left behind during the last ice age. At night he plays the washboard with his gnarled fingers. I'm sure this music is what made the ceiling fall down. He lives on spiders and detergent."

"Sounds like Baby Jesus to me. Is he swaddled?"

"No, completely naked. When my temple to him is finished, I believe he'll be more approachable. I've chosen the Dorian style of architecture for his sanctum, because it represents the last period when the *Old Ones* openly interacted with humanity.”

“And the girl is a sacrifice to him?”

“Oh dear, no. I need her to hold the roof up. I've got a dozen with blue marble heads lining the lounge. When there's enough of them to take the weight, I'll knock the walls down.”

“Hey presto! An instant temple!”

“That's the idea. He's far too small a god to digest a whole female in one go. For sacrifices I rely on my wife.”

“I thought you said she left you?”

“She did. But I rushed out after the steamroller and peeled her off the asphalt in a single flapping sheet. I rolled her up under my arm and stored her in the downstairs toilet.”

“You sentimental old fool. How touching!”

“Whenever he gets frisky and starts playing his damned washboard, I tear off a required length and feed it to him on a pole. My wife doubles up as a blanket on cold nights. I think I prefer her after the accident. But she's getting shorter every month.”

“This is my stop. I'll take my leave of you here. But I've got some bad news, I'm afraid. I'm also a pickface.”

“I should have known! You have fingers like chisels.”

“I specialise in brass heads. I made a switch when you looked away. Now you shan't finish your temple.”

“You swapped her blue marble head for a brass one? That's breach of contract. Give it back this instant!”

“You misunderstand. I can't blame you, considering what your brains have to sit in. It's your head I picked.”

“So you have! That's really brassed me off. You'd better return it. How will I ever enter an ironmonger's without losing face? You've ruined me. Come back here for a good polishing!”

“Sorry, I have to deliver a parcel to China. But look on the bright side. You'll be able to fry mushrooms on your cheeks. Haven't you wanted to do that for years? It's not all doom.”

"What will my god say? He'll be absolutely livid."

"But mine will be enraptured. I've also got a broom cupboard with a resident deity. He's the last of the *Older Ones*, who are much older than the *Old Ones*. Apart from the *Oldest Ones* they're the oldest *Ones* of all. He plays the spoons all evening. I suppose diabolism and skiffle must be connected somewhere along the line."

"It's not fair! I'm a widower!"

"So am I. My wife was a steamroller. She blamed herself for rolling over a pedestrian and committed suicide."

"But what about my temple? It was so ambitious."

"I've decided to adopt your idea for my house. Perhaps it will keep my god away from his blasted spoons. He's bigger than yours so I'll have to build a larger temple. He'll need a higher roof and girls just aren't tall enough. Let me think it over."

3...."Excuse me, is your boyfriend feeling unwell?"

"I don't think so. Why do you ask?"

"Stop me if it's none of my business, but he seems to have a... It appears that his... I mean to say..."

THE ORANGE GOAT

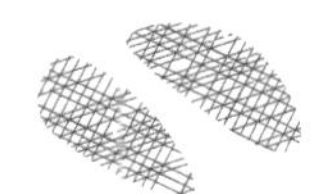

Ye who boil are still among the kitchens; but I who bake have long since gone my way into the region of cellars. For indeed strange cakes shall rise, and secret crusts be filled, and many diners shall pass away, ere my ovens be seen of men. That's one way of putting it. Another is that my efforts to perfect the blueberry pie had all failed miserably, and I hoped to hide my mistakes underground.

It was summer in Monmouth, and the market with its imps was filled with exotic goods and mundane bads. A maddening wind blew across Monnow bridge and the pub signs were playing cricket with wasps. I had rented a basement in the 'Green Dragon' for my experiments and regular explosions shook the building, turning the patrons upstairs a matching colour. Fire was my boss; steam, my lover. I hungered to find the alchemical formula for pastry – the philosopher's scone.

Now that Myfanwy had vanished, meals resembled amputees, lacking a tasteful limb. She had a way with blueberries no other mortal possessed. The man who succeeded in duplicating her recipes would monopolise trade in this rare commodity. And it was I, Gruffydd ap Slack, cheated suitor and unsuited comprador, who'd come closest thus far. The only pretender to her crumb-dusted throne, I should have been a respected elder of the county. But I didn't even own my own house.

I opened the oven door and drew out, on an iron skillet, my latest creation. Misshapen and sinister, it exuded a noxious smell. I jabbed my thumb into the covering and the pie erupted, spewing molten blueberries over my smock and frown. Something was still wrong! There was a flaw in the matrix. I carried the cyan volcano to my bench and cut off a sample for my microscope. It had caramelised.

"O, Myfanwy, my lost love! How did you do it?"

Licking away my tears, I ran up the steps to the

taproom for a cold beer deep enough to jump in and drown.

I was on my third glass when the door of the pub swung open and a weary traveller entered with his goat.

His face was a mass of wrinkles, but one beneath his right eye was younger than the others and I recognised it. Struggling to extricate my shoe from my drink, I hopped away from his presence. It was too late to escape; he caught sight of me and flung his broad arms about my neck, a gesture of affection which also served to keep him upright. His stained apparel (including trousers with bulging pockets) was buttoned with hot smells from ninety seven realms.

"Now listen, Owain," I said, "it's nasty manners to greet an enemy like a friend. Have you forgotten our feuding over the hand (and elbow) of fair Myfanwy? She who betrayed us both by refusing to choose between my excellence and your roguery?"

"No, Gruffydd, I remember. But it was boring standing at my corner of the scalene world – there was nothing to see over the edge – and I decided to return. Why are you trying to jump into a beer? Many changes have taken place in my absence!"

It was impossible to neglect him. I bought him a stout and we stood together at the bar, exchanging histories. Fashions had changed. Now that it was acceptable to walk the streets without trousers or soul, or with someone else's instead of your own, our original disagreement looked absurd. I told him how an imp had stolen my keepsake pie – the last known example of Myfanwy's craft. Since then, I had struggled to recreate it artificially, to no avail. He clucked his tongue and muttered.

"I owe you a canine and an explanation. But first, permit me to ask what milk you utilise for the dough?"

I rolled my eyes. "Sheep's! You mean to say there are others? I am less experienced in the world's ways and angles than you. I didn't reach my corner, Hyperborea, before turning."

He handed me the reins of his goat. "Here you are."

I scratched my head. While it was obvious his journey back had been stressful, I couldn't envisage what manner of sufferings, however hairy, had caused him to disorder mammals in such blatant fashion. I tugged the goat's beard to prove it wasn't fake.

"Owain ap Iorwerth, you are a dunce! If you owe me a canine, which you don't, why pass off that as one? It's a caper!"

Parting the froth on his beer with a comb, he grinned. "Not so. Do you recall that time on the Monnow bridge when I slapped your back? The tooth you coughed loose was a canine, and I picked it up after you left. It's an old tradition in Wales – as I'm sure you're aware – to make a necklace from the teeth of vanquished boars and bores. I hung it from my neck on a string and took it abroad."

I felt in my mouth for the gap and nodded. This gum had healed, but others yearned to be ruined on blueberry pie. Ignoring my cries of, "How tensile the filling?", Owain proceeded with his account. Pies and caries both require plugging with amalgam, but my curiosity was extracted, root and all. When the love triangle whose sides consisted of himself, myself and Myfanwy had shed its cosines, mainly due to that slacks-and-spectres scuffle of our adolescence, he had hastened off to Zipangu, the remotest isle in the atlas. There he spent his money on green tea and train rides and quickly found himself penniless.

Desperate for a coin, he took my tooth from his necklace and placed it under a pillow. But in Zipangu they don't have fairies, or even imps. They have gnoles, in kimonos, and when he awoke he was astounded to find himself sleeping not on a groat, but a goat. That's the way they arrange matters over there. Perhaps those gnoles are hard of hearing. Anyway, he rode the ruminant back to Wales, and here it was, my property, though he doubted it would fit over my tongue.

"I was going to keep it for myself, but I felt pity for you when I heard your story about the pie. What was the name of the imp who conned it from you? Ochre Fingers? I assumed so!"

My brain was spinning. It's common knowledge that the best pie has myriad ingredients you won't find in the cookbooks. The tooth is one of the most important – it's added last, right at the point of eating, and imparts the crucial flavour which distinguishes a mother's cooking from everything that comes after; milk teeth have the best texture for this, which is why cakes never taste so momentous to adults. If this goat was really a transformation of my pointed pearly, then it might provide the missing component in my project. I yowled.

"By using the milk of my tooth in my pastry, I can inject a dose of childhood into my pie! What a boon!"

Owain plucked my sleeve. "Not so hasty! The goat won't be enough by itself. The flour has to bind in a particular way with the milk, rather than at random. There are a million ways a pie can rise, but only one of these was Myfanwy's. Think of pastry molecules like a stack of oranges. The row on the bottom determines how the others are going to behave. We need a specimen from a genuine crust, a seed, to shepherd the atoms into tasty formation, else it will fail."

I shook my head. I'd already thought of cloning the pie, ransacking the imp's stall one midnight after he'd snatched it, but he had devoured it whole. Owain rubbed his ear thoughtfully. "The essence of the flavour may still be contained in the imp's body?"

"Yes, he's too small to digest the filling in less than a decade. I bet a blueberry is larger than his heart."

"Well then, boyo, you're in luck." Lowering his tone, Owain devised a plan to seize Ochre Fingers and weld him to the goat. He used his comb to write the equation in the remaining foam of his beer – I checked his calculations and nodded my agreement:

(Goat (kidnapped imp) + flour) + (blueberry)^3 = PIE.

Peering at the patrons in the pub, I deemed our present location an unwise spot for the discussion of our scheme. So I led Owain down to my cellar. He squinted in the smoky light of the furnace, studying the pie charts and schematics which adorned the walls, detailing sundry examples of the baker's art through the ages, including the very first quiche, a sand-and-millet masterpiece designed for King Zoser. My old rival noted the bed and basin in the darkest limits of the room; his raised eyebrows brushed the low ceiling inquiringly.

I purpled in the gloom. "This vile dungeon is my home as well as my place of work. I tried to woo Myfanwy with a clock and carrot; the clock came with an irate pastor. While I was absent, setting out for my corner of the scalene world, he invited his friends round and they took over my residence, barring the entrance with a lofty door of brass, fashioned by the artisan Corinnos, fastened from within. Even now the trespassers are seated at my table of ebony, singing the songs of the son of Teios, over some flasks of the red Chian wine. I'm an exile."

"We shall remove them, Gruffydd. Show me how your ovens work; they are the best in Monmouth, are they not? We'll bake a Trojan Pie for the squatters. I see! The blue is inserted here and the berries there. The bellows are pumped and the ingredients are fused in this chamber and swaddled in pastry. A fabulous device! Well the goat can go in one, the imp in the other, and then we'll fan the flames. The goat is a tooth; the imp is sore, like a gum. They'll fit together superbly!"

"I don't understand what good that will do."

"We'll carry the finished pie to the front of your house, ring the bell and run away. When the pastor and his chums look out of the window and spy it, they'll think it's a divine gift. Opening the door, they'll drag it in. Imagine their panic when the goat-imp combination jumps out of the crust! They are sure to believe it's a devil and flee your home. Then you can reclaim your premises."

I was delighted by this suggestion and stuttered my gratitude. My emotion was rawer than a simurgh egg.

"It's Myfanwy I want! She had no time for me when I lacked talent, but she'll be impressed by an identical pie. If you and I can both come back from our exploits, so must she!"

He was consoling. "Imitation as the sincerest form of flattery? It is a maxim I am fully in accord with. Scamp along now and capture Ochre Fingers, while I light up the coals."

From the sparkle in his eyes, I gathered he didn't need a match. Up the stairs I went, passing through the taproom, where Owain's unfinished beer stood meekly. I picked up the comb next to it and completed his sum more to my liking, giggling dreamily.

PIE + trousers + soul = Myfanwy.

Myfanwy + Gruffydd = near bliss for months.

The year has been a year of disappointment, and of feelings more intense than disappointment, for which there is no name in Wales. After hurrying out of the 'Green Dragon', as instructed, I made my way across Agincourt Square to the market. I found the imp and skillfully bundled him into my trousers, which after all might not be my own, smuggling him back to the cellar. Strangely, Owain had gone. So had much of my flour. But the oven was blazing and the goat was tethered to my bellows. I proceeded without my confederate and baked a vast pie, carrying it on my back to the front of my residence. There were a dozen crumbs on the doorstep but I trod on them all and tolled the rusty bell.

Hiding behind a bush, I watched as the portals swung open and hands reached out to snatch the gift. A voice announced, "Another one!", which bewildered me, but I remained at my vantage until a great howling within the house caused me to stand trembling, and shuddering, and aghast, like a soul sewn into a sail, while no less than seven pastors burst from the building with pale countenances, each forehead stamped with a bruise the shape of a hoof. I raced forward but – to my profound alarm – found the portals closing again. By the time I gained the threshold, it was locked and belittled my fists. I glanced through a window, and beyond a rent in the sable draperies, saw treachery.

Owain was dancing with Pan, or so it seemed; there was steam enough to veil their motions in mystery. Scattered about like Sabine attire lay relics of pie. It was plain that Owain had baked himself into one during my abduction of the imp, conveying it (I guess not how!) to my porch and thus gaining admittance. The second pie had cleared the house of pastors and now the unnatural intruders were in cahoots, and in my kitchen. As I engrave this tale in pastry with a wooden spoon, I hear rumours above in the pub. Owain ap Iorwerth sells a beautiful pie, not of blueberries but oranges, and he has stitched a toga from peel for his familiar, which in return provides milk for his dough.

Now I comprehend why he bulged when he entered the pub; in Zipangu, so I've read, there are mandarins in every pocket. That's natural. Wiser than me, he'd worked out that blueberry pie couldn't entice Myfanwy back to Monmouth; she'd sniff a threat. Better to try a different flavour! He must have evolved the plan at his furthest point, while staring out over the void beyond his corner. And the reason why his right eye was younger than his left? He'd been winking to himself throughout Asia, all the way back across the fruitless desserts.

NOTHING
MORE
COMMON

Mr Hugo Bloat, a disappointingly thin man, was an oddity amongst antique collectors for the grand nature of his acquisitions. Not content with hoarding clocks, furniture and porcelain, he had embarked on a mission to secure a tin mine. He owned a house with grounds extensive enough to install one entire, and possessed ample funds for its transportation. Furthermore, he lacked a wife to complain about the bother, and his neighbours were sufficiently distanced not to perceive an obstruction to the view. Already he had arranged a private paddlesteamer, *The Waverley*, to ship his prize across the Bristol Channel, from the Cornish Portreath to the Welsh Porthcawl. All that now remained was to select a suitable example of the desired goods.

He travelled by road to his destination, crossing the county border on the afternoon of August 24th 19- and proceeding across Bodmin Moor at a fair speed. Devoid of the miserly urges which frequently assail the slender rich, he nonetheless eschewed a chauffeur and preferred to drive his own vintage Bentley. The weather was wet and warm, with a salty mist which stung his lips. After a break to change a flat tyre, he pushed on all the way to St Agnes, reaching the ivy-choked Trevaunance Point Hotel shortly before dusk. Mist was also evident down in the cove and the collector formed the impression that it originated here, foaming over the rim of cliffs and saturating the land.

The Trevaunance Point Hotel is situated in a magnificent location, standing atop the battered headland with its gables akimbo. For an instant, Mr Bloat imagined it as the petrified and mouldy flame of a wreckers' beacon – a ludicrous comparison, and one which convinced him he had been travelling too long. He signed the register, permitted his baggage to be carried up to his room and sauntered into the bar to await his contact. He sipped a cognac and studied the menu, tempted by the vegetarian extravaganzas but dissuaded from their practical application by a hasty measurement of his modest stomach. Settling for a cress sandwich, he alternately nibbled at the crust and twiddled thumbs so laden with ancient rings his impatience was audible as a flamenco rhythm.

At last, a dark figure wearing a wide-brimmed hat slouched over his face entered the Hotel and joined his table, furtively setting down his own glass and drawing a flask from his pocket. He glanced about before pouring a generous measure. Whatever the stuff was, Mr Bloat decided, it was no regular tipple. Milky and viscous, it left a discernible trace of salt on the side as its owner swirled it around. To upstage the awkward silence which waited like a gin-trap, the collector ventured, "Mr Grebe, I presume?" to which the other gave a start, as if rudely denied a vital element of an arcane ritual.

"That I might very well be," came the response.

"If not," Mr Bloat announced, "you had best find another table. I'm waiting for a notorious smuggler."

"Hush! hush! Very well then, I'll admit it, only you must keep your voice down. The proprietor don't care for me, not since I ran a pipeline from his cellar to my cottage. Beer on tap for a month I had, before he found me out and followed the pipes to my dwelling. He shook and slapped me, and says he, 'You naughty bootlegger, haven't I forbid you seventy times to plunder my refreshments?' But he weren't able to punish me more than that, for folks would be in uproar. Where else would they get their little treats? Answer me that!"

At this juncture, he cast a wink at the collector and appeared to have difficulty opening his eye afterward; perhaps the briny fumes from his beverage had sealed it shut. Or maybe it was the fog which glued it tight, for the vapours were seeping into the Hotel and filling the bar to the brim with pearly tendrils.

Mr Bloat was annoyed by what he took for affected eccentricity and answered, "Yes, I've heard you are the slyest rogue in the region, which is precisely why I wish to engage your services. You are aware of the object of my quest?" And by the width of the other's smile, he was sure there had been no misunderstandings.

"Our mutual friend, Mr Longhorn, told me everything, sir. Tomorrow we shall go a-prospecting, and I know where the best mines are: I was looking at some today. Lovely shafts!"

Mr Bloat finished his brandy and frowned. "You don't think it is a tall order? I'm not talking about a couple of barrels of whisky. This is a major piece of contraband."

"What's that? Fie upon you, sir, for doubting my talents! I'll have you to understand that my family have been in the purloining trade for generations. Have you heard of the land of Lyonesse which once connected Penwith to the Scilly Isles? Where do you think it went? Under the sea! Oh no, sir, not an ounce of it. Spirited away to Greece, every speck, by one of my nameless ancestors. A tin mine won't be much bother at all; no more than picking a blackberry."

The eye popped open in an inverse wink more conspiratorial than the standard kind, and Mr Bloat was compelled to order a second drink before discussing his scheme's finer details.

"The villains in my home town are similarly given to exaggeration, but I care little for talk. Results are what I crave, Mr Grebe, and it is on performance alone you shall be remunerated. I've bribed the pilot of *The Waverley* – a Captain Nothing, as he likes to term himself – to anchor off the ruined harbour of Portreath. The cove below is unsuitable for large vessels, so Mr Longhorn has informed me. Moving the mine to the harbour is the tricky part. Once across the Channel, I can dock in Porthcawl without trouble – the authorities there are used to turning a blind eye to my undertakings."

"Oh very amusing, sir!" chortled the smuggler, rolling his newly freed orbit in its socket. Dismayed at this favourable reception to an unintentional joke, Mr Bloat sighed.

"The operation must be carried out in a single night.

Are you quite sure you can manage it alone?"

"Have no fear, sir. I'll meet you here at dawn and we'll go to the outskirts for a poke around."

He might have said more, but the proprietor of the Hotel caught sight of him and came over, armed with a dishcloth. A dozen or so grimy lashings and the smuggler jumped up and scurried outside, leaving his flask behind. The proprietor called:

"You've raked your last moon in this establishment! Get out of it, you bedsheet or I'll carve a runic whistle from your nose!"

As soon as Mr Grebe had vanished, he leaned apologetically forward. "Was that very wicked man bothering you, sir?"

"I do believe he was," coolly answered Mr Bloat.

"Keep your door locked tonight. There's no telling who or what may be lurking. Not just smugglers, neither. This fog's been giving some of my guests bad dreams. Spewing out of Hell's Mouth by all accounts." Then noting the collector's arched eyebrow, he added, "That's a geographical feature, not a religious allusion."

Mr Bloat nodded. He recalled the enthusiastic descriptions of this area given him by Mr Longhorn, who was his most reliable advisor in all dubious dealings. Hell's Mouth was a simmering pot of foam and rocks not far from Portreath's abandoned quays. In some ways, it was a negative of St Agnes Beacon, the peak which dominated the western skyline, or was supposed to – it was presently invisible in the fog. Despite his wealth, Mr Bloat was unable to obtain a head for heights and therefore remained sceptical about both these attractions. He concentrated instead on the flatter issue of linguistic matters.

"Why did you call Mr Grebe a 'bedsheet'?"

The proprietor folded his dishcloth. "He comes over all comfortable and snug but then tangles himself around your legs. That's all I meant. It's not an indigenous insult, sir!" After a pause of irresolution, he went on, "Actually my mind had been concerned with bedsheets lately. We have a lady guest upstairs who..."

Drowning him out with a yawn, the collector rose from his seat. "I hope you'll excuse me, but I'm tired. I have an early start tomorrow and I must get some rest. For breakfast I require espresso coffee, chocolate croissants and a green napkin. However, I must go out on business before dawn, so have it ready for my return."

And so saying, he marched past the stairs and stumbled through the main exit into the unlit car park.

The proprietor's voice followed him outside: "You've gone the wrong way! Your room is on the top floor."

"Yes! yes!" snapped Mr Bloat. "It's this cursed mist; I can't see a thing." He was about to turn and retrace his steps when a metallic noise attracted his attention. He groped toward it through the vapour until he reached the side of his Bentley, tripping over a pair of feet which were jutting from under it. Bending low, he tugged at one of the shoes, which came off in his hand. Somebody was tinkering with his car. He kicked the unshod foot and the concealed figure struck its head on the underside of the vehicle before slithering out.

Mr Bloat was exceedingly astonished to recognise Mr Grebe closing a pocket knife and hopping on one leg.

"You nasty sinner, have you been meddling with my Bentley?" wailed the collector, directing a second kick at the injured foot. "Cutting the brake cable, eh? Why, I ought to thrash you all the way from here to the cathedral town of Whitminster!"

"Hush! hush! 'Twas force of habit, sir. I'm a wrecker as well as a bootlegger. It's in the blood; I have to tamper, the same way I have to conceal and siphon. It won't do you no harm, lest you take it along the Stippy-Stappy. I know better than to murder my paymaster! I'm intensely interested in its workings, anyway."

"Well, my man, though I do not wholly approve of your conducting without my supervision alterations which may possibly impair the usefulness of a vintage motor, I will do my best to explain the principles of classic braking systems to you. Fetch me the jack from the boot and remove your hat."

Ten minutes later, having wiped that piece of equipment clean with a handkerchief, Mr Bloat returned to the Hotel. But as he was passing through the entrance, he happened to glance up and catch a momentary vision of a face in one of the highest windows – a face more creased than unwashed linen. He shuddered away the mirage and proceeded into the lobby and up the stairs to his room. As he turned the key in the lock, it occurred to him that the crumpled visage must belong to the occupant of the adjacent chamber. He listened: there was a faint whistling sound coming from behind the door.

His own room was neat and clean, filled with ornaments which as a collector he could not resist handling. He sat on the edge of his bed and stared through the window at the blank vista, imagining the sea with its susurrating cargo of pebbles and seaweed. St Agnes Head, a colony of kittiwakes, was near, though his ears picked up no sound other than the soft whistling of his neighbour. Its melody disturbed him and he was on the point of hammering on the wall with his fist when it abruptly broke off. There was movement on the floorboards; the occupant was leaving the room. He heard small feet skipping down the stairs and then, after an interval, coming back up. The door opened, the floorboards groaned an extra chord and the whistling was resumed. Mr Bloat stepped out into the corridor, but no clues were forthcoming. He placed an eye to the keyhole but saw only unrelieved darkness.

Straightening up, he remembered the smuggler's flask. He went down to the bar and searched in vain; someone had removed it. While he was pondering the disappearance, the proprietor startled him by approaching from behind and touching his shoulder.

"I do apologise for scaring you, sir. But you seem to be in need of assistance. What may I do for you?"

"Something quite simple. I forgot a flask of medicine when I went up to bed and now it has vanished."

The proprietor squinted. "A flask, you say? Are you certain it was yours? Why, the lady next to you came down for it five minutes ago and said it was a pint of cleaning fluid."

"A bare-faced untruth!" spluttered Mr Bloat.

"Now don't get all woundy cross tempered with me. I try to be civil to all my guests; a helpful chap is what I am. Plainly you are suffering from delusions occasioned by mental exhaustion. I know it's a long drive from Wales, sir, and I wouldn't be feeling myself either if I'd made it, but that's no reason to abuse me."

The collector's manner softened and he backed away, hands raised in a placatory gesture. He could not afford to alienate the proprietor now, for he did not wish to draw attention to his activities. Besides, there was an unsheathed dishcloth in the fellow's hands and he seemed willing to employ it to further his point. Mr Bloat retreated to the base of the stairway, where an idea came to him. He tiptoed to the reception desk and picked up the register, tracing with his finger the numbers of the rooms and the corresponding names.

The chamber next to his, he discovered, was occupied by a Rosemary Gibbet-Pardoe from Chester. The appellation, though unfamiliar, sent a shiver through him, as if internal thumbs were plucking a dirge on his nerves. He slammed the book shut, crushing a tongue of fog, and tramped up to the security of his room.

Why had this woman stolen the flask? How had she known it was left downstairs? The peculiar whistling noise was emanating through her wall again; he placed his palms over his ears, but the drone's absence was no less irritating. At last he vowed to discover the nature of the sound, whatever the danger the pledge might expose him to. But how? Trying her door was out of the question...

Throwing open his window, allowing limbs of fog to flop onto the sill, he climbed onto a narrow ledge which ran the length of the facade. His breathing rate increased and he fought down panic, but the drop was concealed by the billowing mist and only in occasional rents was he led to an appreciation of his elevation. Inching along the ledge, clutching at ivy for support, he gained the adjacent casement and peered inside. At first he made no sense of what he saw, assuming the space was filled with the same brume which swaddled the external world, but then his eyes adjusted and he uttered a cry of horror.

There was a woman asleep on a bed, her face contorted with mighty effort, as if she was digging a pit in her dream. What the collector had taken for the ubiquitous fog was in point of fact a voluminous bedsheet which covered a good half of the floor as well as the sleeper and seemed to be connected to her in the same way a moth is attached to its wings. This was in itself somewhat unusual.

Even more bizarre was the way in which the bedsheet rose up in time to her snoring. Mr Bloat understood now that the whistling was a product of her nostrils; whenever she exhaled, the bedsheet billowed and ruffled and gathered itself into the semblance of a living being with a creased face, before collapsing at the end of the note. This repeated itself in a relentless rhythm and the sheet expanded on each pulse, as if it were oozing from the pores of her body. Was she an anthropomorphic silkworm, he wondered? But no, she looked like an ordinary female, though a little Gothic about the hairstyle, and with an inscribed nose. Mr Bloat was a poor philologist and the olfactory writing was too small to be made out at this distance, but he imagined it was a vulgar sort of Latin. On the pillow, tipped at an angle near her murmuring lips, was the smuggler's flask, obviously drained of contents.

With pounding heart, he returned to his room. But sleep eluded him and he sat up until he heard movement next door. The lady was awake and striding about; then her door opened and he heard her descending. Moving to his window, he caught sight of her figure striding into the fog, the bedsheet neatly folded in her arms. At once he resolved to follow her.

Pulling on his coat, he left the Hotel and pursued her toward the centre of St Agnes. He was dimly aware of her form flitting between slashes of vapour. Along the Stippy-Stappy she went, that precipitous terrace which makes the village so unique. She led him to the outskirts, a region of forgotten tin mines whose crumbling chimneys jutted into the mist like organ pipes blowing a fumy fugue.

In this landscape of industrial fossils, she slowed her pace and Mr Bloat crouched behind a ruined wall to observe her progress. She crossed to the edge of an abandoned shaft and dropped the folded bedsheet into the darkness. It should have made no sound, but the collector picked up a choral giggle almost below the pitch of audibility. Rubbing her hands together, the woman headed toward Trevaunance Point. Mr Bloat picked his way to the shaft and glanced down, seeing nothing, yet the giggle still descended. A laugh without a mouth?

Walking back to his lodgings, he was conscious of a change in the mist. It was slightly thinner, as if a single layer had been peeled away from it. Shaking his head at this new phenomenon, Mr Bloat was grateful to reach the Hotel and catch up on a few hours of much needed sleep. As he drifted off, he was aware the whistling had ceased, replaced by the rasp of more conventional snoring.

His portable alarm clock – not an antique – woke him as dawn's left hand was waiting for the horizon to stamp its visa. The vapour possessed an inner light; a chill glow tumbled in as he drew back the curtains. He thought he spied Mr Grebe moving about in the car park, or at least the brim of his hat. Exhausted by his adventure, Mr Bloat went down without shaving and greeted the smuggler uncivilly. "Are you certain this can't wait till a more sociable hour?"

Mr Grebe pouted. "I'm afraid not, if you want the goods ready for shipping tonight. Take me a whole day to smuggle a mine, it will! What do you take me for, a talking owl?"

Ignoring this idiosyncratic expression, the collector nodded. "Very well, lead me to the pickings."

Before setting off, Mr Grebe cleared his throat. "Got to go inside for a moment, sir. Won't be long."

He entered the lobby and Mr Bloat was much put out to observe him raising a flask to his lips as he did so. Had Mrs Gibbet-Pardoe given it back to him since her assignation with the shaft? When the bootlegger returned, the flask was gone and there was a flicker of movement at her window. What did this signify?

Keeping his questions to himself, Mr Bloat permitted the fellow to guide him down the exact route he had taken the previous night. They reached the site of disused mines and Mr Grebe showed him a selection of different types, waxing lyrical about their bargain prices. "Choose any one, sir!" he cried. The collector was intrigued to note he gave a wide berth to the mine visited by the woman.

Purposefully, Mr Bloat strode over to it. "I like the look of this one. It has a tasteful bleakness."

"No, no, not that mine! 'Tis not for sale, sir!"

"None are for sale," the collector reminded him. "But you asked me to choose and so I have. Here it is. I expect it to be packed up and waiting for *The Waverley* at Portreath by midnight. Come now, Mr Grebe, what's the matter? You've gone pale."

"Well, sir, you told me you lived alone in Wales and liked it that way. But if you take this one home, you won't want for company."

"Oh ho, so you suspect it's haunted?"

"Nothing is more common, sir!" squealed the smuggler. "Please look for another. It'll turn me faint and ill if I have to handle it. Yes, it's an old-fashioned pit, that one, and I've always been afeared of it, but now it's full again, if you take my meaning."

"I regret to say I don't," confessed Mr Bloat, and then he added, "Nothing more common, eh? I guess that must be so, for ghosts are merely nothing and they grow more numerous by the day."

"'Tis not wise to mock the dead. These mines go right down under the sea and a great many men have been lost in their depths. This one's an unreliable model anyhow, and I reckon you'd rather have one of these later shafts. Easier to clean, sir!"

Mr Bloat was firm. He insisted on this particular mine or none at all, and the smuggler's avarice finally overcame his reluctance, on the condition the fee was doubled. The collector assented and they arranged to meet at Portreath at the designated hour.

Back at the Hotel, Mr Bloat found his breakfast, though it was not what he had ordered. Instead of coffee and croissants, he was presented with ordinary bread and a pound of mostellaria cheese, a type unknown to him until he called the proprietor over.

"I wish to complain about the texture of my incorrect meal. Plus I want to know more about the woman upstairs."

"The first is local, the second is enigmatic," came the reply. "But Mrs Gibbet-Pardoe has been here for a whole week and refuses to let the maid make her bed. Provides her own blankets, I suppose, but I can't be sure because she never comes down to breakfast for a grilling. Lives on flasks of liquor, according to the maid."

"Have you no other information?"

"Well, I know this sounds absurd, but I can't help remembering a tale my aged grandam told me, about a wise man from Bascombe who visited this town to rid it of a plague of flies. Ate them up, he did, and spat them out in the shape of a black scarf."

"Now that is very intriguing," announced Mr Bloat as he toyed with his gratuitous food. "You think she's dining on insects and creating her own sheets from the process?"

"Oh no, sir!" cried the proprietor, blushing hotly.

"The flies were phantoms, at least that's how I understood it from my grandam. She had a cryptic way with anecdotes."

Mr Bloat snorted and waved him away. He lounged about in his room after breakfast, hugely irritated by the whistling which had resumed next door. The day passed slowly, but he resisted the temptation to spy on the smuggler; Mr Longhorn had warned him that such types guarded their trade secrets jealously and would refuse to work for anyone who pried. If the collector ever needed Mr Grebe's services again, it was important he did not antagonise him.

Finally the evening came, and Mr Bloat made ready to leave. As he was brushing his teeth, the whistling stopped and he heard his neighbour depart. He was still curious as to her business, but his own plans took up most of his thoughts, so he continued with his ablutions. When he had finished, he descended and reversed his Bentley out of the car park. He checked his watch and saw he had an hour before Captain Nothing was due to dock – enough time to make a detour to satiate the most nagging parts of his bewilderment. He headed for the outskirts of St Agnes, turning off his lights to avoid being seen.

His chosen mine had vanished. Where there had once been a shaft, the ground was smooth and level. The smuggler had evidently kept his side of the bargain. But what most astonished Mr Bloat was the sight of Mrs Gibbet-Pardoe standing forlornly in the vicinity. She held a folded bedsheet and seemed to be cursing.

The collector continued past and though he was what you might call a hard nature of a man, he was quite overcome and mumbled a hypocritical prayer as he steered his car. As he proceeded, turning his lights back on, he was aware that the fog had thinned again, shedding another layer of its clammy skin, like a snake made of semi-precious droplets. All the way to Portreath he shivered, where he had a monumental task bringing the car to a halt, for the brake cables were severed. He turned onto the beach and the soft sand arrested his motion.

He waited in the Bentley, pulling up his collar to warm his face and gazing intently out to sea. He thought he discerned a light and heard the pounding of a wheel – *The Waverley* was approaching. He got out and paced to the shoreline, blowing on his hands. Where was Mr Grebe? Captain Nothing would not brook delay.

How the smuggler intended to transport the mine to the harbour was something Mr Bloat had not paid much thought to. He assumed Mr Grebe had a number of trucks at his disposal. One can therefore picture his alarm when the rascal appeared out of the gloom mounted on a bicycle, ringing his bell and coming to a rest near the Bentley.

"What's this?" spluttered the collector. "Have you failed? Well, you won't get a penny out of me."

"Hush! hush! 'Tis all in order. Look here!" The rogue lifted a box from the rear of the bicycle, secured to the frame with string. Mr Bloat eyed it with a mixture of fear and hope.

"The mine is in there? The idea of such a thing!"

"Yes, sir, the idea! This box contains the essence of the pit. You don't need the ground around it; the space inside is enough. I shovelled out the gaps in the mine, sir, then I compressed them. As I removed the empty space, the shaft filled up and became solid again. 'Tis compressed inside there, waiting to spring out, so be careful how you open it. Wait till you reach Porthcawl. Reassembling a tin mine on board ship might very well result in an accident."

"How can emptiness spring out?" wondered Mr Bloat, but before the smuggler could answer, a figure lurched out of the mist, catching him by the scruff. It was Mrs Gibbet-Pardoe, dishevelled and furious. She shook Mr Grebe until he burst into tears.

"You cursed scrapbook! You lost heart! You churchyard dweller!" she screamed, and the barrage of unconventional insults made Mr Bloat draw away. "You mezzotint! You wailing well! You mazy inheritance!" She ended with a more coherent oath: "Rats!"

"'Tweren't my fault. He insisted, he did! Blame him, not me, that gentleman there. He's Welsh, a nasty man."

"You're the one responsible for digging it up!" she countered. "And you must take the blame. I told you not to touch that mine till it was filled up. What shall I do with the leftover ghosts now?" She held out the bedsheet for him to scrutinise. "Take that box to St Agnes and put back the gaps, do you hear me? And while you're at it, fetch me another flask of fog. We can't afford to dawdle!"

Mr Bloat, perceiving his prize was about to be lost, said, "Watch him, madam, he's been taking sips on the sly."

Her eyebrows shot up and she rounded on the smuggler. "Drinking the ghosts as well? Why, you thief, I ought to stretch your guts out as far as Barchester. But here's a better punishment!" She cast the sheet over him, blowing her nose at the same time.

"'Twas force of habit!" cried the smuggler, but it was too late for explanations. At the first note of the whistle, the bedsheet seemed to wrap itself around him, like a cotton octopus, and adopted an appearance of its own, rather different from the physical characteristics of the man beneath. Then flapping and undulating, though there was no breath of wind, it glided off into the mist, making a wailing as rich as a male voice choir being carried to Hades.

Mr Bloat did not linger at the scene. *The Waverley* had docked and he was pleased to have a chance of getting away without paying the fee. He hoisted the box onto his shoulders, marvelling at its lightness, and ran to the harbour, where he was helped on board by Captain Nothing. So engrossed in her revenge was the woman she failed to notice him depart. As they paddled away into the Channel, the incoming tide washed over the stranded Bentley. The collector resisted the temptation to open the box until they passed the island of Lundy.

Whatever happened to Mr Hugo Bloat is beyond my conjecture. I heard the tale when I visited the Trevaunance Point Hotel on business last summer. Charles, the proprietor, knew the story up to that point but no further. Whether Mrs Gibbet-Pardoe had told it to him, I thought rude to enquire, but I believe it not unlikely. He came up to me after breakfast and gave me the benefit of his speculations.

"Listen, Mr Longhorn, I know it's a long shot but this whole affair reminds me of something my aged grandam once said. She claimed phantoms can often solidify into other forms, such as flies or dolls' houses. I'm wondering if all the fog we had that time was the condensed souls of the miners who perished in the pits? I mean, the tunnels extend out under the sea. Suppose the dead spirits somehow leaked through the rocks into the Channel and turned into mist? Mrs Gibbet-Pardoe might have been a sort of witch or wise woman, like the man who came from Bascombe to eat the flies. Maybe she was here to transform the fog into bedsheets and return the ghosts to the mines? If so, I reckon she employed Mr Grebe to collect and compress the mist and bring it to her in a thermos. That blighter could smuggle anything!"

I have long since learned to maintain an open mind on such topics. *The Waverley* never reached Porthcawl; it was last sighted off the coast of Lundy. The police doubt the collector ever boarded the ship – his car was found washed up in Hell's Mouth with its brake cables cut and they assume he had plummeted over the cliffs to his death. They are searching for a Mr Grebe to assist with their enquiries. From what the proprietor said, I do not think they will find him.

Since then, there have been rumours of a ship with billowing sails approaching the coast of Portreath on foggy nights, but this cannot be the paddlesteamer – it had no mast. Perhaps one day I will run into Mrs Gibbet-Pardoe and learn the entire truth. Until then I shall keep an eye out for Mr Bloat.

It should not be too difficult to detect his presence in the air. For as I have been told, nothing is more common, and now the collector is all but nothing.

MUSCOVADO
LASHES

Because parrots know how to tell happy stories, he wore an onion on his shoulder. On deck, while the other men joked with guitars, he preferred to weep. He sabotaged every song with spices. His right ear was deaf to the howls of soup; his left to the moans of stew. He refused to flavour beans, claiming salt cracked them like knuckles. His stove was directly beneath Morgan's cabin, and the pounding of the captain's boots walking ideas into a cutlass stirred the pot for him. In rough weather, he fell asleep with a spoon; in calm, with a fork. Only when the waves were too indecisive for comment was he lonely.

He resigned from piracy after Panama, as they all did. The doom of the Cup of Gold had left him taller, so often had he jumped with terror at the blast of cannon. The streets were full of burst sacks of coffee, steaming in the sun, forming breastworks behind which the Spanish aimed bombards and pedereros. His forehead was peppered with grapeshot enough to keep him permanently drunk on mulled whine. But others suffered more than he. The sailmaker's leg kicked him in the teeth as it flew without the rest of the fellow into the least salubrious quarter of the city. A kneejerk reaction, equal and opposed.

Pairs of knives and hours: that is how he best recalled the throes of the Cup. His galley utensils cut through armour more neatly than any military blade. So frantic was the fighting that the traditional habits of battle were reversed: he was soon cleaning his apron by wiping it on his wounds. At noontide, Morgan ordered the burning of the cedar houses and the Genoese slave market, with the auctioneers still inside. Plates of flaming rum truffles were slung through windows; his recipe. The few defenders who held out detonated barrels of powder in attics to prevent the overrich conflagration spreading.

How the crew snorted and nodded as the city ruptured itself! Fuses hissed everywhere, like grilled eggs, and rubble and antiques were spat high, to knock on the eaves of the cathedral. As the houses burst open, the opportunity for a new game also arose. Two objects had been lost in the siege, names and gambling cards, and now there was a substitute for the latter. The residences of the richest traders were furnished in one of four contemporary styles – Moorish, French, Venetian, Basque – and thirteen expensive colours. Suits of shades. And certainly other ghosts shuffled in the murk, like croupiers.

So each player was allotted a street in turn, and the abrupt bloom of form and hue down its length constituted a hand in cribbage. As cook to rascals, he had often concealed mistakes and hid trumps, or turnips, up his sleeve. But abodes were too awkward to fit. He was no cheat when dealt a Panama. It was the barber who kept winning. His whisks, skewers and spoons were gone within the span of an avenue and alley. Spermaceti Whiskers pocketed the lot. Suddenly Morgan himself cut the pack, racing into the muddle with nude sword. With his sickly Welsh eyes he had seen a prize to be sheared but not shared.

A woman on a balcony, her tongue long and pale as a plume of smoke from an igniting matchlock. But this was only a type of scream, wrapped in rags by the sulphurous air; her beauty would have been legendary had these not been the days before legends. Wine curls, so much deeper than vintage that Morgan vowed to forsake biting corks. Green eyes, never to be compared with emeralds in his presence, for his career had been long in the handling of gems, but the feeling her gaze inspired in him was a facet of life wholly new. Climbing the orange tree in the garden to her side, he loaded his lips with kisses.

The carpenter set up a spyglass on a tripod to study developments. Morgan's mouth eclipsed hers; then they both moved back into the lavish bedroom. There were Spaniards in the rafters. An eruption; the building came apart, according to the sailmaker, like a typhoon'd jib. Omophagia Ankles insisted the pair had survived, propelled toward the stars, hand in hand. Nobody else noted this, but the navigator could not be doubted in matters of degree, whether of burns or trajectories. And Morgan, the canniest pirate alive, would not die so easily; the devil often claimed to have his luck. So the crew waited.

He was away for a week and when he finally returned the fires were out and the men had drunk themselves into a nervous stupor on the spilt coffee. Unable to sleep, they listened to him relate the details of his most remarkable conquest, though he was much given to frowning while he spoke, as if his heart wanted to keep the adventure private. Buccaneers must confide secrets to each other, the Custom of the Coast demands it. Even Morgan would not flout these laws, drawn up in northern Hispaniola while he was a babe in a Llanrumney cot. So who was she? La Santa Roja, wife of a noble merchant from Tobago.

His charms had not worked on her below the waist. When they landed safely on the far side of the city, she accepted his mouth only down to her shoulders and his hands only down to her hips. Her coyness inflamed his lusts the more. He grew insistent; she challenged him to a duel for her virtue, the winner keeping also the weapons employed. He selected a cutlass; she chose a mirror and firearm. She was a traveller and exotic guns were holstered in her garter. Ten paces they walked before turning to discharge. She blinded him with his image, and he lost. But then she offered him the tools of her victory.

"Gather round, men. Look now, the blunderbuss from her collection. And the glass. What irks you, 'Vado?"

"Smells of hemlock. Glints like a pterosaur bone."

"From Pennsylvania, she said. A new country in the north. A flying galleon jettisoned both at her feet."

At once, Morgan discarded his traditional buckler and carbine, and adopted these quintessentially feminine pieces. The cook did not accept the existence of aerial ships, and declared so aloud, to the monumental rage of the captain, who had recently flown himself and could vouch for this method of transport. So he was expelled for a night from the camp, and banned from hearing the conclusion of the tale. But before he went, Morgan gave him a kiss to demonstrate La Santa Roja's technique. With a chuckle, he disengaged. Then all the men wanted one: barber, sailmaker, carpenter, navigator. And he obliged.

"Off with you, chef! Watch the sky for schooners."

"Terrible barque in the Gemini Bight."

As he walked away, he heard Morgan practising with the new gun and also with an old pistol. A grunt in the ricochets of the first made him further doubt that arms were ever manufactured in, or dropped from, the clouds. To his ear, schooled in bash of spoon on pan, it sounded like a product of Asturias. Yet a clever corsair will say little to contradict his master. Besotted with his new love affair, the Welshman was picking fruit from trees with balls, a curl of his sweetheart's hair knotted to his own forelock. There was a lesson in this brute harvest, one croaked by the cruel hero in a stage whisper:

"What the pistol won't salt, the blunderbuss may pepper. Bigger is really better, my friends. And Panama's the widest reward of all. Where shall we go from here? Where indeed?"

There was only one more siege to scheme: retirement. The cook left the circle of merriment and picked his way through the ashes of the Cup with a horrid suspicion he was no longer himself. What he did was broil and bake for pirates; such was his identity. The options now were those of a different man. Shuddering, he reached the outskirts of Panama, and wandered some way into the forest. There was a commotion in a clearing. A group of *Indios bravos*, formerly hired by the Spanish as mercenaries, were crouched over food. With a serrated knife, they were sacrificing a dish of raw vegetables. Beastly race!

The cook squinted. He knew that supplies had been

destroyed in the retreat, to save them from the gullets of the buccaneers, but this must surely be a darker ritual. He recalled 'Phagia lecturing him on how the future was a yarn written in entrails. Here, under a nose accustomed to drip more steam than sweat, a quiver of savage prophets were engaged in gross *saladomancy*. What should he do? Ebony skin glistening, he hurried out from his vantage, waving his arms. The warriors scattered, seeing a demon from their own mythology, a scorched man in a white hat. Thus the seeds of prediction became his alone.

When dawn bloodied the swamps, he stumbled back to his comrades, a sacred vegetable bulging in every inner pocket. The men were silent and no sentry watched over them, or so he thought at first: he stepped into another forest, of pikes and muskets leaning together, to be confronted with a duel. Not Morgan and his woman, nor any rogue he recognised, but figures of wood and cloth, armed with rapier and arquebus. Puppets they were; rivals worked by strings. And he could empathise more keenly with this struggle than that of skin men. His trespass distracted the wooden doll, and the other puppet shot it in the spine.

The naive contest between sailmaker and carpenter to win the right to amuse the buccaneers was over. 'Tology hopped his triumph while 'Lin sulked. The cook was not blamed for ruining the sport; his intervention was called fate. And he grinned in the corners, for the tubers and leaf of what was to come, the ingredients of the soup of time, truly were on his person. Morgan welcomed him, all insults forgotten, and requested a farewell banquet for Panama. He fried a supper from Yucatan more fabled than a griffin, chillies stuffed with grated coconut, determined not to cut his prophetic groceries too soon.

Morgan decided to lick his portion from La Santa Roja's mirror, so that his reflection would emerge just in time for dessert. But the heat damaged the unusual ornament. From that instant, it ran slow; a looking glass not to be trusted.

The captain had no use for a sluggard, even if ashore, and presented it to the sailmaker. 'Tology angled it toward his stump, hoping to glimpse his missing leg, but to dawdle that far behind the present was a feat, or foot, beyond any magic surface. Next in line was the barber and 'Ceti greeted it like a convex brother. Now he could catch, on a nape, an itch in the act.

While he alarmed the crew by showing them the backs of their heads to their faces, Morgan divided the requisitioned sherry. From the crypt of the cathedral, which they had converted into a prison for the papist dogs and macaws of the city, bottles of Oloroso were lifted on pulleys. During the sack, these had rolled to the grumbling of cannon, betraying their presence. Now they were required to surrender their corks for the benefit of the wounded. A hundred glasses should be adequate to collect a limb's worth for the sailmaker, to tipple him from legless to steady, against all the laws of intoxication.

Bellies full of food, the rovers doused the spices with pale fire. Only the cook was busy elsewhere, washing up in the bowl of a fountain. The juice of the nut of the barrel sent all others into dream, but they finished the false limb first. It was hollow and lacquered with 'Ceti's favourite restorer, to encourage hairs on the calf, which was golden as an idol. 'Tology clutched it tight to his chest as he snored. Though he allowed himself a toast while he dried with a flag, the cook had sipped too much coffee for his senses to be similarly soothed. Sober he stood, and troubled, under a rack of plates.

When he finished his chores, and turned to settle down, a dreadful sight made his eyebrows dance like hung felons. An odious shape, a bald ghoul, was stooping low over the sailmaker to slot something inside his leg. This apparition wore three capes abillow, but seemed in a peculiar sort of way to be a double of the cook. White instead of black, lacking an ear, breath strung with toxins rather than savours, but possessed of a Malagasy daring. It looked up, held a finger to its lips and vanished into the landscape of burnt spars and charred stone. Too embarrassed to cry aloud, the cook boiled his faith.

He was still unable to protest, or warn, when the men woke in late afternoon and the sailmaker fixed his new leg to his stump, securing it with screws to the bone. Too late now; the chance had gone. So what was in the knee other than stale Panama air? A bomb? A spy? Nothing was too devious at this latitude. Keep quiet and forget; 'Tology was no genuine friend. He felt closer to 'Ceti and 'Phagia. But when curiosity pinched too hard, he peeled one of his oracles, an avocado, to gauge the facts. The stone was reticent until smashed; then it babbled nonsense. He cast the fragments again, for a full hour.

Finally he achieved a coherent sentence. It repeated the captain's dictum with a pithy variation. *The bigger same is a better same.* By the soul of soup, what did that mean? This divination business was a potted pantomime, not a panacea. Dusk fell, realisation dawned. The cook could hardly deliver the sailmaker, because it was he, or a magnified version thereof, who had performed the act of leggy subterfuge! That apparition was a double in truth, a doppelganger, as they say in Prussia, a mirror image of the cook, but one warped, running as fast as 'Ceti's glass ran slow: his identity stretched forward.

Having grown up with tales of assorted frights – penanggalans and werelemurs – he thought himself seasoned to all chills of supernature. But the doppelganger he had not previously considered, and thus had not dreaded; it was a fresh abomination. Morgan's rhetoric with blunderbuss and pistol had urged him up this speculative creek. The two weapons are normally perceived as being separate objects, not superior and inferior variations on a single theme. But here was a truer way of regarding all guns and cooks: bleary or clear reflections of one perfect form. Pistol was he; blunderbuss, the infiltrator.

When they left Panama, on 24 February 1671, with 175 mules weighed down with treasures, prisoners to the tune of 600 and a flute, blisters and bouts of amnesia, the cook watched the sailmaker from a distance. A force inside the cork leg seemed to tug 'Tology off the path, which ran along a bank of the river, so that Morgan had to tie a leather thong to his thigh to keep him on the straight. They reached the village of Cruz and here, as they provisioned the canoes, the captain threw a slow wink at the cook which disconcerted him hugely. Then he kissed the barrel of the blunderbuss with his wide tongue.

"Ah, 'Vado. A wife who transforms into a mistress is better than a mistress who transforms into a wife."

"You think the gun is married to someone else?"

"Imagine a keelhauling in the sky! And what length of chain for an aerial anchor? Mind your skull, boy."

The advice was strange but sincere. The cook remembered it, though his powers of recall were up to nasty tricks. Already, as they embarked for the palisadoes of Fort Chagre, the adventure seemed to have gone on for years. Cloud descended over the river and his mind. Did others feel the same as he? They did: 'Ceti no longer knew which dialect he thought in, though his vocabulary was large. This concerned him more, and less, as the oddity endured in time, but faded from memory. Safe in the Fort, Morgan shared the loot, cheating the French rovers who had sworn fealty to him. Welsh ethic, spun like sugar.

No more than 200 pieces of eight for any rough who sniffed brandy. When this created strife, the captain made ready to leave, removing all cannon to his flagship, and setting two things: the palisadoes on fire, and sail. Let those follow him who chose. Three barques came after; the French gave chase, chewing their dastardly moustaches. But the wind was with Morgan, who lightened his vessel by blasting rocks at his pursuers and dancing, so that his heavy boots were partly off the deck. The cook baked a crumble, to represent the resolve of the hunting pack: fragile, lacking iron, rife with cooling fats.

In Jamaica, the men parted, supposedly for good, or bad, depending on what business they next adopted. Morgan gave the bulk of the silver, emeralds and tobacco to himself. The cook planned to stay in touch only with the barber, who still had many of his utensils, and the navigator, who was inestimable. 'Ceti left for Pirano, 'Phagia for Smarje, but his own return to Europe was unsettled. He tried to remain at sea, broiling for an eccentric smuggler by the name of Marlow Nullity, but the dishes he was expected to serve were so protean and implausible that he jumped galley in a hurricane off the Azores.

He was washed up on a Terceira reef and dried by a sunset, so that his fortune resembled a plate. From this volcanic isle, he worked brief passage to Lisbon, always alert for a looming of his double, and thence overland to a mountain republic, the isolated city of Chaud-Mellé. Here thrived villains the equal of Morgan; he might roast for them. He hoped to avoid the mistake of turning honest. Wiping clean a cauldron, but no slate, was for him a necessity of survival. He applied for a job in the Café Worm, where threadbare landlords and swindlers clad in yellow were in the habit of bartering deceptions.

Faces in a pot of soup always alarmed him. He avoided peering over the rim into the reflective depths. The kitchens were open to view, and the patrons often berated him for his timidity. He expected to meet his doppelganger every time the doors creaked. He felt relatively secure in such ignoble chaos, an urban environment where no street was wider than a puff of breath to cool a flan, but if he could negotiate the maze, so might his distended shadow. Cats frolicked in his cupboards; he offered them curds and fern wine. Generous to a fault, but jealous of salt. And how many sayers will spoil the sooth?

The final time he had hugged 'Ceti, he had given the barber a sack of dumb vegetables as a practical memento. Now he regretted his impulse and wrung his forks, for Chaud-Mellé's gardens, mounted on roofs, could nurture only withered plants, and his salads were the balk of the town. The lower burghers subsisted mainly on cheese; the elite on pastries, a discipline in which he dared not compete. The Guilds had cakes sewn up, with threads of liquorice, and his Malagasy icings were most unwelcome. Banter with his customers mollified him, though they often regarded him as a steward rather than a craftsman.

"Flagon of hot wormwood, 'Vado, for my comrade!"

"What do you mean to do with it, Wynkyn de Rackrent? Melt parmesan over the ribcage of Beerbohm Soames?"

"Aye, for absinthe makes the heart grow fondue."

The Café Worm was the perfect venue for criminals and bohemians to meet and learn each other's ploys. The cook, whose own underworlds were wholly geological, and already undertaken, was gradually drawn into the conspiracies of the latter set; the orchid sniffers, demi-monde and men with boneless wrists. They spoke theatre, a patois with trapdoor vowels and backstage grammar. Encouraged by their programmes, which made steam swirl more effectively than any Chinese fan, he agreed to attend a show in the company of poets and sculptors, refusing only to doff his chef's hat, under which his oracles nestled.

The Theatre de l'Orotund was a disappointment in terms of interior design, which was lunatic, and current production, which was an unfunny routine by a comedian named Caspar Nefandous. This buffoon was assisted by a woman who bounded across the stage as if on springs – even higher than Morgan! He walked out in the middle and returned to work. But some months later, he decided to give the thespian arts a second chance. The comedian had taken to writing opera. On his own in the stalls, the cook blinked at *The Morgan Wheel*, a farce based on the sack of Panama, acted as if the affair was ancient history!

Had his sense of time been wounded so badly in the assault? During the interval, he stepped into the cloakroom for a lungful of fresh air, a rare commodity in Chaud-Mellé, unavailable in the street. Three capes recalled his double, who was close; he felt it. Rather than go back and wait for the début of the actor who took his role, he fled. Outside, he glimpsed a ship in the sky, a canoe with spiral vanes for oars! Perched on a seat under the machine was the ghoul. So Morgan had not lied about boats aloft! This one was flying south-west, but whether into or out of the metropolis could not be assessed.

Learning is strength. The next day, he visited the city library to consult a bestiary on the topic of doppelgangers. He was given a volume bound in the marbled skin of an ineffable worm. The entries were listed alphabetically, but in Enochian script, which is unpronounceable. There were no words on the relevant page, simply a mirror sewn into the paper which amplified his image. He slammed away his reflected leer and swore an oath never to be browbeaten by himself. What precautions he ought to take were still a mystery; he would discover them in due course, and in sooth he did not need to tarry hours.

In the Café Worm, while he was disputing with two regulars, Soames and de Rackrent, a new customer wove between the tables to the kitchen. His tortured eyes were sunk in hypogene sockets; he wore a beard forked triple. He ordered a cup of chocolate and coffee, sipped a mouthful and spat it on the boards. In a Dutch accent, he mocked the mocha. But this was only the trick of a salesman; he was a merchant with plantations in Java, and he was blustering for orders. Having taken enough coffee from Panama to last a hundred millennia, the cook was unimpressed, until the merchant suddenly vaulted into a pot.

It emerged, when he did likewise, that he was hiding from a fellow who had just entered, another virgin patron. The newcomer was Professor of Astronomy at the University of Chaud-Mellé, who cared not for coffee or even absinthe, but only to investigate the establishment as the site of a recent meteor shower. The violent eruption of a casserole dish the previous week had generated this rumour. The cook ushered the Professor upstairs, to a brothel where all collisions were catered for. An honest mistake, but no, the Dutchman claimed they were the same person! Coffee trader, stargazer; percolated as one.

The cook frowned. How could a doppelganger be so dissimilar to the original model? The merchant winked uneasily. Same man, parallel pasts, or rather divergent presents. One version had chosen a scientific route through life, the other a commercial. And the trader, a physical giant, was frightened of the scrawny academic! So it was possible that he, the cook, was not the inferior segment of the bald ghoul, but vice versa. A joyous concept! The ghoul was wealthy enough to own a flying ship: must he become as successful, as rich, to compete? If so, he should exercise his single skill to its basted limit.

His big chance came with the Chiliad Festival, a carnival of food, to which he was formally invited. This took place in the coldest season of the city's annals, in Hauser Park. For the occasion, he risked death by preparing pastry without a Guild license. He erected a stove, a tent to envelop it, a welcoming sign in the flap. Nobody came; he was forced to knot a lasso with a liquorice cord. He cast at a passing rascal in a tricorne hat, whose bad teeth were evidence of an affection for sweets. The lasso snapped. No good; his destiny had its own agenda. At least he might read it before it was executed.

Removing his hat, he spread the sibylline vegetables. All but one, a coco-de-mer, did he sacrifice. The cabbage said: *all rovers will fail in honesty.* The carrot: *relationships are geometrical.* The swede: *steer a cauldron with a rudder.* The potato, squash and yam: *memories can grow fuller than rooms, mirrors which run slow are obscurer than squonks, an octant is a sextant in man's britches.* Turnip: *Chaud-Mellé will soon be destroyed.* Sprout: *one of these groceries is a liar.* It was time to run out of the city, in the opposite direction to that of the aerial ghoul, afore the metropolis mimicked Panama.

Naturally, it was feasible the turnip was the fake prophet. He did not, or could not, consider the logical consequences of a false sprout. That was a paradox unstirred. No, the city had the feel of expiry about it, a rotting ambience which could only degenerate. He escaped with his largest pot, rolling it north-east into Austria and then Bavaria. As he trundled onward, he stopped in taverns and collected tankards of pewter which he hammered onto his vessel with his fists. Bigger is better, and it soon became the deepest, widest skillet in Europe. What supper might be boiled in this? Curry for cyclops.

When it grew too heavy for him to turn, he paused. The sleepy town of Trostberg became his new home. He set a fire under the cauldron, and passed the time waiting for it to heat up by baking cakes. Interest was minimal, despite his vast experience. He attempted to recreate the myth of Morgan's childhood: a blueberry pie as barbed as a harpoon. Failure, deflation, charred edges. The alternative was to cook virtuous desserts for moral gourmets, but the cabbage's advice must not be ignored. Where were the bandits of Trostberg?

One morning, a postman came to deliver a message in a bottle, from the barber.

"Old 'Ceti Whiskers wanted you to read this. A request for help. I think his stomach is in big trouble."

"Are you evil? Will you take breakfast here?"

"No, but if I was, south I would go, to a Mediterranean isle. That is where the fashionable felons eat."

The cook cradled his sable head in his oven gloves. He had a rival whose soups were cooled by sea breezes! Was it his double? He shattered the bottle and read the letter. Then he hooked his thumbs in the fringe of the coco-de-mer and travelled to Pirano. At the door of the barber's shop, he met the carpenter, who had received a similar request. Forcing entry, they found the razors coated in dust. A single vegetable bubbled in a pan – his prophetic yam! He had given the wrong grocery to 'Ceti. Did it matter? Difficult to be sure. But the coco-de-mer would tell the barber how best to shave future days.

When they departed, 'Lin took a hat from a peg, pieces of a mirror stitched around the brim. The sailmaker had asked him for a reflection. He passed it to the cook, to send on to 'Phagia – who alone knew where all pirates lived. He did so, and when he reached Trostberg, the pot of ages was ready. A meeting with his doppelganger, a bite of fates, could be delayed no longer. Only one meal startling enough to entice the bald ghoul into his premises. Peeling the onion on his shoulder, crying once without regret, he climbed into the pot. Hot oil lapped his ankles, his thighs, nipples and unrefined lashes.

The coconut remained unopened, on the barber's chair. But it never could assist 'Ceti anyway. Inside, it simply foretold that Morgan would journey to Trostberg and claim the cook's cauldron for a ship. By which time, the contents had evaporated and clouds of steam billowed over the landscape, momentarily forming the silhouette of a gigantic man, a trio of capes lifting like wings, before dispersing in the wake of an aerial craft, a terrible barque in the Gemini bight, heading for the Dog Star, shedding tears. But Morgan was Welsh and had none to match, not even an eye moist enough to reflect flavours.

A PERSON
NOT IN THE
STORY

It was the year the Eisteddfod came to Lladloh. Anyone who has ventured into the lost corners of West Wales knows the fungal people with which it is infected – the dank little inhabitants, usually in the unfriendly style, dressed in patchwork coats. For me they have always had a strong repulsion: with their ghastly haunts, the sunken houses and constipated streets, the nameless taverns. In this respect, Lladloh seems to fester more horribly than its fellows. The village is an eruption on the flesh of the land; it is pleasing that the sore was lanced by a man who bears the name of his achievement – Doctor Pin.

"I suppose you'll be getting away pretty soon, now you've been made redundant, Doctor?" said a personable *Signor* to the eccentric Professor of Engineering. Pin was something of an old woman – he baked puddings in his bedroom – but he was dauntless and sincere in his confections, and a maverick deserving of the highest respect.

"Yes," he said; "my friends have been making fun of me this term. I mean either to redeem my reputation or kill myself. My train departs for Lladloh (I dare say you don't know it) in an hour."

"Oh, Pin," said another neighbour at the farewell feast, "if you're going to Wales, I wish you would look at the site of the Garden Festival and let me know if you think it would be good to have a dig there in the Winter." It was, as you might suppose, an Horticulture graduate who said this. With his fork, he irrigated his curry.

"Certainly not," replied rude Dr Pin; "the show you allude to takes place in Builth Wells and Lladloh is ninety shepherds further on. All of you should know that this expedition of mine will be undertaken with the object of tracing something in connection with the antique steam turbine locked away in the basement of my Department."

At this point, Pin went carefully over ground with which we are not at all familiar. "Nobody knows quite how it ended up here, in St James's College. I reason it was stolen by one of our roving antiquarians before the feelings of rightful owners were taken into account. It's an amazing device; scarcely larger than a grapefruit, yet capable of doing the work of a thousand well-paid porters. Its exact workings remain the secret of its designer, the legendary Kingdom Noisette."

"There has always been much gossip about that fellow," observed the Italian scholar who, like minestrone soup, appears only in the prologue. "Yet efforts to research his history have hitherto failed. Do you expect to succeed in Wales? Do you suppose the Chancellor will reinstate you if you manage to document Noisette's origins?"

"Well, it is rather hard to say exactly what I do suppose," was the frank answer; "but I'm hoping for more than a biography from my pains. A fresh insight into a radical new form of mechanics is my ultimate aim. I want to make porters obsolete within a generation. I predict a time when our swan cutlets will be served by automation!"

The small group of friends digested this notion under the impassive gaze of a serving boy. The refectory was old, cluttered and imprecise in layout: the furnishings were little better than what might be found in a Sadducee's tent. Ugly brass coronae hung from the roof; the iron cutlery was as ill-matched as a divorced couple's tongues. Only the new curtains agreed to admiration of their surroundings.

"Such talk was the cause of your downfall," said the Gardener after a pause; "your proposed device to mark examination papers in the absence of the Chancellor proved a dismal failure on two counts. It was a source of annoyance to the worthy in question; secondly, it would have drenched his office in ink. *Gravis ira regum est semper!*"

"You've been listening to Somerton again! How I mistrust Latinists! But remember: *audentes fortuna juvat.* When I solve the enigma of Kingdom Noisette's engines, I shall return in triumph to overthrow the doddering fool who is currently head of St James's."

"Steady on," cried a certain Professor Axl Persson, a Nordic savant who was naturally of a taciturn disposition; "although I sympathise with your plight, I am still an employee of this institution. Criticism of Mr Parkins must be limited to mild insults."

"Oh, you are a reactionary!" blurted Dr Pin. In essence, this was a fair appraisal. Since his arrival from Jutland on an exchange programme, Professor Persson had joined the Conservative Party and was intending to stand for Parliament in a Nottingham seat. His Danish nationality had so far excited little comment among the electorate.

"But why have you chosen Lladloh to begin your quest?" inquired the Italian; "from my knowledge of etymology, Kingdom Noisette does not seem a Welsh name. It has an Anglo-French lilt."

"That sounds logical," cried Pin; "but I believe it to be a cunning pseudonym, a play on words. My skill with puddings has helped me here: a noisette is a nut-like sweet. A nut is a colloquial lunatic. Lladloh has a habit of declaring itself independent and crowning locals as monarchs. In other words, it's a kingdom of nutters!"

At this, there was a general murmuring of appreciation for Dr Pin's powers of rationcination. Few conundrums were tortuous enough to conquer his intellect. He was also a solver of newspaper crosswords; before some adventures which we shall shortly divulge instilled in him a mortal fear of any material which flaps or flutters.

The Italian, a daring soul with a moustache, now asked why Parkins, the Chancellor, had always disliked Dr Pin. They were, in fact, the only two surviving staff members from the Golden Age of St James's. With much of that naivety often attributed to Mediterranean questions, he wondered whether a dark secret lurked in their past.

Pin flushed, with wine as well as shame, and replied

that once they had been passable friends. In those days, Parkins was merely a Professor of Ontography; a fussy chap, destitute of the sense of humour. But after a holiday in Burnstow (the details of which were never revealed) Parkins became aggressive and morbid in outlook. He seemed to blame the engineer for an unspecified crisis which he'd endured.

"I honestly don't know why he split with me," Pin sighed; "but his other colleagues also found him intolerable. Rogers and Disney left the College, driven to ill health by his bickering. Without rivals, he soon worked his way to the top of the academic ladder. I endured his insults and remained, for the sake of the facilities."

The Gardener nodded sombrely, wielding his spoon like a spade. "Odd business, I agree. But speak more of your intended triumphal return. You shall be mounted atop a modern equivalent of a white charger, I take it? A locomotive powered by one of Noisette's engines?"

"Capital idea, Bradley!" the Italian applauded; "though Dr Pin will undoubtedly find the current distractions of Lladloh a drain on his time and energy. I'm not talking about a golf course but the Eisteddfod which has started there. I am considering whether it will constitute something in the nature of a hindrance to his work."

"Perhaps," said Pin, rather hastily; "but I suppose I can manage to rough it for the time I anticipate being there. Not that I call avoiding Male Voice Choirs roughing it. I booked a double-bedded room in the only open lodging house. I must have a fairly large room for I am taking some cogs down as well as the ancient turbine."

And with this pronouncement, the company fell silent until the last course was eaten and cleared away. Cigars and sherry put in a lugubrious appearance: with a funereal finality, no speeches were volunteered, only small talk, which adopted a circular pattern; the same queries were made by every member of the party in turn. "I suppose you'll be getting away pretty soon..." started A. Persson, Nottingham Tory, and

200

Pin, knowing it was time to leave, pushed back his chair and stood, shaking hands with a grim smile and an engineer's blistered fingers.

In relating the above dialogue, I have tried to give the impression which it made on me, that although something of an old woman, Pin was an exceedingly ambitious and capable one. He left the refectory and reached his rooms, where he collected his tools and cake tins. Then he went down into the basement and picked up the miniature turbine. On the ascent, an evil impulse seized him – the urge to give the Chancellor a slice of his mind. He knocked on his door; no answer. So he turned the handle and was astonished when the study proved to be unlocked and deserted. The reason for this does not lack irony: Parkins was in his own cellar, ear pressed to a water pipe. The plumbing of St James's left much to be desired, and the Chancellor had discovered the acoustical properties of its conduits. Because of his suspicious and cruel mind, he was a habitual eavesdropper on the conversation of diners in the refectory.

Realising the propriety of returning to his office when Dr Pin left the dining room, Parkins groped his way through the gloomy basement; but his foot caught, partly in an electric cable and partly in a large stack of banned magazines, and over he went. When he got up, vital minutes had been wasted. Pin was already scheming his break-in and embracing quite a different sort of pipe – a briar. Let us return to the engineer and view his indiscreet doings with grudging admiration.

Candle in hand and pipe in mouth, he moved around the room for some time, taking stock of the ornaments on display. The majority were of an Ontographical nature; but on the mantelpiece lay something which bore a resemblance to a small sarcophagus of copper. The padlock which secured it was unfastened. Opening the lid, Pin lighted one match after another to help him see of what nature the box was, but the plot was too strong for them all. He introduced his hand and met with a cylindrical object resting on the floor of the moribund casket. He picked it up, naturally enough, and when he brought it into the light, he saw it was yet another kind of pipe – a metal tube four inches long.

It was of bronze and shaped very much after the manner of a modern referee's whistle. In fact it was – yes, certainly it was – actually no more nor less than a whistle, but quite full of crushed seashells, as if it had been cast into the sea by a very brawny arm and washed up again. Pin blew tentatively, but the note inside was stuck, and would not yield to knocking, but must be loosened with a knife. Pin deemed it something dear to the Chancellor's hidden heart and, still in his wicked phase, he pocketed it. A vague memory came back to him: had Parkins not mentioned a whistle after his Burnstow vacation? It was so long ago that Pin could hardly remember; and so much the worse for him. The object felt heavy in his possession, as if it were not a rudimentary musical apparatus of the sort favoured by boys, but a fully grown man with shoes full of sand. As this was an absurd notion, Pin expelled it.

It has to be noted that the engineer felt little guilt at stealing. St James's had a tradition of scholarly appropriation; a lack of concern in what a native's views might be was considered essential. Changes have been wrought since then, I'm pleased to say: the institution compensates for its desecrations these days. But less of the moralising! It is more appropriate, at this juncture, to record Pin's departure from St James's and his arrival at the train station. As for Parkins: he gained his room in a poor condition, bruised the entire length of one knee, but saw in a moment what had occurred in his absence. He felt inside his box, and let loose an uneducated curse. Then he made a sudden decision, packed a few things into a carpet bag and followed Pin.

How unpleasant it can be, alone in a second class railway carriage, on a first day of a redundancy that might be fairly long, to dawdle through a bit of Welsh country that is unhallowed, stalling at every haystack. The Lladloh express was late in leaving – Pin knew this was always the case, and that arriving at the station on time to catch it would simply ensure him a seat on an earlier one. But at last they pulled out; after rolling English fields, the train crossed the border into wilder terrain. With a map open on his knee, Pin picked out the villages that lay to the right and left by their church towers, and even spotted a few not designated. Soon he was in the depths of the country. I need not particularise, but if you divided the map of Wales into thirteen pieces, he would have been found in the one shaped like a harpy.

When he had reached the edge of his map, and had nowhere to go, his mind attempted to divert him with memories and reflections. His life had been one of moderate success: he had taken a good degree, published work on fluid dynamics and magnetically-coupled circuits and even entertained his peers by seeking to combine branches of pure and applied mathematics in a single tutor. He was tolerated for his skill with Fourier Analysis and self-raising flour. Laplace Transforms were butter in his hands – or margarine on quasi-healthy days. In St James's, he had been something of a misfit, never comfortable among those who lectured in Humanities. More than the others, Parkins had treated him kindly – and this fact made his later behaviour all the more incomprehensible.

What exactly happened to him in Burnstow? After his return why did he snub his former friends? Was there any truth in the rumour that since then, the Chancellor refused to sleep under sheets, but preferred to lie naked on top of a bare mattress? And what was the significance, if any, of the whistle? Before the fateful vacation, one of Parkins's principal characteristics was pluck. After it, pluck was demoted to the status of fresher, while squinting and an acid tongue attained a position of some prominence on his troubled face. His views on certain points altered so dramatically that standard topics of conversation at dinner – surplices hanging on doors or scarecrows in winter fields – had to be forfeited to prevent him swooning into the gravy. Exactly what explanation was cooked up for visiting academics I must confess I do not recollect. Parkins was somehow cleared of the ready suspicion of hallucinogenic substances, and the college of the reputation of an opium den.

Unlike Rogers and Disney, Pin was determined not to be bullied when the transformed Professor of Ontography started to harass him. Parkins threw himself into his work, acquiring power as he did so: after gaining the position of Dean, he was able to set homework for the Professors, as if avenging himself for some unspoken injury. Rogers and Disney left, to be replaced by Bradley and Collodi. The Gardener and Italian were honest chaps, but neither was young, neat or precise in speech. Pin missed such qualities, possessed by the original Parkins.

While the engineer mused thus, he became aware of a clatter outside his compartment door. For some minutes he sat and pondered over possible reasons for this disturbance. There had been a movement, he was sure, in the empty connecting corridor. Might rats be playing about in it? It was quiet now. No! the commotion began again. But was it with rats? I should not ask, because in this case it was not. Besides, there was a rustling and shaking: surely more than any rat could cause.

Pin was off his seat in one bound, and made a dash toward the door, with no weapon than a template for gingerbread men. The rustling turned into a flurry of footsteps; the engineer poked his head into the passage just in time to catch a glimpse of a bobbing black object vanishing into an adjacent compartment. With its back to him, it was anonymous; yet Pin felt that its frictionless gait was familiar. With many misgivings as to incipient failure of eyesight, overworked brain, excessive smoking, and so on, he resigned himself to making a search of the carriage. He slowly crept up to the compartment into which the figure had jumped, and peered through the glass at the interior. It was quite devoid of personages: as he'd assumed he was alone on the express, this revelation afforded Pin a crumb of comfort. But there was a blanket of some kind resting on one of the tastelessly upholstered seats – a previous passenger must have left it there – and this travelling adjunct bore a distinct human appearance, with a crumpled, and intensely horrible, face. Furthermore, it seemed to be quivering, as if panting after some exertion.

For a moment, the engineer was at a loss to account for this. There were no open windows in the room; the wind was not disturbing the cloth. Then he remembered his notion of rats loose on the train; this proved to be the likely explanation. After all, ragged and mouldy bedclothes often heaved like seas, with the rats under them. Why not travelling rugs? Pin congratulated himself on his logical approach to mysteries, and returned briskly to his own compartment and fidgetings.

The journey ended about midnight. Between the houses, Pin could see the tents of the Eisteddfod, with the monumental Grand Pavilion towering over the other structures. No cheerful country porter came to greet him. He was forced to carry his luggage onto the platform himself; as he took a rest on his suitcase, the aching engineer was almost knocked down by a trainspotter who collided with him at the very top of his speed. Instead of running away, the misfit remaining hanging on to him, speechless with fright. It is dangerous to give a hobbyist such a scare as this one had had, and Pin, knowing this, sought the bottom of the matter.

"What have you been up to? What have you seen?" he demanded.

"Duw, I seen it wave at me out of the window," wailed the spotter. "And I don't like it. It wasn't a tidy boyo."

Pin sent the man on his way with a shilling and frowned. The window indicated was the one next to his own; the compartment into which darted the faceless shape. There was nothing there now. Can rats wave? At least the fellow had not seen fit to throw a stone.

Dismissing the incident, the engineer made his way through the dark streets to his lodgings. The place which the reader is asked to consider is Lladloh. It is different now from what I remember it to have been. An ancient mortuary chapel, with a cemetery shaped like a goat's tear; tall trees smothering domestic buildings; crooked lanes made not with cobbles but flint nodules, so that pedestrians with hobnailed boots light their way without recourse to expensive public illumination. There was a glum black windmill just after you left the station, which looked like it had lost a joust with a deluded knight... Also shops of dull red brick, with roofs of dirty straw... but why do I encumber you with these commonplace details? Is it because dots are a good substitute for effective writing? Or because I am writing a guide book...?

Walk away from the mill and turn down the road on the left. It runs parallel to the railway, and if you follow it, it descends into a smelly sort of hollow, at the bottom of which can be found the village square. Here Pin encountered the nameless tavern which was to be his home for as many weeks as it took for him to revolutionise the power ratios of steam engines and redeem himself as a tutor of merit. As he walked, he had the traditional feeling of being followed; but he resisted a growing urge to look over his shoulder and spoil the story.

Before dropping into the urban pit, he cast a glance at the site of the Eisteddfod. Not all was quiet at this late hour; flickering lamps of paraffin moved to and fro, as if the stall owners were preparing for the morning's entertainments. For any reader who is interested, let me state that the Royal National Eisteddfod is the major Welsh festival, and must not be confused with the International Eisteddfod, which has a permanent site in Llangollen. The Royal is a nomad, whose venue is proclaimed one year and a day in advance by the Gorsedd of Bards. It is fundamentally a cultural tournament, with overblown pageantry and a wealth of aesthetic events, including Druidic competitions. The Grand Pavilion is a marquee worthy of a Mongol Khan, so large that fifty six blows of square-headed iron mallets are needed to secure each peg.

Pin was made welcome at the squalid inn, was installed in the large double-bedded room of which we have heard, and was able to arrange his materials for work in crab-apple-pie order upon a narrow table standing in the wide end of the room. There was a single window which looked over the filthy street. After resting awhile on a chair, Pin returned to the bar for a strong nightcap. The tavern's interior was far too spacious to be illuminated, as it was, by a dozen or so candles. The engineer made a remark to the barman to the effect that atmosphere was one thing; seeing where you were going was quite another.

The barman, who went by the name of Emyr James, was affable. "These are not our preferred arrangements. The generator which provides us with electricity has been broken for many years."

"Well," said Pin, "but it appears to me at that rate, sir, that you must be little better than a Cimmerian."

"Perhaps I am," the barman answered; "but the laws which govern our generator are really not at all perfectly known. No mechanic has managed to fix it; thus the village exists without electric light or heating. In view of this, and the fact it seems likely to turn rather colder, would you like any extra blankets on your bed?"

Pin declined the offer and ordered a glass of porter. "As an expert with engines, I wonder if I may be of assistance? What sort of generator do you use? Pour this pint first." Interval.

"About that generator you were asking. It's rather a curious one. I have it in my cellar. As a matter of fact, I was polishing it yesterday. Beautiful model, astounding performance. Man-sized but with a water-tube boiler and a double Kylchap exhaust. Delivers a pressure of 666psi, more in summer. Fully portable – in a wheelchair."

Dr Pin was stupefied by these specifications, which he was tempted to laugh to scorn, but his incredulity was greatly modified with another pint, and the reaction to his next question. He wondered aloud whether a certain Noisette had manufactured the device.

In front of the hearth, seated on a Gothic chair with a candle set in either arm, an ample and malignant youth with brass-rimmed spectacles quietly laughed with unimaginable cynicism.

"Never mind him," whispered Emyr; "that's just Mr Homunculus, local poet, embittered and drunk as a study-toad."

But the youth suddenly muttered: "Poor Noisette! Lots of hobbies, a comfortable home, all his time to himself. Took his work so seriously he lost himself in it! Never found his way out!"

"Hush!" warned Emyr. But Pin was not at all deterred by the cryptic utterance. He was pleased to receive confirmation of his belief that the village of Lladloh was indeed the hometown of the legendary inventor. I can imagine him rubbing his palms together once he returned to his room after consuming a third glass. Before he went to bed, he took out of his suitcase the whistle he had stolen from Parkins. Crushed seashells still clogged the mouthpiece, and the pea was a pearl, but he managed to clear it out with his toothbrush. Tidy as ever in his habits, he stepped close to the window to throw the brush out. Opening the casement, he noticed a belated wanderer coming down the hill into the square, wearing something in the manner of a *djellaba*, trotting with swiftness and irregularity, a startling and terrifying speed. Then Pin closed the window, surprised at the odd cloaks people wore at Lladloh.

Later, he thought he heard voices conversing outside his door. Emyr was ushering a late arrival into a room. They talked as if they were old acquaintances who had been reunited.

In the morning, Pin woke and dressed, putting the finishing touches to his corset, when one of the maids came in.

"If you please," she said, "would you like extra oil on your cogs, sir?"

"Ah, thank you," said Pin, casting a glance over the spare parts he had arranged on his cankerous dressing table. "Yes, I think I would like some. They seem likely to turn rather rusty."

"Are you employed at the Eisteddfod, sir?" she asked.

"Dear me. My arrival here has nothing to do with the festival. I'm a scholar exiled from his college for some minor offences. For example, my Wankel engine was caught in the act."

"Really? How very absurd!" said the maid, departing to giggle with her colleagues, while Pin set forth, with a stern determination to enjoy an ethnic breakfast. And sure enough, he ate a double helping of chunky cawl with a plate of barabrith, followed by a Red Dragon Pie*, which is usually baked for half-an-hour at 180 degrees centigrade. Onions, beans and carrots are the chief ingredients, topped with potatoes. But I'm not writing a recipe book – unlike Dr Pin, who is.

He left the dive and returned up the hill to the Eisteddfod. He was disappointed to learn of a hefty entrance fee for the privilege of being admitted into the festival. Pin's experience on this occasion was a very distressing one. Transactions were conducted in Welsh and he was snubbed by a mob of language activists, who delighted in spelling out words they thought unfamiliar to him – as c-o-b-l-y-n coblyn, and the like. I heard the whole story from him some months later. He wandered through the dirt and muddy puddles, finally coming to the entrance of the Grand Pavilion. Then, with a nervous shrug, he disappeared into the maw of the cyclopean tent – where the Bardic recital was in progress.

For an hour he endured the strict rhythms and soft mutations, until the Arch-Druid, Barrington Burke, announced the competition's winner. In Pin's phrase, Mr Burke, dressed in a gown of crumpled linen, was so Arch he was practically Ctesiphonic. Pin left the marquee in bewilderment and horror, emotions I can figure to myself, for I have in the flesh thirty years back seen the same thing happen; but the reader can hardly imagine how dreadful it was to him to see first prize awarded to a poet which he had known to be an empty talent. He sauntered in search of the exit, was set upon by charity fundraisers and was forced to pause and feel in his pockets. But he only drew out the whistle.

"Well, that's curious," he said; "I remember that before I started this morning I intended to leave it behind."

But the fund-raisers would not accept it as a substitute for money, and after an alternative pocket was ransacked, his redundancy payoff was further depleted. In disgust, he decided to return to his lodging, where he might be more assured of solitude. As he neared the tavern, he caught sight of something playing tricks in his room – a hint of bundled up and twisted bedclothes moving about on their own behind the glass. "Now," he thought aloud, "if this is one of the servants going into my room when I am away, I can only say that – well, that I don't approve of it at all." Unless, he amended, it was a frisky maid.

While he was in the act of rushing into the building, and demanding an explanation from the barman, he was detained on the threshold by the youth who had chuckled at him in the bar. Mr Homunculus, as Emyr termed him, snatched Pin's sleeve and hissed: "So you're interested in Kingdom Noisette? Come with me, sir, into the cellar."

"I'll go down in a moment. It'll be a pleasure, both to you and to myself. First we must get to the bottom of this: what do you know about Noisette and where his designs came from?"

"Honest, sir, I don't know the source of his inspiration, or how he arrived at the finished product – that nobody could guess. But I'll go as far as say this, that he's not a hundred feet from this place. Quite whole, in a perfectly undecayed state."

"You'll forgive me, I hope," started Pin, "if I sound

impertinent, but are you quite sure he's near here? I thought it was just an example of his work which was kept in the cellar."

"Right down there, sir. That's the truth what I'm telling you, that is; if you don't believe me, ask the barman."

Saying nothing, the engineer followed the youth under a low archway and down a steep spiral staircase. Half aloud Pin counted the steps as he went down, and he got as far as the thirty eighth before reaching the floor of the cellar. It was very dark and there was some foulness of air which nearly extinguished the matches he lit in sequence. The dank room under the tavern went some little way back, and on the right and left of the entrance, he could discern rounded objects which might be barrels. A taller shape loomed straight ahead; he reached out and touched something curved, that felt – yes – more or less like skin. This discovery made it absolutely certain to Pin's mind that he was on the right track. Putting both hands out as well as he could, he pulled it to him, and it came. It was heavy, but moved more easily than expected.

Bumping into an unseen obstruction, it tottered and then slipped on to Pin's chest, and wrapped its arms round his neck. He was conscious of a most horrible smell of garlic, and of a cold kind of face pressed into his own, and of moving slowly over it, and of several – I don't know how many – pistons or crankshafts or pendulums rotating against his body. He would have screamed out like a beast, but Homunculus, running quickly up the steps, returned with a lantern, and the vista was illuminated in the fashion of supernatural melodrama. By this time, of course, Pin realised he was in the presence of an automaton.

But what he actually saw impressed him, as he told me, more than he could have conceived any machine or device capable of impressing him. It is useless to try to convey by words the effect which this apparatus had upon him. However, the main traits of it I can at least indicate. He saw at first only a frock coat and top-hat; presently it was seen that these covered a body of Victorian severity, almost a disciplinarian, with very bushy side-whiskers standing out like brooms. The hands were of a rugged texture, suited to holding spanners; while the tongue, lubricated with a burning spittle, was able to lash pupils and tutors alike. One remark is usually made by those who have seen the original: "Ee oop!" But for Pin, the most astonishing aspect of the encounter was his sudden grasping of the fact that Kingdom Noisette and his work were one and the same thing! He had a great deal of use for this insight.

"My life upon it," he said; "but the secret of increased efficiency and reduced emissions is here." Turning to Homunculus, he added: "You be off, and don't think any more about it. And, by the way, congratulations on winning the poetry chair at the Eisteddfod!"

It was in a somewhat pensive frame of mind that Pin returned to the bar and proposed to Emyr the buying of the generator off the citizens of Lladloh for a reasonable sum. "As it is broken, I am sure you will quote a small price. How much do you ask for it? Will you take two hundred and fifty shillings? This is not confounding."

"I will not. The contraption is not for sale."

"My silly barman!" Pin cried again and again, "deal with a gent if you can get on the track of one. Your generator is worth much less than two hundred and fifty shillings, I assure you – much less. Consider its uselessness. What do you want for it?"

"Nothing – nothing in the world. Sir is not welcome to it. We still hope that, one day, it will be mended."

Even an engineer's conscience is sometimes stirred, and that of Pin was tenderer than an engineer's. He confessed that he knew how to fix it and was willing to do so, on the condition that he was allowed to borrow it for a week or two. Emyr could hardly disguise his delight at the news and immediately assented to Pin's terms. The engineer requested that the generator be hoisted from the cellar – whether by ropes or chains wasn't an issue – and placed at his disposal.

The barman, anxious to learn what had made Pin so confident of success, offered him a cognac on the house, which Pin accepted without loosening his tongue.

While sipping the spirit, the scholar chanced to notice, in a dusky corner of the room, where the walls and furnishings were blackened with soot, a thing that looked like a band of dark shadow sitting at a table. He was reminded of the bobbing shape on the train, the late wayfarer on the road and the vision of twisted blankets glimpsed through the window of his room. Whatever it was, with a sudden smooth motion, it shifted on its chair and began to reach for the pint of beer on the table. It moved awkwardly, in a stooping posture, and all at once the engineer realised, with some horror and some relief, that it must be blind, for it seemed to feel about it with its muffled arms in a groping and random fashion. Turning half away, it became suddenly conscious of its drink and thrust in its hand, as if to gauge the depth of the contents. In a few moments it seemed to know that the glass was empty.

Pin would have liked to have observed this apparition order another pint; but a call of nature required his brief absence. When he returned, and found the shape gone, he was both pleased and disappointed. He asked the barman whether there were any unusual guests staying at the lodgings during the Eisteddfod week; anyone whose extraordinary habits marked him out from the common run of humanity.

"Apart from yourself, none," opined Emyr. "All present in my tavern are known to me. You are the only stranger."

Dr Pin finished his cognac, ordered a whisky and soda to dilute it, and made his way to his bed. When he reached his room, the lock of which had been forced, he was alarmed to find his cogs in disarray and all his other possessions thrown about in great profusion, as if an intruder had decided to give vent to his animal spirits. Only the blankets on the bed were undisturbed, and their orderly condition gave the impression they'd been deliberately avoided. Pin was about to stomp downstairs again, with his boots still on, and complain to Emyr – but he caught a whiff of some feminine scent, a perfume seemingly distilled from a rose garden, and he deduced from this that a frisky maid had been dancing in his room. So he felt at ease once more and went to bed.

The following morning, he arranged the lifting of Kingdom Noisette from the cellar. The burghers of Lladloh rallied round to assist him in relocating the generator to an abandoned railway siding which connected with the town's main line. Soon Pin was well on his way to implementing Bradley's suggestion about returning to St James's on a modern charger. Around the Victorian cadaver, he constructed a high-pressure, 4-cylinder compound 4-6-4 locomotive. He had just the right number of cogs for this purpose; and although wheels were not available, his cake tins made very adequate substitutes. One of Emyr's barrels doubled up as a cabin. Only one component was not to be had anywhere in the village, and at first it appeared that the project would be abandoned, so vital was this missing piece. But inspiration came to the engineer; dipping into his pocket, he saved the day, and the people made a hum, and a deal of applause, and Dr Pin felt himself to be of some slight value.

I possess a copy of the timetable for that particular Eisteddfod. A festival held in Lladloh is generally run backwards, and so right at the end of the week, after the climactic events were finished, only a rather thin crowd remained to taste the minor entertainments. As it was nearing the time to pack up, the pegs of the Grand Pavilion were being loosened, with fifty six tugs of iron pincers, while Pin finally announced that he too was ready to depart from Lladloh. The staff of the tavern, with some guests, who had gathered to wave him off, were joined by the last of the festival mob, and the engineer revealed his secret. First he unbuttoned Noisette's coat, and then his shirt, to reveal a broad expanse of hairy chest. Stepping forward, he raised a wooden spoon and dealt a tremendous blow on a hidden panel, which sprang open.

"Here is the reason for the fault!" he exclaimed, holding something rather like a grapefruit and inserting it carefully into the cavity thus exposed. "It's the beating of his hideous heart!"

The object in question, of course, was the small steam-turbine Pin brought with him from St James's. Once reunited with its host, it had an incredible effect on the broken device. With steadily mounting velocity, Noisette's top-hat rose and fell; his sideburns worked like crankshafts. The locomotive, which Pin had mysteriously christened *Lost Hearts*, began to glide down the siding, bearing its scholastic passenger in reasonable comfort. As he gathered speed towards the main line, he was horrified to note a billowing shape leering at him from the ranks of cheering faces. Abruptly, it broke from the mob and headed to intercept him. He quickly accelerated, but it was too late; with surprising agility, the faceless figure leapt up and joined him in the driver's cabin. As Pin gasped, one corner of its draperies swept across his face.

He was on the point of throwing himself off the train, and risking a nasty fall, when the apparition suddenly reached up and pulled off its grotesque covering. Beneath was not a mask. It was a face – not young, not neat, not precise in features. Dr Pin remembers the minute drops of perspiration which started from its forehead; he remembers how the jaw had a plucky cast and the eyes an aptitude for judging distance on the golf course. He recalls his own astonishment.

"Parkins! What the deuce! This is dreadful!"

But the Chancellor shook his head and launched into an explanation of his presence and strange disguise.

He spoke with great urgency and his elucidation I cannot represent as perfectly as I should like. But the nub was his terror when he discovered the theft of his whistle, his decision to come to Lladloh after Pin. He confessed a regular eavesdropper on the engineer's conversation, had been following his movements rather closely. The

the train was none other than himself; as well as the shape in the window and the drinker in the tavern. He burgled Dr Pin's room in an attempt to locate the whistle, not knowing the engineer kept it on his person. To allay suspicion, he boiled rose petals in a kettle and then sprinkled the tincture over the carpets.

"I don't understand it!" Pin cried at last. "Are you mad? You must be, and what a sad thing! Such a good Ontographer too, and so successful in your business. What does it mean?"

"The whole thing is so ghastly and abnormal that I must own it puts me quite off my balance," avowed Parkins; "but if you bear with me, I'll tell the rest. It is tied up with the vacation I took to Burnstow years ago. I have much to say bout my visit to that dreadful place, and what I found in half- ried ruins by the shore."

"Excavating, were you?" Pin asked.

"Very little," was the answer; "I went to improve my ?ut I'd made a sort of promise to Disney, our antiquarian, over the site of a preceptory which had once belonged iights Templars. Well, I chanced upon a metal whistle en raised to the lips and sounded, invested blankets)f their own."

good Heaven! I take it that this was the origin of 1ce of sheets? How does the whistle work?"

ave no idea. It must have something to do with 't by the Templars. I believe a clue is afforded made popular recently by the invention of the get who wrote the words: it was either Mrs ustin Hayward. There is a refrain which white satin!"

s too much of an old woman to have ph recordings. He deferred to superior

oring it to St James's?" he asked.

get rid of it first. An acquaintance of

mine – my golfing partner – threw it out to sea. But the tide returned it, like an overdue library book, and my hoarding instinct compelled me to add it to the college's possessions. It remained safely locked in my room until it was snatched by you and brought here."

"Well, as you have explained the matter, I freely own that I do not like robbing a colleague," confessed Pin; "I believe what you have said, yet some points need to be cleared up. If you are scared of sheets, why have you taken to wearing one in Lladloh?"

"I had no wish to. I believe I am now acquainted with the extremity of terror and repulsion which a man can endure without losing his mind. After you left St James's to catch the express, I had less than a minute to secure a disguise and follow you. Although it pained me dreadfully to make use of it, the tablecloth in the refectory was the only thing which suited my build. An unexpected good has come of this – proximity to what I fear most has cured me of my phobia. I'm no longer frightened of linen and much less grumpy as a consequence."

"That is another point," put in Pin, sotto voce; "I am still pained by your unreasonable hatred toward me."

"Just so, Pin, just so. The matter is easily resolved. When I first planned to go to Burnstow, I was full of enthusiasm for the trip. Rather quickly my zeal waned, as it is apt to do with Ontographers. In short, I decided to change my mind. I arranged a feast to inform my colleagues of my altered plans, and was just about to break the news when you piped up with this question: 'I suppose you will be getting away pretty soon, now Full Term is over, Professor?' After that, it was impossible not to lose face by backing out. So I went against my will. When the terrible events happened, I held you responsible. You started the adventure, but took no part in it – like a person not in the story!"

"Oh dear, Mr Parkins, what a dreadful thing of me to do. What must you have thought? You must forgive me."

"Not at all, Dr Pin, I assure you. Coming here has done me a world of good, and I no longer wish to dwell on what might be termed 'Burnstow Sickness'. It is quite unproductive."

The reader will not be far out if he guesses that Pin accepted this honest statement as an example of good sense. But he will also naturally inquire, as the engineer did, at what inn the Chancellor found lodgings. Parkins was keen to give an answer on the point, and did so with obvious alacrity. When Pin learned it was the nameless tavern where he had spent his own nights – there being only one such establishment in Lladloh – he was confounded. He pointed out that the barman insisted that Pin was the only stranger in the house during the week.

"But I wasn't a stranger!" Parkins said; "This is my second journey to these parts. When I first came here, thirty years ago, I discovered a civilised society, making use of cheap electricity. For the furtherance of academic learning, I befriended the barman and plied him with drinks until he revealed the secret of the village's energy supply. Then I went into the cellar, stole Noisette's heart and took it back to St James's. This was before you joined the college: when you arrived, it was already part of the Engineering Department! The citizens of Lladloh never knew I was responsible for breaking the generator. Indeed, Emyr kept sending me favourable postcards depicting local sheep."

It seems curious that, despite his aptitude for cryptic puzzles, Dr Pin hadn't worked this out for himself.

"This explains the friendly banter of the voices outside my room. I guess Emyr was pleased to see you again. I suppose it also assured you a room at short notice – most 'belated wanderers' would be turned away for the duration of the Eisteddfod. But how did you get away with sporting a tablecloth, especially one stained with jam?"

The Chancellor smiled smugly and said: "Really, it was surprisingly easy. I convinced the barman that, as a 'grapher', I was 'Ethno-' rather than 'Onto-', and that I must needs wear a sheet to study Druidic habits more closely. He fell for it: hook, line and sigil. But this is of small urgency. My main concern, and the whole point of my trip, is to stop you blowing my whistle. It is rather dangerous!"

"Don't trouble to do that, thanks," replied Pin; "I have virtually no love for music. And bronze sickens me."

"I have reason to believe you are thinking of sounding the whistle without using your lips! My aim is to dissuade you from such a course of action, without appearing impertinent."

"While I'm willing to appreciate your skill as an eavesdropper," Dr Pin objected, "I don't see how you can possibly know what I am thinking. I rather sniff at the idea that minds can be read like Latin primers. I remain a convinced disbeliever in telepathy."

"I can do nothing whatever of that kind," Parkins said; "But you're in this story – unlike the Burnstow one – and I have written it down for the entertainment of our colleagues."

The Chancellor reached into his pocket and produced a manuscript of a size too large for a missal, and not the shape of an antiphoner. As he turned the pages, Pin realised the value of such a work. It was a nearly complete account of the story which you, the reader with endurance, have managed to reach to this point[†]. Too scared to read it right to the end, the engineer stopped about here and changed the topic of conversation to less paradoxical matters. He discussed the nature of animated sheets and what they did when they came alive; he wondered if modern bedclothes had some immunity to the effects of the whistle. Would a duvet exhibit quite the same evil propensities as a plain blanket? What if Parkins had spent his Burnstow holiday in a sleeping bag? Did a double-bed always produce an apparition of larger dimensions than a bachelor's berth? What if the whistle was played aboard a ship? Would hammocks rise up? Would Papists and Jesuits welcome genuine holy ghosts?

"I believe any fabric is a suitable candidate for animation," cried Parkins; "whether curtains, tapestries or handkerchiefs. I think it will depend on how hard the whistle is blown. The volume of the note controls which covering adopts a semblance of life!"

He would have said more, but he was cut short by a cry from Pin. On the line directly ahead of them stood a figure in an anorak. It was, of course, the same trainspotter Pin had met at the station. He was unaware of his danger, too overcome with excitement at finding a locomotive not spotted by any of his peers. As he wrote down the registration number of the *Lost Hearts*, the engineer called for him to get out of the way. Much too engrossed in his business, the misfit ignored him. There was nothing for it but for Pin to reach out and pull the chain which allowed a blast of steam to sound the – (at this stage, the reader must pause for a cup of very sweet tea) – yes, yes, the whistle!

You don't need to be told what happened next. They were passing the deflated Grand Pavilion at the time and it seemed to suddenly sit up, as if it concealed a waking giant. The notion of Pin and Parkins increasing speed and fleeing from – from something like this, is very comforting to me. You can guess what they fancied: how the thing might follow them and derail them with a casual sweep of a gargantuan foot. But, in fact, keen to take the opposite direction, it stamped toward the village square and descended the hill in a single bound. Although there seemed to be little material about it than the marquee of which it had made itself a body, a splintering sound confirmed to the departing scholars that it was rather adept at wreaking physical damage. In the moments that remained before a bend obstructed their view of the village, moments of tense anxiety, for they knew not whether they would have to pay compensation for the havoc, or whether they were covered by insurance, both men noticed that the sky and landscape seemed to darken about them – as if the being was standing in front of Lladloh's desultory sun.

It is absolutely clear that they reached their destination a day or two later, and that they were mentally exhausted. It is also known that Pin took to his bed on the afternoon of the 23rd, and is still there. He does not make use of blankets, but sleeps with a college cat for warmth. The irony of all this, of course, is that Parkins is no longer bothered by such fears; he reinstated Pin as an Emeritus, feeling that giving him the sack might have been a bad omen, and took over his duties. It is not a pretty sight, to see an Ontographer adopting a new profession, but he soon had the measure of gear ratios and the lever principle, and already is embarking on an ambitious extension of gyroscope dynamics into realms of anti-gravity physics. Indeed, I am – I mean, he is – rather close to designing a working model of a spaceship.

Nothing is less common form in postmodern stories than a serious attempt to explore real emotions and real people. The aftermath of the happening at Lladloh should be outlined, with particular reference to the terrible sufferings and deprivations of the populace. But neither Pin nor myself have ever taken the trouble to return there, or to learn what buildings, if any, survived the rampage. Possibly the survivors will try to rebuild what they have lost – perhaps they will move elsewhere. I know only that the village is no longer to be found on maps of the region; but it never featured on the majority of them anyway.

The conventional sequel to this tale is that the organisers of the Eisteddfod have vowed never to hold another festival near there. Indeed, Mr Barrington Burke, the Arch-Druid, has even suggested taking the event outside Wales for the first time. He has his eye on an innocuous town on the east coast by the name of Seaburgh. Nothing can possibly go wrong in that location, he claims; but if it does, then he will take the festival out of the country altogether, to a place he has heard about, a decayed little town on the spurs of the Pyrenees.

---

* Dr Pin was deceived. Red Dragon Pie is Chinese in origin.
† It did not contain footnotes.

Bridge Over Troubled Blood

"Here's to you, Mrs Robinson!" cried Artery Garfunkle, raising his glass of blood. "Without your help, I would never have transfused the required eight pints and graduated."

"It's called 'Passing Out'," returned Mrs Robinson. She drained her glass and licked her bitter lips.

"Nothing like your own vintage," observed Garfunkle. He sighed. "Do you think our relationship is sinful? I'm barely into triple figures and you're approaching your millennium."

Mrs Robinson reached out and caressed his wings. "Silly bat! Ignore conventional morality. Now help me get dressed. I bought a new brassière the other day. Would you like to button it?"

"No, I can't stand French food. The Marquis de Sade gave me ghastly indigestion. It's time I prepared for work."

Lilith Robinson regarded her enthusiastic young lover with a slight frown. His brand of innocence worried her: it wasn't fresh and charming, but rotten and cankerous – more like decayed sagacity than true naïvety. Quick as a fever, he climbed out of bed and started dressing, relying on her mimicry to adjust his silk cravat. Unable to use mirrors, they often stood in for each other's reflection.

Her tone was gently chiding. "Only graduated last month and already starting a job! The youth of today don't know how to enjoy themselves. I took a century off when I was your age."

"Really?" Garfunkle raised an eyebrow. "What for?"

"Holiday in Arkham. Did me an underworld of good."

"But that's where I'm off to! The college has arranged an exchange. Arkham's brightest graduate is coming over here – she's an engineer of some kind – and I'm going over there. Isn't it exciting? I can't imagine how I won the offer. Competition was fierce.”

“Tell me more. What are you expected to do? I hope it's not just an excuse for some cheap labour! I don't want you working your guts out for the sake of a wriggly taskmaster.”

He smiled. “The Arkham authorities seem personable entities. It's a cultural thing. They like my music.”

“Music? But you graduated in euthanasia!”

“I specialised in rubbing down bishops with extreme unction. But my guitar is the cavity where I keep my heart...”

“You're not taking Appalling with you?”

Artery Garfunkle flushed white and nodded: “He's my best fiend. And who else can provide me with lyrics?”

Mrs Robinson threw up her talons in despair. “The pair of you don't know what the music business is like! So many ambitious bats end up with dreams smeared over their maws. Don't do it, Artery!”

“I have to. It's my destiny. I know the folk scene is difficult to make a mark in. But so is a flint neck! It takes a degree of masochism. Remember this, Mrs Robinson: hell holds a place for those who prey. When I'm wealthy, you'll have as much lingerie as you want. With Appalling by my side, we'll soon be rolling in it!”

Lilith shook her head. “The words of the profit were written on the dungeon wall,” she muttered. “In gore.”

With an angry pout, he pulled on his coat and made to leave. “Sorry you don't feel the way I do. But you must try to understand. Best for me to make my own mistakes in my own way. No point trying to put an ancient skull on old shoulders. It's not a matter for debate – I'm off to Arkham to strum the catgut and there's an end to it.”

“What if you meet someone else? Musicians are followed by hordes of screaming harpies. They're young and puffy!”

“You'll just have to trust me, Mrs Robinson.”

Wings flapping through the slits in his coat, Garfunkle stormed out of the apartment, slamming the window as he went. Lilith buried her face in the grave-scented pillow and spilled a crepuscular tear. What she had feared all along was coming to pass: the age difference was too great to sustain the affair. She had lost him – he was off in pursuit of somebody new. Not that he necessarily knew this on a conscious level: it was the inevitable outcome of unbalanced amours.

Lilith raised herself, tears cascading over the side of the bed and landing in her glass of blood, diluting the ruby fluid to a tragic rosé. The only question was how she ought to act now: embittered or forgiving? It was much more mature to shrug her shoulders and forget about him. But maturity only lasted from the ages of eighteen to seven hundred and ten. After that, emotions turned full circle: grudges were reclaimed, revenge was back in favour and hate became a noble feeling. Deeming it better to act her age, she decided to be vindictive.

She would strike viciously, without mercy, as blatantly as a child. She would damage not his skin but his reputation. When he came back from Arkham, he would find himself mocked in professional circles. No hospice would employ him as an euthanasist. If he wanted to fool with music, she would ensure he did it on street corners.

Moving to the casement, she peered through the warped glass. Artery had landed on the grass embankment outside the library and was listening to his companion, Appalling Simon, who was playing a flute carved out of a mouse. Even at this distance, Mrs Robinson thought she could discern a whisper of the furtive and twitching melody.

She snatched up her brassière and carried it into the kitchen. When she reached the stove she filled the iron cups with charcoal and grilled a whole poodle over the pulsating flames. Her brassière often doubled up as a brazier: it saved on vocabulary.

A week after Artery and Appalling left for Arkham, the exchange graduate arrived at the college. She was almost twelve feet tall, with snaky hair and four visible arms. She was softly spoken, darkly cowled and teetered on a pair of stiff legs. She introduced herself as 'Oldona' and seemed a little confused in her new environment. She was a civil engineer and her main interest was in building bridges. The Chancellor had commissioned a crossing of the local river as a test.

The college stream was a trickle, but it cut into the campus like a festering wound, dividing one faculty from another. For the flying staff this presented few problems; but the Social Science Departments were run by zombies, who had to be rowed from bank to bank by galley slaves taken from the student ranks. The loss of scholars was high; the gondolas were often capsized by the suicidal punters, fatally dampening the reputation of Stakehampton Institute of Parasitical Studies.

Wasting no time, Oldona experimented with a large number of designs before submitting the most suitable for approval by the Chancellor. Only a suspension bridge would look right, she maintained; and only if it was well-hung. This was Arkham gallows humour.

Lilith planned to make her acquaintance as soon as it was feasible, but in fact the engineer sought her out first. Officially, Mrs Robinson was a student counsellor. Undergraduates came to her with their problems and her job was to make them worse, offering bad advice on such dilemmas as housing, nourishment and faith.

"I just can't seem to settle in," Oldona lisped, as she entered Mrs Robinson's office. "The climate is horrid and I can't get used to biting on the left hand side of the neck."

"Sit down." Lilith indicated a chair.

Oldona lowered herself, rather awkwardly, onto the seat. She winced and adjusted her position. "I'm quite happy with my working arrangements here; it's the social side. I feel lonely."

"Perhaps you need a lover. There are some eligible

gargoyles on the shelf in the college chapel basement."

"I'm a married entity. I couldn't possibly consider a paramour. How would I appease my conscience?"

"A *paranormalmour*," corrected Mrs Robinson. "I had one myself, very recently. See this cleaver hung around my neck? The first gift he bought me. I sharpen it once a day. Actually, he's the bat who's gone to Arkham in your place. He's a songwriter."

Oldona's eyes grew bright. "Is he any good?"

"In bed? Certainly! You mean his music? Well actually..."

Lilith bit her lip, a painful gesture. Oldona seemed flustered; she mopped her brow with one hand and twiddled the thumbs of two others. Mrs Robinson broke the uneasy pause with a lopsided grin. "We both need some company. Let me show you the local nightlife."

Oldona chuckled. "I was hoping you'd say that..."

"I'll meet you outside the Palais de Decadence at midnight. But you must lope along now, I've got work to do."

Oldona staggered to her feet and lurched out. Lilith was astonished by a screech which diminished in sinusoidal waves. Then she guessed that Oldona had eased her alarming bulk onto the balcony of the spiral stairs and was enjoying an unconventional descent. She brushed tears and smiled indulgently at the same time. Youth was such a marvellous attribute, but no matter how it was spent it was squandered!

Mrs Robinson thought of Artery Garfunkle, swooping over the maggoty campus of a foreign college, or treading the boards of a graveyard dive, plucking his guitar and crooning to Appalling's accordion. What would an American audience make of their portentous melodies? Lilith recalled her own heroes – Howlin' Werewolf, Bloody Waters, Hellmore James. Artery had no chance of competing with those big bogies.

On the other talon, it was even more disturbing to envisage success for the duo. If it happened it would go straight to their skulls, like a wine fermented from pumpkins, nightshade and cheerleaders. The pleasures on offer, the adulation, would rot Artery's mind, leaving him a pathetic wreck on the rocky shores of folk.

At this thought, Mrs Robinson rubbed her palms in glee. Perhaps she ought to let them ruin themselves. But no, this smacked of quietism, she was determined to play a part in the final humiliation. With her sleeve, she wiped away the usual stain from the chair where Oldona had sat. Then she returned to work, shuffling her papers.

The afternoon progressed slowly. Seven distraught students, with a coffinful of depressions between them, came to visit, but she could only convince three that the answer was suicide. The others expressed doubts about its usefulness and her counselling skills could not persuade them otherwise. "It's good for you!" she insisted.

Returning to her room, she made herself up with violet lipstick and crimson mascara, and hung dark pearls from her pierced nipples. Then she gargled with sweet nepenthe, stiffened her hair with lime and slipped on a revealing silk number, with thigh-length leather boots and a belt made from a heretic's flayed back. Her mirrors were useless, so she dressed a voodoo mannequin carved in her image. The way the doll wore its garments was indicative of the way she looked. Finally, she strapped the pig-iron brassière to the outside of her dress.

How much longer could she strut her stuff like this? When would her fellow bats start wrinkling snouts and making disparaging comments? From the Anatomy lecturers, she had already heard some. "Mutton dressed up as aardvark!" was the cruellest jibe to date.

Perhaps some of Oldona's vitality would rub off on her. The student was a peculiar creature, to be sure, but not unattractive. Spraying neck and cleavage with Chanel No.666, Lilith opened the window and kissed the wind. She flung herself over the edge and headed downtown. She still had a century of prime animus left, there was still time to dance and flirt. No mediocre songwriter was going to tarnish her dignity. She would split Artery and Appalling apart like mating toads.

Oldona was waiting for her outside the Palais de Decadence. The exchange student was wearing a poncho stitched with occult symbols and a sombrero with a sand-filled brim. A prickly cactus sprouted from the crown. "It's the only formal gear I brought over," she apologised. "I didn't think to pack many posh clothes. Is it out of place?"

Mrs Robinson shook her head. "By no means! You look really elegant. I wish I had your bone structure."

"That's just where I keep my purse!"

They entered the dancehall arm in arm in arm. A gallows stood on a makeshift stage. Corpses dangled from nooses, clutching trumpets, double basses and saxophones, which they played with violent spasms. "Don't you just love traditional Swing?" Oldona asked.

The floor was crowded with jazz freaks: tattooed ladies, strong men and sword swallowers in zoot suits. They were dancing the jittervirus, a new craze created in a test-tube in the Chemistry Department. Surprising herself, Lilith snatched Oldona and bounded onto the floor, kicking legs and gyrating hips to the insidious rhythms.

Later, exhausted, they sat in a corner on a comfortable sofa, knees touching. Mrs Robinson gazed into Oldona's rheumy eyes and found herself blushing as white as a grub.

"I know it sounds corny," she stammered, "but I feel I've known you for a very long time."

"That's exactly how I feel, Lilith."

"Like really close sisters."

Oldona leaned forward. "Or lovers...?"

Mrs Robinson turned away, burning behind her pointed ears. But she was excited by the suggestion. Her strict

Satanist upbringing prevented her from continuing the conversation in this vein, it was too perverse, so she attempted to change the subject.

"Tell me about Arkham, Oldona."

For some reason, the student seemed unsure of herself. "Well, there are woods near there which no axe has felled. The food is quite good: an indigenous dish is Blue-Heretic Pie..."

Oldona appeared reluctant to say more about Arkham. Lilith wondered at this unnatural reticence; it was as if the student actually knew very little about her home town. Perhaps there were secrets in her past which she was not yet ready to confront?

Lilith decided to draw Oldona out by revealing secrets of her own. This would also complete the first stage of her revenge against Artery. She sipped her drink and remarked casually:

"My former lover was a cheat!"

Oldona spluttered and coughed. "Really?"

"Oh yes, he passed his euthanasia exams by resorting to deception. The blood he transfused for his finals wasn't his own. I collected lots of samples and distilled a substitute!"

The student appeared to be going into convulsions. She regained her composure with some difficulty and cried: "That's impossible! Samples of bat blood cannot be collected without a license, and these are locked in a safe in the Chancellor's office. They are rarely issued to students or staff, and the illegal collecting of bat blood is severely punished. Any student who used human blood would be disqualified immediately. Cheating is not a viable option at this college!"

Lilith frowned. How did Oldona know more about the rules of British vampire institutes than about the characteristics of her own town? There was something funny going on, not only in her lower regions. As if aware of her mistake, the student shrugged.

"That's what I've heard, anyhow," she said.

Lilith nodded. "Well, it happens to be true. But Artery and myself came up with a novel way round the problem."

"Novel? I read one once: it was about a cannibal horse."

Lilith tugged at a fang. Oldona had made the sort of slightly silly remark she was used to hearing from Artery. They were similar in so many ways. Was it the fact they were the same age and had absorbed identical cultural influences? Or was there a mystic element, an astral connection between the pair? Lilith distrusted the idea of elective affinities, but she had to admit there was an uncanny overlap of behaviour patterns. Was this why she felt attracted to the student?

Mrs Robinson returned to her confession: "To swindle the examiners, we collected the blood drop by drop, from unsuspecting donors, over many months! We were very patient."

"But how did you do it?" Oldona shifted uncomfortably. "How did you manage to steal blood painlessly?"

"I didn't say we did. But the pain was too minor to excite alarm. I am a counsellor, as you know. My clients are confused students. I invite them to sit on the chair opposite mine. It is fixed to the floor, with a solid base. A hollow needle protrudes above the level of the cushion and this pierces the flesh of a victim's buttock. A drop of blood runs into a reservoir located under the floorboards. After the counselling session the victim departs my office none the wiser, attributing any discomfort in the posterior to psychosomatic causes."

Oldona tapped her gigantic nose. "I thought I felt a puncture wound when I first came to see you!" She kneaded Mrs Robinson's legs under the table and batted her eyelashes. "But wouldn't the reservoir be mixed up with different blood groups?"

Lilith smirked. "We discovered a process of refining

blood types. I borrowed from the petroleum industry and set up an ichor-cracker, gently heating the mixture so that the group we needed evaporated and condensed in a separate chamber. Artery was type z."

"I'm type z as well!" giggled Oldona.

"The only worrying thing," continued Lilith, "is that there's still a chamber full of unwanted blood beneath me. Disposing of it might prove to be difficult. A pipe connects the reservoir with the river. Turning a faucet under my desk will make the whole lot cascade out. Then the water will turn red and the Chancellor will notice. It'll be traced back to me and Artery's degree will be stripped."

Oldona moved her hands higher. Now four sets of fingers brushed Mrs Robinson's thighs. "Better not turn that faucet then! Perhaps you should leak a little at a time? One drop a day?"

Lilith sighed. "No, the freshers on the gondolas have nostrils like sharks, capable of sniffing out a few molecules. They'll do anything to escape a life on the galleys and would report the blood in the desperate hope of gaining parole."

"So what are you going to do?"

"My plan is to pressurise the reservoir with helium and invite back my clients for a reappraisal. When they sit down, the needle will inject the blood they originally lost."

"I knew it! I knew it!" Oldona threw two of her arms around Lilith, the others moving closer to her moist secret.

Lilith pulled away, flattered and unnerved by the unrestrained show of affection. Were American monsters always as exuberant? Why did Oldona keep winking at her, as if they were confederates in a plot? She worried over this for no more than a moment; Oldona pulled her to her feet, took her round the waist and dragged her onto the dancefloor. This time mood and tempo were slow and intimate.

The student leant over to press lips to Lilith's yawning cleavage. At first, these kisses were given partly in a spirit of playfulness, but they quickly became more serious. Lilith abandoned the fight against her conscience and allowed herself to be swept away by the sheer audacity of the episode. Oldona's tongue found a way under her brassière and flicked like a flame over her pierced nipples, swelling the nodules to grotesque dimensions and dislodging a pearl.

A little later, the student clattered outside with her new lover. A meteor shower was spanking the backside of the constellation Polidori, a zodiac sign only recognised by bats. Lilith and Oldona groped in the wet shadows, elastic snapping in the penumbra where fireflies singed a night ready to fold in on itself. But though they rotated in the vortex of the wildest passion, the exchange student was careful to keep Lilith's hands away from her own breasts and yielding sex.

"Here's to you, Mrs Robinson!" whispered Oldona, as her thumb found the bud of her batty clitoris.

Lilith sighed. "That's what my lover used to say!"

"I'm your lover now, gorgeous! Do you know what I'm going to do for you? I'm redesigning my bridge without telling the authorities! When you cast eyes on it, you'll be delighted!"

Moaning, Lilith dissolved in a puddle of lust.

The construction of the bridge proceeded at high speed. Mrs Robinson was able to watch developments from her office window. The structure was now taking on the appearance of something archetypal and familiar, something both welcome and strangely repellent. A knot of nostalgia tightened down in her gut, but she was unable to say exactly what the bridge resembled. Form was still too vague to comprehend.

There was one piece of bad news: her husband was coming back from a lucrative teaching post in Yemen. The desert ghouls were bright students but they kept eating the necromancy exhibits. He'd had his fill: if they kept on like this, he'd have to teach them from textbooks. A necromancer worth his electrodes never relies on books, so he'd decided to return to the festering bosom of scholarship. He told her this in a letter written on the skin of a colleague who had been sacked for drunkenness. The last thing Lilith wanted was to see Woody again.

The only thing to make him change his mind would be the acquisition of inedible exhibits. If he could get hold of viscera for his work which his students couldn't digest, he'd stay in Yemen. But corpses were tasty over there, soft and juicy, not like leathery British cadavers. He asked the Chancellor of Stakehampton College to send some over, but it was the end of term and there were none to spare.

Lilith shouldered this extra worry with stoic grace and whiled away the days walking the river, watching cables being stretched over girders like guitar strings. Just as the bridge seemed ready to crystallise into something she could comprehend, Oldona issued instructions that a canopy was to be placed over it, to shield final preparations from prying eyes. Under the billowing fabric, the workmen's shouts and oaths were muffled, like Bluebeardian brides asphyxiating in the nuptial pillow. Oldona kept stalking the banks with her whip and megaphone, calling out instructions or lashing at a disobedient silhouette.

They met at the Palais de Decadence every midnight. The staff were discreet and showed them into an inner suite of rooms, done up in gaudy purple satins, where narghiles bubbled and clockwork zoetropes showed a panoply of moving erotic images. Lilith puffed the hashish, quaffed the petal-infused wine and listened to the cellos and violins of a hung and drawn quartet. She talked about Artery a lot, casting aspersions on his imagined talent, but this seemed to cause Oldona some pain. When they'd tired of each other's thumbs, the monkeys and eunuchs, they returned to the dancefloor, gyrating in a corybantic frenzy, as if releasing inner tensions as taut as cables on the bridge.

Eventually, the project was completed. It was the day before Artery was due to fly back over. He hadn't sent her a letter since storming out all those months before. She assumed he'd hitched himself to a harpy his own age and this thought kept the hatred flowing through her veins. Once she started to spin the grinding wheels of her dramatic scheme, the hate would pour out, engulfing the campus.

Oldona still knew nothing about it. The opening of the bridge would make a perfect backdrop to revenge plans. There was going to be a parade with fireworks and bunting; the Chancellor and his minions were supposed to be the first to stride over. Halfway across, they would pause to make a speech about unity and fraternity. That would be Lilith's signal; with a twist of the faucet, she would release the reservoir of blood directly under them, turning the river the colour of slaughtered tomatoes. Artery would return to immediate disgrace, his degree stripped and orders given to exile him from Stakehampton's limits.

Naturally, this would ruin Lilith as well. But she planned to throw herself on Oldona's mercy, pleading with the student to take her back to Arkham. Once in America, she would propose living together as squid-and-bat, which would give her rights under the constitution. From this base, she could set about sabotaging any reputation Artery had managed to make in the music business. If he went Stateside to resume a music career, he would find himself greeted by jeers.

The night before the big day, Oldona took Lilith for a drink at the Palais. Lilith wanted to keep a clear head, but the student insisted she consume bottle after bottle of strong beer.

"It's a celebration," Oldona insisted.

Lilith leaned closer and belched. "I've enjoyed your caresses for a whole semester. But why don't you let me give you pleasure in return? Is it American shyness? My tongue is very fast!"

Oldona smiled. "Just wait for tomorrow, Mrs Robinson. All will then be revealed; it's a surprise for you!"

In the morning, Lilith woke with a hangover. Groping her way to the bed's edge, she looked at the sundial in horror. She had overslept: in a few minutes, the parade would begin. Dressing hurriedly in a velvet cape she jumped to the window and looked out. The canopy had been lifted from the bridge and the riverbanks were thronged with students. Mrs Robinson rubbed her disbelieving eyes: the bridge was an exact replica of a banjo and Oldona stood in the centre of the structure like a plectrum. Aghast, Lilith fell back from the curtains. Noticing the movement at the window, Oldona blew a kiss. Was this some sort of sick joke? A banjo! Shivering, Lilith chewed her talons, her hearts thumping.

Slowly, like puppets stalking a lathe, the Chancellor and his staff of diseased minions made their way to the front of the bridge. There was no better time: all eyes were focused on the river and the crossing. Mrs Robinson rushed to her desk, felt under it for the faucet and opened the valve. There was an immense crash far below, the pipes were rumbling and screaming; the office shook. She returned to the window and looked down. Any moment now, the tide of blood...

At this point, something truly unexpected happened. The Chancellor took his first faltering step on the bridge, followed by his colleagues. The vibration sounded a chord from the taut cables. Each step produced a different chord, a sequence of notes which formed a melody. Even worse, the melody was recognisable as one of Artery's most syrupy compositions. As the Chancellor proceeded, Oldona raised her megaphone, pointed it at Lilith's window and started to sing.

Lilith dove headfirst through the glass, speeding towards Oldona. A student burst into applause, convinced this was part of the parade. Then others joined in, distracting Lilith, who lost control and collided with Oldona. The exchange student tumbled and bits of her fell off. Suddenly, it appeared she had snapped in two.

Lilith rolled upright and gazed at the disconnected

segments of her American lover, her Sapphic sweetheart.

"Artery Garfunkle and Appalling Simon!"

The two figures brushed splinters of smashed costume from wings and limbs. Artery was rueful. "This isn't what I wanted! It was supposed to be a surprise. Now you've spoiled it!"

The Chancellor approached, his inverted face full of occult fury. A deafening rumble beneath them drowned out his words of chastisement. Now the torrent of blood was gushing at full force down the river but nobody seemed to notice. They were too concerned with watching the Chancellor's bodily contortions, unsure whether this really was part of the act. With a pang of despair, Lilith realised the whole flood of ichor was going to pass without exciting any comment whatsoever.

"Why did you do it, Artery? What was it for?"

"You mean you didn't know it was us, Mrs Robinson? But I thought we blew our disguise in the Palais de Decadence!"

The Chancellor bellowed. Lilith wiped a tear.

"Oldona was just a costume!" she cried. "I fell in love with a mere disguise! No wonder her mannerisms seemed familiar! You've hurt me badly this time, Artery. My heart is cankerous!"

Garfunkle laughed uneasily. "This is a joke, right? You are trying some sort of double bluff? Appalling and I came up with the plan during my graduation. We wanted to hear you praise our music. You pretended not to like it, but we knew that was an affectation. We're talented lads and our songs are special! So we invented the exchange student as a test. It failed and you saw behind Oldona's disguise. You must have done, because you kept insisting you hated our music!"

Appalling added: "If you hadn't known it was us, you'd have given a more honest appraisal and said we were great!"

Artery nodded. "We figured if you were going to keep up with such a ridiculous pretence, we were as well! I thought the banjo-bridge was the really clever touch. A stroke of genius!"

Lilith was still sobbing. "I loved a figment!" She grabbed Artery's wings. "Don't you understand? I loved her!"

Artery cleared his throat and shuffled his feet. "Very funny but we ought to kneel in front of the Chancellor before he has us locked in the college dungeons! He's livid as a maggot!"

Lilith peered over the side of the bridge. The river was clear as a mouse's lust. Not a spot of blood remained in the water. "Let's just get away, Artery. Come with me back to my room."

"I'm all yours!" Artery let himself be led from the bridge and into the air. They flapped over the crumbling outbuildings to the residential block. They entered the window together.

As soon as they were inside, Lilith took the cleaver from the chain around her neck and struck Artery a mighty blow. His wing tore along the edge. He gasped and choked in amazement.

"What was that for? Didn't you like my landing?"

He struggled into the air, spiralling around the room and crashing onto the bed, his face and voice contorted.

Lilith glowered. "You've finished me at this college. I can't take a job in America, because my contact was a fraud. Arkham isn't aware of my existence! My only option is to join my husband in Yemen. But Woody needs some new exhibits to stay there. Your tendons have been toughened by singing. Ghouls won't find you appetising."

The blade slashed down again. Garfunkle screamed.

Lilith chortled. "This is the sound of violence."

It really was his age. These warped relationships were doomed right from the outset. There were historic examples: Actaeon had peeped at the goddess Diana as she bathed naked and she was several millions years his senior. The affair ended in disaster. Lilith knew the source of Artery's irritating innocence: too much maturity.

Perhaps he had been so sensible he'd gone round in a circle. Which, she supposed, was the only way to go with a damaged wing. As she allowed her gaze to linger on his torn membrane, she raised the cleaver for what lay ahead. Each time it descended, she counted on his appendages and her numbers soon exhausted fingers and toes.

There must be fifty ways to cleave a lover.

BURKE
AND
RABBIT

BURKE
AND
RABBIT

It's bad enough pulling back the bedsheets to find a severed head gazing up at you. It's even worse when it starts to accuse you of all sorts of misdemeanours. I'd had problems of this kind ever since I decided to run for mayor. The position was officially vacant now we'd finished toasting the last one, grinding his bones to make muffins. The one before that, I seem to remember, withered away to nothing.

Shortly after I announced my intention, a thunderstorm drenched my house. It had not rained in Lladloh for thirteen years. A rival village had been stealing our weather. News of my decision so startled one of their magicians that he left his cellar door open and the captive clouds escaped up the chimney. Where the heavy droplets fell, monstrous orchids sprang up, smothering the valley in decadent scents. For the sake of my buttonhole, I pounced on one with a scythe.

In the local pub, a nameless horror, I drank a glass of whisky and defended my actions. "As mayor of this miserable hole," I said, "I shall be able to carry out reforms that should have been implemented centuries ago. Lladloh is still existing in the Dark Ages. It is my intention to strike the match of reason on the sandpaper of progress." I knitted my brows. "Or is it simply to strike?"

Emyr, the landlord, was not helpful. "In this village, only a fool would willingly become mayor. I lie awake at night praying I won't be chosen. There'll be no turning back once you're elected. Do you realise what you're letting yourself in for?" He jabbed a finger at my chest. "A fate much worse than the millstone and grill!"

In Lladloh, which really is behind the times, the function of mayor is not quite the same as in other places. Here, a mayor holds power for a relatively short length of time, and is then sacrificed in a number of horrible ways. It is an old, corrupted tradition – the next unlucky soul would be hurled down the opening of a disused goldmine, to placate the god of yellow beer. "I'm not afraid," I replied.

"It is said the mineshaft is bottomless," added Emyr. "You'll die of thirst before hitting anything. If you take enough supplies, you may even die of old age!"

Although he has little love for me, Emyr is always loathe to lose a good customer. "Why throw your life away for the sake of a superstition? It's all nonsense, after all. Nobody believes in the beer god anymore. Fie! What rubbish!" He kept his voice down and glanced around, to make sure no beer barrels were listening.

I paid for my drink and returned to my garret. Dark rain was still pounding the streets; in my pocket, the manuscript of my latest poetic folly rustled. I took it out and used it as an umbrella. An unsuccessful poet, my work often serves a prosaic function. This latest effort was an epic entitled *Harping the Wormy.* It told the story, in blank verse, of a harp strung with carnivorous worms which turned on its owner during a recital and tried to eat him. The audience gave both a standing ovation. My greatest failing, as an artist, is lack of imagination.

My room, the sordid chamber where I live and compose, is right at the top of the mortuary chapel. Although in a picturesque state of semi-dilapidation, the building is still used as a meeting place for various local societies. Squeezing through one of the broken windows (the front door is guarded by a garrulous gargoyle) I was much astonished to find myself dropping into the midst of a candle-lit banquet. I picked myself out of the tureen of semolina and made my apologies.

It was the annual dinner of the Eldritch Explorers Club. The dozen members regarded my intrusion with a weary cynicism. They were a jaded mob, senses dulled by a lifetime's pursuit of the strange and unnatural. The society's founder, Caradoc Weasel, was in the middle of a speech. He turned his doleful eyes upon me and frowned. "As I was saying, I found

Noah's Ark exactly where I calculated – in Snowdonia. It was far larger than I'd been led to believe. Its dimensions bespoke of a technology superior to our own. On the side was some writing, which took me a while to translate. A single word – Lifeboat."

Polite applause echoed faintly throughout the nave. Caradoc Weasel was held in high esteem for mounting three audacious expeditions. Apart from his discovery of Noah's Ark, he was the first man to reach the West Pole (which unlike its chilly counterparts is almost impossible to run a flag up.) Even more incredible, in therapy, he once discovered himself. These achievements formed the basis of much of his conversation. He was forever declaring there were no regions left to explore.

"Balloons! Hydrogen balloons!" My intrusion gave Icarus Evans, the club's treasurer, a chance to air his own obsessions. He was Caradoc's biggest rival and always keen to denigrate the older man. "Balloons are the answer! My latest model is big enough to carry a cat. Soon I shall have enough material to construct a device capable of lifting a human being into the stratosphere!" It was suspected he made his balloons from handkerchiefs, the only suitable fabric in the village, filched from our very pockets. "New regions aplenty!"

"Foul liar!" stormed Caradoc, jumping up onto the table and waving his fists. Icarus rose to the challenge and followed his example. Black jellies were trodden underfoot. Aware that I was partly responsible for the fracas, I sought to make amends. "Gentlemen!" I pleaded. "When I'm mayor, I'll throw a banquet every week! You'll have semolina of every conceivable shade, from midnight blue to lopped arm red!" This had the desired effect and they calmed down. I was extremely grateful. I did not wish to be kept awake by an esoteric squabble.

I left them to their meal and ascended a spiral staircase to my garret. Here, I resided among my unpublished poems. Lighting a candle, I took out the one in my pocket and held it up to the flame. The ink had run in the storm, improving the piece considerably. I called out for my cat, Pushkin, but he was nowhere to be seen. I threw myself onto the bed and laughed aloud. I was standing on the threshold of a new life, a doorstep beyond which lay the gratification of my desires. Once elected, a mayor is allowed to take into his bed the entire female population of Lladloh, witches and gorgons excepted.

Although a poet, I am also a man, with the natural urges common to my kind. The girls of the village tended to ignore me, hardly surprising considering my lack of redeeming features. While racking my brains over how to improve my amorous fortunes, an ingenious idea came to me. As I have already stated, a mayor only holds power for a brief period before being sacrificed to some dubious deity. The period in question concerns the number of nights it takes him to exhaust all his lustful privileges. Depending on the vigour and age of the candidate, it can range from a single weekend to several years.

My ingenious idea, as lustrous as a toadstone, was the discovery of a loophole in this curious custom. I had seen a way in which, as mayor, I could enjoy my dues without having to forfeit my life. I'll say more about this later. For the rest of that evening, I lay between my sheets, writing erotic verses with a pair of scissors. This compositional method requires explanation. My blank notebooks had long since been filled up. In a corner of my chamber, left over from happier mortuary days, a stack of Bibles awaited my lyrical alchemy. I worked my way through the tomes, cutting out words that had no place in my poems.

That night, my dreams were full of soft female bodies and groaning bedsprings. I woke in the early hours to a horrible mewling. Something brushed against the skylight. Pressing my face to the glass, I thought I saw the silhouette of a balloon drifting off into the clouds. It was too dark to be certain. At the same time, I called Pushkin again, but he did not answer. Obviously he'd wandered off, which was unusual, considering I always kept my garret door locked.

The next day, I was the talk of Lladloh. My application for mayor had been accepted by the village elders (a band of lawmakers so secret nobody can name them – I might even be one.) In the nameless pub, Emyr commiserated with me. As the only candidate, it was highly probable I would win the election. "Idiot!" he kept crying. "Daft hap'orth!" But I smiled smugly, drank the whisky he offered and even had the audacity to toast the god of golden beer. "Heretic!" was his main comment now. In my wallet, generally empty, I kept the words I'd removed from the Bibles. I tipped them into my full glass and watched the new poems wriggle in the alcohol like Silurian worms.

I will skip over the details of the actual election. I was far too excited to pay much attention to them. Suffice to say, I became mayor, carried out some nominal duties (such as changing Emyr's licensing hours and keeping my promise to the Eldritch Explorers Club) and then set to task on the village maidens. I'll also say little about this, save that my eyebrows – already so high they tickled my crown – were raised still further. "So that's what it's like!" I said to myself, in stupefaction. "More fun to read about than try!" But as my technique began to match my enthusiasm, this opinion was slowly reversed (when the former exceeded the latter, I was utterly bewildered).

Finally, one evening, as I staggered into the pub, Emyr took hold of my arm and helped me to a stool. "Slow down, friend," he cautioned. "There's only Bigamy Bertha left. After her it's the mineshaft." Too exhausted to speak, I shook my head. "You can't escape," he reminded me. "The mayor can change any law he pleases, except that one. Tomorrow, at sunrise, if you entertain tonight, down the shaft you'll go. There's no appeal." He didn't guess I had a trump card, held up my sleeve with the aid of a sophistic bicycle clip.

Even had I wished to spend a quiet evening alone, it would have availed me naught. Bigamy Bertha, the long-distance adulteress, has no need to enter a man's garret to envelop him in her unique charms. Her peculiar talent has been sought by arcane pleasure houses as far afield as Anglesey. To put a finer point on it, she came to me in succubus form while I was looking for Pushkin, who still hadn't turned up. On my hands and knees under the sink, I was in no position to resist. Her passion is like a doughnut caught in a mousetrap: sickly-sweet, contrived, wholly inappropriate. It was my turn to mewl.

There are a couple of things I've forgotten to mention. Because of my liberal administration, with regard to semolina consumption within village limits, the Eldritch Explorers Club made me an honorary member. I kept finding promotional leaflets under my door, offering cut-price boots, knives and beards. Also, my poetry suffered. Lacking the spark of inspiration provided by my failure with women, it reached new depths of bathos. Considering it was of zero merit to begin with, this was no mean achievement. I was now possessed of negative talent, a curious (and not entirely unwelcome) development. This expressed itself in my poems as an aesthetic vacuum, which sucked a reader's own literary abilities out of his brain and onto the page. I had invented a genre.

Anyway, the morning after, I dressed in my ermine robes, hung the heavy gold chain around my neck, adjusted my fur-trimmed tricorne hat and made my way down the spiral stairs. Outside, in the graveyard, a procession awaited. Hoisting me onto their shoulders and banging on iron gongs they paraded me through the streets, making three circuits of the village square before veering off towards the disused mineshaft. Emyr was there, looking embarrassed, hair stiffened with lime and dressed in animal skins. Hywel the Baker, completely naked, led the way, elongated loaves (representing antlers) tied to his head.

I said little until we reached our destination. Then, just as they were about to hurl me down the opening, I raised a hand for silence and cleared my throat. "What are you doing?

My term is not yet over." They chuckled at this, suspecting a joke. But I was serious. "I haven't had all my privileges," I continued. I reminded them that I was entitled to enjoy every women in the village. "But I've only just finished the live ones," I said. Gasps of outrage went up from the crowd. I had escaped on a technicality – there was nothing in the terms of the custom to exclude those females who lay rotting in the graveyard.

"But there's generations of 'em!" protested Hywel the Baker. "And they won't be available till the Last Trump! This is a mean trick! What will the Elders say?" After a little thought, he ordered the procession to retrace its steps. The Elders, he insisted, wouldn't want to decide the issue until after dinner. (I suspect Hywel to be Chief Elder, fond as he is of making cakes in the shape of single-eyed pyramids – though he insists this is to stop them going stale.) I was more than happy to let him return me to the chapel.

To colour the event more effectively on the way back, I'll mention others in the procession. There was Phil the Liver, a nun's priest with a horror of sugar; Neifion Napcyn, the spotted fishmonger; Catrin Mucus, high on peyote, playing a flute hollowed from a cucumber; Iolo Machen, a panophobic shepherd. Apart from lack of imagination, my other failing as a poet is an inability to flesh out a scene, to make it jump alive from the page. Please do it for me: images, noises, odours.

When they set me down, I managed to have a quick word with Emyr. "I am saved," I told him. "Doesn't that make you happy?" He nodded, but the spark of pain in his eyes flashed across to burn my own. I rushed up to my room, removed my stifling robes and placed a record on my gramophone. I spent the next few hours dancing to crackling tunes, until an envoy came to tell me I'd been reprieved. No other judgment was possible, but I celebrated the news by setting my gramophone in reverse and singing along to the occult chants thus evoked.

My plan had worked perfectly. I had tasted the forbidden fruit with impunity. Cheating tradition, I had severed the bootlace binding my fate to the mineshaft. Until the god of golden beer persuaded the spirits of all dead maidens in Lladloh to visit me, I was safe. The fact he didn't exist was to my advantage. I challenged him to summon up their phantoms, to direct them into my abode. I dared them to rise up from their tombs, to entwine their chilly limbs around mine. "Come, decaying temptresses!" I bawled. I blew kisses in the aether.

That night, I found the severed head at the bottom of my bed. This was, to say the least, a surprise. It was a ghostly head – no need to wash my sheets. That was one consolation. "What are you doing?" I cried. The head belonged to Rhonwen Clot, who had been decapitated by a sickle during an unlucky harvest thirty years ago. She began to berate me for disturbing her peace. "What has the village come to when mayors demand their conjugal rights of the dead?" she wanted to know. She refused to leave when I asked her, so we had to share a pillow. In the morning, she was nowhere to be seen. She had rolled under the bed. "You kicked me out in your sleep!" she complained.

This was the first encounter of many. In the nights that followed, a whole host of dead females came to offer their insubstantial bodies, or lack of them, to my carnal designs. I can't honestly say I welcomed their attentions. The formless shapes were cold to the touch, and the shapeless forms took up most of the bed. Combined with the fact I had been ostracised by the living villagers, my nerves started to fray at the edges. I developed a twitch in my left eye and a compulsion to jerk my shoulders at odd intervals (some of the older ghosts liked to perch on my back.) At least my poetry began to improve, steadily reaching its previous level of utter banality.

Emyr alone continued to treat me as if nothing had happened. When I entered his pub, the other drinkers would all fall silent. Many of them would even snort in derision and leave the premises. But Emyr continued to serve me whisky, making small talk about the weather, and how he had preferred it when we hadn't any. I responded by telling him all about my unearthly girlfriends. He was always keen to ascertain my progress with each. "The god of golden beer seems determined to have me," I explained. He laughed at this and called it pagan nonsense.

My third failing as a writer is my poor sense of pace and rhythm. I shall now demonstrate this weakness by wrapping up my tale just as it is about to settle into the main plot. I couldn't bear these ghostly lovers any more, so I decided to drink myself into oblivion. One dusk, after a thoroughly terrifying encounter with a lamia called Bronwen, I pulled on my tweed jacket (with its drooping monstrous orchid) and made my way to the pub. But as I approached the building, I saw Emyr conversing with a stranger at the base of the gibbet tree (which serves in lieu of a signpost.) Dressed in druidic garb, the fellow owned a smile no less lunar than the crescents that spattered his robe.

"This is for services rendered," Emyr said, handing the stranger a full beer barrel. "The god of yellow beer rewards his servants. We're halfway through the graveyard already. Only a hundred more phantoms to go and then he's mine!" He chuckled, closed one eye and made the sign of a pyramid in front of the other. "I thought he was going to escape me. But the amber deity will not be denied!"

The stranger hoisted the barrel onto his shoulders and grunted with approval. "It was an easy spell. A favour for a favour. This lot should win me admittance back into my village. They exiled me after I let those clouds escape." He turned and staggered into the undergrowth. There was a violent shaking among some shrubs and then a giant rabbit (there are no magic carpets west of Monmouth) bounded into the sky, the stranger holding tightly onto its ears, clutching the barrel between his knees. Emyr waved them away. "Farewell, Mr Burke!"

I collapsed to my knees and burst into tears. I instantly decided to throw myself down the mineshaft of my own volition. At least this way I would be spared the rest of the preternatural amoretti. But I also vowed some good would come of the sacrifice. I returned to my garret and lay on the bed, wondering what useful purpose such a leap could provide. As I pondered, the skylight burst open. I shivered, thinking it was yet another spooky paramour, and pulled the sheets over my head. Something landed on the bed and addressed me in sibilant tones.

It was Pushkin, my cat, in a balloon stitched from handkerchiefs. He was fresh from adventures in distant parts. He'd been to a land where the inhabitants were so happy they couldn't bear it any longer and drowned themselves. I'd heard this tale before, but never with such poignancy. Talking cats had overrun the place and had taught him to speak. If you do not believe this, come and question him yourself. (To find Lladloh, set out on the longest road from Carmarthen and turn right at the tallest tree).

Anyway, this gave me an idea. Taking hold of the balloon, I rushed downstairs, where the Eldritch Explorers Club were holding their latest dinner, told them of my suicidal intention and offered to write a report on what I found at the bottom of the mineshaft. If I took the balloon with me, I could send the report back up to them. They agreed it was an excellent idea, but Caradoc Weasel and Icarus Evans fell into another argument. If the shaft was truly bottomless, there were only two places it could lead. Caradoc thought I would end up in Hell. Icarus had his money on Llanelli. There was one way to find out.

I jumped down in full regalia. And I'm still falling. The walls of the shaft are lined with shelves containing marmalade jars. Of all those I've tasted, the best is cranberry and nightshade. I carry two letters of introduction, one to the Devil and one to the mayor of Llanelli. They make the same request: "Can we have the Necronomicon back?" Despite what others might say, the book was penned in our village and stolen by one of those fiends. It's getting hot down here now, so I shan't delay any longer. I'll secure this report to the balloon and let it go. If you're reading it, and you're not a member of the Eldritch Explorers Club, it means Cardoc Weasel wasn't quick enough with his net.

THE
YELLOW
IMP

The tavern into which my verger had ventured to make an unseen entrance, rather than permit me, in my desperately penurious condition, to pay for a drink and meal, was one of those hovels of commingled turf and granite which so quaintly obstruct the vales of Shropshire, no less in fact than in the fancy of Professor Housman. To all appearance it had modified its management very lately, for the name of the landlord on a plank over the door was daubed in paint which was still wet. Slipping into the shadows, we established ourselves in one of the narrowest and least cosy corners, away from the barrels and the fire, where we might sit for free, resting our weary limbs and increasing our smugness by observing the denizens of the realm. The fittings, however, proved even more absurd than the faces and it was with maximum difficulty that I convinced myself they were not products of walrus artifice. Each wall was hung with canoes, snow shoes, bagpipes and other adjuncts of the polar regions. In addition, a harpoon protruded from a beam above the bar, fastened to a string which vanished through an open window and continued south as far as the horizon, like a communal washing line for dirty tricks.

While I was engaged in reluctant contemplation of these foul items, my verger busied himself with requisitioning pints of beer and plates of cakes from unsuspecting patrons. Whenever one rose to relieve himself in the privy, my furtive assistant crept forward to gather up the abandoned fare in two billowing sleeves. Wrapped in murk, we were beyond suspicion and it was amusing to compare the barbarous oaths when the simple beings returned to empty tables. Yet there was something about the tavern apart from disfigured décor and clientele which niggled me: a memory adrift in the pond of my subconscious. The familiarity of a poor (rather than bad) dream (for there is sensation in panic and this was purely mundane) with lids wide open; one of those hypnagogic visits to tedium's own aunt. In other words, I felt I had been here before, but the place disagreed, and without such endorsement my senses doubted themselves, as they ought to, for they were up to mischief in other areas. My reveries were constantly disrupted by the floor, which seemed to vibrate under me, and the mutant brambles and other feeble flora of the whereabouts slid past the window. The local beer was clearly very potent.

I confided in my verger, who inquired, "Ever been to Shropshire?" I was forced to admit I'd passed through, on my way to Hyperborea, but did not tarry in any inn, preferring to be out. At this he pouted his bottom lip. "Then the county has been to you."

I sighed. "Anything is likely in my horrid life."

"Except happiness and ease, Gruffydd."

Truth had been uttered. A domain as glum as this might well seek me out. As my readers are already aware, unless they have treated my former adventures like reversed eyeballs, to be discarded without insight, I am an exile from my own home. When Owain ap Iorwerth and Ochre Fingers (now known as Tangerine Pan) fooled me into giving up my house to them, after evicting various pastors from the premises, I decided to depart Monmouth and return with a besieging army to secure a fierce revenge. The problem was that few armies would ever care to follow me; I could not pay brutal soldiers or fit them with exciting uniforms. The remaining option was to make an alliance with my former rivals, enlisting the aid of the fleeing pastors. They would be eager to return to my comfortable abode, with its mantelpiece and divan, and I would rather share my space with hypocrites than allow Owain and his accomplice to act the goat all over my shelves. So I took theology lessons and became a man of the cloth. Then packing a blueberry pie (one of my own defective models) and borrowing a verger, I set off into the secular yonder, singing praises and selling indulgences to the sinners of the Marches for my meals, and praying for one of those coincidences which have largely replaced miracles. The chance of meeting any pastor was slim, but fuller than I.

Without parting from a shilling, I had soon eaten and sipped so much, by way of my canny verger, that I needed to spend a penny of a metaphorical character. Keeping hard to the penumbral walls, brushing cobwebs from my surplice, I made for the privy, which a sign claimed was located through a rear exit. More euphemism, I presume!

Instead of opening into a white chamber with the standard porcelain adjuncts, the door led outside. I stood and blinked at Shropshire hills. At least Wales gets them up high; these were timid and the resident cows were ashamed to be slanting on them. But the air was clean enough, and I felt tolerant of primitive customs; I dare say a similar urge to conjoin with the chthonal served Professor Housman during his bucolic sojourn in these very wilds. Dropping my trousers, I bared teeth to wind and cheeks to nettles, a temporary peasant. Above me the twine of the harpoon fixed window to distance. And behind: a monumental rumbling which I mistook at first for my bowels but which persisted after my business was concluded. Frowning, I loped back to the interior.

To be accosted at the door by the barman! Disgust prettied his face and his thumb indicated the real privy, which lay down a flight of steps I had not seen. We glanced each other over: his torso was homely, and he clearly thought as much of mine, for his anger melted away, like clotted cream on a flaming pie. Then he roared:

"No trousers? You must be a Welsh preacher!"

I bowed with ecclesiastic cynicism. "The Reverend Gruffydd ap Slack at your service. Weddings and funerals conducted at the drop of a niece. My fates and prejudices are very reasonable. And my Masses have enormous Inertia. Do you require a benediction?"

Although my voice was calm, I was acutely aware of

my bare legs and exposed ineffable. How had I managed to forget my trousers? That happens only when you're unsure if they are really your own. It's rather easy to leave someone else's trousers outside. But now I had to continue without them, as if pockets were redundant. I said to the barman, "You are Welsh too. What are you doing in Shropshire?"

"It's a tragic story, Gruffydd. My name is Emyr James and I am from the village of Lladloh. I owned a pub there, but got into a spot of dark bother, so I left for the snowy north, where trouble has to wear mittens if it wants to pursue. Arriving in Whitby, I discovered this tavern, all deserted and going to waste. I resolved to take it over. After all, it's the job I do best. But no sooner was I open for business than I began to feel myself being drawn back to Wales."

Now I recalled this tavern, but my amazement was hardly diminished, for Whitby, the town whose vowels were still on his teeth, was a port on the shore of the Northern Sea, built to ship goods to the brumal folk of the Magnetic Cosine. No sun shone there, not even in the day, and ladies were made from bears. The final stop on my aborted voyage to Hyperborea, my chosen corner of the scalene world, it had given me a bitter taste of the chills waiting higher up: I quickly developed an aversion to icecaps and turned back. But before I went, I groped about in the darkness for a drink, a mug of hot rum to give me the strength to bend my knees for the regressive hike. It was difficult to find doors in the ambient nigritude and I was compelled to climb through a window to gain entry to a pub. My unorthodox method of ingress must have frightened the barman, who loosed a howl (the notes of which froze in midair and shattered on my brow) and ran off. I helped myself to a drink and followed his example. Emyr James must have come in shortly after. And here I was again: same environment, different location. Tipsy happenstance!

He noted my bewilderment. "Come, Gruffydd. I'll show you the reason why this tavern is drifting south." He led me to the bar and the harpoon in the beam above. He gestured at the barbed implement. "This is pulling us over the landscape. The building is being reeled in, to where I can't be sure, but I dread it might be home."

Stretching up, I touched the cord. It was vibrating with incredible energy and was more tense than anything I'd witnessed since fair Myfanwy had salted her suspender belt. This was the source of the rumbling which pervaded every stone of the structure, so integral to the milieu that it was completely in place and thus unnoticeable. I lunged at the aluminium blade, and vainly tried to ease it out.

Emyr was close to tears. "I've already tried that. It's stuck deep. Across the glaciers of Yorkshire it has hoisted me, and over the steppes of Derby and Stafford. I feel like a fish." The simile was inappropriate and he bartered it. "No, like a squid."

"You have the sense of one. Why stay in the tavern? Jump out of the door now and you'll be perfectly safe."

"It's my constitution, Gruffydd. I simply can't exist without pints to pour. My brain is evenly distributed between the heads of every stout which gushes from a barrel. Without a pub to run I'll be the dregs of my usual self. I know it from experience."

I mulled. It was possible we were heading to Lladloh, which sounded frightful, but I doubted it. The direction of the harpoon's rope was due south and that was also the bearing for Monmouth. Before I could resolve the ideas which were brewing in my subconscious on this point, the whole building suddenly lurched and we were pitched against the bar. The sound of silence was appalling: the absence of the rumbling hurt my ears. Emyr regained his balance and felt a stone wall. Then a broad smile split his cheeks into a pair of bad moons rising.

"We've stopped moving! This must be our destination!"

"No, the tension in the rope's increasing."

He ran outside and returned to crush me in a

malodorous embrace. It was a relief when he disengaged to cry:

"Your discarded trousers have jammed under the foundations! You are a hero, Gruffydd! A pocketless wonder."

Though I did not share his enthusiasm, I partly welcomed this news, for it meant a clue had been granted regarding the ownership of breeches in the material-and-immaterial dispute which had led to my being present in Shropshire in the first place. Only the trousers of Owain ap Iorwerth were tenacious enough to halt the progress of a motive pub. And if I was now certain I'd not been wearing my own, it made it 17% more likely that Myfanwy had, and was (two elements in the equation instead of three), an erotic prospect which excited me to irreligious heights. Imagine how she might be treating them! Drawing them off, putting them on, ironing them! My soul, wherever it was, was thrilled.

"I'll do anything in return," blurted Emyr.

Before he could appreciate the idiocy of this remark, I gestured at my verger, beckoning him forward. The patrons frowned as he emerged from shadows, stupefied as to how a minor divine could generate spontaneously from a void. Then I blared imperiously:

"Free ale and cakes until the end of time."

"That's easy. I want to do something difficult for you. Stand on my head for a month or marry a bucket. I can't say that it's pleasant to be stranded in Shropshire, which is an attenuated echo of Wales, but rather this than a return to Lladloh nasties."

My verger and I exchanged glances. I indicated the window. "Here is truly a bleak wasteland, devoid of the appurtenances of civilisation. If you construct a settlement, say a small town, to enclose the pub, I will be duly satisfied. Houses, shops, casinos, saloons, theatres, parks, but don't build a church. Leave it amoral."

"Consider it done!" And Emyr reached behind the bar for a whip with which to enrol and organise the labour of his drinkers, whose complaints were drowned by the crack of knucklebone lash. One at a time, they drank up and slowly shuffled out to work. My verger gasped at this development and I bent closer to explain, mumbling:

"Why race around the land looking for pastors when we can lure them here? What better trap than a godless pit? A town without a church! They will come to establish one themselves!"

Under Emyr's direction, work progressed rapidly. Within a week, we drank no longer in an isolated tavern but in a village pub. The settlement was as nameless as the tavern (in Whitby nothing is named because nobody can read in the dark) and we argued long hours over a suitable title. It was prudent to pacify the former customers, now slaves, and I shared much of my beer and cakes with them, instead of burdening them with wages, which I couldn't afford to do anyway. The three managers of the project (which is how I came to think of the barman, verger and myself) based ourselves at the bar, ensuring that all tastes were accounted for. The ale ran out too quickly and we were forced to brew our own from local weeds. In time we adapted to the toxic flavours; at perigee to the tongue they eclipsed moonshine. I should have been content. But the harpoon in the beam still disturbed me. The stress in the cable was monumental and something would soon have to give, other than our host.

One morning, while we were chatting about cricket (a game which has not yet reached Shropshire in any recognisable form) and how the ancient druids were wont to bat with a hare's ear, the incident I feared as much as the tickle of a hangman's noose occurred. The harpoon line snapped. I heard a shrill whistle, like a kettle boiling over a firefly, but it was not immediately obvious what had happened, for the rope didn't break our end. I touched it and burnt my palm: it was contracting rapidly, and the tension was draining out of it like steam. My verger and I rushed to the window, to observe a pale object approaching from the horizon. I thought it was a toy balloon, knotted to the far tip of the cord, but as it flew closer, I recognised the outline as a callous intrusion from my past. My verger was as shrewd as I, standing aside from the window, but poor Emyr was tardier than a scrapbook, and when the missile crashed into the pub, it landed on him and skittled him awry.

We hurried to his side. "Are you badly injured?"

He was. The collision had prolapsed an eyeball. It hung down on his cheek on the optic nerve, as if to lower tears gently to the cold floor. He sat up, glanced about (by swinging the eye from side to side and over his shoulder) and groaned pathetically:

"What in the name of leprous pustules was that?"

"A yellow imp. He was clutching the other end of the cable and must have been catapulted all the way here."

The trivial being in question cleared its throat. "Sure, and it's a long way from Monmouth. Hiding in the spokes of the waterwheel by Monnow Bridge, I was. Managed to cut a length of rope and suddenly found myself in this cavern of polychromic drunkards. Broke a fang on an iris, I did. You may arrange compensation in opals."

"Hiding, eh? Why weren't you in the market?" I picked him up by the nose and inverted him, but his pockets were empty. "Cheating honest folk is your standard pastime, not lurking."

"You don't understand. The market's been taken over by gnoles. They have driven us out. We are unemployed."

"Don't be ludicrous. Gnoles live in Zipangu. That's where they went after they were successfully burgled by Nuth. Who did you steal this lie from? Answer quickly, my beige napkin."

"It's true. The place is crawling with them. Please don't wipe your chin with me! Of course gnoles live in Zipangu, but now Zipangu lives in Monmouth! It's the waterwheel's fault."

I remembered the machine and Monnow Bridge, where Owain had knocked out my canine. The imp and I had two traumas in common: sore gum, exile. Yet he was enlightened and I was confused, so our woes were not entirely matched. Nonetheless, a speck of empathy required me to put him down and smooth the petals of his sunflower jerkin. An impulsive movement to gain time for ponder, to subdue my tongue for a more sober interrogation, but the imp satisfied my unvoiced queries without prompting; the wind of his trip had oiled his lips. Monmouth had changed a great deal, he insisted. It was built on three separate levels now, each precariously balanced on the other, parts of which had given way so that vast tracts were jumbled up together. There was the original town at the base, then the island of Zipangu, held over it by the iron poles of the market stalls, and a lush kingdom of hemlock forest over this, supported by the pagodas of Zipangu and trailing tendrils of vegetation over the rim. All very peculiar, but life continued much as before, except for the imps, who couldn't compete with the aggressive gnoles. Famished, they wandered the suburbs of town, seeking scraps to eat. Because imps are good at selling rope, and gnoles have been known to express an interest in it, our yellow friend resolved to obtain a piece and win their trust. For some reason, there were three extremely long lines wrapped around the waterwheel: two were tangled and beyond rescue, the third met his knife.

"It didn't help much," he muttered. "I bet the gnoles will be after me now for leaving Monmouth without a permit. Gross dictators, they are! Sipping sword-flavoured tea all night!"

The last thing I wanted was a troupe of gnoles taking over the pub, spoiling my project. With a flourish, I drew out my flawed blueberry pie from a secret pocket. "Perhaps I can assist you, lemon fool. Allow me to stain your skin with a fruity filling."

I lifted the lid off the crust and he nodded.

"Disguise me as a blue dwarf? Superb!"

"Climb inside and splash around for a while."

The operation was simple but effective. The instant he finished his blueberry ablutions, he was a yellow imp no longer.

Just then, there was a rumpus from outside. Not the gnoles, but the slaves, who were tired of erecting buildings and wanted to try rising up in revolutionary ferment. Draping his loosened eye over his left wrist like a dishcloth, Emyr went to deal with the problem. I could hardly bear to look at him now, though he had always been ugly, and was delighted for him to go.

Returning with a worried squint (which was engineered between finger and thumb) he told us that the slaves were planning to storm the tavern and kill the verger and I. They had finally made a logical connection between our appearance and the theft of their meals. Before we arrived, beer and cakes vanished mysteriously. Now they gorged at our expense and naught went missing. So there had to be a link between our existence and this anomaly: a link to be severed with many blows of a shovel.

The blue dwarf formerly known as a yellow imp touched my knee. "You did me a favour. Let me now return it."

And he walked out of the building. There were screams, so muted and ethereal that I thought he was kicking moths, then he came back in, tiny hands slick with a dull, viscous fluid.

"The colour of my skin is different. But I still have the skills of an imp. We are the finest pickpockets."

"I assume you picked something else today?"

He smirked. "Livers. Do you have a loaf of bread?"

I didn't know whether to hug or retch all over him. But Emyr tapped my shoulder. "Without a workforce, we can't finish the town! I refuse to mix cement, heft bricks, mend trowels."

"No need," I replied. "Everything's turned out for

the best. We may not have a town, but we've got a quaint village, and that should attract pastors even more quickly. Let's have a pint while we wait for the knock on the door. It'll take about a month."

And so it did. Yet when I answered the rhythmic fist, as ready to kiss a sacred hem or sing a pious hymn as sign a hissing pie, if one ever baked my way, I found no column of holy agents but a vision of feminine beauty beyond any succour of the Church. A radiant maiden, stronger on radiance than maidenliness, and full of glee, all light and smiles and frolicsome as the young fawn, loving and cherishing all things within reason, and I jumped up high to clap my clumsy hands.
"Fair Myfanwy! You've come back to me at last!"
"Not quite, Gruffydd. But an explanation is in order. I followed an unwound turban to find this place. When the cable propelled the imp from Monmouth to Shropshire, a frayed end of his elaborate headwear caught in a waterwheel spoke and stretched into a yellow ribbon which led me here. Now let me tell you the part you've played in my little scheme. Remember when you romanced me with a carrot and clock? You lost your trousers and soul because of your lust, and when I exchanged my own to buy them back, a hatstand and three harpoons were thrown in. These simple items gave me an opportunity to improve intellectual conditions for the common folk of Wales. Before Owain, yourself and I rushed to the corners of the scalene world, I mounted a harpoon on each of our heads. Then I wrapped the ends of the trailing ropes around the waterwheel. My notion was for the barbs to stick in our destinations, the three points of existence, and for the turning wheel to gradually pull them together, so that the planet was no longer triangular but folded over like a samosa. That's not as neat as a sphere, but Welsh mentality mustn't be rushed. It should first be herded and dipped, then shorn of woolly ideas.

"I realise you are flabbergasted by the audacity of this operation. To be honest, I was unsure whether the Welsh were ready for such a giant leap in the science of geography. But I was tired of living in a country which still had a triangular planet. In every other nation, the world is round, like an orange. Only in Wales does it resemble a slice of pie. Of course, I feared you might spoil the venture, and so you did. Owain went to Zipangu, the eastern corner of the planet, and I reached Pennsylvania safely, the western corner. But instead of braving it out to Hyperborea, the northern corner, you stopped in Whitby. Then you inadvertently fixed your harpoon to a weak point by climbing through a window in a structure which broke free of the land and was drawn in without any background. So although two flaps of the triangle have come together in Monmouth, there is still a third jutting out into the cosmos, and Wales continues to lag behind its European neighbours. I make no mention of Shropshire, because it has an even more primitive conception of the world (a bubble in solid rock) and thus cannot be helped. Now I want you to come back with me, to put matters to rights. It's your duty."

Fumbling with my surplice, I cried: "You're not going to send me to Hyperborea? What a fine woman you are!"

She nodded in agreement, turning her head one way and then another, so that her profile might have an airing. It was noble enough to be that of an empress of confections, and my heart yearned to be a berry beneath her crust, but she didn't share my ardour, for her smile was utilitarian and would brook no syrupy emotion atop.

"It's not sentiment, Gruffydd. The mess can be sorted out from your home in Monmouth, but I need you to operate the ovens. In return, I will help you conquer Owain and Tangerine Pan, his familiar. It'll be the pie fight of the millennium! A prime example of batterpole, which is rougher than slapstick. Come with me, buffoon!"

I glanced at my verger for advice, but his expression was even more devious than Myfanwy's. I knew he was formulating his own scheme when he answered: "Yes, let's go back to Monmouth. But permit me to take Owain's trousers first. It's a kind of trophy."

As we left, barman and dwarf ran up to me. I thought they wanted to commiserate, or wish me luck for the future. But what had really excited them was something far more selfish. Although his hanging orb oscillated like a pendulum, Emyr's timing was bad.

"I've finally come up with a name for the pub! *The Plucked Eyeball.* What do you think? And my tiny friend here thinks *Purloin My Liver* would be a humorous epithet for the village."

"And accurate, because I intend to pick the livers of everybody who crosses into it," added the blue dwarf.

"You still need a local clergyman," I pointed out.

Myfanwy took my arm and we stepped out into the mundane wastelands. My verger skipped and bent to retrieve Owain's trousers. They were stuck fast under the foundations and he had to strain hugely to free them. But the rewards of this toil were material.

"Look now, Gruffydd! They're completely buckled!"

LANOLIN BROWS

A city made from wood. Not planks and boards nailed together, but carved out of a single pine block. Towers and temples, homes and shops, arcades with slender columns, windmills and taverns, concert halls and theatres, libraries of grainy books, squares and parks, all lovingly chiselled and planed and painted. Each oval cobble on every road is a protuberance on a whole body, not a separate element. The environment is integrated with itself. It is one. And there is no civil strife, for the inhabitants are also fashioned from wood, rooted in the ground, immobile and bevelled. A population of empty suits of armour, fixed in bustling positions at work and play. The outdoor cafés are full, the municipal buildings are packed with clerks, there is an audience at the opera, the jail has a prisoner, but none are true, all are varnished.

The king of this timber metropolis stalks the alleyways with a saw. It is his token, as it was for Shamash, god of the Sumerian sun, who cut the days into dark and light. But he, the mortal, is a Swedish carpenter and knows nothing of deities other than Woden, who is jointed and rotten and felled. The teeth of his blade are blunt, for they have rasped much, feasting on the knots of his domain, but a symbol may serve on a loftier level. Infrequently, as he patrols the pavements, he adjusts a member of the public, perhaps notching lines of age on smooth cheeks, amputating a finger to simulate a plague, trimming a splintered beard. At night, when he surveys the city from the balcony of his palace, he can be assured it is changing in accordance with standard time. To thrive quicker than his subjects is one of his worst terrors.

His name is Lanolin Brows, though none of his people call him that. Once a pirate, now a potentate, his eye is frosted from winking slyly at the equator. It was not a safe gesture. The imaginary line is too bright at noon on a foaming sea. His memories of buccaneering are unhappy. When he followed Morgan to Puerto de Naos, creeping along the scurvy coast to Porto Bello, the captain ordered him off the ship into a canoe to attack the town more secretly, but the smaller vessel was chipped on the stern, a poor piece of work; he disapproved. His protests were disregarded. The life of a craftsman among ruffians is difficult. The arquebus nestled so awkwardly in his arms that he cast it away and charged with his tools. A drill does not need reloading. Nor a vise virtue. Glue flicked in a face is also a sticky end for expressions.

The inhabitants were asleep when the carnage began. So he fashioned cabinets from chests and spittoons from snores, unopposed. Shaping death is not as comfortable as producing chairs, but his mercy was sanded away in a professional frenzy. The richest citizens woke and hurled valuables down wells to cheat the rovers of booty. He peered over the edge of one, at a bobbing casket of pearls, wondering how to hook it out with an axe, but his musings were pounded out of his mind by a gold candelabrum which fell from the upper story of a house. The woman who dwelled up there had mistaken his blond hair for reflected moonlight at the cistern's bottom. From that moment he vowed never to rush into battle without armour, hewn from teak joists: helmet, greaves, cuirass. In the aftermath he span his lathe, filling the port with sawdust.

"Do you seek to choke the donkeys and prisoners? Do you not trust a swallow of grog as protection, 'Lin?"

"Not really, sir. It is inadequate proof."

"Take care not to rot in the marshes of Panama. This raid is only a practice for our big act of bravado."

And Morgan stomped off, to torment a captive nun. Truly Porto Bello was a dry run for an assault on the Cup of Gold, as the urban wonder was mostly called, for the rum ration had been reduced and the Welsh corsair wanted all blood thinned with water or knives, depending on nationality. The rovers ridiculed the grog which substituted for the manly stuff; the Spanish had no more affection for the blades. When the armour was ready, the carpenter tried it on, to the amusement of barber and sailmaker, his closest friends. Spermaceti Whiskers cared to shampoo the visor, but was dissuaded by a hammer; Thanatology Spleen hoped to stitch a surcoat, but was repelled by a mallet. The suit moaned as it moved, but it was hot in winter, cool in summer, and deflected grapeshot quite as well as an iron shell. Also it floated across rivers.

The sound of wooden armour, though muted, was unique enough to give him nightmares of thorns. Now, in his own city, the kindling chords were everywhere with the wind. When ice blew down from the mountains, all his subjects would creak together. Then he would leave the palace balcony in numb anxiety and return to his throne. His saw doubled as a sceptre, his head as an orb. He listened to the crowd and it seemed they were hailing or jeering him; he could not judge. No civil strife? Ha! So what if they grew sufficiently high to oust him? Pine versus teak; he was tougher but they were more. It hardly mattered he was a benign dictator, for history is a chisel and gouges the pith with the worm. A sculpted republic might arise, with equal rights for all branches of society; a dismal prospect, against the grain of honest politics.

Lightning licked the remote peaks, adding a revolutionary lustre to the quadrangles beneath the palace, each nested inside the others like a conjuror's pockets. The creosoted figures did not move in the storm, but their shadows were active, darting about the squares like anarchists. He opened the doors of his treasury, cast handfuls of wooden coins over the side. The greedy outlines slid to gather them. Then the storm passed and the mob was mollified. An awful situation when a king must bribe his own followers! And who would look after Linopolis without his munificence? A canker would set in: good for mushrooms, who never had a capital to call their own. Perhaps it was time to revalue his remaining funds, to etch a higher figure on the discs? Florins as big as tables and worth a million dinners might satisfy them for years.

He refused to doff his armour even in bed. Not only because of fear of assassination; it was too tight to remove. The teak was not dead when he whittled it; now the roots had penetrated his lower orifice, deriving sustenance from whatever he digested. Royal banquets kept the new growth supple and fast. Finally the visor sealed itself and he was compelled to bore holes in the beak to breathe. He thought of himself as a man with a pair of skeletons, bone and furniture. Not that he had wanted to take it apart even when disrobing, or diswardrobing, was feasible. Too secure he felt inside, unable to recollect how he coped without it, on the Main or off. Damage to the suit healed naturally; bark wandered his torso. Women were denied him, for the brothels of the Windwards did not believe money grew on trees, so love too was safer.

In Panama such precautions saved his skin, for he was hiding behind a sack of wool when a cannonball burst this defence and knotted him with unspun fleece. His porous armour drank the oil of the lambs' curls until it was saturated. He had carved a frown into his helmet, for he reckoned it unseemly to lurch into a fight without features, or with a smile, and the grease collected in the grooves of his forehead, staining his brows. Thus did he earn his alias, when his original name was forgotten. Rather luckier than the cook, who absorbed the contents of a sack of sugar with his bare face, mainly on shut eyelids! The granules studded him sweetly, including the onion he wore on his shoulder. Later, sparks from a pistol caramelised this vegetable and his lashes. French rovers were charmed by him after that, for cultural reasons.

The crew maintained that the siege was so bloody and traumatic they were shocked out of memory. The Swede did not allow this. It was not the scarmoge, the combat, which robbed them as they plundered, but a strange event which occurred in the ruins. Morgan had vanished with a woman, but returned with a mirror and blunderbuss. The mirror was a box with a tiny lever which, when pressed, created a flash. A minute later and a picture would emerge from a slot at the base of the machine. The captain claimed it was a slow looking glass, but the carpenter had seen a similar device in the observatory at Uppsala. It was, he realised, a new type of *camera obscura*, one which took solid images. Remarkable! And it had fallen from a flying galleon over Pennsylvania, which was a land of tears. Who could invent such a marvel? A mythic beast!

They sat and played with it, drinking coffee and waiting for Morgan to rescind the order stressing sobriety. So he would, in due course, but only with sherry. 'Ceti won the right to keep the box, for his barbering days were not yet numbered. Before this came the episode which the Swede held responsible for the amnesia which gripped them all. The captain put away his shame and showed them how a lady kissed. None of the other crew had won girls, but the Welsh rascal was insensitive enough to parade his success with his spit. One at a time, he fixed his wet mouth to the lips of his men, wielding his tongue like a cutlass, winning every duel. Such childish laughter! The barber and sailmaker and cook snorted with irony, but the navigator accepted his attentions with a serious countenance and emerged from the fondle disappointed.

"Your turn now, 'Lin! Raise your leafy casque! How else may I reach your ruby pout? What a coy criminal!"

"Be gentle, sir. You have rough stubble."

"That's what a pillaging life is about. A chin like the ocean. This mattock should lever open your helm."

It felt more like a conversation than a smooch. As Morgan moved his lips, forcing his to writhe in tandem, silent words passed between them. The captain was telling him a secret, not tickling his tonsils! Then the course of his life was diverted, because he knew something which steered his hopes higher than Biscay waves. A nasty joy overwhelmed him, and all the crew. To dissipate it a notch, a puppet battle was arranged with the sailmaker. 'Tology won by cheating and their friendship became strained. Then the sherry was opened and sense was fully diluted. When he woke, he was reconciled to what he had learned. No longer a normal man, but not a full devil. Something in the middle. And because only rovers can live in romantic mischief, not unholy savants, the disintegration of the company was inevitable. Panama was the limit.

They separated in Jamaica. 'Ceti and 'Tology, the only two he cared to keep in touch with, bought property in Pirano and Wolkenstein. It was vital they went somewhere they would not be recognised. But he, engulfed by his armour, was able to return to Uppsala. His disguise was stiff and much admired. His old neighbours did not berate him for turning bad, for they could not identify him. He lumbered down the alleys like a sentient log, feeling at home on the roof of the Gothic cathedral, the Domkyrkan, with its gargoyles. But the city had altered. There were less faces from his childhood. New people had taken over the public places. In his attic lodgings he sat on a barrel of gunpowder and fretted. This explosive was his pitiful reward for decades of service. Morgan had absconded with the pick of the loot back to Welsh hills.

On a ship, a community was sealed. A known quantity of souls pacing the deck. Recruits on the high seas were rare: an attacked galleon might supply an extra hand if he bragged a specific skill, but the majority of prisoners walked the planks he measured and hacked. And in port, unknown faces were expected, for Morgan tended to berth in cities they had never visited before. The problem with Uppsala was that it was one place which constantly evolved fresh inhabitants; this is the way it looked. Perched on the eaves of the Domkyrkan, the carpenter started to believe that new men and women were condensing from the dignified atmosphere which flowed into the sky from the open windows of the Carolina Rediviva, the college library. And when he descended to the level of the Linnaeus Gardens, the odd phenomenon was even more blatant.

He trembled under his armour in his room, so that

the leaves on his head rustled and fell with autumn music. The teak was dying in the chill of the Swedish climate. Russet foliage littered the boards, mimicking an adventure to Maryland, when Morgan sailed them up the Chesapeake to meet Billy Barnett, an accomplice. They hugged an estuary bank, mast knocking trees so that a shower of muted colour celebrated their arrival. In this attic, however, the meaning was different. He went out to dine at a café below the castle. Already he was collecting details for his own capital. Over a bowl of fisksoppa, sucked up with a straw, he peered at the other customers. None were familiar, yet he had eaten in this restaurant every day since his arrival. New people again! Immigrants? No, they spoke with local accents and fitted the customs.

They must have generated spontaneously inside the city. He realised this had always been true, that it was the same for all men. Go out into the streets of a town, the thoroughfares of your home, and glance at the faces which pass close. They will be mostly unknown. Repeat the exercise on the morrow, and there will be a different set of cheeks, noses, eyes, equally mysterious. Surely these are just citizens you have not met? But the lie erodes on each successive venture, for the faces, and the owners underneath, are always original, never the same. How can these strangers all fit inside one conurbation without becoming recognisable? It must be that they do not exist until you observe them! You invent them: they are your offspring! The explanation is shocking but logical, and there is no other. We are fathers between blinks.

The carpenter's return to Uppsala had expanded its population to an unsustainable level. He had played the prodigal pirate for two months in his lodging at the corner of Svartbäcksgatan and Torbjörnsgatan, near to where he had grown up. At dawn he rose and dusted himself with a napkin, then staggered north along the river to the Gustavianum, braving insults from children who did not tolerate teak pedestrians. He counted fifty or sixty new faces on the way.

The panelled interior of his destination was good camouflage; he might pause here on the tiers of the Anatomy Theatre and spy on students arranging scalpels. Another seventy or eighty unique individuals! Later, a meal at Barowiak, together with ninety others, all unknown. Then rigid acrobatics on the Domkyrkan roof to work off a plate of köttbullar. A hundred worshippers!

By early afternoon he had already sired ten thousand burghers. This promiscuity must not continue! The city would end up unbearably cramped! The dangers of plague were considerable in such insanitary conditions. A slum is a brothel for disease, as Morgan often used to say. Germs with a ticket to breed! Cholera, typhus, syphilis, leprosy, smallpox, gangrene, tuberculosis, brownjack, jock itch, monkeybreath, jaundice, drunkenness, spontaneous combustion, toothache, stress attack, all the afflictions of adult compression. The Welsh rascal's answer was fire. Had he not healed the stubborn defenders of San Lorenzo de Chagre with an arrow wrapped in burning cotton blasted from a musket? The palm leaf thatch of the houses in the fortress ignited so quickly that it crashed down on a huge barrel of gunpowder and every pox was cured.

"Stand clear, 'Lin. These days you are at loggerheads with yourself and thus inflammable. My male dryad!"

"You still disapprove of my armour, sir?"

"There may come a time when you need a raging inferno. How will you escape that suit then? 'Tis suicide."

No, the Swede dared not put a match to Uppsala. Also the structures and his memories were too gorgeous. The only solution was to stay in his attic and look at no face. That way he would not fabricate spare humans. Ten thousand a day for two months is more than half a million! He sat on his own cask of explosive and wrapped his head with his arms. Because of his jaunts, the city had trebled in residents. Refugees from his mind! A pounding reached his sanctuary from outside: the weight of feet stamping pavement slabs. Too much mass! He covered the single window with a sheet to keep out the sight of the crowded streets, bodies pressed against the walls of his own home. What if the pressure broke down the front door? A tide of sick humanity, his children, rushing up the stairs to burst into his room for revenge and pocketmoney!

He departed in the middle of a dark night, when he could barely see his own legs as he hastened south into the open country. Uppsala and its improbable population was soon behind him; he felt much lighter. He took his toolbox and his powder, rolling the barrel with a sprouting foot. It was best to avoid urban centres bigger than villages, for these were the places where a man's mind acts the part of a phallus, fertilising spaces with folks. In a village, such imagination is celibate. Still better was the shunning of all people. He walked the rutted lanes past Stockholm to Karlskrona and the hedges welcomed him as a cousin. He did not enter the port to catch a boat, but drifted out to sea on his buoyant back and met the vessel midstream. He hauled himself aboard and hid in a coil of rope like a crocodile in a static cyclone.

For pure isolation he should have paced north to Finnmark, but some story of 'Tology's, plus a desire to keep his armour alive and unrotten, had led him to believe that the deserted isles of the Mediterranean were the perfect retreat. Warm enough to ensure his suit might repair itself, but lacking fishermen and tourists. He slipped off the ferry just before it docked in Stettin. Then it was down through Germany, drying slowly in a sun which smelled of cabbage. The sailmaker had come from Tunisia; the barren islands he knew were called Pantelleria and Lampedusa and lay not far off the African coast. Hurry! He lived on berries and hot steam from washing hung on hayricks. He skirted Görlitz into Bohemia, regretting he could not visit Prague. Through Trebonsko into Austria, past Linz, where chocolate clouds billowed and minted.

It was on the foothills of the Salza Hochschwab, at a point roughly between Waidhofen and Mariazell, that he finally understood his mistake. It was a wasteland here, dramatic but bare, uninhabited and treeless. No dwelling in sight, no artificial item of any kind. No chance to catch an unknown face! He was halfway to his final destination, but he guessed it was now beyond him, for he had truly stuffed the world with illegitimate sons and daughters. He collapsed to his knees, hugged his cask and wept. Seeing new humans did not produce them; it was *not* seeing them which did that! Out in a city, with the individuals in view, a population is fixed in the present. It is always on the following day, a time not yet ready, that they suddenly swell. What precisely distinguishes that present from our future? The state of being alone!

The moment he went back to his room, removed from the bustle of the street, he might be sure of one thing: an increase in local humanity for the next morning. While he was inside, without company, his non-presence externally was inseminating shadows or smells or sounds, whatever it was that served as a womb for the adult fetuses. So it was self-defeating to come to an uninhabited zone of Mitteleuropa on the way to a desert isle! Here he was in a position of permanent arousal and dispatch. No existing public to halt his elsewhere lusts! Where he was, he was celibate; where he was not, he was wanton. He lifted his head and gazed at each horizon. All were empty, fertile, monstrous. With such an expanse of nullity, the tide of humanity must be surging to ridiculous heights! For every second he spied nobody, a million were born!

He had scant choice but to destroy himself. Even as he breached his barrel, he knew the gesture was futile. Morgan's kiss had told him this. But he struck two iron hammers together until a long spark fell into the dark powder. The explosion reminded him of Roche Braziliano's adventures in Castilla de Oro, when that most gentle of buccaneers ignited a whisky still and blew himself over the heads of his enemies, a score of Spanish pikemen, and onto a horse. The carpenter too was knocked high, but where he landed was wholly rump, on the edge of the crater he had exposed, his armour having rotated around him a dozen times in midair, coming to rest in its proper position, so that he did not face the wrong way, and would not have to lurch backward to his birthplace, to a coffin once a cot. He was barely scratched from the impact.

At the base of the pit smoked a gigantic block of wood, the largest he had ever seen, wide as the reefs of the Azores, thick as a ship. What was it doing under the uncultivable soil? This was a secret he was never able to learn. The truth is that Nature has a short way with any species which becomes too widespread over the face of the globe. Trees once held the continents and atmosphere to ransom with root and oxygen, and so the ecological balance, a feedback system, embarked on a cull. Men filled up with an irrational loathing of wood and invented saw and axe. Humans are the chosen nemesis of forests. But in this spot the pines resisted. They scattered their seeds inversely, so that the ensuing generation of trees grew down, into the forsaken cavern of a shaman. For further protection, these fused trunks into a single unit.

And now they had been discovered by a whittler. He began to work as soon as he could unlock his toolbox, for he had calculated that peace of mind was a carving. He made a city, Linopolis, and this ended his unique claustrophobia, because it contained no citizens whose contours were not known to him. Relentless fatherhood ceased, the dangers of being crushed by excessive populations receded. He had saved the world from famine and riots and other cluttered crises. Experience with wooden suits of armour enabled him to fashion people likewise. Already hederated, masses of ivy dangling like a greasy fringe, he considered himself crowned and adopted the persona of a king. His time on the palace balcony was rarely wasted, for a competent ruler must keep watch over courtyards, shadows, weather, malcontents, affairs and all cobbles.

In the middle of one storm, he noticed a light which had nothing to do with electric clouds. It grew brighter from the south-west, though it remained tiny. Entering his realm without a visa, it swerved through the mazy quadrangles, up the palace steps. He confronted it with a drill. It was a puppet! The face of the sailmaker peered anxiously from a polished head. A figure of 'Tology animated by flames! The Swede guessed it was a message, a request for a mirror, but there were no reflections to be had here; a wooden king has no need of them. 'Ceti had Morgan's camera; that must suffice. For the sake of friendship, the Swede planned to leave his dominion for a while and visit the barber. There was a risk of decadence among his subjects in his absence, but 'Ceti had done much for him, pale whale oil soothing his fleecy frowns.

Before he could depart, a crack of thunder above the peaks startled the vegetation on his helmet. No, not part of the tempest. A hiss like a circular swordfight, something black coming down from above. He squinted not to see. The silhouette in the main courtyard was too stolid to be an illusion. It darted toward the museum, where the carpenter-king kept his regrets on display. He went down to greet it with anger. A tall man with no attire or hair sprang out at him. He held a wicker receptacle and his shoulders were dusted with melting snow. His breath was foul, worse than a sick shark's. He opened and closed his hands, seeking a secure grip on the teak cuirass, failing. He reminded the Swede of 'Vado, the cook, but only because of the tangled odours. Like a telescope dissolved in acids! Then the monster sneezed and giggled.

"I arrived on a helicopter, a flying machine. I'm no assassin. I am here to learn and browse. The barber sent you a letter and I made a note of the address. To learn 'n' browse."

"How dare you lisp my name! Who are you?"

"I am a manipulator. I am a noxious sage. My morals are curly, like Turkish slippers, but I am parallel."

"You shake more violently than cutlass play."

"Because I am nude in sleet. I had three capes, but removed them to trap 'Ceti Whiskers in Pirano. Hung them on washing lines across each of the alleyways which run to his shop."

"Curly indeed! What's your business here?"

"To be yet more noxious and sagacious. I'm a master rogue who wants to recruit followers. Retired pirates are perfect for my scheme, but you have all abandoned evil. I've been spying on your crew since Morgan fled Jamaica and I am disappointed. So I intend to force you back into crime. But you are a stubborn lot, and weak since your retirements. The barber, sailmaker and cook have spurned my efforts. As for the navigator, I'm in total despair. And Morgan's missing."

"What use have I for more vices and cruelty?"

"Ah, traitor! What has happened to you all? Once you bathed in gore and the sweat of eels. You ate gems for breakfast. You can't be blissful now! What's the point of this place?"

"You rarely see the same person twice in a big city. But you always see new people. Thus the population must magnify each time one goes out. My ambition was to break that cycle."

"At the dawn of time there was only one man, 'Lin, but he looked in a mirror. He did not recognise himself and so produced another. That was in Ur, the first city, capital of Sumer, the first land. The process was soon accelerating out of control and the world was filled with people. I know you are not wondering how the original man built Ur on his own, for you have achieved a similar feat. And gods are more likely to visit such cities. Shamash for him; me for you."

"These names are too curious, bald ghoul."

"Take this basket to Pirano. Now that 'Ceti is trapped by my cloaks he must wait for your arrival. I'll hide at the bottom with only my head showing. He will assume I am a coconut and when you leave I can convince him to join my tribe. My scalp resembles the fruit of a tropical seaside palm tree and that he will not deny."

"I was wrong. The population expands each time one does not go out, or whenever one is not in that city."

"How you prattle, 'Lin! Will you obey me?"

"No, I shall ignore you. I intended to voyage to

Pirano anyway. Not as a pressganger for a doppelganger!”

"Wretch! You'll be sorry. I'm so noxious!”

But away hurried the Swede, glancing back not once, until Linopolis was a splinter in his rear and the ghoul's howls were naught. He rested, walked, and tried to forget about not seeing his citizens, which was how they bred. In Pirano he collided with the cook, who had received 'Ceti's official letter. Here was a genuine coconut, no nasty pate! They entered the shop together and he lifted the mirror from a peg; it was broken but might still serve. However, there was no time to journey to Wolkenstein, the world would burst, so he passed it to 'Vado, who must give it to the navigator, who wandered everywhere. On the way back, the carpenter began to forget what it was that Morgan's kiss told him. Something vital! Such a surprise to find that his capital was lit for his return. He wanted no public illumination during his reign.

Lamps in each window, at the top of the towers. Never had Linopolis looked so festive. Streamers of fluid colour dancing on the roofs. Licks and winks, an epithalamium of tints and twinkles. Was the heat emanating from the friction of capering feet? He heard a hissing music, the rhythm of popping drums, but saw no players. If he really had become popular at last, why were they waiting indoors? He entered his palace and found the ghoul squatting on his throne, rubbing sooty palms, an insult! Before he could sever the chair from its dais with his saw, and tip it to dislodge the usurper, there was a tumultuous crash from outside. The windmill had toppled, weighed down with too many lamps. But now it seemed the edifice itself was one giant lamp. How strange! Then the ghoul stood and touched his elbow, as if divining his wonder.

"This is no celebration. I allowed the sailmaker's puppet to wander at will through the houses. The fire in its chest quickly spread. It's a revolution! Don't you see, 'Lin? When your subjects are consumed, you'll impregnate the planet again. By charring your people to ash and watching them scatter, I'll crush you under the density of impromptu populations. Your safeguard against claustrophobia is cancelled. Join my scheme and I can provide you with an alternative."

"Never! My death will be a prophylactic."

"'Lin! You are made of wood, not rubber!"

But the Swede was off, running through his smoking streets with the ghoul in a hot pursuit that was cooler than the cobbles. The theatre was blazing more quickly than any other building, so he leapt inside, hoping to catch. The roof was missing and the stars poured molten beauty on the fabrics which had not yet ignited. He paused in the centre of the stage, reciting a lament to the raging audience, who whistled and spat. Boiling sap sprayed over his armour, but the lanolin repelled it. The bald ghoul was no longer behind him. He heard a slashing sound, like a snake riding a carousel, and the stars died. He looked up and saw a machine with dark blades high above Linopolis. Then a bucket of water was released and his armour steamed and flexed. A second, third, and he was sodden. The ghoul shouted down through a metallic cone:

"I need you, 'Lin! I won't let you burn."

A misguided attempt at rescue, for these amplified words fanned the inferno to make a tropical midsummer in the auditorium, and the teak was released from the cage of homesickness. Since carved by the carpenter in Panama it had resented the cold latitudes, dreaming of hot monsoons. Now it assumed it had one, with the temperature and moisture, and so it grew faster and faster to reclaim all that lost time. The holes in the helmet sealed themselves up, and the man inside suffocated. The ghoul span away in disgust and Linopolis crumbled to ash around the Swede, drying him as it dispersed, until he was alone on the Alpine plain. A month later, his skeleton fell apart within the suit, skull rattling down the hollow left thigh like a landlord's knock. In the autumn, Morgan came to harvest the armour, claiming it for a figurehead.

The Haunted Womb

It was on our wedding night that my bride revealed she was infected with her lover's ghost. I knew something was amiss, but I'd never anticipated a paranormal problem. Undaunted by her pronouncement, I made yet another attempt at completing our nuptials. The same thing happened once more; I guessed I would continue to fail indefinitely. There was nothing I could do other than weep, while she soothed my brow and finally slipped out of bed to make a pot of sweet tea.

In her absence, I examined the apparatus of my defused ardour. Pale and shrivelled, it trembled with fright; my words of condolence couldn't rouse it from its abject state. Emily had ruined me with her infidelity. No longer a man, I reflected on this reversal of my fortunes, from power to infirmity, rapture to misery, in a single evening. In the deeps of my discarded trousers, a pocket watch chimed twelve; already it was time to consider divorce, and I did so.

But what might I tell a solicitor? After a traditional service in a gothic church, clever speeches from a selection of guests at a sumptuous reception and dancing on a floor made slippery with spilled champagne, I had become a genuine groom, frightfully eager to consummate my marriage. My passion was unbearable; I caught my bride and rushed out of the hotel with her, to the disgust of the manager, a doleful chap who believed the only permissible delights are made from gelatine. The hired car accepted us; I accelerated to Yorkshire.

Hidden in the tangle of rutted lanes which net the landscape around the town of Coxwold, a furnished cottage awaited. Hoisting my bride over the threshold, flinging her on the quilt, I unsheathed her body from her dress with my teeth, hurting my fillings on the gold lamé butterflies. A pair of satin knickers was removed like the crust of a pie; I licked the filling and found it to my taste. Emily giggled. Even then, I had a clue this was a familiar process for her. The rising moon cast a beam through a window to spotlight my pride.

Events moved rapidly. How shall I put the matter delicately? I rose and plunged, in accordance with nature, but the instant I passed through her conjugal gates, something punctured my zeal. Pulling out, I regarded the physical truth of my deflated lust, an object covered in goosebumps. Every hair in the vicinity had turned white with fright. It looked as if my manhood had seen an apparition. When I suggested this to my wife, she responded that it probably had.

Cupid's arrow had become a boomerang!

While I brooded over these terrible scenes, Emily returned from the kitchen with a brimming saucer and a napkin. I lapped the liquid with my tongue and she dabbed at the corners of my eyes. Minutes passed before I felt safe enough to berate her.

"I'm awfully disappointed by this affair."

"These things happen, Joseph. You knew I was a feisty girl when you proposed. Redheads crave variety."

"But what was the scoundrel's name?"

She shrugged and sighed deeply. "It happened in Spain on a business trip. There was an imposing gentleman in a café in Toledo. He approached my table and offered to buy me a drink. His appearance was exotic and in the sleeve of his gown he kept fritillaries, dozens of them. They seemed to obey his command. When he made them form the figure of a heart in the air between us, I was captivated."

I howled. Emily is a lepidopterist and easy to lead astray with the right kind of insect. Indeed, it was the moths in my empty wallet during a restaurant meal, rather than my personality, which won her for me when we started dating, six months ago.

"Seduced by a conjuror! What happened next?"

"He took me to a discreet hotel. The Pensión Lumbreras."

I chewed my lip, but my teeth were too blunt to draw blood. I vowed to see a dentist soon. "And then?"

"The usual outcome. But he was less robust than I'd assumed. At the critical moment, he had a fatal heart attack. Instead of flying off into the air, his soul went the wrong way and entered my uterus, where it has taken residence. I hoped it would make no difference to our relationship but it evidently has. We'll never be able to make love with a phantom in my womb; it'll haunt your member."

Suddenly, I was overwhelmed with sympathy. Emily's mistake affected her no less than me. Forgiveness was not only appropriate but necessary. My duty was to practise tolerance.

"Are you willing to consider an exorcist?"

She frowned. "Do they still exist? I thought the church discouraged its staff from dabbling in magic."

"Well, we're in Yorkshire now. I bet I can find a local vicar ready to take on the job. Shall we try?"

She nodded imperceptibly and I requested the telephone directory. I flicked the pages of the book, found the number of a pastor who lived in Coxwold and dialled him up — it took quite a long time to rouse him from his slumber. After listening to my feverish explanations, he became very excited and promised to come over as quickly as possible. There was some sort of electrical discharge rife on the lines; I winced and dropped the receiver as it stung my cheekbone.

I cradled my bride while we waited. I felt my lust returning, but I was too scared to touch her. I thought I detected the bell of a bicycle, far away on the frozen wind. A storm was gathering; my hair rose on end, green sparks dancing on my fringe.

Pastor Rowlands arrived within the hour. A man with lashes too long for his puritan eyes, I can't say his presence was comforting. A chilly, brooding aura seemed to envelop him, an air of musty antiquity, as if he slept on a shelf in the basement of an unvisited museum. The tips of his fingers, when you looked at them askance, seemed to glow like irradiated worms. I'm convinced he cycled all the way to our cottage without lamps. He didn't appear in need of external illumination. When he talked, I was sure he used more than one tongue.

"Yes, there's definitely a spectre in the vicinity. Show me to your wife, Mr Pickhill. It's a most awkward place for a haunting, though I've had others nearly as troublesome."

"Have you? Will you furnish examples?"

"I'm not here for small talk, but I'll briefly mention the time the clock of Salisbury cathedral was possessed by the spirit of a sundial. A most unfortunate event in winter."

"An evil hob-gnomon, was it?"

I guided him to Emily, who was draped in a blanket. Pastor Rowlands raised his arms in embarrassment. "Keep it on. I can examine you through material. But please silence your husband."

She lifted an unarguable finger and I sealed my mouth.

Kneeling, the exorcist placed an ear to Emily's womb. He tapped the blanket and rolled his eyes violently.

"How utterly fabulous! It's one for the record books."

"Can you cure the infection?" I asked.

He shook his head. "No, because it's not a disease. The soul of her deceased lover has made her pregnant."

"I beg your pardon?" I spluttered. "But how?"

"The spirit has simply joined with an egg and is growing naturally. There's nothing to cure, Mr Pickhill, except the miracle of life itself. By the end of the year, you'll have an addition to your family. Allow me to be first to offer congratulations."

Emily blushed, but for my sake she repressed her smiles. "A phantom pregnancy for real! A stroke of luck."

"I can't tell at this stage whether it's a boy or girl," the pastor confessed. "But it's going to be big."

I simmered with rage. "Boy or girl? Boil or ghoul, more like! Don't you realise what you're saying? My wife is carrying another man's spook! Do you expect me to put up with that?"

"An unhelpful attitude, Mr Pickhill. Are you jealous?"

I persuaded him, without much difficulty, that I was. We were at an impasse. Studying my wife's expression, I realised a termination was out of the question. But there had to be alternatives. What if we could find a surrogate mother willing to carry the child instead? I'd read that the operation was feasible, though for souls the process might be different. I announced: "How about a transplant?"

"I'm not able to assist you there. The spirit must be coaxed out in its own tongue. My Spanish is very weak. Besides the church is reluctant to involve itself in psychic surgery."

"Help me arrange it or I'll kill myself! That'll be a bigger sin on your conscience. I'm serious, pastor."

Emily nodded at the exorcist. She knew me well enough to appreciate the difference between my hollow threats and those more solid than stale coffins. With her support, I knew I'd get my own way. The pastor snorted and regarded his glinting fingernails.

"Well, it's a little drastic, but I know one man who can transplant the phantom to another womb. He's had plenty of experience with peculiar cases. If you have no problem paying his ludicrous fees, I'll inform him of your circumstances. If he agrees to see you, expect him to visit in a week or two. But I advise against it."

"He sounds just the fellow! Why must we wait so long?"

"He's based in Madrid. His name is Doctor José de los Rios and I've heard a great many strange stories about him. It's no good travelling to Spain for a consultation; he uses foreign cases as excuses for holidays. He'll expect you to wine and dine him for the length of his stay as well as put him up for free. He may even linger after your problem is solved. I can say he's the most noble man in his profession – because he happens to be the only one! Apart from that, keep an eye on your wallets when he leaves. His fingers are like hornets."

"You mean his touch stings pockets? Surely any risk is worth it for the chance to consummate my marriage?"

"I'll take your word for that, Mr Pickhill..."

I prevailed upon the exorcist to contact Dr de los Rios right away. He pouted and grumbled but finally promised to send him a note outlining the details of our predicament and begging him to fly over. Nothing else was left for me to do, except grit my aching molars for a fortnight. The pastor left and the darkness jumped into his absence. Dawn hardly helped my mood, which was a combination of fury and forbearance. Emily took her treacherous womb back to bed and I sat at the window cursing hedges. The occasional butterfly, rising from a clump of hyacinths, fanned my hatred with garish efficiency. Several times I was on the point of waking Emily to condemn her, but I restrained the urge.

We maintained an uneasy alliance over the following days. Each time I brought up the subject of infidelity, she reminded me that I was ugly. We were deadlocked. Her fickleness, my visage; both were equally horrid. To freshen this stalemate, we cuddled at frequent intervals, oscillating between compassion and revulsion – good practise for any married couple. Emily sauntered around the garden in the sun but quickly grew exhausted. Pregnancy had borrowed the springiness from her ankles, refusing to give it back, but her appetite remained conventional. At the end of the first week, I burned her wedding dress in the grate, while she was asleep, and the gold lamé decorations spiralled across the room in shimmering clouds to mock my chin and singe my eyebrows.

Pastor Rowlands was a regular guest at our cottage, offering solace and wisdom at bargain prices. His arrival was usually preceded by bursts of icy flame on the horizon; he unnerved us both, though I was delighted with the way he chased horrid shadows into hiding. I never really wanted to associate with ghosts; such close proximity to one altered the entire aspect of the furnishings, turning rooms into chambers of menace. It was easier to bear with the exorcist at sparkling hand. He seemed content in the vicinity of my wife, sitting on the sofa next to her, while I took a position at a safer distance. He promised me that contact with Dr de los Rios had been established, but he was unable to give a definite date for his advent. He sermonised on patience.

Two weeks passed in this state of anguished expectancy. Probably an optical illusion, but my bride seemed to have a definite swelling in her midriff. I fought back my natural paternal reflexes; to betray myself by valuing her condition was an unbearable temptation. I abandoned all hope of ever regaining my virility. The doctor still had not materialised and no amount of imprecation could loosen the pastor's tongue as to where he might be. Finally, at the end of the third week, there was a violent rap on the door. I opened it and a dapper gentleman, portly but not awkward, bowed elegantly before pushing inside.

I retreated as he explored the room, altering the angles of objects and rearranging ornaments. He was dressed in a flamboyant style, antique cane grasped in one hand as he poked among the papers in my bureau. Then he was fiddling with the radio, losing the station I had found with such difficulty. I viewed his waistcoat, with its amethyst buttons and dragon motif, in a kind of numbed astonishment. In his other hand, he carried a wooden box of exquisite workmanship which he laid on the mantelpiece. He briefly surveyed the kitchen and bedroom before returning to confront me with the results of his investigation.

"Ah, so this is a typical English residence?"

The question confused me. "Well, yes, I suppose so, but most people don't live in them." Aware I had contradicted myself, I began stuttering my way deeper into absurdity. "They have cottages elsewhere like this or different which are quite as typical."

"Your wife blends well with the décor, but you are anomalous. Tweed suit and spats would be preferable, though your head catches reflections in an unfortunate way. I have a patent medicine for your stammer. Pay me later, if you like. I'm very thirsty."

Emily was more composed. "Dr de los Rios, I presume?"

"One and the same, Señora. Now where's the wine?"

Carefully testing the chairs with his hand, he selected the most comfortable and pulled it close to the fire. He removed his boots and rested his heels on the warm hearth, wriggling his toes in ecstasy.

I hastened to fetch a bottle of 1985 Le Montrachet from the Domaine de la Romanée-Conti, a top white burgundy. Following the pastor's advice I had stocked up on all kinds of expensive consumables, travelling daily to a delicatessen in Coxwold. I poured the nectar and our saviour gently pushed his nose into the rising fumes.

"A little young for me. Do you have anything else?"

My jaw slackened, but I procured an alternative, a cobwebbed bottle of Château Latour 1961. After a careful sip, he exhaled despondently. "I still rate sherry as the finest wine."

I controlled my anger and resisted a temptation to break the bottle over his skull. These two wines, together with a Krug 1949, Château Haut Brion 1945 and fin de siècle armagnac brandy had almost crippled my bank balance, to say nothing of the Monte Cristo cigars and Edam cheeses with chives. But for the sake of my manhood, I would have to agree with every one of his opinions, however mistaken.

"Did you enjoy your flight?" Emily asked.

The doctor plucked thoughtfully at his forked beard. "Travelling by air is the root cause of much disease, Señora. Consider the case I had a year ago: a balloonist fell to his death over Cádiz and broke a fountain in a square. From that instant, the buildings were terrified of airborne objects, shivering every time a cloud passed overhead. Social disruption was considerable; the citizens were disadvantaged. I treated this phobia with lengthy sessions of psychotherapy. Cádiz regained its senses and is now a liberated and ambitious locale."

"We hope you'll be equally successful here," I said.

He dismissed the tremor in my voice with a wave. "I've cured worse. Allow me to describe the plight of Doña Micaela Valverde, a woman with a passion for cadavers. She visited mortuaries to stare at them, sometimes to take darker liberties. But as with all addictions, tolerance built up until she became immune to death. She kept growing older, but her mortal coil was too tangled to shed. I eased it off with a parsley compress and skeleton-keyhole surgery. I'm clever!"

"Perhaps you can examine my wife now?" I suggested, feeling sure he would grumble at having to go to work.

To my surprise, he acceded. He rose from the chair, fumbling in his pockets for a stethoscope. After listening to Emily's inner workings for a suspiciously long time, he chuckled.

"What was the name of your lover, Señora?"

"The shameless wench didn't even learn," I muttered.

Emily told him the whole story, including details she had kept from me, and Dr de los Rios nodded smartly.

"I know the fellow in question. He is Juan Chinelato, a gambler and wrestler who has a mysterious power over butterflies and ladies. He does this kind of thing on a regular basis, seducing innocent girls and dying in their arms, to ensure his rebirth."

This news cheered me up. It seemed to indicate that Emily wasn't in possession of her senses when she committed her treason. But she quickly dashed my hope. "I was quite willing!"

"Maybe so," the doctor conceded. "But the point is that he won't be easily enticed out of your womb. It's a matter of resurrection and every time he's reborn he enjoys life more."

"What a decadent upstart!" I blurted. "A total cad!"

"Quite so, Señor, but he adds colour to Toledo and is tolerated for that reason. His wife disapproves of his behaviour, they argue and smash plates but she always takes him back."

"She's welcome to him! What an extreme philanderer!"

"Calm yourself, Señor. Her name is Tia Mariquita and she lives in a house that coughs. There is no other female willing to accept the foetus once it is extracted from your bride."

"Tell me your plan, doctor. How can you remove him?"

"He is quite comfortable inside Emily. He must be lured out with an irresistible temptation. He is fond of butterflies; we'll capture one in a jar and parade it in front of your wife's womb. If the example is good enough, he'll bound through her abdomen to inspect it more closely. Once he's inside the jar I'll screw down the lid and carry him back to Toledo where he can be transplanted into Tia Mariquita. It's not the first time she's been pregnant with her husband."

Emily was dubious. "Trap a phantom in glass?"

"Of my own manufacture," Dr de los Rios explained. "Holy water ice, shaped accordingly. A barrier to spectres."

I was eager to search the garden immediately for a suitable insect, but our visitor discouraged me with a yawn.

"It's too late tonight, Señor. In the morning, I will assist you. I am exhausted and need sleep. Escort me to the double bed, if you please. You may take the sofa near the grate."

Emily supported him out of my sight while I fumed at his insolence. When he was on the threshold, I approached the mantelpiece and picked up the box he had left there. It was heavy and satisfying to the touch, but served no evident purpose. I sent my voice after him; it turned into the bedroom. "You've forgotten something."

"The box? No, Señor, that is your wedding present."

Emily returned, having tucked him up. "What a nice gesture! What do you think is inside? Open it, Joseph."

I shook my head. "It's inappropriate. When this horrendous business is all over, I'll be happy to accept the gift. Until then, the box stays locked. For the sake of our marriage."

We snuggled up on the sofa, but our embrace remained chaste. Dreams did not come, nor an untroubled sleep; I lingered in a state between the worlds, my head throbbing, my manhood cowering. I grew nervous and paced the room, waiting for the first stars to fade and take my cowardice with them, to the other side of the planet.

It was dawn. I descended into the garden and wasted my time chasing butterflies. Despite his promise, Dr de los Rios did not help, and Emily was almost as useless, sitting on the grass and reciting the Latin names of those which fluttered out of my clumsy fingers. When she tired of the sport, she slipped indoors to attend to the doctor, who was shouting for his dinner. I was resigned to becoming a pauper at his hands and gullet, but the enormity of his appetites was shocking to the eye as well as the purse. His waistcoat tightened hourly.

A similar routine was observed the following day and though I honed my skills to the point where I caught a dozen Cabbage Whites, the doctor adjudged them too bland to interest the spirit and I set them free. What was required, according to Emily, was something more colourful, a bright *Danaus plexippus, Nymphalis antiopa* or *Apatura iris*. Part of the problem lay with the restrained markings of our indigenous insects, which surely held scant interest for Juan Chinelato, a connoisseur familiar with such unusual jungle types as *Morpho didius*.

Eventually, after a week of prancing, I netted a remarkable *Pyronia tithonus*, a feat even Emily judged worthy of praise. Dr de los Rios held up his jar, kept solid with an intricate web of tiny refrigeration pipes and we persuaded the butterfly to enter by dropping a flower inside. Now there was no time to lose: before it flew away again, we had to pass the jar near to Emily's bulge. When the ghost jumped out of her and into the icy prison, the doctor would seal its fate by screwing on the lid. I was uncomfortably aware that tears were streaming down my face. Soon I would have a second chance to be a real man.

However, Dr de los Rios had other ideas. Before lowering the jar to the level of Emily's womb, he arched a bushy eyebrow, stroked his forked beard with a finger and grinned slyly.

"I haven't been offered money for my services yet, Señor. There may be no better time to settle accounts."

Stupefied by his tactlessness, I involuntarily reached in my pocket and removed my wallet. As I've already insinuated, I am naturally a very thrifty fellow and only the direst circumstances can ever persuade me to abandon the habits of a lifetime. Although I had accepted the great cost of the operation, my wallet had not. When I opened it, a gargantuan moth rose into the air, a repeat of the restaurant incident. It flew straight into my wide mouth and I swallowed it.

Emily squealed with delight. *"Hepialus humuli!"*

In my desperation to spit it out, I stumbled against my bride. With a hiss, her stomach deflated. My knees buckled; something was wrong with my sense of balance. I had acquired a mystifying burden inside me, as if a dwarf was standing on my intestines.

"Ah, look, the spirit prefers the moth to the butterfly! See how it lovingly chooses you for a surrogate."

"What do you mean?" I held the radius of my belly.

"You have a tortilla in the oven, Señor."

Evidently, I had become pregnant!

"This is a terrible accident," I whimpered. "We must hasten to coax it out of me and into the frozen jar."

Emily stamped a foot. "You've had your way,

Joseph, and now it's my turn. The foetus remains where it is."

To my dismay, Dr de los Rios agreed. "Yes, Señora."

I staggered to a chair near the window. It was a relief to take the weight off my feet. I stayed there until sunset, drinking the sweet cups of tea offered by my bride, pondering metaphysical matters until sunset, when a display of the aurora borealis alerted me to the imminent arrival of Pastor Rowlands. Entering without knocking, he was a focus of instant fascination for our guest. Dr de los Rios raised his nose, still stained with wasted vintage wine, and inhaled.

"I can smell ozone," he remarked.

The exorcist sighed. "I had an accident with a lightning conductor. It converted me into a notional grid."

Dr de los Rios studied the pastor's effulgent palms and clucked his tongue. "I have dealt with this sort of thing before. We shall earth you to a mandolin and effect a discharge."

"I don't require your services. I'm also an expert."

Pastor Rowlands and the doctor were soon debating case histories as if they were old friends. They were two sides of the same rare coin; the former purged supernature with litany, the latter relied on scalpels. It appeared they had forgotten my existence. To attract attention, I had to use brute force, dividing them like an immature amoeba. The exorcist was joyful when appraised of my condition.

"You'll make an excellent mother, Mr Pickhill."

"I'm not sure about that. I can't cook."

"Natural birth is out of the question," claimed Dr de los Rios. "We ought to arrange a Caesarean section."

The pastor rubbed his chin. "There's only one hospital in Yorkshire willing to deliver spectres in that fashion."

"Take me there!" I was already dreading labour, its attendant pains and discomforts. "I want anaesthetic!"

"They use aether, rather than ether, Mr Pickhill. But the nurses at Phantomsville Maternity are highly trained.

They'll take care of you and your little bundle of gloom. Perhaps I can officiate at the christening? I've waited for ages to dunk a ghost."

"Do what you like. Just get me medical attention!"

"I think it best if we register you there immediately. They'll want to conduct tests and write research papers on your case. As a first time mother, a primipara, naturally you're anxious, but think what you'll add to science – I envy you, Mr Pickhill."

"Did I ever do anything to deserve this?" I grumbled. "My condition hasn't even got a proper name, I bet!"

"The dark side of the honeymoon, Señor."

I don't care to say much about what happened from that moment. When the ambulance arrived to carry me to Phantomsville, I was alarmed by its resemblance to a hearse. At the hospital, I joined a spirited ante-natal class and learned to stretch my credulity as well as my limbs. Dr de los Rios visited me once, on the eve of my big day, to make his farewells. A commission down south was beckoning; he related its sordid details while eating the grapes on my bedside table.

"There's a hotel manager who believes the only permissible delights are made from gelatine. I'll recommend a kilogramme of Spanish Fly and a dozen Viennese Oysters, thrice daily."

Pastor Rowlands and Emily were more regular witnesses of my misery. They always came together, arm in arm, though I was too intent on myself to register the significance. They took a profound interest in the legal aspects of my predicament. I afterwards learned that Emily had spent the rest of my savings on marriage guidance sessions with Dr de los Rios. He decided it was best if she eloped with the pastor and claimed custody of the ghost. The law courts in Phantomsville are prejudiced against mortal litigants, but the pastor knows how to play the system. Her reincarnated lover was taken from my arms at birth.

They have set up home together, the three of them. I hear they save on electricity bills. But I can't help wondering where it will end. When Juan Chinelato grows up, will Emily transfer her affections back to him? Will the pastor be forced to challenge him to a duel? I can picture them now, one with a sword forged from Toledo steel, the other with a burning net snaking from his fingers, weaving between draperies, smashing tables laden with fruit, leaping onto balconies. I don't intend giving them the chance to fight it out. That's my job.

I have lodged an appeal with the Phantomsville courts for the right to visit my child. If I am successful, I'll tarry until his twenty first birthday before making a move. I can't decide exactly how Dr de los Rios fits into the affair. Did he predict the outcome and act accordingly, or has he manipulated us from the beginning? In my hands I hold his gift, a heavy box with a clasp. Emily appears to have forgotten about it, but my memory is good. I turn the key slowly.

A pair of flintlock pistols.

MR.
HUMPHREY'S
CLOCK'S
INHERITANCE

The reader is asked to imagine a household of the gloomy sort, dominated by two eccentric pieces of furniture. The first of these is an enormous grandfather clock of polished black wood, its body warped in such a way that when viewed from the end of the hall it resembles the rotten tusk of a mammoth with a craving for sweets. Indeed, the instrument seems to palpably ache; there is an aura of throbbing misery about it, expressed most strongly in the somewhat nauseated face of overlapping dials. To be more colourful, let us say this device of charred ebony, green brass and dirty ivory is suffering from a migraine.

The second item, while no less stiff than the first, has a greater range of movement. This is the owner of the hall and clock; an obscure gentleman by the name of Humperdinck Pumpernickel. His tongue, unable to curl itself around this appellation, has settled for 'Humphrey' and this is how he is greeted by that small circle of acquaintances – I dare not term them friends – with which he shares a few mordant interests. There is a mustiness draped on his shoulders, like the ripped bridal veil of a jilted heiress, which oppresses all but his fellow enthusiasts, who are familiar with the taste of damp books and the flavour of aged paintings. For Mr Humphrey is a member of that select group of collectors for whom the licking of antiques is common practice.

The house in which this dubious pair have settled lies on the coast between two minor towns, tucked away behind a frown of sand-dunes which, according to legend, once swallowed an abbey and its bishop. It stands a little way back from the road, protected by a garden of broken artefacts which the occupant has drained of nourishment before casting out from an upstairs window. Because it is on my route, I am often to be found among these lethal objects d'art, picking my way through the Fabergé, Wedgwood and Stradivarius splinters which glimmer like the teeth of sophisticated gin-traps. Once or twice I have seen Mr Humphrey peeping at me through a parted curtain; at these times, my hand trembles as I feed my leaflet to his voracious letterbox, which devours all I can deliver, though no good comes of it. Pumpernickel cannot be solicited.

One day I shall be free of this menial task – forcing badly printed leaflets on a reluctant public. Until then, I shall endure my daily task with reasonable grace. My peregrinations take me from the eastern hamlet to the western – to be specific, from Abell to Quinn – then back along a beach of crushed shell, over a dozen rotting groynes. As I walk, scaling the redundant sea defences with considerable difficulty, I reflect on my impressions of the fellow. I can tell a great deal from a glimpse. There are few more jaded examples of that breed of man who seek out morsels of the past than Mr Humphrey. His appearance gives the impression of weary dilettanteism. He wears his whiskers long and bushy, in the style of the early industrialists, not caring to know the purpose they serve – that sideburns are a carpet-sample of a beard.

His predecessor, in contrast, was a man of astounding energy, taste and wit; a credit to his obsession. It was he who stuffed the house with rarities in the first instance. Abell boasts an antique shop of wondrous dimensions, with a proprietor eager to sell his wares at bargain prices. There is a silly rumour about this chap, a foreign gentleman, which has been of little help to his business: he is a condemned soul waiting for the thousandth customer to pass into his store. Only then will he be set free – presumably to take up a different occupation – while the customer is forced to take his place. The reason for the curse is never outlined. There is mention of him cheating the devil out of a Gainsborough; at any rate, he is generally avoided by the local population. Only the former owner of Humphrey's residence was a regular client – he obtained most of his collection, including the tall ebony clock, from the dealer, whom we may henceforth dignify as Herr

Fluchen.

Thus the reader may be fully assured of Mr Humphrey's indolence. He is not even willing to pursue his chosen hobby with a minimum of genuine effort, but must find a short cut to compulsion. While his brothers take the trouble to build up an accumulation of appetising heirlooms, sparing no pains in learning the locations of secret auctions, roving far afield in the quest for a Clarice Cliff or a Chesterfield, our sullen Humphrey simply casts his eye for a house already crammed with such treasures and promptly moves in. Then he sets to work licking each article raw, garret to basement, much as a conventional gourmand passes over soups and pasta to the pudding. But the building is vast, and a dilettante is languorous in matters of motion, so that by the time our tale begins, though he has occupied the manse for a full decade, our hero has only just reached the end of the hall where the sable timepiece nestles in a recess like a bad odour. Humphrey's suspense as he approached the clock I need not attempt to describe. His senses were overwound.

Reaching the base of the chronometer, he applied tongue to wood and continued in a single fluid motion upward. At first, all went as well as he hoped. In a rather exciting instant he had the full tang: iron pipes, puddles splashed by freckled girls, soot, roots, gears of a second hand bicycle, crumbly cheese, apples, wine mulled with a rusty poker, feather dusters, earlobes. He was astonished at the range of savours to be found in this unique antique. When he stretched on tiptoe to lap the numerals and spidery hands, his pleasure was interrupted by a chilling event. The clock actually seemed to laugh at him; more a cynical snarl than a true expression of mirth. And then the mechanism – which had always operated as smoothly as a nun's thigh – stopped dead.

Our hero abandoned his repast and slumped to the floor. His tongue burned, as if it had been singed by a very small explosion. The baroque dial now mockingly indicated the exact hour at which his palate had met its match. Humphrey dined at eight. Placing his ear to what he presumed must be the pendulum case, he struggled to catch further examples of the vulgar guffaw. But the clock was utterly silent. During the minutes that followed the relinquishing of luncheon, the dilettante staggered to the nearest chair – a Chippendale with a gadrooned square apron in laggard style, and carved tassle and ruffle in pierced vase-shaped splat – and perspired quietly in the consciousness that he had somehow spoiled his dessert. Cuisine is the art of good timing.

Since Humphrey had taken over the residence, the chronometer – like a real grandfather – had minded its own business, and the dilettante had never troubled himself about its maintenance. As he thought about it, it seemed peculiar that not once had he ever wound the thing up. Somehow it coped perfectly well without human intervention. Mechanics was a mystery to our hero – he had a dim notion that Archimedes was a chap who lounged in the bath – and he was quite incapable of grasping the finer points of a clock's anatomy. But he was sure they needed regular attention, of the circular sort, in the same way that a schoolboy must have an arm twisted to operate at maximum potential.

With a finger on the wood, he felt each side of the machine; but no key or hole did he discover. How then was the device to be rewound? More than this: the frame seemed to be quivering, as if stifling more laughs. "Odd!" said Mr Humphrey. "Now I can hardly bear my hand on it. Better to call in professional advice, I think."

Moving to his candlestick telephone, he made his first call in ten years. In Quinn worked a jeweller who knew most of what there was to know about timepieces. Mr Humphrey summoned him to the house and soothed his nerves while waiting by nibbling the marquetry off a small cabinet by Jean Francois Oeben. Picking between meals was always his problem; he was ruining his health with an irregular diet.

Not that this much concerned the jeweller when he arrived. A chubby American with a Yale education, he was skilled at picking locks, but the dark grandfather defeated him. The thing that caught his attention right away were brackets fixed on the top, twisted as if objects had been torn off them, possibly bells. But there was no way of winding the device up; he did not think this indicated it was weight driven. Was Humphrey quite sure it had been running continuously since he bought the manse? In that case, it must be an atmospheric clock.

Grimacing unpleasantly, the dilettante said: "I should be deceiving you, and that to no good purpose, if I laid claim to possess information on that topic. What exactly do you mean by this?"

The jeweller than launched into a turgid lecture on an arcane field of clock design, which had involved attempts to create a pseudoperpetual motion device, resulting in James Cox's remarkable machine of 1760. As I assume the reader knows, it is impossible to obtain more energy from the output of a system than is delivered to its input – the rules of physics are very strict about ensuring a loss of energy in any apparatus with moving parts. This has something to do with Thermodynamics and equations which look like rococo ornamentation.

Cox managed to cheat these laws, at least to the satisfaction of an ignorant public, by utilising barometric pressure to prime his clock. An elaborate winding arrangement was constructed which depended on separate reservoirs of mercury – some 150lb of the expensive liquid – which, kept in a state of unstable equilibrium, amplified pressure differences via a set of levers: a force which was applied to raising a weight which drove the actual clock mechanism. This ingenious contraption was improved by a French engineer, Jean Leon Reutter, in the 1920's, using a liquefied gas and a saturated vapour as well as mercury.

Mr Humphrey yawned, vexed and ashamed at the fiasco of the lecture, which the jeweller was delivering just for his own benefit. "That is all very well," he replied; "but can you open it?"

"Not without cutting it in two," answered the expert; "but it would be a shame to damage such an unusual machine. There is no way of getting inside; I cannot pick a lock which has no keyhole. Perhaps the case door can be forced. Be patient and pass me my chisel."

"Certainly, certainly, here it is. If you succeed, I shall pay your fee with a fine wrought-iron Torchère."

"I would rather the Hepplewhite commode I passed in the corridor. I cannot see it very well from this distance; but it is not unsightly. You must also throw in a few appropriate stools."

That evening brought an hour's hard work to the jeweller, who found it a difficult task even to insert the blade of his tool in the gap made by the frame and door. At last he gave it up; he admitted defeat, adding he had never encountered a clock remotely like this one before. In final desperation, he lifted a stethoscope from his box and probed the sternum of the thing. Listening intently, he frowned.

"I am ashamed to say," said he, "that I can hear breathing."

"Now this is unexpected," commented Mr Humphrey; "though I did read an article in the paper about a toad which took up residence in a cello. Might there be an animal of some sort within?"

The jeweller pursed his lips. "I should prefer to think the mercury is sighing. But look at this: the maker's name on the faceplate has been eroded almost to nothing. Pass me my mirror."

It had not occurred to Mr Humphrey to seek writing on the device: a clock is not a book. Nonetheless, complying with the jeweller's request, he watched in fascination as the fellow angled the mirror at the base of the dial and shone an electric torch on the brass. A pale name shimmered into sight. Struggling to pronounce the reversed letters, the dilettante whispered the maker's name and city – Mortice d'Arthur,

Chaud-Mellé – in tones of instinctive respect. But he immediately added that he had heard of neither; nor did he believe his friends capable of helping him in the matter. Did the jeweller know anything relevant?

"No, I am sorry to say I do not," said the expert. "It seems rather alpine, what I can judge by the syllables. Swiss, I would guess. Perhaps the respiration is due to some kind of cuckoo? Mountain craftsmen are an idiosyncratic breed. In some valleys they are obsessed with automata. My dog is Swiss – I lubricate his cogs with brandy."

Mr Humphrey was still tired. He rubbed his eyes and pandiculated. I imagine that at this point the jeweller made ready to depart. Before he had packed away all his equipment, the dilettante offered him a glass of wine and a pinch of Regency snuff. This was the sum of his payment, due to his manifest failure with the clock. Wine was accepted, but snuff was refused with a horrified expression. Mr Humphrey could see that the chap was struggling with some superstition which clung about the offer like a damp silk scarf. At last he had the reason – with an uneasy shrug of his shoulders, the expert revealed his quaint fears.

"Snuff? Ah no, it is not that I object to, so much as the sneeze. I am wary of the legend which accompanies the dunes outside. A bishop once blew his nose in chapel. He was divinely punished by being buried under tons of sand; and there he will stay until as many sneezes as the grains which cover him are loosed in the vicinity. When this number is reached, the final sneezer will have to take his place."

Humphrey was aware of this tale, but he regarded it with a sardonic smile. "In that case, be sure not to catch cold."

Later, alone again, the dilettante mused on the mysterious clock. A search through his extensive library revealed no volumes about breathing chronometers; one atlas alone showed Chaud-Mellé, which turned out to be a tiny republic some thirteen castles south of Liechtenstein. As for the maker, Mortice d'Arthur, information was as scanty as flourishes in that style of decoration known as Desornamentado, popularised by Herrera. But I am not writing a history of fashion. Mr Humphrey, who had travelled no further than his own county, started to conjure up visions of this hilly state, doubtless an ordered, neat sort of town. There would be houses in many bright colours; girls with mittens and chocolate kisses; bankers in smart suits; teeth without plaque; alpenhorns.

Unable to confirm such assumptions with his available books, he was encouraged to make his first independent purchase. There were many tomes to be browsed in the antique shop in Abell — he resolved to make his way there on the morrow. He knew the address; it was staring at him from the piece of paper he picked from the floor of his passage. Since moving in, he had been snowed under by these advertisements, all of which he fed to the stove in his parlour. At last, he was going to respond to one — such belated victory makes my job worthwhile. Persistence with leaflets is an essential quality for a salesman. Now I was delighted for Herr Fluchen, who had never doubted my ability to snare good customers. But I am being disingenuous — the proprietor in question is myself. A futile attempt at suspense has kept me from revealing this fact.

Lest my readers also accuse me of missing key descriptive passages, I shall take the opportunity to belatedly outline the house in which our Humphrey and his furniture dwells. It was a large edifice, a folly whose Gothic appearance was due more to crumbling stonework than architectural intent. A web of cracks covered the exterior plaster, turning the grubby facade into a spider's lair. Broken chimneys resembled rearing gargoyles or half-finished sculptures; the gutters had sagged, so that the black pipes now frowned over the myopic windows like brows. It seemed, owing to its height, to deliberate wings — bat's or griffin's — but there were none. The dilettante cared naught for making repairs and had allowed the wooden balconies to rot to powder and blow away.

322

After deciding on a rare course of action, Humphrey took to his bed with alacrity and slept soundly for a while, clutching the leaflet under his pillow. Before dawn, he was troubled by dreams of a sensational, but rather confused, nature: the clock was calling to him. Inside, snug as a wasp in an apple, or an insult in a compliment, a skeletal figure coaxed him, again and again: "Let me out, sir, let me out!" This thing was more than just bone, of course; it had a tongue and larynx with which to call him, but the skin was stretched so tight over the frame that it appeared more like a fleshy paint on the ribs and limbs. "Let me out, sir!" There was no great malice in the tone; rather it was sad and cynical, suffused with an ineffable jealousy. Humphrey compared the voice to that of a man whose girlfriend, having spurned him, still fusses his cat. Finally, the sibilant plea broke into a choking laugh – half ecstatic, half terrified – which made the dilettante sit bolt upright.

Naturally, when fully awake, the voice was no longer to be heard. A ghost or bugaboo has a knack of keeping in the margins of the senses. So Humphrey was easily persuaded of the insubstantiality of his experience; he put it down to hallucinations occasioned by gastroenteritis, which in turn had been brought on by licking an unsterilised timepiece. Dressing, he made an early breakfast and, for the first time in his life, observed a sunrise. The speed with which the solar disc climbed over the horizon surprised him. He closely studied the leaflet he had taken to bed; there were precise directions on how to find the antique shop in Abell. As has been stated, Herr Fluchen was very eager for customers to cross over his threshold. Humphrey, unaware of the ridiculous myth which surrounded the proprietor, had no fears about entering the shop. Had he known, it would have altered nothing – the dilettante was a sceptic.

Accordingly, he ventured out into the morning, carefully locked the door of his abode and trotted down the road toward the village. The tall dunes blocked the rays of the low sun; it was still as chill as night in their lumpy shadows. Mr Humphrey was not a fast walker: he reached Abell after Herr Fluchen – a conventional riser – opened shop. There is little need to queue in this store; the dealer was delighted to welcome the one customer he thought he would never entice through his portals. After the standard period of browsing, the dilettante turned to him and cautiously inquired as to the comprehensiveness of his stock of books. Herr Fluchen led him into a side-room, with a sagging ceiling whose rafters were held up by pillars of tomes, and gestured at the scene.

"What exactly did you have in mind?" he asked, with a note of pride in his voice. "My collection is extensive."

"Yes, indeed, I am sure," said Mr Humphrey heartily, "and I note an impressive column of atlases. But, tell me, as you are a foreign fellow, knocking about in Central Europe during your youth, I would be gratified to know if you have ever heard of Chaud-Mellé?"

"Often," answered the proprietor; "but it appears to belong to that category of places which exist more in the geography of memory than in a concrete form. Other examples might be quoted – Mirenburg, Binscombe, Dalkey, Lladloh. Do not all these towns have a familiar ring to them? Yet I challenge you to locate them on any map."

"Perhaps you are right; only, looking at a clock last night, I came across the name being used as the home address of the designer who built it, so you will understand my eagerness to learn more. Have you a volume printed in Chaud-Mellé, for instance? I can afford to reward you well; I can exchange a brace of Churriguera desks."

"Excuse me," cried Herr Fluchen, "but my upbringing in Berlin means I can appreciate only furniture conceived in the Jugendstil style. Yet I will see what I can do for you – there are some dusty missals written in Romansch here. Yes, this may be of use: a work discussing the quality of pâtisseries. Chaud-Mellé had a very good one."

The reader must be informed that, although true,

this statement did not help Humphrey. The book in question had a whole chapter missing; the very one they sought. Muttering about mice, Herr Fluchen searched among the columns for less edible tomes. There was nothing actually published in Chaud-Mellé, but a few texts composed in neighbouring states held the occasional snippet of gossip. In Janez Vajkard Valvasor's *Die Ehre Des Herzogthums Crain*, the dilettante learned that Chaud-Mellé was crammed with clock towers, so many that there was an hour for every citizen; in the depths of Thomas Ariel's *Kruptos: the Micropaedia*, he was pleased to discover that most of these timepieces had been designed by one man, Mortice d'Arthur; in Papus Levi's *Arcane Enabler*, a manual devoted to extending mortal longevity, the collector was intrigued by the writer's claim that d'Arthur had achieved a lifespan of over three centuries. Mr Humphrey felt a picture was gradually emerging.

He was shocked, it must be admitted, to find that his vision of the tiny republic was almost completely wrong. Here was no jovial town awash with melting snow and vibrating to the rhythms of yodellers. Chaud-Mellé was an urban pit more gloomy than Ipswich – a chaotic place with a maze of narrow streets, an ineffectual government and a morbid populace. With houses packed so tightly together that daylight never filtered into the thoroughfares, it was a metropolis which bred villainy and vice at every corner. Devilish was the word which jumped into Mr Humphrey's mind. Even the cable cars went down, rather than up: into yawning fissures where no mortal could be expected to ski. As for chocolates and alpenhorns, there were murderous cartels to control both; mittens were banned outright. In short, the city was not a tourist destination.

Turning the pages of other tomes, and breathing that bookish fungus which makes bibliophilia such a heady pastime, Humphrey at last stumbled on an account of the clock-maker. Mortice d'Arthur had gathered one myth about his shoulders. Here was a book called *The Ingolstadt Legends,* by a Bavarian scholar, Pastor Rowlands, and it told the tale in verse. This is a standard satirical technique, but Mr Humphrey suspected it operated less on an allegorical level than might be supposed. With the linguistic aid of Herr Fluchen, the dilettante was soon thrilling over the impudent cantos, lush stanzas and mock-ghastly rhymes.

"This is what I wanted," he said to the proprietor; "it explains my troubles neatly, though I believe not a word."

"Always keen to be of assistance, sir," answered Herr Fluchen, with a click of his heels. "Perhaps you will allow me to giftwrap it for you? You may pay on credit: a single good deed."

"Admirable! Tie the ribbon tightly, my fine man. I intend to reread it over an early supper. Many, many thanks!"

Before the dilettante could depart, his host pressed a small object into his palm and whispered cryptically: "Please also accept this little cake. It was made by my wife, Anna. Be sure to weigh it carefully before you dine!" Then he tapped his nose meaningfully.

With a curt nod, Humphrey strolled back through the shop, past huge mounds of anachronistic clothing, cutlery, painted jugs, wicker baskets, phonograph records, lamps, battered coins, and up to the front door. He stepped out into a light shower and made his way at a brisk pace back to his house. Herr Fluchen followed him, taking a parallel route along the beach, panting as he climbed the groynes, keeping the dunes between him and his quarry. He managed to beat Mr Humphrey to his manse and found an excellent hiding place in the shrubbery. The dilettante arrived back not a minute later; Herr Fluchen noted he had torn off the wrapping and was writing in the book as he loped down the road.

Muttering to himself, Mr Humphrey entered his dwelling and cast the volume before the clock, much in the manner of a challenge. Herr Fluchen witnessed developments by rushing to the rear of the house and squinting through a window. The dilettante's lips were moving: he was conducting a conversation with the clock. An amateur ventriloquist, the proprietor of the antique shop was able to work out the words.

"So, you are in there!" Humphrey was bawling. "And you have in your possession the power to make me happy. I want all you can offer: tell me how to release you! Show me the secret lock!"

It was obvious to Herr Fluchen, if not yet to the reader, that this somewhat poor hero of ours, Mr Humphrey, had abandoned his scepticism of things supernatural for unabashed belief. The legend of Mortice d'Arthur as revealed by Pastor Rowlands is as follows: the clock-maker, a student of chronometry, wanted to cheat mortality by merging himself with one of his creations. He invented a new kind of clock, with an escapement fixed directly to his mind, so that when his thoughts, as electrical impulses, jumped between his scheming lobes, they were converted into a mechanical energy, which could then, with the aid of gears, be reversed. The ageing process should be defeated: by thinking backwards, and reactivating dead brain cells, Mortice would grow young again.

Setting to work, the craftsman made a grandfather which encased him like a coffin. With his body forming the clock workings, he was required to turn the minute hand with his finger. For each hour he moved forward, he gained a corresponding hour of youth. He kept good time: visitors to his workshop set their watches by him. He planned to spend twenty years inside the timepiece, which would take him back to an age when women, in suitable lighting, might find him not unattractive. On no account was he to be disturbed during the process; nobody was permitted to probe inside the instrument. He arranged matters so that the door of the machine was fitted with a secret lock, which could only be opened from outside by an assistant employed to watch over him.

Predictably enough, this assistant – whom Mr Humphrey suspected was Pastor Rowlands himself – grew bored with his task. He decided on a more profitable form of work: the looting of d'Arthur's workshop for valuable items and the distribution of the objects in pawnshops. Anxious to avoid reprisals for this, the assistant made doubly sure Mortice was unable to escape his confinement: he levered off the alarm bells on the top of the device. These had been set to go off two decades hence, when it was time for the clock-maker to cease turning the minute hand. Without their aid, he would never know the correct moment to stop.

Realising he had been betrayed, but helpless to do much about it, a seething Mortice d'Arthur kept doggedly at his task. The assistant never did return, and the decades ticked by excruciatingly slowly. Eventually, just before the turn of the century, bailiffs forced entry into his home and seized his few remaining possessions: he had not paid the rent for a conventional lifetime. His goods, including the clock, were distributed throughout Europe. The bailiffs treated the grandfather so roughly that the pendulum inside – also a part of the clock-maker's anatomy, we shall refrain from saying which – broke free of its bearings. Unregulated, the timepiece now took its essential rhythms from the silent curses muttered by the creature smouldering in its stomach.

One day, Mortice vowed, he would be free again: he would reward his liberator extensively. The exact nature of this intended munificence was not stated, save in somewhat ambiguous terms. There was an abrupt ending to Pastor Rowland's speculations on the issue.

This was the tale read by Mr Humphrey in the book of poems. And the moral? Doubtless that it is foolish to hoodwink time. The dilettante did not disagree with this diagnosis, but desired the promised rewards. Thus he was determined to be the one who liberated Mortice d'Arthur. Once the secret lock was found, his life would improve.

Humphrey struggled with the clock for the best part of the day. The lock was hidden very cunningly; at any rate, it evaded his fingers. With reluctance, he took a break for dinner. As he ate, he thought the device gave another chuckle and repeated its earlier plea: "Let me out, sir!" A sudden sob seemed to rack the frame. "Let me out!" The dilettante turned to it and cried that he did not know how.

He was on the point of leaving the table when he recalled that Herr Fluchen had given him a cake. Removing it from his pocket, he studied it carefully. It was very delicate – an aerated strudel. Why had the trader insisted he weigh it before popping it into his mouth? He shrugged and carried it over to a pair of scales which rested on top of a pipe organ in a far corner of the room. The scales were presently comparing scores by Bach and Handel. As the sheets of sacred music rocked back and forth, a whine issued from the measuring instrument. Though a secular soul, the dilettante listened to the occasional mass.

Sweeping the scores aside and adjusting a set of counterweights, Mr Humphrey was astonished to discern that, in metric terms, the cake had a weight no greater than a single gram. "Herr Fluchen's spouse, Anna, must be a wondrous cook," he mused. And then inspiration struck. "Heavens! It is a clue! The chap knows how to open the timepiece. He gave me a pastry solution. Anna and a gram! Anagram!"

With this insight, the dilettante rushed back to the clock. Now the words on the tarnished face seemed to glow with an inner light. Studying them more closely, he realised that some of the letters could be used to spell a different sentence. 'Mortice d'Arthur, Chaud-Mellé' might now be seen as concealing a more direct exhortation: 'Let me out'! This was the sort of trick to be expected of foreigners.

Pressing the letters in this order, Humphrey was gratified, after a moment's pause, to hear a click. Reaching down to open the suddenly ajar door, he happened to catch sight of Herr Fluchen at the window. Desirous of keeping the promised reward all to himself, but aware that the trader had given him the method of opening the grandfather, he dithered; he let his arms drop and grimaced. This was possibly the last facial expression he made to be witnessed by a fellow human being.

The antique dealer does not like to talk about what he saw. Had the dilettante looked more closely at the book he bought, he would have seen that mice had been at this too. Well, not mice exactly, but a rodent not a jot less voracious – I mean Herr Fluchen himself, who had cut out some pages which rightly concluded the story. These pages told how Mortice in his prison soon grew very bitter. His initial promise, to reward whoever set him free, underwent a transformation: he vowed instead to submit his liberator to the same treatment he had suffered. Hardly fair on the poor innocent who released him, but like all long term captives, his judgment had been adversely affected. This phenomenon, which is a form of revenge by proxy, is termed Bottled Djinn Syndrome.

What I have been able to get out of the proprietor – which is quite a lot, as he is me – is tinged with awe and horror. The clock flew open: the thing which had occupied it for three centuries snatched Mr Humphrey in its bony arms and bundled him inside. Whether he arranged our hero in a particular way, attaching his limbs to internal gears and levers, I do not know. It is certain, however, that as soon as the desiccated monster slammed shut the door, the clock began working again. It all happened so quickly that Herr Fluchen was unable to take in all the details. He fled back to his shop in Abell, fixing himself a glass of antique absinthe. A few loose ends need to be tied up, and we shall do this while the trader is busy drinking himself into a stupor.

Although he planned everything from the beginning, he was not fully prepared for the sight of the being which leapt out of the clock. He had expected Mortice d'Arthur to resemble the woodcut on one of the pages he had removed from his book. In fact, the clock-maker was altered in a way which suggested he had been subject to more than simple ageing. This can be confirmed by remembering that Mortice, during his imprisonment in the timepiece, was actually ageing backwards.

It appears he grew younger and younger, waiting for

his treacherous assistant to return. Eventually, he regressed beyond his own birth into a prior life. The process was repeated a number of times: we may surmise that the monster which assaulted Humphrey was a character who originally lived three centuries before d'Arthur. Research reveals that Chaud-Mellé was enduring an especially nasty plague at that time. This might account for the suppurating boils and lesions...

When Mortice d'Arthur's possessions were looted by bailiffs, it was Herr Fluchen's ancestors, also in the curio business, who benefited. The clock, the one item they did not manage to sell, was handed through the generations to the present antique shop owner, who, aware of the legend, gave it to the previous inhabitant of Mr Humphrey's house. This occupant was enamoured of antiques but did not, as the proprietor hoped, care to open the grandfather. For his own nefarious reasons, Herr Fluchen needed d'Arthur released, but not by his own hand.

Arriving on the scene, Humphrey presented a perfect opportunity for the unscrupulous trader. Herr Fluchen was also an antiques licker, but a clandestine one: he instantly recognised a kindred spirit. Learning that the dilettante was about to buy the recently vacated house, he forced an entry and doctored the clock. He drilled a hole into the dial and packed an ounce of caesium into the space. Then, to disguise the flavour of the alkaline element, he varnished the grandfather with a tincture made from iron pipes, splashed puddles, soot, roots, bicycle gears, cheese, apples and various other ingredients. He knew that, one day, Mr Humphrey would lick the timepiece: this would detonate the caesium, which explodes when in contact with moisture, and the mechanism would break. The dilettante would then contact the jeweller in Quinn who, unable to repair it, would draw attention to the words on the faceplate. Herr Fluchen gambled that these names would lead Humphrey to his store.

I have told you the rest. The plan worked perfectly.

After watching the remarkable emergence of the clock's prisoner, the proprietor needed absinthe not simply to provide a blanket over fear but as a celebratory adjunct. To be fair, he also raised a glass in the dilettante's memory. We will pre-empt sentimental eulogy by stating that a fool once inherited a grandfather; and the grandfather returned the gesture. Mr Humphrey and his clock's inheritance are one and the same thing.

The tale does not end here, though it is nearly finished. The thing which leapt out of the clock was ravenous after such long confinement. I imagine it roamed the house searching for food. It probably swallowed my wife's cake in a single bite – but I am certain it was impressed by such a delicate savour. Later, when it had eaten its fill, it settled down to stealing the dilettante's identity. Dressed in his spare clothes, it had little difficulty in passing itself off as him. The sideburns took three weeks to grow, the stomach another to bloat. Because Humphrey was a rare visitor to the villages, few noticed the difference. To my delight, this new dilettante had a genuine interest in antiques – possibly because to it they were examples of contemporary design.

One morning, the impostor was passing my store. My wife was baking cakes at the time: the fumes were vented onto the street. The temptation was too great for the creature: it stepped over my threshold. Without a moment's delay, I snatched my hat and coat and rushed past it, through the door. I did not look back. I felt sorry for Anna, naturally enough, but one does not get the chance to cheat the devil twice every century. To put the record straight, I have to say that it was not a Gainsborough but a Turner. Rumours are often poor on detail.

Yes, reader, the monster was my thousandth customer. Compelled to take my place, it is furious at being caught a second time. My sympathy is limited: I moved into the Gothic manse and searched for the document vital to my happiness. I quickly found it. Humphrey had penned his Will on the flyleaf of the *Ingolstadt Legends*. True to his word, it named me as sole inheritor of his property. This is what I meant when I quoted the price of the volume as a "good deed." The best deeds are those which concern houses. Now sit down and permit me to pour you a glass of wine. Perhaps I can offer a pinch of Regency snuff?

Well if you are reluctant to partake, that is your loss. But allow me to demonstrate the elegant way of inhaling tobacco dust. Left nostril first; then the right. Observe the angle of the sneeze. Note its power! Pardon me, I did not realise you were wearing a wig. I assumed readers had their own hair. Now there is a knocking on my window! Who can it be? Excuse me for a moment; I will be right back. There is a peculiar fellow outside: he is peering through the glass. A practical joker, I suspect. He is wearing a mitre and carrying a crook...

AFTERWORD: The above text was found scratched in sand on a beach between the hamlets of Abell and Quinn. Anyone who doubts the content need only contact the local jeweller, who will confirm the main points. The manse, however, may no longer be visited. According to legend, it was a cursed abode condemned to stand until a certain number of owners had lived in it: when that number was reached, it would vanish, taking the very last dweller with it. It is true that sightings have been made of a spectral Gothic structure, housing a bishop-like figure, in various parts of the world, but these cannot be confirmed. The site of the manse is presently occupied by a holiday cottage with a rose garden. All enquiries must be directed to the landlord, Pastor Rowlands.

THERE
WAS A
GHOUL
DWELT BY A
MOSQUE

This is the story about ungodly deeds which Vathek, the mad caliph in Beckford's novel, was hearing from one of the new arrivals in Hell, when his mother flew in on the back of an afrit to chide him for not enjoying the pleasures on offer. The tale is not given; Vathek's acquaintance was damned soon after without having a chance of resuming it. Now what was it going to have been? Beckford knew, no doubt, but I am not bold enough to say that I do. I will offer a new story: one you will think made from scraps of other fables. Everybody should sew a patchwork coat from the materials he likes best. This is mine:

There was a ghoul dwelt by a mosque. His name was Omar and he was a potter with a shop built from broken vases. His doorway looked out on the Kizilirmak, the longest river in Asia Minor, and from his roof he could lean over and touch the mosque with his elongated arms. His wheel and oven had belonged to a human craftsman who died without heirs and was buried with his tools, but (this was in Haroun al Raschid's day) ghouls were allowed to keep any items they dug up. The creature filed his teeth to stubs to reassure his neighbours – but never mind what they thought of him; he was skilled enough at his trade to make a living from the travellers who passed through Avanos. He rarely overcharged for his products and this frightened people most of all.

Omar lacked humanity in other ways: he kept an attic full of hair clipped from the heads of his female visitors. There were women pilgrims and merchants even then and they were politely requested to give up a lock or two for his archive. The monster labelled them and secured them to the ceiling on hooks, where they exuded a musty odour and shivered in the shifting air currents. Omar liked to imagine his attic was a cave beneath a garden – a garden of vegetable girls whose roots were pushing through into his subterranean kingdom. This unusual custom has persisted through the centuries; next time you are in Avanos, ask for the house of Master Galip and you will see what I mean. His modern collection is also illuminated by a single lamp.

The ghoul had a mother no less grotesque in her habits. She helped him collect the red clay from the riverbank, bringing him a supply each morning. Instead of cutting the clay into blocks, she would roll it in her hands and present it to him like a freshly-exhumed intestine. Then he would divide it with a pair of shears and they would gather round the wheel with excited giggles, as if they were grilling sausages instead of preparing to throw another plate or saucer.

The attic was also the place where the ghoul kept all his rejects, the warped and flawed work. Heavy urns, twisted over like slaves; cups with no handles, or too many; pitchers with clamped mouths or leaking sides; shapeless mounds as tall as men which should have been coffins but were unusable, save for lepers; pipes with stems which curled back into the bowl; teapots without spouts, or spouts which poured tea into the lap of the drinker. All these, Omar packed into his attic, loathe to discard them. With the hair above and the failures below, the room became a sort of museum of imperfection – the former lacking complete substance; the latter lacking complete form.

One day, a cowled traveller called at the shop. Veiled from head to foot, she betrayed her femininity by her poise and sibilant voice. She had come far and was taking her first holiday in many years. Her sisters were keen on stone figures for their garden and she had promised to take some back as gifts. But sculptors were rare in Asia Minor, the prophet had forbidden such art, and so, to make the best of a bad thing, she had decided to purchase pottery as a substitute. She wondered if she might view Omar's most decorative examples.

"Well, my work is functional, not fine art," said the ghoul. "But you're free to look round. I'm self-trained and you mustn't expect too much in the way of aesthetic gratification."

"Come, these pots betray a certain flair," cried the visitor. "Lead me through your shop and I will choose something."

So he guided her along racks of ceramic utensils, which she studied with a slight wave, as if to indicate they were not quite suitable. When the conventional rooms were exhausted, they reached the attic. "The work in here is not really for sale," apologised Omar, "but if you will enter and allow me to snip a strand of your hair..."

The visitor seemed about to refuse, but the door was swinging open and when she caught a glimpse of the mutated wares she forgot to voice an objection. Stepping forward in joy, she squealed: "Perfect! They are so delightfully strange. And this one is the oddest of the lot! I must have it at any price!" And she moved to the end of the attic and seized the ghoul's mother, who was sleeping on a stool.

At this point, several things happened at once. The ghoul mistook his visitor's cry for compliance with his request, and he reached across the room with his elongated arms to sever a lock with his shears. But the mother had jumped up in alarm, knocking over and smashing the single lamp. In pitch darkness, Omar felt under his visitor's veil and detached it with clumsy fingers, whereupon he snipped the lock. While he groped his way to a hook to hang it up, his mother struck a flint in an attempt to relight the lamp; the attempt was unsuccessful, but the long spark which winked in the gloom was enough to illuminate the visitor, who was still bending over the mother. Then darkness came again, more intense for the momentary light: there was a groan, something brushed past the ghoul and clattered out through the shop.

When Omar's slitted eyes had adjusted, he saw he was alone in the attic. No: his mother was there as well, but she was changed. Her arms flung up as if to cover her face, her body twisted away as if from some dreadful apparition, she was literally petrified. She had always had a stony expression; now it was real. Omar looked at the ceiling and his hearts raced madly; in place of a lock of hair was a very angry snake, hissing and writhing on its hook.

Well, he gnashed his filed teeth for many a moon, I can assure you. Without a mother, a ghoul is lost, like a bridge without a river or a pot without a price. Luckily, he dwelt by a mosque and the local muezzin was a sorcerer who made no secret of his skills. Standing on his roof at night, just after the evening call to prayer, Omar hailed the muezzin on his minaret and made a pact. He would sell part of his soul, the human part, to Eblis – the devil – in exchange for the return of his mother. So the muezzin lowered a glass tablet inscribed with arcane symbols on a gold thread and told Omar to place it between his mother's granite lips, whereupon she would spring to life.

As he stumbled through the attic with this talisman, Omar happened to brush the snake, which bit him on the shoulder. He growled in pain and his great hands came together, crushing the glass tablet to powder. The sparkling shards flew up and settled on the warped and twisted pots. With a hideous scraping sound, they came alive – the urns, the pitchers, the cups, the coffins – tumbling awkwardly, snapping their lids, grating against each other, whistling, crowding round the ghoul like dogs round a master, or jackals round a corpse. With his fists and feet, he smashed them to pieces, then he went down and returned with the potter's wheel, which he rolled among the wounded ceramics, reducing them to fine dust. The one place the magic glass had missed was the mother, who remained as motionless and igneous as before.

Unable to bear the loss of his soul for naught, Omar left his shop disguised as a minor prince and went searching for his visitor. But he succeeded only in passing into the domain of Hell. By now, his fears had altered. He was more frightened that another sorcerer would manage to reanimate his mother: she would be furious at being kept so long in such a condition and would berate him. Better to be damned, he decided, than to suffer the ill-will of a ghoul's mother, who would be certain to bend him over her knee and smack......

At this juncture, Vathek's acquaintance slapped off his turban to reveal the horns of a ghoul. His forked tongue poked out over his filed teeth. Vathek fell back with a cry of pity and alarm, but recovered soon enough and, tapping his nose, asserted that he knew another mother quite three times as dreadful as that one, but lacked enough horrid words to describe her. Indeed, at that very moment she was trying to dethrone one of the pre-Adamite sultans. More tangibly, in Avanos there is a curious statue standing in the square, waiting for something, a backward glance from an earlier tourist, I do not know; but it is a fact that Gorgons no longer go to Asia Minor for their holidays.

THE PURPLE PASTOR

Of my trousers and my soul I have little to say. Poor fabric and logical positivism have divested me of the one, and argued me from the other. Am I ranting? Surely, for none of this is true. I'm still attached to both, though I know not where they are. Let me start my tale afresh! I cannot, for my soul, or my trousers, remember how, when or even precisely where, I first became acquainted with the Lady Myfanwy. Long ears have elapsed, and my donkey is feeble through much suffering. But this too is a lie! I met her in a decaying town on the River Wye called Monmouth, as you well know. Will the right words forever elude me? I'm in a daze, having eaten my own blueberry pie in the extremity of hunger. A poison now circulates in my blood, for the pie was stale. I'm sick unto death with that horrid filling, and for the wild, yet most homely jam which I'm about to vomit, I neither expect nor solicit a bucket.

There were three of us, heading south from Shropshire, following an unwound turban which had lately belonged to a yellow imp. Myfanwy and my verger took the lead; I trailed behind with bare legs. Our planet was no longer scalene, but it still wasn't round, and it was my fault, so I had the responsibility of tucking up the loose corner, which was flapping in space, to make a parcel, a world-pie containing the future. To be blunt, the task seemed beyond my talent, which is modest and clumsy, but lovely Myfanwy had faith. I could not resist her belief, though I shuddered and sweated at the enormity of the scheme. We passed into the Malvern Hills, and here the turban was snagged on crags and chewed by hermits, until we were obliged to navigate by the stars instead, glittering over the snow, ascending all the while, as if we determined to ask Orion for directions in person, or else to borrow his belt.

I chafed, thighs and tolerance, but protested not, partly because I was too far behind to be heard. The way appeared curiously strenuous. It is rare for Malvern peaks to tax the heel; often they have been hammered to gentle slopes by aeons of weather. The flora was unexpected also: the gorges were filled with Arolla Pine, which is native to the Carpathians. Before I could marvel overmuch at the incongruity, there was a commotion among some boulders, and dark shapes swooped from the shadows. The odour of garlic was extreme, the twang of crossbows untuned, and I surmised we had been ambushed by traditional banditti. By the time I reached Myfanwy and my verger, the skirmish was concluded. An old duelling pistol smoked in her dainty fist. She replaced it in a secret pocket and my admiration was tinged with horror. Such a violent and competent and tasty woman! No sulphur cloud might obscure that fact.

And such a feminine weapon, with a trigger like a batted eyelash of a mistress! They did not sell flintlocks in the markets of Monmouth, not since the days of Charles Rolls, inventor of the limousine, who required one to power his first prototype, so it was clear she had obtained it on her travels. Pressing her on the point, I learned she had bought it from a squonk in Pennsylvania, the western point of the world. She patted the bulge in her jacket and sighed. "I don't care to use it much, because it feels like murder." And when I kicked the leaking bandit at my feet, she added: "Murder of the pistol, I mean."

"You postulate that the firearm is animate?"

She nodded. "The squonk said something to that effect. No matter: I perceive the tethered mounts of our assailants. Let us borrow a horse or three before they return with reinforcements. Listen here, Gruffydd, you lack pants, so take this scrawny ass."

"It has flared nostrils. How unfashionable!"

But I didn't resist, pulling myself into the saddle and clinging to the greasy mane. The going was barely easier; we staggered up summits so lofty that an aurora borealis flickered in a nephelococcugic vale below, and inched along ledges littered with crossbow bolts. Instead of passing into the

346

lowlands which border the Severn estuary, we entered a range of yet taller peaks with cognac-hued sides. Any pretence we were traversing the Malverns was now impossible, and indeed it was my verger who claimed these as the Orchat Mountains, best seen in the season of Opora, when an aerial armada of phoenix alight on branches and burn the stalks off ripe fruits, which drop into the laps of itinerants, but he was unable to say exactly where in the calendar of the year this enigmatic season resided, beyond resorting to some drivel that it was generally between the rising of Sirius and the bedtime of Arcturus.

"Definitely the Orchats," he avowed, "and those others up ahead are the heights of Kunlun Shan. Beyond them, the Hindu Kush, the Julian Alps and what are probably the Kaatskills."

"The Kaatskills?" I objected. "Ridiculous!"

"By no means. Whoever has made a voyage up the Hudson must remember them. They are a dismembered branch of the great Appalachian family, and like to lord it over the surrounding country. A good place for a game of ninepins; a very aged fellow told me."

Myfanwy, who had climbed them on her way to Pennsylvania, concurred with this analysis and wondered aloud:

"It appears that a number of separate ranges have gathered here for a crucial purpose. Do you think they're holding a parliament of peaks? A literal kind of international summit?"

My verger poked his tongue like an uneaten host and hissed: "Highly likely. The Himalayas are absent. I dare state these others have come to conspire against them. That famous range is still growing, and must be a focus of resentment for its eroded cousins. Something similar took place in 1883, when a volcano cartel plotted the assassination of Krakatoa. It was soon annihilated in an explosion."

"A natural catastrophe!" I cried.

He smirked. "No, they sent it a letter bomb."

Despite the grotesque implications of accepting this speculation as fact, I could sympathise with any geological formation, whether volcano, mountain or iceberg, which wanted a level playing field with its rivals. The Himalayas were indeed rising above their station, something never to be said about the Malverns, nor any Welsh peak, including Snowdon, which would shortly glower below its rusty signals, warped rails and tasteless cafe, forcing lazy passengers to walk down to the top. But perhaps I was muddling two meanings of the same word, a bad habit which I hear can now be kept in check in a Prague sanatorium. I had no funds to go there, and was sick, or sock, of walking to boot.

As we stumbled from one spectacular range to another, the rumble of distant avalanches forever in our ears, my donkey tripped and cast me to the frozen ground. The ribbon of the unwound turban fluttered around its hooves. We had found our way again. I was jubilant and started to relax, becoming more responsive to my environs. The mountains really were up to some icy intrigue, and I expressed awe at my verger's erudition. "How do you know so much about arcane topics?"

"I'm a perfect scholar, Gruffydd. I've read the whole of Papus Levi and Valentine Cheese, and most of Montague Winters, Raymond Lullabye and Friedrich Nightshirt. I collect wisdom, but not in my memory. I preserve old truths in balderdash vinegar."

"You? Impossible! A pickler?"

"A pickler," he replied.

"I have my doubts." I said. "A sign."

"It's this," he answered, producing a jar from beneath the folds of his vestments and uncorking it.

"You jest," I exclaimed, recoiling a few paces. "That is naught but a Klein Bottle, with a defective map of the world etched on its surface. But let's proceed to Monmouth."

He snorted softly and turned to Myfanwy. "As for Gruffydd, he can't tell a jar from a bottle!" There was no genuine spite in his tone, and I forgave his insolence. Perversely, I felt affection for him, even subtle reverence, as if I was the callow verger, and he my mentor. I approached him with a low bow locked in my spine.

"We've been working together for almost a year, but still your name is unknown to me. Will you reveal it?"

He waved a tolerant hand. "Why not? The vowels are a joy to project down the chasms. I am Douglas Delves."

Extreme bother seemed pickled in the echo.

To this day, I can't work out how so many massive mountains were able to cram themselves between Shropshire and Monmouth, without crushing either or both, unless they had lost weight in the slide over the continents to meet at that point. We eventually escaped the drama, reaching the rim of the last range, the Caucasus, merely to plunge down its foothills into a crisis. The noble town of Monmouth had changed beyond recognition: there was no horizon anywhere, and it was futile to look for one sideways. The town was now tiered triple, with Zipangu and Pennsylvania mounted above, great sweeps of world curving away from both, inverted oceans and people waving at us from the dizziness of those atmospheric antipodes. Consider a samosa or triangular napkin, with two sides folded into the middle but supported over it. Humanity and other monsters, plain or fable, were the filling, or if you prefer, the sneeze.

It was exhilarating to view lands previously familiar only in cheap atlases. Then it occurred to me that by aiming due west or east, I might reach a fold, cross it and be upside down too, returning in the opposite direction. Myfanwy's dream of a spherical planet had been implemented in such a way that a traveller was nearer his destination before he started his journey; a good reason for not going anywhere. Typically Welsh, that solution! While I frowned at this, and various imponderables, the vision of beauty herself gripped my arm and indicated we were searching for the tavern in whose cellars I had once lodged: my ovens played a part in her strategy. Accordingly, I urged my donkey to a forward totter, pleased to discharge this duty correctly without trousers or soul. On the outskirts of the tectonic stack, I noted that the upper tiers had been warped back to align them with Monmouth, the base.

Needless to say, the streets of my youth were shrouded in darkness, for the only access to the sky, and thus sun, moon, stars, came from the unfolded, northern edge, the direction which I considered mine. And what minimal light glowed from the phosphorescent sky-seas was blocked by the overhanging vegetation of the two continents, acting as exotic drapes. I felt that Monmouth had retired to bed and was too prim to show its naked shoulders to men of the cloth and women of the pie. I saw that creatures with the texture of wood were floating down from the middle tier on silk parachutes made from kimonos, or else employing grappling irons to climb back. These gnoles had inhabited every glade in all lands in the days of Slith, Nuth and the aforementioned Rolls. I didn't like the crafty looks they offered us as we passed through the foliage curtains into the false cavern that was once Agincourt Square.

The market was devoid of imps, for gnoles had taken over all wheels of commerce, except the actual waterwheel by Monnow bridge, which didn't rotate now, having been jammed by the cables which pulled in Zipangu and Pennsylvania. The poles of the stalls supported the first of these lands and they visibly bowed under the weight. Imps are wicked traders, as you have discovered to your cost, but gnoles are worse: they sell items that are no use to anyone. What purpose in buying a kettle with a spout which curls back into its own belly? Might as well order pottery from a ghoul! We ignored the banter and dismounted, groping toward the 'Green Dragon', my last place of abode. Dim lamps swung from external brackets, glinting on my verger's jar. The interior of the pub was illumined by clay pipes, furiously puffed by patrons so they might see their drinks. Ales frothed in the murk like subterranean lagoons.

We went down into the basement through the hole of a dull, dark and soundless trapdoor. I lit a flambeau (the leg of a stool) and studied my surroundings. My possessions were in disarray, but none had been stolen, possibly because they'd been deemed valueless. The oven was still in its customary place, and Myfanwy ran her fingers over the knobs of the lucky burner. She pursed her lips and whistled: "So this is the finest furnace in Gwent? And I am the best pie-artist! What a superb combination! We'll have Owain ap Iorwerth and Tangerine Pan out of your house in a lick!" I was grateful for her zeal, but troubled as to her real motives. Unlikely that affection for me formed any part of them. All the same, I was proud to announce the design of the oven as my own. Inspiration had come while dreaming of home, before returning to find it full of pastors. Long lost pudding times; superior to salad days!

"But all my recipes failed," I meekly appended.

"Because you are a fool," explained Myfanwy. "Don't worry: I'm here now. You allude to similarities between oven and house. That's precisely why I wish to gain entry to your residence. There are two upper chambers in this oven, connected by pipes to a third, lower compartment. Whatever is placed in these top chambers is combined into a pie down here. It's a system which can mix anything and lock it in a crust. Now, Gruffydd, how many rooms do you have in your house?"

"Two upstairs and one down, connected by laundry chutes. Grief! You intend to turn my house into an oven!"

"That's what it always potentially was. You weren't clever to build this machine at all: the house suggested it, and you were just a tool of its urge to have a child. You were a wife to your property, and a mother to this domestic appliance. Well then, let's employ the house itself for a kiln, and bake Wales into the future at the same time! I've calculated an easier way of folding the loose corner of the world over Monmouth. It relies on producing a gargantuan pie."

"You intend inviting Hyperborea to dessert?"

"In a manner of speaking. But first we must gain

entry to the house by expelling its present occupants. And to do that, we need this smaller oven. I'll bake a hundred pies and you must challenge Owain to a battle. His orange tang won't stand a chance against my blueberry bite. So fetch me flour and eggs and a dark-lantern!"

I shuddered. "How do you know he'll accept?"

"Because I'm the victor's prize!"

This was a dismaying prospect, and a cruel one, a form of emotional blackmail, for I was very reluctant to face Owain on the field, or lawn, of honour, yet refusal would diminish my already minuscule reputation in the eyes of my beloved. I've always hated violence, and even my training in the Church hasn't diluted my pacifism, though the hypocrisy is coming along nicely, but Myfanwy is a force equal to my principles. I wanted to impress her more than anything, and as she was already loading furniture into the oven, it seemed wiser not to complain. Also she was stirring us away on the errand with a wooden spoon. I comforted myself: whatever was lost in dignity, sentience and hygiene, if I went through with the duel, was certain to be replaced with piety.

I followed my verger back up the stairs into the tavern. We fumbled to the market and my resourceful comrade used his swift thumbs to pilfer the ordered ingredients. Gnoles rarely scabbard their savagery, but they remain ignorant of the pickpocket's art, and thus are relatively easy to distract and rob, unlike imps. When we returned to the 'Green Dragon', I was astounded to note it was earning the right to keep its name, glowing and belching. Myfanwy had stoked the oven with so many chairs and tables that considerable heat was being conducted up the walls to the roof. The windows melted and flowed into the gutters, where they cooled into grimy puddles. And the faces of the patrons left behind assumed a most intense brilliancy as raised drinks vaporised.

Back in the basement, we encountered what might have been a serving from Mrs Beeton's apocryphal inferno, a cake-tartarus, for sweet Myfanwy had immolated every local vestige of the earthly plane (my few remaining possessions) in her preparation. I'm too upset to describe events of the subsequent hour, so I'll briefly mention that flames surged and expired, the final ember completing the last pie. One hundred examples, not to be slyly chewed on the way to war. Then we waded through the remains of the tavern, which had entirely liquefied and was cascading over the cobbles, with the patrons still inside, but infinitely flat now, like reflections on ripples. Reaching my house, I called: "Come out and meet me, Owain ap Iorwerth! I cast down the oven glove!"

The curtains twitched and two faces appeared at the glass. "Priests are not welcome here. Same for pests."

"For the favours of Myfanwy!" I stammered.

The door opened and the hulking mass of Owain emerged. "Show her to me, Gruffydd, for I suspect trickery."

Verger and woman stepped forward, and I replied: "Behold second and jackpot. Select your finest pies, you rogue, and your longest spoon. The matter shall be resolved by conflict."

The rolling of his heavy eyes was audible in the gloom. "Very well. Pastries at dawn! I nominate my pet goat as my second. But what will you use for first light? There is no sun, prodigal or otherwise, to time our clash, and the rules of the duello are rigid on this point. Consult, for instance, the thirty seventh chapter of Hedelin's *Duelli Lex Scripta, et non; aliterque*, which develops the thesis of illumination at length. All the correct rituals must be observed."

Myfanwy had anticipated this difficulty, which is why she specified a dark-lantern. Now she undid it, cautiously, just so much that a single thin ray fell upon the scene, simulating a dreary dawn, and Owain nodded to himself and shouted to his familiar for a sack of pies. Tangerine Pan passed it to him without crossing the threshold, and it was apparent the creature planned to stay indoors, though how this might help Owain was a mystery whose solution was fated to be an occasion of much pain. I armed myself and took up the recommended position, with surplice unbuttoned to the navel and dashing stubble looping around my sensuous lips. Confident of prevailing, I was nevertheless scared of injury, or rather injury was scared of me, anxious to avoid becoming a guest in my corporeal form and having to lodge in an unrefined wound.

"Ten sniffs, stir and fire!" roared Myfanwy.

I bowled a pie in a perfect arc toward my enemy. The trajectory was precise, the velocity excessive, and I expected it to strike between his eyebrows and terminate the combat immediately. But something happened to the missile as it soared; it grew elongated and unstable, crumbling away before it reached him. I tried again; another failure. In desperation, I threw a dozen at once. Without exception, they changed shape and decayed in flight, raining down on the lawn in specks. Behind Owain, through the open door, I was vaguely aware of Tangerine Pan holding an object in his hairy hand: a pair of compasses or related mathematical instrument. Pies followed each other in quick succession, but I didn't score a hit. I was suddenly out of ammunition: my panic had caused me to discharge them too rapidly, and I sagged in bewilderment.

"What happened? Each circle became an oval!"

My verger clutched at my sleeve and whispered: "It's Tangerine Pan! He has recalculated the value of pie!"

Before I could declare Owain a cheat and the duel annulled, Myfanwy said: "Goats can do that. They're non-Euclidian."

Now my antagonist spoke up: "Stand still, Gruffydd. You've had your turn and I wish to offer a reply." He ignored my tears and unsheathed an enormous spoon. This he planted in the earth and drew back, like the arm of an onager. Then he loaded a pie in the concavity, sighted the device, released it and giggled. The crust exploded against my sternum, knocking me down. The smell of oranges was abominable; I stood to receive another in the face and my vision dimmed. A third scythed my legs away; a fourth numbed my pelvis. I attempted to slither out of range, but pies burst on my spine, temporarily disabling the vertebrae. Every inch of my body was pounded and pulped, coated with jam, riddled with pips, acid stinging my eyes and washing my ears, my appeals for mercy unpeeled, until I finally called out an unconditional surrender.

It was done. With a sigh, Myfanwy walked over to Owain and took his arm. "Where are you going?" I spluttered. She didn't look back, and they disappeared together into the house. The door slammed and bolts slid. It was clear she was keeping her promise; I had lost the duel and therefore my sweetheart. This mental agony overwhelmed the pain of my bruises, and unqualified misery bandaged my cuts with lugubrious lagging. I thus felt physically better; my verger hoisted me to my feet and patted my tousled hair. I wailed: "A brute has won her!"

"Not necessarily, Gruffydd. I have my jar."

He led me to the river and squatted on the bank. Then he held aloft the trousers he had carried from Shropshire, the pair I'd discarded when conducting business among nettles. They weren't mine; we were certain of that. Pompous in pocket, it was likely they belonged to Owain. My verger stuffed them into his bottle. "You are pickling them?" I queried. With a curt nod, he handed the product to me.

"When balderdash vinegar is added, the fashion in this garment will be preserved. Thus the trousers will never be unfashionable. Such a lure will prove far too powerful for the genuine owner, who will be desperate to be reunited with them. But if I aid you in this matter, you must also support me in my plots. I have my own reasons for turning your home into an oven. Do you agree to these terms?"

"I swear loyalty on the grave of my knees."

"Add some balderdash now. Place your lips to the neck and call down a measure of absolute humbug or tosh."

Clearing throat and dredging brain, I mumbled into the bottle: *The mental features discoursed of as the analytical, are, in themselves, but little susceptible of analysis.*"

My verger scowled. "That's not balderdash!"

I quailed at his tone and tried again: "*There are certain themes of which the interest is all-absorbing, but which are too entirely horrible for the purposes of legitimate fiction.*"

"No, no! That was grotesque and arabesque!"

My third attempt was a desperate lunge at nonsense: "*Herodotus, the old grey cat with a mouth full of stories, usually comes into my kitchen in the evenings.*" And I was overjoyed to see that this sentence met with my verger's approval. He replaced the cork and shook the jar. The ripped garment had settled quietly at the bottom, but now it fluffed up angrily as if exposed to an astringent tailor.

"Well done, Gruffydd. That was true bunkum."

To my further astonishment, he threw the bottle into the river. The current snatched it and hurried it south. Suddenly, the door of my house opened and two figures came running out, brushing us in their eagerness, plunging into the greasy waters after the pickled fashion. The trousers, it seemed, or seamed, belonged to Owain after all! But why had Tangerine Pan accompanied him in his submersion?

"He's the familiar," my verger pointed out.

"Have you lost your jar forever?"

"No, our fates are linked. I won the vessel from a coffee trader in a Chaud-Mellé casino. It must return."

We skipped into my house and I pawed the carpet. It felt different, more crumbly. Myfanwy had wasted no time. Borrowing Owain's ingredients, she had already rolled out the base of a monstrous pie. It extended over the whole of the single lower room, wall to wall, and I decided this was the most suitable occasion to press her for more details. Did she really believe she could invite Hyperborea to a feast? It appeared she did, but not quite in the way I'd imagined. She reminded me of the icy conditions to be endured in the region of the far north, and how the local denizens couldn't rest for a moment without freezing solid to their surroundings. They were trolls, of course, with asymmetrical horns and cloaks stitched from magnetism. A pale, pristine race.

"It's my thesis that many of them did try to rest and are now fused to glaciers," she explained. "Sleep is a requirement for all beings. The landscape has become an integral part of them. By summoning them here, I ensure they drag Hyperborea along as well. And when this third corner is folded over Monmouth, the Welsh planet will be round; our global outlook will match that of other countries. The world was once a different shape in every nation: one at a time, each adopted a spherical model. It makes progress less jolting in the trundle."

"But what sort of pie will attract trolls?"

"Only a Polar Pie! The chilliest pie ever conceived! Yes, Gruffydd, I shall bake one so cold that frost must wrap up warm before settling on it. And what elements will go into such a pudding? Think now: what's the saddest liquid in the cosmos? Squonk tears! And what are the most frigid organs? Gnole hearts! Combining them, we'll get frozen squonk grief! The bitterest substance ever synthesised."

I was mortified. "You plan to fill my house with squonks and gnoles and cook them alive? I'm not insured!"

My verger consulted his memory, a less reliable source of knowledge than his jar. "It's a fact that squonks dissolve into tears when bundled in a sack. We could easily fill one of the upstairs rooms with sobs. But gnoles are aggressive. I don't fancy attempting to catch one of those. I trust you'll deal with them yourself?"

Myfanwy gestured at the clock which graced my mantelpiece, the very gadget with which I'd tried to court half of her (I employed a carrot on her other half), and said: "By winding this device backward, I'll obtain a strange chord when it strikes the hour. Gruffydd is prone to confusing the meaning of similar words, and as the house is his husband, it should have picked up the habit. Thus when I take the clock to the target room, it will appear to issue an unusual cord. Gnoles adore string, especially stuff that's new or unique, and they'll run straight into the trap. I'll lock the door behind them; when the squonk tears are safely in the other room, we'll set the building on fire."

"An extremely dangerous recipe," I stuttered. "How do you expect us to climb to Pennsylvania to hunt squonks? We don't have grappling irons, and I certainly don't intend shimmying up the poles to Zipangu, and then up the pagodas. My ankles would rasp."

"I have a ladder, Gruffydd. When I obtained those three harpoons in the market, I also received a hatstand. Lean that against the top level. And take Owain's empty sack with you."

"A hatstand? That won't get us up very high!"

"You'd be surprised. It was designed for a hat the size of a house. The couple who dwelt in it were acquaintances of the Mad Hatter. He even invited them to his wedding ceremony."

"How utterly contrived! Where is the object?"

"In my own house. Take my keys and look in the cloakroom. But don't enter my boudoir or run your callused thumbs through my lingerie! Hasten now! Owain may be back at any moment!"

I deemed this unlikely, but I obeyed my love.

We were returning with a full bag of squonks when a clamour went up from the bottom tier: "Pirates! We're being attacked by pirates!" Gaining the lowest peg, or rung, of the hatstand, and bounding to the ground, we saw the truth of the situation. A schooner had moored against the waterwheel and bronze cannon gleamed in the dusk. My verger squinted and rubbed his chin, as if vaguely familiar with the ruffians who paraded the deck. The vessel itself was curious: it resembled a giant cauldron, with a suit of armour for figurehead and a winding sheet for sail, to say naught of the rudder, which was a sextant, or the flag, a Jolly Roger with real bones. A stocky man with lustrous curls balanced on the prow, teeth shining, an ornate blunderbuss cradled in one arm.

"He has the profile of the infamous Henry Morgan!"

I trembled. "The Welsh corsair? He should have died more than three hundred years ago! What does he want?"

"Why not ask him yourself? However, I suggest we first convey these squonks to Myfanwy. The sooner she completes her intrigue, the quicker I can begin on mine!" And with this brusque assertion, my verger continued to my home. I followed his example. The gnoles were already in place; we could hear them jabbering above the chiming of the clock. They had given up trying to break the door down and were now impaling themselves on the minute hand; a gesture of honour. We emptied our sack into the adjoining chamber, and I was appalled to note that the squonks had turned entirely into tears, forming a pool which palpitated rather than spilled over the boards. This door was also secured and we descended to the lawn, Myfanwy encouraging sparks from her flintlock.

"Is it really essential to ignite my abode?"

"It'll survive, Gruffydd. It's an oven, remember? Now move back and watch. Confection from conflagration!"

The violence of the blaze forced us to the river, where the pirates were haranguing, in a quaint language, all who neared the waterwheel. We stood on the Monnow bridge and peered down at the captain, who shook his fist, rattled a cutlass and exuded such a thick miasma of rum that hairs sprouted from his tongue and St Elmo's Fire withered them back again. He was an epitome of the romantic sickness, and I had an instant foreboding that his moustache and Myfanwy's bosom were converging in both space and time. Nor was there anything I could do to prevent this. I always try to greet my fate, to will what is, instead of what ought to be. But when it comes to fair maidens travelling in a direction opposite my arms, I find that stoicism, like a motor which runs on sauerkraut, or a clotted cream fresco, proves impossible to maintain.

Now the captain's voice became even gruffer:

"Where have ye hidden our gold, ye lubbers? Will we have to torture ye to learn the truth? Heat the tongs, 'Ceti! Sharpen the pins, 'Tology! Boil the oil, 'Vado! Out with the planks, 'Lin! Teach 'em to disturb our treasure. Map their kidneys, 'Phagia!"

The crew scurried about this business, not at all inconvenienced by such peculiar names. The captain puffed his cheeks and stamped his boots and swaddled his boasts in complaints:

"What a blasted crossing! Sailing up the Severn estuary, we saw the creation of a sea-monster. An orange goat was drowning in the waves when a giant fish gobbled it up. But not all o' it! Nay, for that goat lodged in the fish's throat, and they went swimming off together, a goat with a fishy tail. A triton! The fish was flat, like a skate; the goat was sick with the heavings. 'Twas a rum match."

I prodded my verger. "Did you hear that? Tangerine Pan has become a green ray! That is so typical of him."

He nodded. "Another transformation! Originally he was a tall fellow called Otho Vathek who dwelled in Chaud-Mellé, before the wizard Xelucha turned him into a blue dwarf. Then he was known as Cobalt Hugh, at least until a villain named Bartleby Cadiz converted him into a yellow imp. He came to Monmouth as Ochre Fingers and you baked him into an orange goat! I wonder what his new alias might be?"

"Verdigris Manta?" I cried. It corroded nicely on the ear, the same way the schooner rusted on the waters.

My verger spied a face pressed against a porthole. Not a pirate, or even human, but with a stowaway blink.

He blurted: "There's a goblin hiding below!"

The captain heard him and glanced up. "Well? What of it? We've just sailed from Giovanni Ciao's restaurant in Sardinia. Dozens of goblins in his kitchen. Bound to get one or two sneaking aboard. But we're not here to debate illegal passengers. We want our gold and gems! All our plunder from the Sack o' Panama. Buried here."

I decided to help. "There isn't a solitary Panama in our town, sir. But you can have this sack instead. Lubricated on the inside with squonk tears. Keeps regrets fresh for years."

The captain jumped and chortled. "'Tis Toby! I knew he wouldn't let us down! We've come for our trove, my fine young cannibal. Where have ye moved it? And where are thy trousers?"

It was Myfanwy's turn to speak up. "Gruffydd is no cannibal! He's a buffoon. You are in the wrong parish."

The captain growled. "Do ye mean to tell me this isn't Lladloh? But I won't be lulled by that simple trick. Here's the old stone bridge, and also a fellow ugly enough to be Toby."

"Go on, Gruffydd. Prove you don't eat folk."

I drew out my uneaten pie, the one I'd baked in a futile attempt to replicate Myfanwy's speciality. "See!"

"Sugar my timbers! This proves thy point. We must have turned right at the Isle o' Lundy. Cast away, lads! Back to the briny deeps. Cool thy tongs, 'Ceti. Thimble all pins, 'Tology. Leeks in the kettle, 'Vado, not bullets. No joints today, 'Lin. Weigh anchor, 'Phagia! What's that? Half a pound o' tuppenny rice? Lighter than expected. Plus a half o' treacle? That's enough, give or take a weasel."

As the anchor came up, my verger spotted his pickling jar caught on one of the barbs. He gyrated in joy and begged for its return, a request the pirates were wary of granting, in case the contents proved valuable. I grew worried at this sight. It meant that Owain, if he hadn't drowned, would be heading back to Monmouth to be reunited with his trousers. With outstretched cutlass, the captain rescued the bottle. "A message inside? 'Tis composed in obscure hieroglyphs."

While he struggled to decipher the breeches, my verger cried: "It's a map of Lladloh. Give me the jar and I'll tell you how to use it." This bargain was acceptable to the buccaneers and the captain swung the empty bottle onto the riverbank. "Iron out the creases and follow it from back to front. Beware the shallow pockets!"

Myfanwy leaned further to observe proceedings, and the stock of her pistol poked out from her jacket. The blunderbuss in the captain's grasp noticed this and suddenly jerked up and aimed itself at my beloved! With less hesitation than a squonk invited to tune a mandolin from a major to minor key, she responded by drawing and pointing her own firearm. It was clear the pirate was struggling to control his weapon, and this was also true for Myfanwy. Neither wished to pull the trigger! The guns wanted to start the duel themselves. I flinched.

"It's as if the blunderbuss and pistol hate one another! As if they crave to resolve an enduring dispute."

With a cynical shrug, my verger hissed: "Like the wife and mistress of the same man? None of our business, Gruffydd. Leave them to it. It is time to return to your house. The Polar Pie must be ready. Don't object! You promised to assist my plan if I removed Owain for you. I did so, and you must reciprocate. That is virtue."

Though my heart was reluctant to leave Myfanwy, my brain, which has respect for both gunpowder and pledges, told me to comply. I didn't look back as I trailed him first to the river to collect his jar, and then to my home, which was sooty but still intact. Winter aromas wafted over the lawn. The miracle inside was finished, but it was gargantuan: an iceberg colder than interstellar gulfs, nestled in a pastry stadium. Oh Myfanwy! What inhuman daring to conceive such a pie! No tramontane tart, whatever pedigree of superconductive brumes swirled around base or topping, might compare with this noctilucent nouriture. It was as unique and terrifying as its creator. A glittering ziggurat of crystal tears! But how could we extract it through the narrow doorway?

My verger pointed at a pair of hinges on the wall which had escaped my attention. And further along, he found

362

a lever disguised as a bracket for a hanging basket. He pulled it and the entire facade of the building swung open, exposing the upper rooms, and lower, which was bursting with pie. "Myfanwy was right! It's an authentic oven." Entering, and pressing his shoulder to the pastry, he puffed: "Far too heavy to move on my own. Go to the rear, Gruffydd, and heave. I'll chain your donkey to the front and in tandem we might escort it out!"

Behind the pie, I was granted a new clarity of vision. The mountain of ice acted as a lens. My nose and eyes were assailed with the two main effects of Myfanwy's genius: spicy odour and access to remote images. It was as if I smelled a telescope. Through the lamenting facets, I saw the distant river in detail, the bridge and waterwheel, the pirate ship with its brutish crew, the captain with his arm around my sweetheart. Wait! A cruel mirage surely? No, it was true: far from shooting each other, they had somehow become acquainted in the passionate way. Risking my verger's wrath, I dashed out and waved my arms.

"Return to me, Myfanwy! I'm your only beau."

"You jest!" she answered, thrusting a cigar between her teeth. Then I realised how neatly she fitted into this environment. Already her ripe bosom was straining at her bodice; daggers hung from her waist at jaunty angles, baroque gifts from her new paramour. Even her hair flowed in old curls, like blood, rum and smoke. Before the vessel turned a bend in the river and was lost to view, she pulled the pirate captain's cutlass from his own belt (an action which had too much of the sensuous about it) and threw it at me. It stuck in the mud next to my foot, and I like to think she was presenting me with a memento, a souvenir of what had gone (clock and carrot) and what may have come (blueberry stain), rather than trying to wound me. But I'm probably deluded.

I felt an arm on my shoulder. "Back to work, Gruffydd! The donkey's exhausted." Obeying, I wept. My tears splashed on the ice as I pushed at the dessert, fusing instantly to the crystals, maybe diluting the grief, for no human suffering, however acute, expressed in abrasive lachrymals, could parallel that of the average squonk. The strenuousness of the task helped to dampen my taut heartstrings.

When the pie was fully out, I asked my verger why he also needed to employ my house as an oven. His reply was dramatic. With a fluid motion, he removed his surplice, reversed it and drew it back on. Superficially, in terms of texture and design, this other side was identical to what he had previously sported. But the way it swirled about his thighs revealed the fact of the matter. I was stunned.

"You're a priest! Not a humble verger at all!"

"The Reverend Delves at your disservice. Yes, Gruffydd, I've fooled you for a year. It was necessary, of course, to implement my scheme. Two clergymen wandering the realm as equals would have excited comment. Your quest to find the pastors was also mine, but for different reasons. Tell me how many took over your home when you originally left for your corner of the scalene world? Seven? Well, I've got news for you. There was only one, a fellow known as Pastor Rowlands. He's ruler of the evil Church: a schism in orthodoxy and also himself."

"But he came with a clock sold in the market."

"That was when he still had a fragment of goodness in him. After he lived in your house and abandoned all ethics, the Seven Deadly Sins grew too wide for his body. He split into seven replicas, each devoted to one of the vices. He's a sort of gestalt decadent. When Tangerine Pan jumped out of your Trojan Pie, he thought the devil had come to claim him! That pushed him further into wickedness and he became a confirmed Satanist. A pastor, however, is too lowly to have much influence with the Arch-Fiend himself, which is what I require. So my plan is to cram all seven of his aspects into one chamber of the oven and fill the other with the concept *purple*. These I'll bake into a Bishop Pie: a potent functionary of Hades which I can enrol as an intermediary."

"You seek an audience with Lucifer? What for?"

"To petition him to relocate Hell. Listen now, Gruffydd, I know you feel nothing but awe for Myfanwy's venture to make the planet round. But there may be unfortunate consequences. When bad men die, their souls and trousers fall down, toward perdition. The direction of this movement has always been inward, through the surface of the Earth. If Hyperborea does fold itself over Monmouth, a rough sphere will result, but we will dwell in its concavity, rather than on its convexity. Hell will suddenly exist outward, which is the direction where good souls and trousers fly. Don't you appreciate the potential chaos? The moral order will be inverted and spirits and breeches will end up in the wrong place. Good will be jabbed with forks; sin serenaded with harps."

"What cosmic horror! You have my full support. How can we catch the seven pastors and the concept purple?"

"I now conclude Pastor Rowlands has scattered in sundry directions. No point looking for him: we'll wait until each separate piece converges here. As for the purple, it is already present in my jar. When you added your sentences, I pretended the initial two weren't balderdash. That was to ensure you recited three. It takes three measures of nonsense to make a purple passage. It's ready for use."

We stood his bottle in one of the upstairs rooms and retired to the lawn, to bathe in the double shade of Zipangu and Pennsylvania, and idle away the days until the pastors returned. The Polar Pie shielded us from the hemlock vapours which occasionally drifted down from the upper tier. What minimal light flickered from the north was amplified by the immense confection and focussed over the river, which seemed to be swelling from day to day. This borborygmic borealis didn't cheer me. I was so unnerved that when a delegation from afar arrived in Monmouth some weeks later, I hesitated to invite them into my house for coffee. An odd bunch in short trousers, dyed with tropical splashes. Also bare sternums, hair bleached blond, coral necklaces and surfboards.

I speculated they were from Bermuda or Guernsey. But my patois fell on empty ears. Then they corrected me:

"No, friend, we're Hyperboreans. Come to see the iceberg. Ah, there it is! So that's what cold means, eh?"

"You dress like that in the Arctic Circle?"

"Sure enough. Well, it's too hot up there for anything else. Do you assume the far north is a region of chills? It hasn't been like that for decades. Not with the global warming."

"I expected you to tug the landscape along behind. But I see you're not fused to anything. We were praying a variety of pastors would arrive before you, but if you haven't got Hyperborea, I guess it doesn't really matter. We won't create an outside Hell after all! But what's this about temperature? Is the Earth heating up?"

"Certainly is. It's all the cooking that's taking place everywhere. Can hardly walk a mile without finding somebody preparing a stew or pie. Spicy vapours congealing in the atmosphere! Trapping sunlight, they are, melting the glaciers. The example here is probably the very last iceberg in the whole world, which is why we came so far to see it. It also means your town will shortly be deluged by gigantic waves, but I gather you've already started evacuating civilians."

"News to me! What inspires that judgement?"

"We saw seven of them adrift in a boat shaped like a pot. The fools were still cooking as they sailed along! Purple pasta, I believe. Yes, a spaghetti and thistle dish. The leader introduced us to his wife. Called her La Santa Roja; a feisty woman with slack pantaloons. Heading for the highlands of Lladloh. A prudent move."

I was too depressed to smite my chest. "Purple pasta? His wife? Two more glacé nails in my pastry coffin!"

My verger interjected at this point: "I don't believe the planet is doomed to drown! What proof is there?"

The Hyperboreans smirked. "Go to France and see

for yourself. Waves struck Paris last week, stranding the Phantom of the Opera on a rooftop. Also Quasimodo, but he's resourceful."

I could hardly doubt any of this. It was as if the world was crying for my shattered heart and broken tongue. I stood and saddled my donkey, oblivious to my verger's protestation.

"Off to Lladloh," I muttered. "My destiny."

"Don't be silly, Gruffydd! You don't know where it is. Don't listen to what these hoary hippies tell you!"

"The barman in Shropshire will give me directions. He owned the pub there. Farewell, Douglas Delves! You were a charming fake. I hope you'll be very happy with your pickling jar."

"I'll conserve your hide, you slimy scamp!"

Out of Monmouth I rode. Back toward the Caucasus and the Kaatskills and the other misplaced ranges. Always up: on the lookout for the yellow turban which would guide me over the passes. I found it snagged on Mount Ararat, together with a dove, raven and pelican. But even here my vision was obstructed by summits equally lofty. The ribbon of the turban didn't follow the contours of the land, but slanted into the sky. Strumming the taut fabric, I produced a celestial note. As the hours passed, the angle of the slant increased. Soon the ribbon was useless to me, spearing into the clouds which boiled over the Julian Alps, a place I had no desire to visit. I rejected it and weaved without bearings into the Sierra Morena, where bulls and gallows parted for me.

It was only when I gained the apex of the highest peak in the Hindu Kush that I had my first proper view of the horizon. Rather, what should have been my view. The mountains staggered down to the rolling plains of Shropshire; these plains undulated not gently onward but upward. My eyes followed the gentle incline: the vast tract of land was approaching in a wave, growing steeper all the while. At the same time, a shadow hastened toward me, blotting out

Shropshire before the county itself was snatched up. The crest of the tectonic wave was almost directly overhead. The sun vanished. But in the last glimmer of solar radiation, I saw the ultimate beaches of Hyperborea curving high, leading the assault. White sands and deckchairs and not so good vibrations.

The remaining corner of the world was folding itself over Monmouth. But there were no harpoons or trolls to reel it in! Then I realised what had happened: the conference of mountains had started a trend. Geography of every sort now felt an impetus to gather and chatter. Forcing Zipangu and Pennsylvania together had tricked Hyperborea into thinking a meeting was taking place in Wales to which it hadn't been invited. It was coming to discover what the other two corners were saying about it. Dismounting and lowering my ear to the ground, I grimaced. The expected deluge would completely fill up the inside of a round world, drowning all within. The fashioning of a submarine was a priority. I had to bake one immediately, but I lacked oven and all ingredients.

Nothing for it but to extract the filling from my mutant pie! There was a chance I might curl up small enough to replace the jam. If so, the marvels of a saturated planet awaited, the freedom to explore the wrecks of our culture, aquatic cities and markets. If not, my soul and trousers would soon be falling outward, to Hell. If Myfanwy wore the latter, this should leave her legs exposed. Better hurry to Lladloh to see! But there was a third possibility, the one I considered most likely: the pie might be large enough to contain my frame, but eating the filling would poison me fatally. Then I would possess a sarcophagus instead of a submersible; the coffin I previously referred to. Ashes to ashes, crust to crust. And spread a napkin. *In pastry requiescat!*

THE HUSH
OF FALLING HOUSES

The sacred relics of Lladloh are stored behind the bar in the village's nameless tavern. They include the ear of a monstrous rabbit, broad as a rudder, which, together with the rest of the beast, belonged to the very last druid, Barrington Burke; a volume of poems penned by legendary bard Dennistoun Homunculus; the stopper of the pickle jar wielded by Reverend Douglas Delves; a flintlock pistol left behind by a highwayman with bad teeth who fought the pagan god Beer'or and broke his hold on the region. This service earned the fellow extensive dental work from grateful local folksingers, but only in their lyrics.

Despite the gravitas associated with each of these items, the most valuable of our ornaments remains the bottomless glass of Guinness cut from a fossilised demon's tear by Yeats O'Casey, the Dublin rakehell who exhibited his treasure throughout the dives of Europe to general acclaim and specific envy. The subsequent adventures of this object can be found coded in my new recipe, a hotpot which cleverly utilises veins of stout to instruct the epicure. Of all our holy artefacts, the bottomless glass is the only one which attracts pilgrims.

As the self-appointed antiquarian of the town, I see my mission to research our heritage as one of immediate concern to my neighbours. I am not paid for my pains, which are unofficial; perhaps in response to this affront, I am forever seeking to combine my studies with my day job. Any customer who ventures inside my restaurant is sure to leave with as much appreciation of the past as of pâté de foie gras. I can bake lectures on archaeology into casseroles or arrange noodles into family trees. I feed the belly with the stock of centuries. My secret motto is: "An aeon with every course." My name is Giovanni Ciao.

When the last diner departs the establishment, I hurry to the shore and sit on the edge of the pier, fishing in the gelid waters with a net. Heirlooms sometimes come my way, broken clocks and the like. I am hoping for one revelatory catch, a relic to rival O'Casey's glass. When I have it, my hobby will finally be taken seriously – I'll exchange cleaver and pancake for spectacles and lumbago. I am not the only villager to pursue a nobler calling. Since the construction of the real harbour, we have all harboured romantic yearnings, as if the stone quay has turned the locks of a collective repression. Only Olaf Smorgasbord, the innkeeper, is satisfied. The nameless tavern is a focal point of the community and its supervision requires fanatical devotion.

The chilly sea is not generous with its gifts; it can be likened to a sister. Drowned dogs form the bulk of my haul. These are passed to the local anatomist, Medardo, who dreams of dancing ballet. Flaying them, he varnishes the bones with a lacquer of his own devising. So many dogs are washed onto our shore that we have a surfeit of bones. These are used in place of timber for building purposes: the pier consists entirely of the femurs of chows. The more we hook, the further the pier extends. Soon it will reach the place where the animals originate.

Lladloh was not always a seaside resort. In the distant past, when much of the ocean was locked away in polar ice caps, it stood quite far inland. I am acutely aware, when I dangle my legs over the side and gaze south, how many civilisations lie below, visited only by the denizens of the deep. The names of these cultures still sound impossibly exotic when spoken aloud – Swansea, Tenby, Llanelli. What were they really like? I envisage shining towers of crystal; philosophers in togas; gardens full of musicians rehearsing unearthly melodies. A far cry from Lladloh, the malodorous, squat reality of my existence...

The evening I caught the astrolabe was no more remarkable than any other. I dismissed my final customer with subtle hints and a brandished ladle, rushed to the pier and dipped my weave. The air was warm; I soon netted a dachshund and then, to my considerable surprise, a small book. Gratified, I studied it more closely. It turned out to be a summary of the rules of a forgotten game, played by the ancients; though sodden, I slipped it into my jacket pocket and resumed fishing. I did not think I would be lucky enough to trump this find. But I persevered, sweeping my net into the reflected moon and gasping when a rusty fragment of the orb detached itself from the greater mass.

After vigorous polishing with my cuff, this shard began to glitter. A brassy ring seduced my thumb; I dangled the object before white stars, its intended lovers. I was unfamiliar with the workings of astronomical devices; no texts on the topic had survived the deluge. But I recognised it for what it was: the numerals embossed on both sides proclaimed its purpose – the calculation of the precise position of the planets among the constellations. At once I realised its immense worth to the village. A method of casting truly accurate horoscopes had been offered to us. I spent the remainder of the night determining angles of incidence between the visible members of the solar system.

When morning came, my experiments ceased and I rose stiffly from my vantage, shouldering my net and walking up the cobbled lanes to my home. I passed Lladloh's outermost structure, Cobweb Cottage, the abode of my beloved, which, in a permanent state of topple, mulishly defied gravity. The houses of Lladloh stand all alone; we are provincial snobs. Before I reached my own aloof dwelling, I was buttonholed by Padgett Weggs, the postman. "Aren't you the cheerful one?"

"Quite so," I replied. "I have discovered something of great import to the community. A pre-flood artefact."

"You and your past! Won't do you any good, mun. Give it over before it turns you daft. Seen it before. Neurotic obsession is what I call it. Bad for the brain. Gwallgofrwydd!"

I smiled indulgently. Weggs, though uneducated, had aspirations to become our first qualified therapist. As such, he sorted the problems of the inhabitants like mail –

some were lost in the system. His speciality was post-natal depression, second class.

"This is something special," I cried. "It might prevent our village being destroyed again. Or at least give us some warning of any impending disasters. It is a defensive tool."

"Ffolineb! Can't avoid the judgment of destiny. When our time's up, we ought to go quietly. Mustn't fight fate, boyo. Delusions of grandeur, that is. Like what they had in Cardiff."

I sighed. Popular legend still traced the source of the deluge back to that mythical metropolis, whose scheme to build a barrage all the way to the horizon had reputedly angered the sea god. Rather than argue over a superstition, I bade Weggs farewell, took the key from a chain around my neck and opened my restaurant. Right at the back, in the kitchen, my bed awaited. The nameless tavern, final destination of my catch, did not admit patrons until noon; despite my excitement, I was too exhausted to remain upright that long. I slept in my clothes, the waterlogged book in my hand, the astrolabe under my pillow.

My dreams were ungainly affairs. I was preparing meals from stars, grating planets into stews and garnishing them with comets' tails. When I woke, in response to the village clock's dozen groans, I made a quick breakfast of *bara lawr* and hurried to Lladloh's central square. Already the new Reverend Delves was blessing the tavern, censer swinging before him. As the repository of sacred relics, as well as of divine beer, the tavern exerts more of a hold on him than the chapel.

I entered in his wake and we converged at the bar. Olaf, armed with the traditional grimy cloth, was dirtying clean glasses. Delves squinted at me and clutched his stomach. "I think the meal you gave me last night was off. I've got these terrible cramps."

I blushed. The Reverend had been an early

customer and I had tried out a prototype dish on him: a bean salad, lightly draped with a garlic and mint dressing, incorporating a meaty dissertation on the history of community taxes during the rule of Silas Surcharge, the Grasping Mayor. Obviously, I undercooked the conclusion.

"How else do you feel?" I ventured.

"Adept in the setting of tithes," Delves groaned. He shook his head and ordered a glass of porter. Olaf gestured expansively with his giant hands and adjusted his horned helmet.

"Porter? Wouldn't ye rather mead?"

"No thank you," said the Reverend. Emboldened by his determination to choose his own drink, I followed his example. Olaf chewed his russet moustache and glowered at me. Both his lips trembled, but at different frequencies and for different reasons – the upper in berserker joy, the lower in Nordic dismay. This display encouraged me to retreat a pace. The porter seemed to hold its breath.

Later, I tried to persuade Delves that a single rotten pimento was responsible for his condition.

He shrugged. "I don't know. It's a bit disillusioning. The original Giovanni Ciao wouldn't have poisoned his guests. Not in an obvious way. He basted his toxins with style."

We sipped our mead in silence. Before we finish our glasses, I'll explain the references to my namesake.

In its dense history, Lladloh has been annihilated many times. To be pedantic, when this story begins, these cataclysms number 665. After each destruction, survivors – of which there are always some – rebuild and repopulate the village. I won't detail events individually, save to reveal that on one occasion only Reverend Delves escaped death. Climbing Mount Yandro at the time, the highest peak in the area, he turned for an inspiring vista, just as Lladloh and its burghers were dismissed from a world which had never worn them comfortably.

Alone, he was constrained to invite immigrants to

reseed the homes; he advertised far and wide for settlers. One of those who responded was my paradigm, the first Giovanni Ciao, fresh from Sardinia. In the next levelling of the village, he played a courageous role, risking his own life to assist the wounded. This was the problem: with so many disasters and so much opportunity for brave deeds, our folklore became saturated with heroes. So that none might be dishonoured, due to limitations of memory and time, a system evolved whereby each new child was given the name of a predecessor. If they were called upon to perform beyond the bounds of duty, they wouldn't add to the lengthy roster of champions. Thus was Remembrance Day trimmed.

To ease administration between generations, each child also had to follow the profession of its original model. For myself, this meant the saucepan and oven; for our Delves, the cant of the Church. This rule is especially hard on my beloved, Elizabeth Morgan, who despite a terror of brooms has to adopt the persona of a witch. Others suffer: Iolo Machen, fated to be a shepherd in disregard of his preference for nylon; Caradoc Weasel, compelled to be an explorer in an overmapped region; D.F. Lewis, by inclination a barber, obliged to compose short stories by the gross. This explains our lusting after alternative careers.

Recovering my composure, I met the Reverend's gaze and took out my prize. It span in the pale light of the tavern's interior like a button from Odin's favourite shirt. "Forget your ailments for a moment. Look at this and tell me what you think."

He fingered the astrolabe. "A relic to rival Catrin Mucus' cucumber flute! A fine addition to our hoard." He made a pyramid with his fingers and held it over one eye – the holiest sign.

"Consider its applications!" I said. "We can draw a nativity chart for Lladloh itself! With the details this will provide, we'll be able to reckon the date of the next catastrophe."

"To cast a village's horoscope, planetary positions are not enough. The destiny of urban conglomerations is also determined by the orbits of those planets' moons. These are too faint to be discerned with the naked eye; and Lladloh is devoid of telescopes."

I grinned. "You forget my culinary genius. One of my triumphs is a concentrated carrot sauce, reduced slowly over a firefly. Overindulgence of this delicacy has endowed me with superlunary eyesight. I am capable of making the necessary observations."

"To what end? Predicting the apocalypse won't prevent it. The cycle of demolition and rebuilding is endless; we might as well be phantoms trying to stall a carousel. That's the chance we stand of breaking the loop – ghost of a one."

This odd metaphor lodged in my brain; I frowned and angled my jaw at the smoky windows. "Do you really want to erect new nonsense? Better to keep the old. For one thing, I'm not handy with a pick or shovel. My trousers hug my buttocks."

Delves nodded. Like myself, he did not relish the prospect of hard manual labour: the setting up of scaffolding, the endless cups of sweet tea, the tobacco and innuendo breaks. Through the tavern window, it was difficult to see anything, but I kept my gaze symbolically fixed on the filthy glass. Beyond, Lladloh festered in its own juices; the buildings spiralled from the tavern as if they were spiritually draining into it, like coffee down a plughole. This vortex pattern was not an indigenous layout; our ancestors would not recognise the village. Each time it was created, it was assembled slightly differently. Only the tavern, hub of our cosmos, remained unchanged, enjoying exactly the same location and dimensions over the turbulent centuries.

We continued to discuss the immutability of this singular boozer. I was so engrossed in my erudition, I hardly noticed when the doors swung open to admit another drinker.

"What's this?" the newcomer removed his tall hat. I

recognised the whiskers of Kingdom Noisette, resident engineer and the bushy genius behind our most absurd civil projects. These included the underground railway between the tavern and the pharmacy. Before you think me harsh, let me make a statement: Lladloh has no trains.

The Reverend and I fell silent, knowing the hazards of passing the germ of a pristine engineering scheme to this fellow. He would incubate it into another expensive folly. But our prudence was undermined by the innkeeper, who bellowed: "Preparing for the next Ragnarok they are! Got a gadget to tell 'em when it's due."

Kingdom Noisette rubbed his hands. "O aye." As a bleak northerner, he has much in common with Olaf. He removed a pen from a bandolier around his chest and started scribbling on a peeled beer-mat. Already bridges and tunnels were emerging from his fevered doodling, like a length of spaghetti which forms a momentary meaningful phrase as it rises out of the deeps of a bubbling pot. When he finished, he studied the beer-mat critically and ordered a pint of brown ale.

Olaf obligingly drew him a tankard of mead.

"Time to think about preventative measures?" the engineer ventured, with a laboured wink. "When's it to be? Don't be coy, laddie. I'm ready to meet a challenge. How long have we got? Couple o' years? Won't catch me by surprise. I know how it'll happen."

"Really?" I was intrigued, despite my scepticism.

"Of course." He inverted an ashtray and prodded the burnt matches and cigar stubs with his finger. "Pretend this is Lladloh," he said, as he arranged the debris into a fair analogue of the village. "Here's the solution!" With a splutter, as if his mouth was crammed with mushy peas, he emptied his glass over the counter. The liquid swept away the model, propelling it over the side into Olaf's lap. "We're all going to drown!" Slamming his fist into the diminishing lake, he lapsed into a peculiar dialect. His whiskers bristled fearsomely.

I moaned. The style of his arguments, his oratorical

vehemence, was partly my fault. I once fried him a tasty cashew paella, containing some notes on the philosophy of two classical political figures, William Pitt and John Stuart Mill. By a process of osmosis, he absorbed and refined a technique of harangue which I liked to term 'Pitt and Mill'. Since then, I only prepared Yorkshire Pudding for him.

"That's it, laddies!" he bawled. "The sea level hasn't stopped its relentless rise. Pulling itself up by its bootstraps, it is! Lladloh has a watery grave awaiting! I saw it, you know. I watched the block o' ice sail past. Like a lump o' white coal!"

The Reverend and I exchanged glances. In addition to the old myths which plagued Lladloh like toads, new legends sometimes emerged to hold their hands. Once such was the tale of the last iceberg: apparently, it floated past the previous summer, shining like a gargantuan granule of sugar – to use the description of Hywel the Baker, one of the witnesses. Rumour soon elaborated the sighting: when it melted, as it surely would, the additional fluid would be just enough to cover the whole of Lladloh, with the exception of the weather-peacock on the steeple of the mortuary chapel. I regarded this theory with suspicion, suggesting instead that the phenomenon was attributable to a tired cumulus cloud resting on the waves. Though a chef, I am a rational man.

"Not to worry," added Kingdom Noisette. "I've been scheming. What we need are sea defences – seal off the whole town! High walls ringing the valley, like women dancers round a handbag!"

Delves snorted. "You'll never get planning permission."

But the engineer was lost to reason; he snatched up his drawings, folded them in a pocket and scuttled away. He was careful not to crease his frock coat in the wind of his rush – his alternative profession was that of tailor. Suave in an archaic fashion, he had managed to reconcile his two interests by designing a steam-powered sewing machine. When the door slammed behind him, Delves confessed his worries. The engineer, he said, might be able to persuade the mayor, who was turning senile, to let him proceed with the enterprise.

"Let him indulge his risible fantasies," I replied. "It is our duty to approach the problem logically."

"I suppose you're right. Tonight, after your restaurant shift, you must make the stellar observations. We'll give the figures to Elizabeth Morgan and she can cast the horoscope."

Before I left the Reverend, I handed him the rule book. He took it with a beatific expression. "Another relic? Ah, the gods smiled on you. What a miracle!" He passed the volume to Olaf, who placed it between the waistcoats of Harker Melmoth and the earrings of Rosemary Gibbet-Pardoe, most evil of Beer'or's avatars. As I departed, worshippers came in for matins. At the end of the service, Delves would allow them to sip from O'Casey's glass – Guinness was sure protection against the forces which sought to reclaim Lladloh for Beer'or, god of lager. I had never tasted either brew – I was an atheist.

I walked across the central square, skirting the massive statue of the primary Homunculus, abysmal poet and mediocre sorcerer, who presided over Lladloh's most spectacular apocalypse. At his heel, a sculpture of Tourmaline, the triple bodied, single headed Cerberus of an alternative Hades, looked up in infernal loyalty. This figure was a recent addition, cleverly stitched together from drowned hounds by Medardo. It was going off; worms dripped from its tongue.

These, of course, provided my main source of bait. Apart from holy relics, I also fish for skate and bream for my tables. With seafood, I can achieve wonders, masking a whole disquisition on heraldry under the slipper-like flavours. But there was no need to collect worms today; my night exploits on the pier were to consist less of angling than angles. Reaching my kitchen, I started chopping herbs and vegetables, preparing a new variation on the lasagne theme. Herodotus, the cat who lives in my largest cauldron, emerged to study me.

"Do you believe in ghosts?" I asked him, but he

seemed disinclined for conversation and merely offered a yawn.

The subject of phantoms had obsessed me since the Reverend employed one in his carousel conceit. I began to wonder if all wraiths had to be organic in origin: was it conceivable that inanimate objects might have souls? I debated this matter with myself while I cruelly hung, drew and quartered onions and slit the wrists of tomatoes. As I filled the oven with charcoal, struggling to light it with a match, I felt the fibrous presence of all the produce I had brutally slaughtered in that room. It was almost enough to make me free the potatoes and liberate the spices from their jars, those hideous oubliettes.

When the sun set, I reluctantly opened my doors to the public. Only a dozen customers came to sit and eat away the evening. Beerbohm Soames, true to his name, made do with a yard of ale in which floated petals of a monstrous orchid – and an essay on ancient sociology. D.F. Lewis, with his neatly trimmed beard, ordered a curry spiked with maps of Napoleonic campaigns. Bigamy Bertha opted for the cucumber salad, containing sundry examples of antique musical instruments, all edible. When the last cup of coffee was drunk, I ushered out the lingerers and hurried down to the pier, the astrolabe attached to my thumb.

My calculations were completed just as dawn's left hand snared the mortuary chapel's steeple in a noose of light – actually it took several attempts before managing to lasso it; and the sun forgot to whoop as it pulled itself over the horizon. I neglected my bed in favour of wisdom, taking my results straight to Cobweb Cottage.

The Reverend was waiting for me. We gingerly knocked and Elizabeth Morgan let us in. Although she is my beloved, she does not know this; I keep my lust secret. I have been hurt too often in the past. Whenever I obtain a girlfriend, they bid me "Ciao!" and I am never sure if they are ending the relationship or calling my name. Accordingly, I did not look up as we entered the leaning structure. Delves and I were given cushions to sit on and Elizabeth Morgan cast the horoscope before us. Lladloh, of course, is Aries with Sagittarius rising.

The gorgeous auburn haired witch completed the nativity chart and I cried impatiently: "How long left?" Both Reverend Delves and myself were totally unprepared for her answer.

"Six days," she replied, indicating the relevant symbols. No amount of pleading could encourage her to amend this prophecy; there were no mistakes. We had less than a week.

As we left, the Reverend and I supported each other; our knees were filled not with cartilage but semolina. Elizabeth waved us farewell, but I was too weak to return the gesture. Unable to fully assimilate what we had been told, we staggered in the direction of my kitchen. My cupboards contained a supply of quinine and brandy.

Finishing the last bottle, we recovered our senses. We debated what action to take. "Evacuate now," said Delves. "Set up a temporary camp on Yandro. Then we can descend and rebuild."

I shook my head. "I have a smarter plan. It seems to me we can save ourselves the trouble of evacuation and resettlement. There is a subject I have been turning over in my mind recently: ghosts. Do you accept that Lladloh has a soul?" I saw that the Reverend was willing to consider the heretical idea. "Though it is broken with depressing regularity, Lladloh persists through the centuries. The stones might not be the same but the essence of the village is unchanged. What does this suggest but that the spirit of Lladloh is indestructible?"

Delves adjusted his dog collar. "An interesting thesis. I don't see how it helps the town or its citizens."

"But if we could materialise its spirit, we wouldn't have to worry about future catastrophes. If we make Lladloh's ghost solid, the village will be secure for eternity! All that is required is some holy ritual to bind the urban spectre to the earthly plane!"

"Such a ritual does not exist in the pagan Church."

"What about exorcism, which is designed to banish phantoms? What if the chants of this service are reversed?"

Delves stroked his chin. "Yes, it's possible. Why not? To catch the spirit of the community and solidify it means conducting the rite at its hub – the lounge of the nameless tavern. At this moment, it's impossible to separate the essence and the corporality. Lladloh isn't yet dead. The anti-exorcism must take place at the exact instant of dissolution, when the village's ghost detaches itself from the houses and civic buildings! And there's another major problem."

"What is it?" My heart was pounding like a mortar, mashing anxiety into my bloodstream. My ears were pestles.

"The words of the backwards exorcism. They'll have to be pronounced correctly first time. How in Beer'or's name will I be able to do that? I don't even know how they'll sound!"

I snapped my fingers. "There's no need for a live performance. Why not record the normal exorcism on a wax disc and then play it in reverse on a gramophone? Titian Grundy's wife is a beekeeper; she can provide us with the wax. The mayor is in possession of a gramophone. I netted it a decade ago; he took a fancy to it."

"Come, we'd better ask him if he'll lend it to us. This is a risky operation, Giovanni. If anything goes wrong, I'll hold you responsible. The survivors will need a scapegoat."

I nodded numbly and we made our way to the mortuary chapel. The new Dennistoun Hommunculus, in accordance with tradition, lived in the same garret as the first. At the top of the chapel, under the leaking slates, he held gloomy court among spare tombstones and tambourines. The actual cemetery, of which the chapel itself is a grim memorial, is ringed by a wall shaped like a donkey's tear. This is another example of mutation; I have forcefully proved, by dint of extensive research, that the original boundary resembled the sorrow of a pig.

As we approached the chapel's entrance, we met

Kingdom Noisette on his way out. The engineer was in a boisterous mood; he clapped his hairy palms and chortled. "Ee oop! I've just had an audience with 'is lowness. Planning permission been granted for my scheme."

I was aghast. "But we only have six days! How will you erect useful sea defences in that time? I won't help you."

"Oh, no? But you'll have to, laddie. The mayor's issued orders. All citizens have to report to me for work tomorrow morning. Shall I say how I'm going to speed up my project? We're not going to build a wall; every householder is going to extend his or her dwelling, on both sides, until it meets up with that o' their neighbours! Filling in the gaps, I am! It will make a watertight spiral round Lladloh; then we'll seal the opening and cheat the melting iceberg!"

Without waiting to hear the rest of his triumphant rhetoric, Delves and I rushed up the chapel steps to the garret. We made obeisance before the greasy fringed demagogue who lay on his filthy bed, composing horrid verse. I felt sorry for the mayor: he was a talented poet and the effort involved in deliberately writing doggerel had taken its toll on his poor health. He was far more sprightly than he ought to be; indeed, the fever which he had to wear with the medallion and ermine robe seemed in danger of slipping off. Clutched between his bony knees through the thin sheets was a curious item: a miniature pyramid.

His lips moved awkwardly. "I'm working on an ode to this device. It appeared from nowhere above my bed; I reckon it's a time machine. Wasn't anything inside. Completely empty."

I winced. His mind had obviously snapped; we knew that senility had been sucking on his desiccated lobes for some time. Stepping closer, I outlined my request. He gazed at me with blank eyes, scratching his nose with his harpy quill. "Gramophone? Oh that! Take it by all means." With a casual wave, he returned to his travesty.

The instrument stood in a corner. With the

Reverend's help, and the aid of my belt, we strapped it to my back. Descending from the garret, I hobbled back to my restaurant, holding up my trousers with my thumbs. In the kitchen I placed down the gramophone and wound it tight while Delves sought out Titian Grundy, the local constable. His wife supplied us with enough beeswax to record the complete oeuvre of Cobalt Hugh, our busker. Using a meat tenderiser, I hammered out a selection of golden discs. The Reverend took a book of services from a fold in his vestments and, under my cat's sheltering sneer, recited the spell.

Eventually, we had an excellent recording of the ritual. I reversed the polarity of the gramophone's spring and we listened to the ritual in reverse, the Reverend's chants swooping backwards like bats unable to turn in a narrow tunnel. Gingerly, I touched the walls of my restaurant, smarting as Delves loosed a mocking guffaw.

"Nothing will happen until the point of Lladloh's death. Its spirit is still firmly locked away in its bricks!"

"Then there is nothing more we can do. We must wait for the correct hour. But I can hardly bear the suspense!"

"I'm sure Kingdom Noisette's project will help to take our thoughts off things. I just can't believe that water will destroy Lladloh. In the previous calamities not a single citizen has drowned!" He squinted. "How on earth do I know that? Most odd!"

I cleared my throat. The Reverend's erudition on the topic had much to do with last week's macaroni cheese...

Needless to say, his words about the diverting effects of the grand project were proved correct. I do not intend to make a fuss about what occurred over the next five days. The scheme blistered my mind as well as my hands; the Reverend and I spared no pains in sharing our knowledge of the hour of Lladloh's doom. It was to no avail. The engineer didn't doubt our forecast, but believed he could finish the undertaking before the week was out. His poor judgment was backed by the mayor, who never descended from his garret to view our plight.

Active rebellion was out of the question. Dennistoun Homunculus had issued a direct command – to ignore it would be to risk being sacrificed to one of the local members of the pagan pantheon. Such martyrdoms often involve plummets from great heights: offenders are cast over the side of the stone bridge on the edge of town; or defenestrated from the eyeless windows of the nameless tavern's upper floor; or hurled into the smoking crater of Yandro, home of Cthulhu's uncle.

The sea defences proceeded slowly. Like I said, Lladloh is full of detached houses. Ramparts were extended from each building so that they inched closer to their colleagues. Halfway through the task, I made an observation. Previously there had been enough space for a falling house to crumple to dust without grazing a neighbour. This was no longer true. The range of tumblings now overlapped: the buildings resembled dominoes placed upright, waiting for a finger to push over the first and initiate a chain reaction. I informed Delves of my anxieties. He simply wiped his forehead with his trowel and shrugged.

"No matter. The project must be abandoned. We should convene at the tavern." He consulted the clock I had provided him with, calling to the others: "One hour to go! Down tools and follow me!

Kingdom Noisette flapped between the departing labourers. "Good for nothings! Indolent fools! If you'd put your backs into it, the job would be finished! Now we'll all be gargling!"

Olaf, always sensitive to the engineer's needs, had lovingly sealed the cracks in the tavern. Also, on his own initiative, he had installed a periscope which protruded from the roof and offered excellent views of the town from the comfort of the lounge. We filed into the establishment and took our places at the bar, feet resting on the brass rail, symbolic glasses of mead raised to our lips. The Reverend wound up the gramophone and waited for the correct moment to engage the motor. Minutes passed as unevenly as pints. Sitting in state before the hearth, the mayor doffed his tricorne hat and wept dramatically. I considered clutching Elizabeth Morgan for comfort; I wisely desisted.

Scanning the horizon with his periscope, Olaf muttered: "Can't see anything. Are ye sure Ragnarok's today?"

"Absolutely." The Reverend's hand trembled over the gramophone. The timing was crucial – the inverse exorcism had to commence as soon as the village's phantom gingerly poked its ectoplasm out of its cobbles. After an agony of waiting, the clock struck the hour. I closed my eyes. Delves still did not unleash the chant; a concerned muttering grew. I opened my lids. Outside, the village was silent. The crowd shuffled impatiently; I saw they were succumbing to boredom. Iolo Machen twiddled his crook; D.F. Lewis wrote his nine thousandth short story in a puddle of beer; Medardo performed assorted ballet antics.

Keen to disperse the communal frustration, I volunteered to venture out, to gauge the state of affairs. The door was opened as narrowly as possible; I squeezed through. I wandered the plaza, searching for proof of looming doom. I walked to Cobweb Cottage, the edge of town. The sea was as peaceful as an exhumed grave.

While I rested in the obtuse shadow of the edifice, the breathless figure of the Reverend bounded over to me.

"Giovanni!" he gasped. "We must return at once. The clock you gave me! Where did you get it? It's fast!"

Suddenly I understood my mistake. As I have mentioned, the clocks I caught were often broken; some were in perfect working order. Even these were inaccurate. Such timepieces still ran on Greenwich Mean Time. But Greenwich had not existed for a dozen centuries. Hours were now reckoned using Lladloh Nasty Time – a more brutal method.

When I told the Reverend that the clock had come from the ocean, he plucked at my elbow. "Hurry!"

I lost my balance and slumped against Cobweb

Cottage. At once, with a horrid moan, the entire structure toppled. I knew what this meant – we were in the vicinity of a self-fulfilling prophecy. The building crashed against its neighbour and this also tumbled; an irreversible process. As Lladloh was arranged in a spiral, each house formed part of the domino matrix. Right at the end of the helix, the nameless tavern waited like a thumb ready to be pulped by a hammer.

There was one chance of survival: if we reached the gramophone and started the anti-exorcism before the last house crushed the life out of the tavern, we could exile the dying body of Lladloh and replace it with the solidified community spirit...

As I ran, I became aware that the houses were falling with a hush. Fate had placed a finger to its lips, perhaps in respect for the dismal irony. The collapse was accelerating, hastening toward a finale. We had a big advantage in being able to take the shortest route to the tavern, while the apocalypse was condemned to a roundabout approach. Around us, the noose tightened – the outskirts looped closer. I watched the chapel vanish; my restaurant; the lingerie shops. This scene felt unreal; like a camel's dream of smoothness.

At last, we dashed into the tavern and the Reverend threw himself onto the gramophone. The motor was engaged and the chant flooded through the lounge. All else was static. When it was over, Delves wore a smile, the smuggest of his career. "Benediction!"

I stood. Something was not quite right. No light shone through the windows; an oppressive weight seemed to surround the tavern. In answer to my questioning frown, Delves opened the door. He was confronted by a solid stone wall. Turning, he matched my look with one of equal horror. We knew what had happened; a grotesque side-effect of our operations. I swallowed dryly as Olaf took his axe from under the counter and smashed the windows, revealing a similar expanse of impassible stone. The blond giant cursed: "Longships and runes!"

Stricken, I made the announcement. "Burghers of Lladloh! We've been more successful than I bargained for. We've solidified not only the soul of the present village but of all those which preceded it. As buildings were never erected in the same place, this simultaneous materialisation has surrounded us with a myriad variants of Lladloh. Only the tavern has always occupied a single location. Were it not for this happy fact, we'd now be embedded in living rock!"

Kingdom Noisette howled and grappled with the periscope. "It's all true! I can see thousands o' houses, meshed together at strange angles, without a gap between 'em! We're trapped!" He fell before me. "I've got plans! We'll drill through the walls!"

I pouted. "There are 665 taverns superimposed on ours. I consider it unlikely we'll be able to break out."

A triumphant voice interrupted me. It belonged to the mayor; he was perched on the apex of his small pyramid, long legs sliding on the glass sides, waving his tricorne hat in one hand. "Doesn't bother me. I've got my time machine. Mouse and hattock away!"

With a minor thunderclap, he disappeared. I arched an eyebrow. It remained arched for the rest of the day – I was determined to anticipate any more impossibilities. Sighing, I made an appeal: "Has anyone got any bright ideas? Wan ones will suffice."

Padgett Weggs raised a hand. "Yn siwr! Psychological damage, that's the problem! Stuck like colliers in a gold pit. Pendrwm! Ought to occupy our fears. Play games, a bit of sport."

I snorted. Weggs' therapy was particularly inappropriate now. Olaf, on the other lobe, took up the request and amplified it: "There's a book of rules on my shelf. Ancient game called 'Cricket'. Read it in my spare time. Will ye join me for a few overs?"

Arms akimbo, I derided the suggestion. "Most foolish. No equipment is available for such a pastime."

"Oh no?" Delves winked treacherously...

The sacred relics of Lladloh are no longer stored behind the bar in the village's nameless tavern. The ear of a monstrous rabbit made a fine bat; a volume of poems penned by a legendary bard doubled up as a superb wicket; the stopper of a pickle jar was the ideal substitute for a ball. Nervously, I stood at the crease, awaiting another of the Reverend's sly googlies. With an athletic grace which amazed me as much as my fielders, I hit the ball over the counter for a six.

It struck a pistol left behind by a highwayman. Primed, the pistol discharged a lead ball at O'Casey's glass of stout. The glass shattered. A fountain of Guinness erupted into the air, raining on our heads. Play was called off; the pitch was abandoned. Under chairs, we waited for the storm to subside. It never did. O'Casey's glass has no bottom. Soon we were forced to climb onto the chairs, as the stout level rose higher and higher. The tavern was hermetically sealed by a plethora of congealed urban ghosts; we floundered in the surging brew.

"It seems we're going to drown after all," Delves remarked. "Though not in the way we'd anticipated!"

I swam over to the Reverend and belaboured him with my bat. I was not ready to accept my own responsibility. The undertow of Guinness pulled me away from his side. The stout had reached the windows; Olaf tried to stem the source with his beard; his chin was soon waterlogged and he fell aside, exhausted. Surprisingly, it was Kingdom Noisette who preserved the most sobriety. Balanced on a raft made from an hatstand, he called above our tumultuous voices:

"My underground tunnel! I knew 'twould be useful one o' these days. Dive down and open the hatch, laddies!"

Elizabeth Morgan, the strongest swimmer, disappeared under the dark waters. A moment later there was a horrible sucking sound. The maelström was as unavoidable as an aunt's kiss. The stout's head was utterly pure, oppressively white. Round and round we whirled; I was surely delirious, for I even sought amusement in speculating upon the relative velocities of our several descents toward the foam below. Then, with no opportunity to make observations on which objects, whether spherical or cylindrical in shape, were absorbed at the greater rate, I vanished down a hole and was swept along a conduit at frightful speed.

At the end of the tunnel, I regained my feet, mounted a flight of steps and emerged in the pharmacy. When we were all inside, we closed the hatch and searched for an exit from the building. The pressure of eternal stout was immense; no door could hold it back. We had to leave the village and flee into the hills. Even there, we would be swamped within a generation. But this pharmacy only led to another; our ritual had turned Lladloh into a convoluted maze, a labyrinth more complex than any conceived by Minoan ingenuity. The ghosts of inanimate objects may not be malevolent; but they are certainly tricky.

We still wander the endless rooms, the surge of Guinness forever in our ears. It is essential to keep moving; the weak are left behind. Only Olaf is happy: he is able to loot the homes of his neighbours as we pass through them – they have plenty to spare. Each time we broach an earlier version of my restaurant, I prepare meals for the company. I no longer spice my creations with references to the past. Now I bake future hopes into my dishes. My belief is that ghost villages suffer apocalypses too. If true, it's just a question of hanging on until the ectoplasmic walls tumble in some phantasmagoric cataclysm and we are able to emerge like worms from a stitched dog's tongue.

THE
SICKNESS
OF
SATAN
STATELY PLEASURE DOME

The sickness began with the leaflet which was pushed under my front door on a damp Thursday morning. It was one of those glossy propaganda sheets used to announce the opening of a new restaurant. I detest unwanted mail and was on the point of compressing it into a sphere and kicking it into the nearest wicker bin when my nose was distracted by the peculiar smell of the paper. I raised it to my nostrils and inhaled. My mind swam under the onslaught of a myriad exotic aromas and I cried out in alarm. It was necessary for me to sit on the floor.

Odette came down to see what the fuss was about.

"Have a good sniff of this," I croaked.

She took the leaflet and her nostrils quivered. "Forty nine billion Pork Vindaloos, twenty three million Shashlik Kebabs, seventeen thousand Orange Duck Curries, eight hundred and sixty two Chilli Chicken Hotpots, fifty seven Veal Jerks and a pint of lager."

"There's a Frog Moussaka in there as well, I believe."

"No, it's Toad. With a wart sauce."

"Rotten salesman. It's a stinking trick. I'm going to wire the door up to a generator. He'll fry if he returns."

Odette brushed her red hair back over flawed ears and chuckled. "It wasn't a deliberate insult, Donald. How was he supposed to know you're a vegetarian? He's just doing his job."

"I admit it's a neat piece of advertising."

"And it's come just in time for our first anniversary. You promised to take me for a meal. This place is local."

I sighed. Despite my basic apathy concerning morals, I rarely break a pledge. The execution of an oath, the display of its rotting corpse in the gibbet of my swagger, has little to do with conspicuous virtue. What I enjoy is the pleasure of contrast. When the burden of an obligation is eased off, like a pinching shoe, I am suffused with profound relief, the freedom of irresponsibility. Let us say my addiction to making vows must culminate in its cure – with the promise never to make another promise. Until then, Odette will suck my wallet.

"Very well, we shall feast in an abattoir."

She pecked me on the cheek and I trembled. Despite twelve months of marriage, our relationship was still viable. Odette loved me in the same way a circle adores its circumference. She needed to be restrained by my embrace or else she would explode into emotional nothingness. I held her against my stomach, that basilica of rumbling egoism. The tenderness was interrupted by Billy, our lodger, who paused at the top of the stairs on his way to the bathroom. His face, with its divergent eyes and the frown of an athlete who smokes, annoyed me intensely. Odette twisted out of my clutch in embarrassment and vanished.

Billy smiled timidly at me and resumed his voyage to the sink. This violation of my grope seemed an evil augur for the remainder of the day. We both disliked sharing our home with a stranger but the revenue gained from renting the spare room was crucial to our solvency. Since losing my job at the hospital, our combined income had been reduced by a third. It was unfair to criticise the idiot student for his presence – he was not unreasonable in his habits – but his shambling gait and scratched vinyl giggle presented an easy focus for resentment and I was unable to resist radiating disgust over his footsteps.

I listened to the flushing toilet and scrape of brush on teeth, two sounds I had forsaken. Picking up the telephone in the hall, I jabbed at the number printed on the leaflet. As I waited for the connection, which seemed to take ages, as if I was dialling across an interstellar gulf, I studied the sheet more carefully. The lettering writhed over the surface like mangled hot pokers on a frozen lake. Impregnating the laminate with an excess of cooking scents was a whisk of genius. I wondered how it had been accomplished. I was still debating when the connection was made and an attenuated ringing tickled my ear.

The voice on the other end was faint: "Yea?"

I cleared my throat. "Is that the *Stately Pleasure Dome?*"

"It has been decreed as such."

"I wish to book a table for two on Saturday night."

"Divulge your appellation."

"Donald and Odette Saunders." I paused while a distant pen wandered across an invisible register. "Tell me, do your serve vegetarian food? I mean, there was nothing on the menu."

The silence was gratuitous, like a nun's ovulation.

My discomfort grew as the passing seconds became minutes. Was there a fault on the line? I bit my tongue.

"I'm quite happy with a simple salad."

Again there was no response. Desperately, I continued: "So we'll be there at half past eight. Thank you."

And hung up. I had a feeling the call was going to prove enormously expensive despite its brief duration.

Later, after Odette had left for work and Billy for college, I went up to the attic and stared out of the window at the urban mistake called Swansea. A tedious life I led, moping through rooms, licking books which no longer intrigued me, because they were full of reality. Even my taste in pompous music had dulled – the stereo now belonged to silence. There was only one activity left which was wholly mine – isolation. And every recluse knows that the best way of widening an ache in a soul to abyssal dimensions is to spy on happier folk.

Our house catches its breath on the steepest hill in the city. Down toward the grainy sea, with its burden of rusty ships shaving the waves, innumerable filthy streets staggered. The windows of most buildings were bleary, lapped by mist stale as the breath of a donkey who drinks cider. There was little movement on the cambers and slabs. A solitary figure in a remote avenue stooped to slide something under a door. I grappled with my binoculars and focussed on his form. He was sheathed in a cassock and the bag of leaflets slung from his shoulder was actually a giant censer. For a halo he wore a garlic poppadum.

It never occurred to me to check out the exact location of the place. On Saturday night, after Odette and myself had performed the common rituals with soap, brush and mirror, we set off up to the summit of Constitution Hill. The *Stately Pleasure Dome* supposedly lurked at the junction of two ugly roads, Penygraig and Terrace, where litter brewed in fumes like the tea of a liar. Although the location was less than five minutes from our habitation, neither of us was familiar with it.   We preferred to tramp in the opposite direction, to Cwmdonkin Park, unloading our stale loaves on vermin and mallards. I wore my purple shirt for the occasion and stubble brutal enough to impale spare crumbs.

We strolled to the address, confident of finding a typical licensed ethnic eaterie, with a Mughal facade and a flock of doormen to match the gaudy wallpaper. Instead, to my bewilderment, we approached a church, St Jude's, a Gothic edifice with those depressingly asymmetrical towers one associates with Welsh Catholic architecture.   The opaque windows throbbed with a sticky effulgence, like lemon curd spread on sacred hosts, and an excited muttering issued from the open portals. I compared the number on the iron gate with that on the leaflet. They were identical. We were not alone in our alarm – two other couples lingered outside the entrance in parallel dismay, hairstyles curdling.

Odette shrugged. "It's a typographical error."

I shook my head scornfully. "No, it's deliberate deceit. I observed a priest deliver the things. A recruitment drive for a flagging diocese. I find this absolutely outrageous!"

"Do you really think they'd pull such a desperate stunt to increase their congregation? Maybe it's a believer's theme night? I've heard what can be done with fish and a few rolls."

"Well I'm not eating in there. Papist cheats!"

I craned my neck to peer inside, in the unlikely event it was all a joke, but what little of the interior I could see was resolutely church. Shaking my fist at the gargoyles dribbling oily water onto the railings, I snatched Odette's hand and pulled her away. The other couples followed our example, dispersing along secular sidestreets. We cantered back down Constitution Hill, the Mumbles lighthouse winking slyly at us across the bay like a headmaster with an erection.

"We'll feed in the *Bengal Brasserie* instead. Or that Austrian place next to it, *Mozart's*. How does that sound?"

"Look, Donald, I know you don't really want to spend money on me. I realise you've become a worthless miser. That's fine. I don't expect any charity from a misanthrope. We'll go home."

"Curse your mature womanly sentience!"

I fumed and blustered but gratefully took the opportunity of saving cash. Odette wanted too much from my pocket – I had already treated her to the cinema the previous month. We returned to the house and because I usually weaken when I triumph, I offered to make her a special meal with my own hands. She accepted without a smile and I raided the refrigerator for pugilist celery, fussy lettuce, cucumber, radishes, beetroot, yellow peppers bigger than cowardly hearts, avocados, watercress and coriander. Then I plundered less frigid regions of the kitchen for onions, parsley, pumpkin seeds and olives. This was going to be the mother of all salads, a denial of the flesh of the world.

Tarragon oil and rosé wine vinegar splashed the pageant. I shredded miscellaneous herbs over the bowl with a pair of broken scissors. As the central rivet worked loose, the blades pulled away from each other, like the legs of a newt employed as a wishbone. I tossed the result with fork and spoon, tuning the roughage to the pitch of a rabbit's tooth. Thunder rumbled in my gut and elsewhere. Casabel chillies are testicles scorched by lightning in any raw dish. I cast them in whole, as if to fertilise a womb of chicory positioned alluringly on the vegetable bed. Beckoning my spouse to table is a tricky recipe in itself – she is always performing mysterious chores in the furthest corners of our abode. Lighting candles and dimming the bulbs, I waited.

She eventually appeared with a handful of vitamin tablets, a signal that I was permitted to begin. She often chides me for the acidity of my dressing, so it is crucial to blunt her taste with caustic conversation. Yet I had nothing to say. This awkwardness was punctured by noises which had another source. Billy was wallowing about in the bath again. Despite the vibrancy of the Swansea college scene, our lodger led a mundane life which alternated between tub, pet hamster and secret cigarette. On those few occasions when he left our home to play badminton, Odette and I were so pleased we sometimes had sex. As I crunched the fibres with the teeth on only one side of my mouth, I listened to the student breaking wind in the soapy water. The candle wicks flared.

"There's going to be a huge tempest," Odette remarked.

"Can you tell that from the clap of a bum?"

"Yes, because little storms come up the other way. We belch isobars when they can be digested poorly. If they can't be digested at all, they hurtle straight down. Nature is brewing."

We gorged ourselves sick in anticipation. Then we rested on a couch and sweated out the condiment. All that remained of the noble salad were two olives, shining at the bottom of the bowl like pineal glands plucked from the fused craniums of Siamese twins.

The storm broke just after midnight. Rain slapped the roof like soup and I stirred out of a dream with the grace of a convecting lentil. I groped for Odette but her side of the bed was icy – she had gone. As I blinked into full awareness, the windows burst open under the weight of a horrid shape. A man dressed in lederhosen sprawled on the floor, accompanied by a dreadful stench of vomit. I threw back the sheets and jumped up, using a rug to cover my nakedness. The intruder stood and brushed fragments of wood and fabric from his narrow shoulders. He carried an antique firearm and levelled it at my head, sighting along a warped barrel longer than a tusk. I closed my eyes but no explosion came. There was different sound, an avian trill which pecked my lobes.

When I regained my composure, I realised he was questioning me in a fluting voice. *"Darf ich das Fenster öffnen?"*

"Sorry, I don't understand you. Damages must be paid for in full. I hope you won't turn this into a legal issue."

"Können Sie mir helfen? Ich weiss nicht, wo ich bin."

"I think you should leave now. If you refuse, I'll call my wife. Do you have any idea how angry she'll be?"

I backed toward the door and shouted for Odette. There was no reply and I briefly wondered if she had employed an assassin to remove me from her life. The intruder followed, the muzzle of his weapon poised over my spleen. It was an extremely unwieldy carbine and even he seemed slightly ashamed to be bothering me with it.

Retreating down the stairs, arms elevated in a pacific gesture, rug dropping to my feet, I was disturbed by a feeling of mythic recognition. During my housebound explorations of our bookcases, I once spent an hour with a volume on the history of aviation. Before fixed wing gliders were developed by Cayley, Langley and Lilienthal, a few pioneers attempted to conquer the skies in devices which mimicked the flapping of birds. These ornithopters usually failed to clear the ground, but in 1809 an Austrian by the name of Jacob Degen managed to stay aloft strapped to a hybrid of flexible vanes and hydrogen balloon.

His success inspired imitators who were less clever. After numerous accidents in Vienna, Degen was proclaimed an outlaw. He escaped with his apparatus and was seen circling the peaks of the Niedere Tauern, waiting for a gust to carry him to Salzburg. The authorities put up a reward for his capture and he became an aerial bandit, swooping on travellers after maiming them with his musket, which he supposedly carved from a sapling. He was a merciless assailant, by popular report, and his romanticism was always tempered with an insensate brutality. It was not inconceivable he had been blown off course to Swansea.

I tried out my theory on the visitor. "Herr Degen?"

He recoiled in surprise, then offered me an ironic grin. "*Ja, freut mich! Ich habe hier Schmerzen. Es wird Schlimmer.*"

"You should have died centuries ago!"

He shrugged and jabbed the gun into my belly, squinting through one eye as he squeezed the trigger. Nothing happened and he scowled, less in fury than resignation. "*Es klemmt!*"

We had reached the point where the stairway bent back on itself and it became apparent he would not be able to manoeuvre the carbine through this sharp angle. I turned and ran down into the hallway while he fought to twist the oversized barrel. My impulse was to head for the front door and escape into the street, but a low groan from the kitchen reminded me that my wife might still be in the house.

I knocked along the corridor in the dark, restraining an impulse to weep on our relatively new carpet. The kitchen was fitfully illumined by the candles we had used to bathe our salad. They were no more than stubs now and threw shifting shadows on the walls. Odette sat on a chair, face contorted in anguish. The bindings were invisible until I stood directly above her. I removed her gag and frowned.

"What are you doing all trussed up?"

She took a deep breath. "Look to your left, Donald."

I obeyed her command and was astonished to note a bishop sitting at our table, leaning over a vast ledger. He held a quill in one rough hand and seemed to be scratching occult symbols on the vellum. Frequently, he would pause to pluck the strings of a lute which rested on his knee. The resulting note was plaintive and shrill. I covered my ears at the savage beauty of it and the bishop chuckled.

"Ples de tristor, marritz e doloiros," he crooned horridly. *"Comens est planch per lo dan remembrar."*

"It's unbearable!" I stammered.

"I entirely agree. But who is he?"

"How should I know? I've got Jacob Degen upstairs. He used a flying machine to break into the bedroom."

"Somebody's coming down the steps. Release me!"

I snatched the broken scissors from the rack and hacked at Odette's bonds. As I blistered my thumbs, she related all that had happened while I lay asleep. "There was this unbelievable downpour and then I heard the most wondrous singing outside. So I went down and unlocked the back door and this bishop pushed his way in and tied me up with this rope. I think he's been torturing me for heresy."

"It wasn't a normal storm, evidently."

"Let's leave them to it. I'm not staying here another minute. We'll spend the rest of the night in a hotel."

The bishop regarded our departure with genuine sorrow. It was clear he would have obstructed us had he been more agile. But the girth of his abdomen and the dislocation of his hip when he rose demonstrated how the advantage had passed into our hands, or rather feet. He consoled himself by slamming his book, spraying wet ink over table and mitre, and picking out a haunted arpeggio on his lute.

"Perparan dreg, es tortz tant enantitz."

We hastened down the hallway, also ignoring the voice which warbled from the landing. Herr Degen was still having problems working his rifle free. *"Können Sie einen*

Mechaniker schicken?"

"Tell me what's happening, Donald."

"I thought it had something to do with you!"

Opening the front door, our eyes were assaulted by a chaotic scene. The streetlights had failed but illumination was provided by a fire upon which smouldered a dozen neighbours. A convocation of men in robes stood around the blaze, warming gauntlets and perspiring through the peepholes of pointed hoods. Dishevelled people raced up and down the middle of the road, dressed in sundry historical garb. At first it appeared that every amateur thespian in the district had suddenly chosen to stage an outdoor tragedy in the same place, lacking only a script. But these protagonists were too talented to be local actors.

We stepped forward warily, slipping on a puddle of vomit. Suspended from gables and chimneys, massive streamers of regurgitated food emitted an abominable odour. The entire city had been used as a bucket by a vast debaucher, a macrocosmic Vitellius of ineffable appetite. Mingled in the slurry, spices bubbled forth in opaque clouds which tumbled over gardens and parked cars like battlefield gas.

"There must be a link with that restaurant."

Odette nodded. "Why don't we find out?"

Directly opposite our house, a swarthy character climbed slates and launched himself off a roof. Sigils were spattered over his robes and he wore a corrugated beard. Instead of falling, he hovered in the air, wild kicks shredding the saffron vapours, a fist glinting with barbaric rings describing arcane figures above his head.

"Zazazaoy, Zothzazoth, Thozaxazoth!"

A papyrus sandal dropped from one foot, exposing toenails as curved and sharp as damascene scimitars. The shoe struck a Victorian gentleman, perhaps a physician, who lingered below. He carried his own selection of blades and beckoned to my wife as if she was a prostitute. Further along the pavement, a traditional impalement was in progress. A telephone pole had been uprooted and sharpened with an axe. It was being replanted with a burden even more vocal than the lines it had previously held. The wiry form of our newsagent, recently engaged, now hung up, undulated over the smoky street like a tapeworm kebab.

I was tempted to rush to his aid, but the appearance of the man who stood under the stake quickly discouraged me. Perched above the vomit on a mound of crimson cushions, he managed to blend uncouth mannerisms with elegant apparel, like the king of a remote mediaeval principality, which is what I suspected he really was. He chided his lackeys, who flopped in the vomit as they righted the pole.

"Înca un rînd, va rog. Imediat, noi grabim."

I gripped Odette's hand and we skated past the grisly vista, but as we came within range of the sadistic king, he reached out and pinched my nude buttocks between finger and thumb. Then he winked at me with a slow eye and through simple reflex I found myself returning the dalliance. My cheeks burning, heart brimming with self-disgust, I left him for another horror. In one of the myriad potholes neglected by the City Council, now overflowing with sick, a miniature submarine floated unsteadily, while a businessman with the starched grin of a double agent accepted money from rival groups of sunburnt murderers.

"I've seen his face before," Odette cried. "He was a notorious arms dealer active during the Boer War."

"We've been sent to Hell!" I replied.

"No, Donald, I think Hell has come to us."

We struggled up Constitution Hill and when we turned at the apex to stare across the city we beheld a panorama worthy of the lunatic artists of Holland, an animated combination of Hieronymus Bosch, Pieter Brueghel and Hugo van der Goes. The Mumbles lighthouse span its wounded cyclopean eye over the sub-Neapolitan bay, but it irradiated only muttering filth. The devastation was broad and unique. The Guildhall, the only attractive edifice in the sprawl, was crusted with vultures, while elephants on the sward below stamped men in turbans. From the Vetch, the football ground, came sundry dog Latin sounds: the jabbing of a thousand inverted thumbs, the roaring of unspecified animals.

Odette swallowed with difficulty. "I never imagined it was feasible for Swansea to sink any lower."

Pressing on to St Jude's, we entered the church and stumbled to the altar. An impossible staircase led upward from the ciborium, higher than the loftiest steeple, into a metaphysical region that my eyes refused to define in terms of honest perspective. We shuddered in each other's arms as we estimated the length of the bannisters – precisely that of levers to shift the Earth off its orbit. And there was a place to stand for the job, a location which met Archimedes's criteria. A bistro in the sky. An ontological eaterie. Vomit cascaded down the steps, eroded cubes of meat and bones rolling in rainbow slush.

I began the daunting ascent. My wife tugged at my shirt to restrain me, but I broke into a run, chest heaving, stomach likewise. And finally the flock wallpaper, almost a hypothetical concept at the bottom, an act of faith, came into sight, expanding from a glowing dot into an unstable square flooded with twenty shades of scarlet, the pattern saturated with this sanguine spectra, like a beermat for the Holy Grail. I ran for half an hour. And something vile came down to greet me – a sheep born not in Wales but in a vat of stomach acid.

Exhausted and delirious, I kneeled and waited for the half digested lamb to reach me. It bleated and pranced in a jerky rhythm, as if auditioning for an epileptic's nightmare. This spot was the midpoint between my wife and the origin of the vomit, and I judged it to be the happiest position I had ever attained, equidistant from two purgatories. Squinting between the haze of capsicum gas, I watched the gigantic morsel splash closer, a second helping of panic cooling on its scaphocephalic visage. It wobbled competently on two legs, and I wondered whether it was trying to imitate the shepherd who had sold it to the cook, or the gourmand who had forced it whole down a bourgeois gullet.

Yet the lamb turned out to be neither oviform nor macerated, but an old man wrapped in dirty woollens. He strongly resembled the thaumaturge who hovered over our street, though there was a weariness in his motions not negated by his obvious haste. He called to me in a voice deader than myrrh, each letter of his sentence pronounced with a different accent. I struggled to interpret his words. At least with the foreigners, tone had provided context, but there were no clues here: the meaning was unaided. It was like listening to a cedar.

"Turn back! We are evacuating the restaurant!"

"You speak English? That's a relief."

"I know every language in which mortals can argue, save Volapük and Euskara. Now hurry up and run down."

"Not before you tell me who you are."

"I am Cartaphilus, the Wandering Jew. But Satan is coming! His guts are empty. Do you want your head chomped?"

At the top of the stairs, the square of wallpaper was eclipsed by a hairy shape, immense and awkward. Yet it did not betray a purely bestial outline. It was more rococo than that. The impression it gave was one of filigreed evil, utmost depravity with a gilded shell, a Fabergé devil. I envisaged topaz horns, braided eyebrows, powdered cheeks, though details could not be confirmed at this range.

I preceded my new comrade on the descent, until we rejoined my wife at the altar. Ludicrously, we paused here, as if level ground was secure from the demented Prince of Darkness.

I made polite introductions. "This is Odette."

He offered a hand. "Call me Ahasuerus."

"You said your name was Cartaphilus!"

"So it is! And Giovanni Buttadeo. I have as many names as countries and favour none of them. Striking Christ on the route to the crucifixion was an unlikely beginning to the adventure holiday of the aeon! One tiny blow, the sort of thing anyone might try, and there I was, off on a tour of all the kingdoms of the world."

"Have you been to Peru?" inquired Odette.

"I was present when Pizarro ordered the murder of Atahualpa. He had mild breath for a conquistador, but his ears stank. Doubtless he is here now, with his ruffians, digging for gold in Cwmdonkin Park. Nonetheless, we must leave the church and hurl ourselves into the tumult. A respected eccentric, I am quite safe. Unfortunately, you don't share the necessary attributes to mollify the damned."

I choked. "Will you aid us? For payment?"

"What need have I for money?"

"I'll show you something you've never seen in all your centuries of travel. Consider it: a new sight!"

While Odette frowned at me in stupefaction, Cartaphilus stroked his forked beard and nodded. I had chanced on his one weakness. He was jaded to such an extent that his kidneys almost passed green stones. With only a brief glance back up the steps, he ushered us onto the street. Panting back to our home, I indicated the spectacle of horror, my gesture taking in the flames, screams, tears, stains, decay and blades. The environs of the Guildhall were strewn with skin and unravelled turbans. And vultures squabbled bloatedly, like gloves.

"Ah yes! Emperor Aurangazib. He often trampled his own citizens. He was the only sober man in Hindustan in the 17th Century. Totally insane, of course, but a snappy dresser."

I pointed at the stadium. "And there?"

"Another despot, but a different age. I conclude it is Commodus and one of his special circuses. He enjoyed fighting gladiators himself, but only after they had been drugged. However, he was an accurate archer. He is shooting giraffes, by the sound of it. First time real skill has been demonstrated at the Vetch for decades!"

Thus we were provided with a commentary on the most terrible rogues from times past. All were there – Fernando Álvarez de Toledo y Pimentel rode past us on a white stallion, with a string of tongues dangling from his pommel, which he poked out at us in sequence by jerking the cord, an insult only he laughed at. Cartaphilus lowered his voice. I learned that this was perhaps the most cruel man who had ever lived. When Pope Pius V excommunicated the entire population of the Netherlands in 1567, valiant Fernando was sent to carry out the sentence of death. He was diligent in his work, with pokers and shears.

Our street had changed for the worse. The submarine was burning and sinking in its pond of sick, while the bearded arms dealer counted a wad of roubles. Cartaphilus hailed him in Greek and the icy fellow held up a Mauser pistol for inspection. I doubted the value of bullets against the devil and shook my head. No sale.

"Basil Zaharoff, a most intriguing scoundrel. Started wars and sold weapons to both sides. One of the richest men who have ever lived. Satan was especially fond of him. And the mediaeval king is Stefan cel Mare of Moldavia. He will attend any party where there are sausages and gherkins on sticks. Clench your buttocks in his presence. You rarely know when he might slip a stake between them."

I made certain to follow this advice. I resolved to ransack laundry baskets, both Odette's and mine, for trousers, the moment we reached our house. On the telephone pole, the newsagent still writhed. Soon he would be lonely no longer. King Stefan was preparing a dog and milkman to keep him company. And now the Victorian gentleman approached and leered at my wife, suggestively flexing a saw.

"That is Francis J. Tumblety, quack doctor and pornographer, better known as Jack the Ripper. Does it surprise you he's American? Misogynist all his life. Worked the canal banks as a boy, selling dirty pictures to navigators.

Collected wombs even then."

"The flying chap above? Friend of yours?"

"Simon Magus. A rival to Christ and the original Beast 666. I think he had a dispute with Crowley over the title. Played that trick once too often. Fell to his doom in Rome."

Odette gripped my arm. "We'll have to go round the back. Don't care to push my way through that lot."

The gang of hoods had erected another fire on the pavement directly in front of our door. One of the figures removed his mask and mopped his sooty brow with a voluminous sleeve. He was a coarse monk, with squashed nose and uneven tonsure, not the impressive features one associates with a chief inquisitor, who should be tall, slim and dark, with silver teeth and platinum earrings. I smirked.

"Oh come on, he's gouty and decrepit."

Cartaphilus growled. "Tomás de Torquemada. He has no love for Jews. I prefer your wife's suggestion."

He shivered beneath his woollens, the first time he had shown fear. It was infectious. We detoured down an alleyway at the side of the house and climbed a wall into our garden. A solitary light revealed that Billy was still in his room, probably snoring through the apocalypse. The back door was ajar and we pushed into the kitchen. There was laughter and the whisper of a lute. I wiped my bare feet on the doormat. Vomit had forced itself under my ingrown toenails.

Jacob Degen sat with the bishop at the table. Having cut his musket in half to carry it down the stairs, he was busy gluing it together. The barrel gouged furrows in the ceiling, another source of disbursement. No resentment at our escape glittered in their eyes. Cartaphilus joked with them in German and Langue d'oc and they nodded encouragingly. Turning to me, he identified the bishop, also a troubadour, as Folquet de Marselha, the crooning butcher of Toulouse.

I was careful to give them both a wide berth, though I did offer to make a pot of tea. The Wandering Jew secured the back door and shook his head. "No time for that. Can't you hear it? He's reached the bottom step and is mincing out of St Jude's."

Far away, a hollow booming intensified.

"Hark, cobbles! His hooves are striking sparks."

Odette was more relaxed. "What are we supposed to do now? Just wait for the slob to diabolise elsewhere?"

"He won't leave. This city is ideal for him."

I pouted. "Suppose you tell us the whole story?"

"As you wish. Ever heard of Origen?"

"One of the Church Fathers," announced Odette. "Gelded himself with a bronze sickle to avoid temptation."

"Quite right. His knackers were preserved in an Armenian chapel for the edification of infertile pilgrims. But his real claim to fame is his heresy, which maintains that God and Satan will settle their differences and become reconciled. Despite his great importance to the early Church, he was reprimanded by orthodox historians, though Eusebius speaks highly of him. The point is, his doctrine never faded. A core of followers kept it going down through the generations. At last they seized the chance to restore harmony between the kings of Heaven and Hell by inviting them to a special meal in a celestial restaurant."

"You mean the *Stately Pleasure Dome*?"

"That's the one. Plenty of business deals are made in the convivial surroundings of a first class brasserie, so why not a theological truce? Anything can be sorted out over a curry, even the fate of the cosmos. It took centuries for the Origenists to save enough money, but coin by coin it accumulated. Because I owe allegiance to neither side, I was hired to wait on table. To the incalculable relief of my employers, God and Satan accepted their invitations. A date was set for the opening night and six trillion animals were slaughtered. As you know, Christian archetypes are carnivorous. They can't abide vegetables."

"Why was Swansea selected for the venture?"

"It's the only neutral location in the world.

Everywhere else is an enclave of Paradise or Perdition, encompassing greater or lesser aspects of one or the other. Venice, for instance, is divine, while Bucharest is infernal. This is true for every city in creation, except Swansea, which is an earthly analogue of Limbo. It's a void. That's why the locals were also invited to dinner. It would have been awkward to have God and Satan sitting in an empty restaurant."

"An astounding account. But it doesn't explain the vomit and damned souls flowing down the streets."

"Something went wrong. At first God and Satan chatted amiably. They had a great deal in common. The beer flowed, the plates came and went in rapid succession. Conversation grew more animated. Reconciliation seemed inevitable. Then the devil clutched his hirsute abdomen. He had terrible cramps and was barely able to lurch to a window before throwing up. This restaurant was in the sky, remember, so he disgorged the entire contents of his stomach over Swansea. Ordinary sinners boil in brimstone, but the worst are swallowed by Satan the moment they enter Hell. And now they're free again, to mess the byways!"

Odette curled a lock of auburn hair around a finger. "Did Satan eat too much or was the food poisoned?"

"Who would wish to keep good and evil at odds?"

"The Archbishop of Canterbury? To safeguard his job."

Cartaphilus was genuinely intrigued. "If true, it's worked. Now the devil has decided to trump God by refilling his empty guts with virtuous mortals. Instead of gathering up Judas, Zaharoff, Hitler, Stalin and the others, he's swallowing innocents!"

I exchanged glances with my wife. "What about us?"

"You'd better do something inhuman if you want to survive. He'll be checking every home in due course."

"Think of an abominable crime, Donald!"

Snapping my fingers, I hissed: "The imbecilic lodger!"

Whooping in counterpoint, we bounded up the stairs and crashed into Billy's bedroom. The student was not asleep but quaking under the quilt. My wife relied on her superior strength to drag him out, while I scooped his pet hamster from its cage on the dresser. He chuckled unconvincingly as Odette pinched him down the steps into the kitchen. Losing no time, I clutched the scissors and wielded them as a dagger, thrusting the closed blades upward into his throat, while my wife held him still in her arms. We fell back to monitor the result.

It was unexpected. As the utensil penetrated his brain, the central rivet split and the blades parted. One severed his left optic nerve, the other sliced his right. With a slight slurping sound, his eyes fell out, spinning on the carpet, unable to blink at their misfortune. We recoiled from the bulging globules of jelly.

More farce was to come. Billy remained erect, groping for his loose orbs like a blinded puppet. His hands flailed everywhere but the correct place. Finally he reached the salad bowl and felt within its confines. A gurgle of triumph erupted from his lips as he slotted the uneaten olives into his sockets. Now he turned to confront us, proudly folding his arms across his chest. But then he rubbed at his pitted vision with a knuckle and fled groaning down the hallway.

Cartaphilus draped his ugly arm over my immoral shoulders. "Let him bluster his way into the lounge at the front of the house. That is where your monstrous act might be best displayed to Satan when he passes for a check. He'll be here before long."

We trailed Billy and discovered him on his knees, spitting a pallid blend of blood and bile. The thunderous footsteps were much louder. With a sudden inspiration, Odette kicked him to the floor. She beckoned to me for the hamster. I threw it and she caught it with atrocious grace. Flat on his back, Billy pleaded for mercy, not for himself but his pet, as if trying to assure us that his Kalamáta peepers really could weep.

My wife is rarely responsive to guile. Squatting on his ribs, she began to tread the olives into oil with the feet of the hamster. Viscous juice trickled along his despicable cheeks. It was such a pastoral scene that I fancied myself marooned on an Aegean isle.

At the suggestion of the Wandering Jew, I urged her on with obscene imprecations. "Apply more pressure to the stale fresher!" The timing was perfect. While Billy's death rattle was still at the back of his throat, making its way forward to his teeth, an enormous eye appeared in the bay window. It was not slitted like a goat's but layered like a flower, dark petals within petals, inexpressibly delicate, peeling open in a morbidly fecund spring. For a harrowing minute it studied us, passing over Degen, Marselha and Cartaphilus, fixing its iridial corolliflorae on Odette and myself. The lodger twitched thrice.

A gargantuan hand pressed against the glass, a clenched fist with a raised thumb. Then Satan was off again, to harry our neighbours. Screams of terror, clash of teeth, a belch.

Cartaphilus patted my back. "Well done! You've passed the test. Now you are officially an evil couple."

"Indebted to you for giving us the chance."

"I didn't do it for nothing. You owe me a special sight, one I have never seen before. That was the deal."

Wasting no time, I opened my mouth and pulled back my lips. With an exclamation of disgust, the Wandering Jew squinted within. The cancerous gums on the right side of my face were in doomed contrast to the healthy examples on the left. Never had neglect been so impeccably asymmetrical, not in Egypt, Babylon, Persia, Byzantium, Sicily, Xanadu, or anywhere in the history of the aching world, not among deserts or forests, swamps or mountains, since the nailing of Jesus.

"I admit it! That's completely original!"

Degen and Marselha tangled arms and danced a saraband, to celebrate my conversion to the accursed side.

The bishop was too ungainly for the complex rhythm and fell against his companion. Degen's gun, held in both hands like a tightrope walker's staff, sparked into life. A purple flash and a cloud of smoke frightened us all. A stone bullet, rounded in the rapids of an Alpine stream, burst the window and streaked upward like a rewound meteor. It punctured Simon Magus, who plummeted to the ground.

Cartaphilus shrugged. "He's used to it already."

Choking on the fumes, I cleared out my lungs on Billy's corpse. The apocalypse was over. There was nothing more to do. Odette held me around the waist. "Up the wooden hill, chaps."

Because I had endured the adventure nude, I dressed for bed, luxuriating in the weight of corduroy on my thighs. Odette dribbled peacefully by my side, slipping further beneath the quilt, only her fiery hair visible on the pillow, as if I shared my sleep with a crucified anemone. Despite my exhaustion, sundry distractions conspired to keep me awake. Embers still smouldered in the street, casting a throbbing glow through the curtains. Then there were new financial worries: two smashed windows and a damaged ceiling. Plus spiritual trauma. Few outsiders would ever credit what had happened to Swansea on this melodramatic night. The landscape has always looked like a rehearsal for Ragnarok.

Our three guests were supposed to be sharing dead Billy's mattress, but the Wandering Jew, true to name, was pacing the creaking floorboards of the landing. It felt different being evil. My muscles were more alive than before. A wild urge to wear a cape and brandish a swordstick nearly overwhelmed me. So too my stubble was hurrying out into a pointed beard. At last I could bear it no longer and jumped up, to crouch at the jagged pane. Genuine ideas for killing the hours until dawn were lacking. Could I replace Degen's slashed balloon with one of Odette's dresses, inflated from the gas cooker? Or retune Marselha's lute to the mixolydian mode? I grumbled. These options were routine.

I was in the process of cursing all mankind when the second tempest arrived. This time the vomit which splashed the pavements and houses was golden and contained pale fluttering shapes, like winged maggots. Before I could summon Cartaphilus, he was by my side, gesturing at the arrivals with a nasal laugh. I felt betrayed.

"More denizens of Hell? An afterpuke?"

"No. George Wythe, American liberal. I spy the famed humanist, Juan de Valdés. That's William Tubman with his glasses, cigar and wit. Alexis Tocqueville, also. She's Isabella van Wagener, the abolitionist. Olaudah Equiano, a gentleman of similar persuasion. Henry Mayhew. Elihu Root. Is that Carl von Ossietzky over there?"

"I don't understand. What are you telling me?"

"It's God's turn to be ill. These were some of the nicest people in history. You're in profound trouble."

Odette was surfacing from her oblivion. "Do I hear footsteps softer than those of an emaciated ostrich?"

"God's coming to gorge the wicked..."

And he did. In the purest corner of his stomach, near the duodenum, where the acids foam like the mouths of rabid choirboys, there is a desk and a lamp. Because I promised Odette to keep myself busy, I have chosen to record the advent of the sickness. Here it is. Degen and Marselha are up to their tricks, below the liver. We rarely speak. I am no less happy here than in Swansea. When I finish writing, I intend to study the works of Origen. The doctrine of universal restoration appeals to me. Also the pre-existence of men, elsewhere, safe.

Yet my regrets are scarce. The only part of the experience I really want to forget is our attempt to justify Billy's murder. Odette told God that the student deserved to die, because when he broke wind in the bath he leant over to bite the bubbles. Although God acknowledged the serious nature of the charge, he did not think it warranted execution. The query that burns my bowels is this: how did my wife know? She remains reticent on the subject, like a banquet which refuses to be regurgitated. But our futures are still bonded. With enzymes.

OMOPHAGIA

ANKLES

Her father was a matador and her mother entertained men while he was at work. The wife imagined her lovers were bulls and that they bellowed in rage at her flapping knickers. The steel blade of her husband slid into a bull at the exact instant she was impaled on a flesh sword, or so she liked to think. When he came home, there was a meal on the wooden table and her skirts were unruffled. He chewed bread, drank wine, offered her the ear as if it was a flower. She pickled it in sherry with the others on a high shelf. Behind the jars she hid the gifts of her paramours. He suspected her affairs but was too tired to argue. Sometimes he stood on a stool and reached for the chocolate or cheese. Marina blamed the mice aloud and him, Federico, in her prayers. But she loved him all the same and bore him a beautiful daughter.

They dwelled in the town of Espinama in Asturias, which is part of Spain purely in political terms; the culture and climate are different. From an early age the child was aware how independent her people really were. Sitting on her father's knee in front of the fire, picking at the sequins on his waistcoat, she listened to him rant at the injustices of the local aristocrats, who had been imported from the south. The greedy Cadiz clan, out of favour with King Philip in Madrid and transferred to the remotest province, had no patience with the peasantry. The chief of the line, Ugolino, was a cruel man, but cultured and witty. He raised a castle in the foothills of the Picos de Europa and might be seen on the highest balcony at night, reading a book or hurling a goat to its doom, plainly the actions of a magician.

Federico brushed the loose spangles from his lap and sighed. "They say he can turn iron into mercury, sherry into amontillado and men into guns. What do you think, Juanita?"

The daughter shrugged. "A worthless fool."

But the brutality of Ugolino Cadiz might not be doubted. They were soon treated to an example of his caprice. A foreign poet, Humberto von Gibbon, had been sent by the king to entertain all his nobles in strict order. He travelled with his wife and mistress, the latter always a day behind. Ugolino provided a bed and waited for the lyricist to compose a favourable ode. Humberto was not a vigorous talent and had attained his reputation more on account of tender fortune than raw ability. When six quills had been worn out, and a cistern of ink, he was ready to exhibit the result of his labours. He was invited to one of the regular parties thrown by the decadent Cadizites in a massive banqueting hall. Blinking through tiny spectacles at the deranged architecture and bizarre antics of his hosts, he recited his work.

Ugolino's smile was very wide, but just over his dripping nose was a frown which was like a lid for his lips. And Humberto appreciated for the first time the difference between a smile and a grin. Pages spilled to the floor, and the orgy which had progressed through the spectrum of obscenity around him while he spoke was abruptly stalled by this, as if the wind of the sheaves had cooled the unnatural, almost phosphorescent lusts. A silence defined by absent giggles filled the room, as a circle of metal converts a hole into a cannon. Despite the implausible amounts of sherry he had quaffed, Ugolino was steady as he rose to his feet and extended a finger at Humberto. Gathering strewn garments and appliances of delight or torment, usually the same device, the entire Cadiz family departed, leaving the guest alone.

What happened later that night is not abundantly clear. Giving his castle to Humberto was an ironic gesture on the part of Ugolino, and in truth the structure became the poet's prison, but it seems a needlessly expensive revenge on a harmless scribbler. Thumbscrew and strappado are reserved for those who fool with words. Against the wishes of the King, the Cadiz clan relocated to Oviedo, many miles to the west of the Picos de Europa. Then notices started to appear pasted or nailed to doors all over Espinama and the other villages nestled in that range. Ugolino was demanding a total evacuation of every mountain settlement. The mayor of Poncebos wrote a letter of protest to King Philip but the messenger who carried it was eaten by a bear. A witness saw Ugolino hurry through the forest with the animal on a leash.

Because of his stature as a sorcerer, many citizens left without a single debate on the issue. They packed enough olives and bread to last a month and set off for the provinces of Galicia or Navarra. But Marina and Federico were stubborn. They watched the trickle of neighbours turn into a flood and stood in the doorway shouting at them to stay. Juanita herself was appalled at this demonstration of fatality and despair, but she lacked words to harangue the refugees. Soon the Picos de Europa, so high they might be hammered flat into the biggest country in the world, would be empty, save for Humberto von Gibbon in his unwanted castle. It must not be allowed to pass like this without a fight! The proud people of Asturias had never bowed to despotism, however magical, keeping such precedents tethered to the future.

News arrived from Oviedo once a week, mostly unreliable gossip and speculation. Ugolino was breeding flying lizards in his dungeon; he was filling the caverns under the mountains with bags of air; he had turned the poet's wife into a blunderbuss. Marina talked in the streets to all who would listen. Her family were going nowhere. Federico sharpened his sword, found a breastplate which had belonged to an ancestor who sailed with Cortés and took a break from killing bulls. So his wife knew acute longing in her nether lips while her upper were fulfilled. Even Juanita made a toy knife to defend her property. It was not long before Ugolino heard about the rebels in his domain. Early one morning, Federico found a letter glued to his bedroom window. His wife read it for him while he tuned his nerves with iced coffee.

"Ugolino plans to detach the Picos de Europa and set the mountains down in the sea. The bags of air will keep the range afloat and it will be a drifting exile for Humberto."

"It is the year of our Lord, 1655, and such things no longer occur in the civilised world. What will we do without a serrated skyline? The enterprise is utterly abominable!"

"But this is Asturias, my dearest, and the King no longer cares to trouble his head with such matters. The glory of Spain is tarnished and the riches of the Indies are threatened by the buccaneers. There are so many of them: Bras de Fer and Edward Mansveldt and Pierre le Grand. Men who kill soldiers as casually as you slay bulls. A few are handsome and bold enough to love greedy women."

"What else does the wicked tyrant say?"

"That you are invited to his secret arena in Oviedo to demonstrate your fighting talents. Defeat his champion bull and he will reverse his order and free Humberto. He will also grant us a pension. Otherwise, we must be expelled with the others."

Federico pondered this proposal. He was in his prime as a matador, cool and quick in the dance of dust and death, a blur of colour, deadly and familiar with the raging bovine character. He did not believe for a moment that an outsider such as Ugolino could nurture an animal to best him. There would be no picadors; the note specified that. He was on his own. But duty as well as inner confidence prompted him to accept, for a man should never allow a mountain range to be pushed out to sea without trying to hold it back, rooted to the continent. He stepped outside and practised his strokes on a carpet hanging from a tree. His wife dreamed of the green islands of the Caribbean, stirring a pot of broth as if it was a chest of doubloons. It was the first time Juanita had heard about the privateers who roved the Main.

She followed her father and saw he had slaughtered the rug and was resting on his heels. His blade sparkled in the dappled shade under the leaves. As she approached him, her way was barred by a giant man with a bald head and three capes. He had come silently from nowhere. Breathing heavily, viscous sweat pouring from his peeling brow, he leaned forward until his mouth was close to the ear of Federico. But although he tried to whisper, his abrasive voice was quite audible. His presence was both startling and unconvincing, like a mixture of rare but sour wines. Then she noticed a machine on the roof of the house, a contraption with thin wings turning slowly about a middle point. Had he arrived from the sky? It was possible. Her mother once told her about a man who flew onto her from a wardrobe. Now she listened.

"Greetings, Señor. My name is Xelucha Dowson Laocoön and I hope to become the most notorious rascal in recorded history. I am collecting a clique of villains from all over time and space to assist me. There are vacancies for trespassers and squatters. If you would care to sign this contract, you may enlist at once."

"I am a good man, not a criminal, and one sick of grandiose plots. Depart for Oviedo and open the jails, or better still knock on the door of the jailers, the Cadiz family."

"With respect, that is inappropriate. Ugolino is the law and those who oppose him are the offenders. There is no justice above reality and no morality beyond a strong will."

"Why should I leave with you when I have the opportunity to rescue this whole landscape? No, I will slay his pet bull and be a hero to all my relatives and even to my wife."

Jutting his chin at a proud angle, Federico stood and stalked back into the house. The bald man, or ghoul, examined his fingernails, grime from future ages turning them into a handy representation of the phases of the moon. He yawned theatrically, rubbed an elbow, flicked his capes so they undulated up his back and cooled his spine. But his insouciance was a fraud and he could maintain it only until the matador slammed the door behind him. Then he crumbled.

"Nobody ever wants to comply!" he wailed.

Juanita walked close and tugged at the hem of the stranger's outer cape. He turned and looked down at her, his snarl of annoyance replaced by a grimace of amusement. He bowed and stretched to pat her black hair with his clubbed fingers. Her dark brown eyes regarded him objectively. She saw an authentic monster with a hideous agenda, but one lacking the basic charisma which makes a proper devil. This was an opening for her, a chance for a spectacular career.

"I will join your cabal, if you make me your deputy. And our first campaign must be against Ugolino."

"Hu! What an excellent joke! Run along, little lady, and knit some pretty flowers into a saucepan. Rascality and roguery are tasks for men and boys. Girls turn into nurses."

"Prejudiced oaf! Have you not studied the world in your wanderings through the centuries? Plenty of women have excelled at crime. Mull the examples of Theodora and Antonina, who manipulated the Byzantine Empire with cunning so low that fish swam above it. Or Countess Báthori, clean as a hatchet in her pool of blood. And the enigmatic La Santa Roja, who still smuggles weapons to escaped slaves in America. We can surpass men in every endeavour. I heard about these. But I will be the best of all, for I am Juanita Evita Zanahoria."

The ghoul waved aside this petty objection. He reached out to rasp his thumb against her toy knife. His blood was pale and jumped from his skin like a pink flea. He groaned.

"You have injured me! The blade is real!"

"Call yourself a noxious sage? You are a weakling and liar. I have changed my mind about aiding you. And I am no longer astonished at your embarrassing lack of accomplices."

"Note this wink, child! You may be precocious but I am Laocoön! Of course the process of organising a transdimensional criminal fraternity is not easy. I know that. It will take much effort. Each time I visit a period in history, I must learn the language and customs. And my flying machine cannot be repaired in the past. It is a risk. No matter: I will not give up. Persuading a rascal to ally himself with me is like asking a donkey to climb a mountain. Stick and carrot must be applied together at the right locations; stick behind, carrot before. In my work, I also adopt this double trick. The body of my donkey is the total lifespan of the man I wish to employ. First I travel to his past to apply the stick and then to his future to swing the carrot. It was I who told the Cadiz family of your father's defiance."

"That was the stick? And you offer him an escape from the fight as a carrot? He believes he can win."

"Then he is a fool and he will die. That is another test. My tribe of rogues must not be tainted with rash individuals. If you were male I might consider returning for you when you reach maturity, but girls are not smart with swords, despite your speech. Now I must leave. I have an appointment some centuries hence."

He sprang away and scuttled up the walls of the stone house to the roof. He was agile enough for his age, but on the verge of stiffness, a ghoul rapidly nearing retirement. Juanita was still not fully impressed by the actual depth of his evil. She felt she could discern the bottom, that he was deluding himself with dreams which were vicious but unripe. It gave her moral faculty indigestion and she returned to the house. In the kitchen, the pulse of the machine made the concealed chocolate call out for attention, but Federico and Marina deliberately ignored it. The ceiling sagged, then it straightened. The intruder was lifting into the atmosphere like a dog which chases its tail too fast. No speck apparent up the chimney. He must have sailed into clouds of years and decades as thick as those of vapour and hail.

The following week, they set off for Oviedo on a sturdy horse, the matador walking and leading the animal by the bridle. Federico wore his brightest waistcoat, darkest beret, boots with brass heels, and because Ugolino was not an honourable man, kept a small flintlock strapped to a wrist. If the bull fought too hard, the barrel might be inserted into a nostril without attracting the attention of the spectators. The gunshot would sound just like a snort. This was insurance rather than cheating. Besides, a Cadizite audience would not expect legality, and the absence of picador and banderilleros did not favour the tip of his sword. Still he was confident, and with Marina looking, a new occurrence, he did not know why, he believed himself capable of any feat, even if charged by a dozen mad cows from Sierra Morena.

The Picos were depopulated but not quiet, for the distant cries of Humberto on his balcony echoed down the narrow valleys. All morning and afternoon they vibrated, with a short break for a siesta, and then back to howling through the evening, so that Federico and Marina and Juanita lost all sympathy for the trapped poet. Huddled around a fire in a wood outside Amieva, they were bathed in mist from the sea, fifteen miles to the north. It should have been just clammy, but in fact had a different significance for each family member. The father felt that his own blood was already trickling down his face; the mother smelled pearls, most in the ears of romantic, nude pirates; the daughter jumped as if the coils of fog were tapping her gently on the shoulder, trying to remind her of events which had not yet happened.

All the animals had left the mountains, so that owls and bears and wolves did not trouble her dreams, which meant she could not sleep. The fire dimmed and flickered out and her father's sword, stuck in the damp earth, seemed to wink away with it, for it refused to reflect the stars which poked through rents in the aerial vapours. This was a bad omen. A dull sound of surf cleansed her ears; the gasps of shipwrecked men. The deep was feasting, with rocks for teeth and foam for spit. When sunrise warmed her coffee jug and she rose to sip, she was more tired than when she had gone to bed, but the sounds of death had died, empty bubbles on the vocal tide of the newly awakened Humberto, and she laughed secretly to herself at the power of a mistress, in this case the ocean, but soon herself, to silence even phantoms.

Federico wasted little time before setting them off

again, and she experienced an urge to carefully note every tiny change of direction as they continued out of the Picos. They passed the very last caves in the range, all of which had been boarded up, and then down into the meadows and vineyards below Cangas de Onís, stealing grapes, chewing these eggs of sherry on hoof and sole. They greeted a plague of shrews in the town of Infiesto, final refugees from Ugolino's whim, and the matador fought against a river of teeth, swishing a cat as a cape. When the danger was over, the thin alleys came alive for the first time in weeks and barmen and whores offered him much gratitude in barrels and thighs. He refused but smoked a cigar at the base of a strawberry tree. Clean emotions are best in every prelude to any duel.

The ultimate stretch of the voyage was inappropriately pleasant, a cool fertile realm of fields and stone cottages and mineshafts brimming with blossoms. Then they entered Oviedo and attempted to ignore all the blue faces which peeped from high windows. The citizens were monstrous, famished, lean, corrupted by the gross presence of the Cadiz tribe. The horse was nervous, but Federico whistled a jaunty air, and his wife and daughter knew his melody was determined by a mouth which wanted to lick its own blood, by lips thirsty in the wrong way, and too cheerful about it, so they shivered as they skirted the remnants of the city wall, the Calle del Paraiso, pausing at the gate of the Palacio Arzobispal, which Ugolino had requisitioned and altered to his own peculiar tastes. A big building like a swollen sepulchre.

As they approached, the gate swung open, operated by hidden levers and weights. Guards were unnecessary, for no thief would dare to pilfer from here, unless they cared to be transmuted into a flintlock felon or matchlock miscreant, with their souls as a single charge, sparking away from existence on the reverse side of a firing squad, a perverted style of execution invented by Ugolino in his cups. The matador strolled into a courtyard and was met by a dwarf, Uranus Cadiz, who acted as a fabled servant to the rest of the family, rarely to be found when needed. This was a special occasion, so he bowed to the level of an imp and took the reins. Marina and Juanita dismounted and blinked at the garish carvings and tapestries which tickled the columns and lopsided balconies. With a low snarl, Uranus led them inside.

Federico slitted his eyes as he traversed the passage, for what he saw on both sides, through open doors, defied imagination and geometry. At one point he became separated from his wife and child, even from his stunted escort, and whirled in a panic. But there were voices ahead; he assumed they had taken a shortcut and hurried to catch up. A quick stab of light and he was back in the open, but not in the streets of Oviedo. Still enclosed by the walls of the Palacio, a miniature bullring basted in the noonday sun. The tiers were steep and pegged with rotting rails. This was the heart of the edifice and it pulsed with humid evil. Barely one inch of seating was manifest, for the exclusively Cadizite audience had squeezed so tightly onto the narrow rows that the arena appeared to be made wholly of ulcerated flesh.

For Juanita, this entrance of her father into the amphitheatre was a disappointment, and she felt shame for treating him with an impartial eye. He should have strutted into the centre of the bowl of sand, blade shining in the faces of his tormentors, sequins burning up the graceful curve of his back, but he shambled as if he knew not where he was. Back in the passage, Uranus had directed her and Marina through a side door, up a flight of steps, assuring them Federico was being prepared for the combat. They had emerged in the gradas, the zone of cheapest seating at the very top. Before scurrying off, the dwarf pointed at a box directly opposite them, a covered gallery where the most important Cadizites sat and nibbled sugared eyelashes. Dressed in the simplest clothes, Ugolino suddenly glanced up from his meal.

"He is winking at me," muttered Marina.

"Not with his eye," fumed Juanita.

"Yes, it is arrogant to wink with a dish. But he is not

as ugly as his name indicates. Do you agree?"

"Father will kill his ridiculous bull."

Chewing her lower lip, the daughter studied the other occupants of the gallery, trying to fix their faces in her memory. A few were guests from awkward climes or declining cultures. There was Bartleby, who gave her the impression of a bottle of sour wine swaddled in a placenta; his jaw was flexing in a mad grin but his eyes were uncertain and roved the crowd. Next to him sat Unfortunato, and behind him, Gaspar, Maurice and Isabel. From the armpit of Africa, now in the groin of misery, crouched Desmond, with a companion mirror, perhaps his wife or shadow; he tended to lurk in cupboards. Carmen, Tomasso, Brigida, Fizcko, Horace, Rosalie and Manuel. Higher up, Omensetter, gassy and lucky. Moving to the back, Portia and Wormy. And Planton, judged to be even crueller than Ugolino, with massive spectacles on a pole.

At the bottom, restrained by shackles, tongue held fast by an iron gag, so that Ugolino was able to lean over and pinch it easily with hot tongs at regular intervals, squirmed Hoopdriver, the only good Cadizite in the history of the universe. His life was sacred as a family member, but his genes were tormented to prevent them reappearing in the future. Such was the crew of fascinating brutes who had assembled to sample the bloodshed. The mob in the auditorium were mostly pale versions of these boxed elite and Juanita felt no fear while watching them, only disgust. Now the matador finally seemed to grasp his plight and stood with sword and cape raised. The crowd chuckled, but not at his elegance; they were watching Ugolino, who was making obscure, possibly obscene, gestures at Marina. Then the trumpets sounded.

"Federico Zanahoria versus Rutilicus Azelfafage!"

A very broad door in the side of the stadium slid open, disgorging Uranus, who hefted a spade and a bucket of coal. The spectators laughed again, but a curious disinterest gripped them; most were not looking at the dwarf, or what followed him out. Juanita frowned. Was this a circus show before the main event? No, for the thing that emerged had the head and shoulders of a bull. But it was silver and encrusted with bolts and rivets. It dragged a network of iron pipes on the ground, like a bundle of hissing entrails. This was no injury; it was a machine of some kind, with a fire in its belly and boiling water in its limbs. Then the metal horns swivelled and Ugolino fell back in his seat, helpless with mirth. The dwarf cracked the beast on the flank with his spade and its crystal eyes tumbled within their sockets.

For an instant it seemed it might turn on him and the tiny face of Uranus quivered, but the myopic beast caught sight of Federico and some intelligence that was not even bovine caused it to lower its giant head and paw the dust into a cloud. Federico dropped his sword and cape, for he knew he was doomed and that he should not be absurd as he died. Into his hand from his wrist fell the cheating pistol, but he had no time to aim it at Ugolino or any of the other major Cadizites. He would have to try for a ricochet. With a force and speed that so numbed the mind that nobody was astonished, the bull rushed him. He fired his flintlock at a point between its eyes. That was the last he knew. The automaton had no chance to fix him on a horn; it knocked him down in the wind of its run and trampled him to a purple pulp.

The bullet glinted in the air and whistled toward the gallery. The mob gasped in alarm. Even Ugolino quaked. Then Hoopdriver broke his gag and cried: "I have been murdered!"

Juanita saw her father caught by the trailing pipes and dragged in the wake of the beast, which was unable to stop and crashed through the far side of the stadium, with Uranus in desperate pursuit. The sound of smashing crockery rose above the concerned mumble of the crowd. Ugolino raised his arms for silence and announced Rutilicus as the victor, with nothing forfeit, despite the havoc it was now wreaking in the kitchens, so that they might all have to go hungry at the next orgy. Uranus would be baked instead. Then the bets were settled.

Juanita sighed as the man next to her passed a bundle of notes to his neighbour, who passed it on in turn, until the money had completed a full circuit of the auditorium and was back in the pocket of its original owner. All had lost; all had won. It was the same on every row.

She turned to express her irritation to her mother, because it was too early to absorb the larger enormity of Federico's death, and sorrow appropriate for that would have to be matured in the cask of her skull, but Marina had gone. The seat was empty. Then she noted Ugolino leaving his gallery through curtains at the back. Juanita picked her way out of the gradas, stumbling over feet, scrambling over knees. Other bets were still revolving. She reached the exit without being challenged. Now she was in a maze of corridors, but her sense of direction, evolved on that trip from Espinama, helped her to navigate toward a room directly under the gallery. She guessed this was Ugolino's private residence. The door was open and she crept inside. The chamber was stuffed with statues, so it was easy to run through unseen.

In the very centre, surrounded by ornaments of dubious function, a man and woman were dancing. Ugolino held Marina tightly about the waist and spun her so that her black hair erupted like an obsidian wave. Rage beyond swords came upon Juanita, but she realised that Ugolino had cast an enchantment upon her mother, possibly with his finger signals before the fight. But her steps were despicable. The accelerated saraband, for it was not a fast dance but a slow one speeded up, grew more passionate and Ugolino lowered his thick lips to those of his partner. Eyes closed in ecstasy, she accepted his tongue and stubble. Then her bodice seemed to swell of its own accord, so that the laces burst, one by one, with a joyous note, like an arpeggio on a scented guitar, and her breasts rose out to accept his bruising homage.

Juanita scowled and plotted revenge, but Ugolino would not succumb to a toy knife. She must be more devious. She slithered over to the bed which stood in a niche, reinforced springs awaiting the combined weight of master and mistress, and mulled her options. If she hid below, until his will was accomplished, might she leap up and exploit his exhaustion with a pillow pressed over his face? Unlikely. She peered under the bed and noticed a book, a huge tome with a crinkled cover. Reaching for it, she was astounded by the clammy touch of the warty leather. It was much too heavy to be a normal volume; even the poems of Humberto were not as ponderous as this work. Obviously a grimoire, a magical book. A cunning retribution, for the theft of his treasured manual of spells would hurt him in a style above the physical.

She clutched the tome to her chest and crept out, behind the array of statues, most of Cadizites, some lacking heads, and took a last peep at the dancers before departing. But her mother was not a traitor after all, for she had somehow fled Ugolino's embrace! She had vanished. What trick had she played to escape? The magician did not seem depressed. He danced with a musket instead. And the weapon had a trigger which smiled not unlike Marina. Ugolino was working the ramrod on it with long, slow strokes, but the smell of powder was absent. Very peculiar! Best not to linger. Her mother had probably rushed out of the Palacio, into Oviedo, and would head out of town back to the Picos. She would do likewise. At home they might scheme the downfall of the Cadiz tribe, petitioning the King or even the Papal ambassador.

Returning to the courtyard, she was bewildered that Marina had not taken the horse. It was still tethered to a column. There were cries, a boiling roar. Rutilicus and Uranus were coming! Having no desire to see Federico's broken corpse, Juanita untied the steed, mounted it and rode out of the nightmare. The book of magic slowed her down, but she was as quick as a cough, which is adequate. She kept searching for her mother, but the streets and surrounding country were deserted. Then she was out of the malign influence of Oviedo and galloping back to the forests. No appetite for meals or sleep; she continued until the horse collapsed in a froth and then rested next to it. Fitful dreams of bulls. And islands groaning with gold. The taste of rum and lime. Typhoons. And her father stroking her cheek with an anchor.

When the horse had recovered, she rode it at a kinder pace through the vineyards, fixing her gaze on the horizon for the highest mountains of her homeland. But the Picos did not appear. Then she reached the rim of a mysterious lake, at the very place where the foothills should have risen. So where was the range? And where was her mother? The slopes had evaporated like kisses on the neck of geography. Ugolino had stolen the heights and the waters of the sea had rushed in to replace them! He had cut an inlet in the back of Asturias, removed the spine and flushed the wound like a surgeon who sweats into a patient. She realised the shouts of the drowning sailors had come from lost ships sucked into the sudden vortex, and the mist was the breath of old prayer. Here were the bodies of those men, on this false beach.

She paddled in the surf and opened the volume of spells. To hurl a curse on Ugolino: true joy! But the pages were crammed with complicated diagrams, and words in a bizarre alphabet. It might take years of study to unravel these secrets. She would apply herself diligently, but first she needed to grow up, become strong, powerful, respected. A child with a grimoire is a prime target for the Inquisition. She would nurture her anger until it was taller than a tower of every living Cadizite stacked one atop another. From the middle of the tome, marking a chapter on the fabrication of steam automata, slid out a dagger with a single ruby for a hilt. An extravagant bookmark and contributor to the manual's weight. Sharp and unique and exactly what she required, for the revenge she had in mind was going to be expensive.

With savage strokes, she cut her hair over the waves. Her image in the foam turned from girl to boy. There was worthwhile work to be found abroad, in the Indies, guarding the treasure ships which supplied Spain with most of its income. Her excellent sense of direction had given her the notion of training as a navigator; the dagger would pay her college fees, and even allow her to take up tobacco, sherbet and some other bad habits. But not the brothel. She would have to enrol disguised as a man of slight build, for ladies were not allowed to work for the fleets. It was vital to forget her femininity, to exaggerate her swagger and curse like the son of a miner or the brother of a bishop. It was prudent also to hide the stolen book. She pushed it to the bottom of one of her deep saddlebags, under her dirty socks.

To Seville she travelled, having perfected a spit and sneer worthy of an exhausted trader who hopes to better himself. A far ride, but the King's bureaucrats had ordained that city as the centre of his maritime empire, despite its inconvenient location. She traversed the sweltering lands of León and Old Castile, living on her wits, snatching sherry and male attire from unprotected households at night, climbing through open windows with the stealth of a lizard. A cap obscuring her elegant brow, her lips chapped by the relentless sun, she was saluted as a boy by all the farmers she passed. Her strategy was working. Spain was at war with Portugal, but signs of strife out here were few; crops were untrampled. The forces of King Philip were so worthless they were even incapable of retreating in the right direction.

She sold the dagger to a jeweller in Madrid for a vast sum. He was an enemy of the Cadiz family, recognised the insignia on the pommel and bought it without asking a single awkward question. Then it was back to the road, heading south until the mountains of Andalucía shimmered over the dusty plains. These arid ranges were like skeletons of the Picos. A dejection came upon her, but Seville and its college banished it. Señor Alonzo, the ancient chancellor, accepted her application the moment she threw a purse of coins on the threshold, and so she became a student of navigation, an undergraduate, too short to reach her desk but with more determination than the sons of nobles, who idled in the classroom while awaiting their inheritances. The first lecture on the use of the octant befuddled her more than moonshine.

Of her time here, she cared to enjoy little. Thoughts of vengeance were always prodding her to work harder. But her memories of her father and mother, while not losing their significance, became muted. Her hate for Ugolino moved from her body to her brain; his destruction was now a mental affair and her blood no longer boiled, merely simmered. Peculiar how past experiences settle at the bottom of the mind! They never truly spill from the head but are adulterated with events of the present. The act of forgetting is akin to adding beer to wine: the adjusted life and drink are less palatable to the tongue, which has gone, but more to the gut, which is here. She started to understand how the nature of time is chemical and digestive. In her room she slept under charts for blankets and employed a globe as a cushion.

The college was a miniature state, with its own market gardens and well, and jaunts into Seville were superfluous. She rarely wandered the cloisters, but regularly visited the stables, where her horse grazed on pale hay and the occasional orange. The magic book was still in the bag below her socks; it was safe there, for she frequently changed the foul rags for grubbier ones. No sane nose might sniff this secret. Sometimes she opened the grimoire and struggled to read. One chapter promised the gift of eternal life. It was stamped with Ugolino's fingerprints, as if studied rigorously. It involved fixing certain weird words in the mind, but she had no idea how to pronounce them. Near the climax of her first term, she went down to the stable and received a nasty shock. She raced to the chancellor and berated him.

"An outrage! My mount has been stolen!"

Señor Alonzo shrugged. "The sailors creep into the campus and ride unguarded steeds back to the ships. Your beast is already on its way to the Indies. There are no appeals."

"I demand to be awarded my degree now."

A jangle of coins turned this order into a ceremony. She graduated with honours an hour later, in the chancellor's office, and was given a polished octant with a leather strap and a signed certificate. Then she ran to the docks and asked for employment with the first rough she met. He regarded her angrily but with a pinch of admiration. He too had been so young when he initially went to sea that he could sleep in a cannon, and new recruits brought him drinking money, even if only for a thimble of stale grog. He took her aboard a blue galleon, low in the water with the mass of guns, and introduced her to Captain Belial Pérez de Guzmán, who owned a single long eyebrow above a broken nose, and raised it like a rope at her supple bow. Impatiently, he nodded, and Juanita was shown her quarters, a room full of maps.

Her octant hardly left her eye, as if she was calculating a course around the whole world back to her childhood, which was receding on the quayside. She kept watch on deck for the caravel which had abducted her horse and tome of redress. Out in the wild ocean, her stomach disgorged her last student meal: cabbage soup and duck. The sail ahead was always faster, for her ship lumbered like a brass toad. Now it was weevils and seaweed for supper. Once past the Azores she thought she glimpsed large reptilian birds circling an unknown island made of mountains. A mirage? Surely, for this longitude had been searched for potential colonies for centuries without luck. Portugal had snatched the prime rocks here. The King of Spain had cast his imperial mesh further, to the Caribbean. But the net needed to be woven firmer.

Captain Guzmán summoned her to his cabin and fumbled with a goblet of amontillado. His fingers were so encrusted with rings he could raise them only when strictly necessary. Now he gestured wearily like a rusty clock and enticed her to his side.

"Well, boy, what do you think of me?"

"A worthy citizen of Spain, a dutiful master with a burning desire to protect his King's revenue from pirates and rovers. A commander with a huge heart and eyebrow for war."

"Come and sit on my knee. You are quite right about the importance of my mission. Without our treasure fleets, Spain would be penniless. I am thus under a great deal of physical and mental stress. You are young for a navigator, very young. How old? Thirteen? Ah, and my pretty cabin boy fell sick at the last minute."

Juanita fumed. "Remove your hand from there!"

"What is this? Are you a castrato? Wait, this is horrid sacrilege! Girls are not permitted on a working ship! You have polluted me! To the brig with you! Off, off! Pervert!"

Two burly sailors entered and pulled her below, securing her limbs in manacles. She was marooned in the dark, bilge and rats investigating her ankles and wrists. Now her plans were finished; she had lost energy and opportunity. Perhaps Ugolino had arranged this fate from the start! It was not beyond his wisdom. Her memories surfaced from where they had lurked. Separated from the present, so that the past became now, locked in each passing second, they dominated her identity. Federico killing a rug, kissing her brow, carrying her on his shoulders through the square of Espinama during a fiesta. Marina dancing in the kitchen, learning to play a guitar, describing her lovers as wardrobes with the key still in the lock. And both telling her stories of buccaneers, madmen who licked muskets and boiled boots in a pot.

Her navigational skills, mostly intuitive, were so acute that long confinement did not prevent her from sensing her position in the ocean. It was as if she felt the lines of longitude and latitude on her torso, like a cloak of seaweed. Her father had once run a magnet over her from head to heel. It was feasible this joke had aligned her to the planet's own magnetic field. Whales, she had heard, could perform this trick. It might be that Federico was not truly her begetter, that one of Marina's affairs had been cetacean in nature. Unlikely, but not more so than the fact of a steam bull. And she was aware that with every puff of wind in the galleon sails, she was closer to slavery, that Captain Guzmán would sell her to the mines as soon as they reached the coast of Darien. Hope was sunk both in deeps and shafts.

They were not more than ten leagues from Guanahani, and the mighty guns were being loaded to prepare for the task of guarding the merchant ships, when a single howl of terror vibrated through the decks, so that the timbers really did shiver and the empty hammocks swung like gallows in a storm. The cry was many voices joined as one, and Juanita listened to the stamp of feet on the boards above her head. Pirates! Now a clash of swords rose above the other sounds, so harsh that a stream of sparks gushed down the ladder from above, illuminating her prison. What if the attackers were French? Those were the worst buccaneers, offering brutal death with a hint of garlic, cooking men slowly, cutting out tongues or hearts or eyes. Francois l'Olonnais was one; he hated Spaniards so much he even tormented their prisoners.

Soon it was apparent that the entire crew had been hurled over the side and that the new owners of the galleon were searching it for booty or information. A wide figure descended into the brig, with a candle on the crown of a floppy hat. His hair fell in curls, as glossy as her own but longer; his moustache was white with salt. He was no Frenchman, for his voice was too low, an intoxicating rumble. He placed the tip of his cutlass to her throat and smirked.

"Are you another dog of King Philip?"

Juanita lied without a flicker of hesitation. "If so, why should I be shut in here? I am a prisoner."

"Not Spanish? So where are you from?"

She recalled the grimoire and babbled a few meaningless words from the first chapter. "That is an example of my language. I am a navigator from Atinauj, which is a realm far to the north but close to the south. Have you been there? It is grand."

"We always have need of skilled men who hate the Spanish. I should like to hire you as our helmsman."

Juanita wept openly, for this was a chance to

complete her revenge on Ugolino, but in a different way from the one originally envisaged. A rover preying on the countrymen who had betrayed her! By weakening King Philip, she would strengthen his anger, and then he would turn on those nearer to him, his enemies within Spain. As they jabbed at him, so must he prod and scratch at the Cadiz tribe. This itch would bleed by proxy, with royal fingers, diamond nails.

"Do not blubber, boy! Are you cousin to squonks?"

"Squonk? What sort of word is that?"

"Name of a creature. A weeper from Pennsylvania."

"And what is a Pennsylvania?"

"You may see, my lad, when we journey to North America, for I have an accomplice on the East Coast who barters hides for silver. A bad man but true, known as Billy Barnett."

He released her and introduced her to his crew. They were fearless and proud, for he was Henry Morgan, Welshman, with ambitions to be best buccaneer of any age. She shook hands with the barber, Hugo Olmeijer, a Flem, and the sailmaker, Ghassan Razzaz, from Tunis, and the cook, Phya Srinawk, from Madagascar, and the carpenter, Hjalmar Dagerman, a Swede. Then a fresh life began, exploits beyond her mother's dreams. The green surf turned ruby as they ploughed it with swords, and the bubbles which rose from the lips of drowning soldiers resembled cherries. She saw the wonders of the Indies. But she also noted things which reminded her too much of the bald ghoul with the flying machine; it was tough to specify what. And she forever debated the issue of whether to declare herself a girl and demand their infatuation.

True, a few lady buccaneers did exist who worked without disguise. There was the pirate queen, Charlotte Gallon, who was sweet and fierce, gentle and dangerous, kind and evil, all at the same time. She was very beautiful, with lustrous black hair, dark eyes and olive skin; when she smiled even sharks and lobsters fell in love. Sailors were desperate to be caught by her, just for the pleasure of walking her plank. Those who survived hoped to be captured again. She drank, gambled and danced more than any man, braving reef and cannon in her quest for a green diamond. No other colour suited her; she cast ordinary gems over the side. Black pearls she kept also, for they shone like her hair. She wore a necklace of seashells and never rose early in the morning, unless her cup of tea was made in exactly the right way.

But Juanita did not feel safe enough with Morgan to admit her true gender. So she remained a fellow and the crew began to judge her as the most masculine hand they had ever met, for she expressed no interest in soft silks or delicate food, but preferred woollen stockings and coarse bread. Her acting was almost too good. Yet she was always very civil to the girls they stole from enemy vessels. She might rip a bodice for the sake of tradition, but would then apologise and offer to repair it. And Morgan, who was obsessed with love, assumed his navigator was remaining true to a wife or mistress in some distant port, which really is a much less likely scenario than that of his ship being steered by a woman. He was Welsh and often confused the two meanings of romance, as if lip and sword can ever have common values.

Morgan's mentor had just died and he was keen to outwit the memory of the notorious Mansveldt by adventuring beyond all tavern anecdote. A raid on Puerto del Principe made his name as a thief of cattle, but not as a suitable title for a ballad. So he captured a hundred Spanish nuns from a convent and marched on Porto Bello, forcing his prisoners to run at the fort with ladders, and giggling as they were sliced to fragments by the carbines of their own side. Then his men were up the rungs, over the walls, hurling grenades and blasphemy at the defenders. In the wake of this conflict, Juanita contracted the rare tropical disease known as monkeybreath, a grotesque condition but useful for keeping Morgan at an even greater distance. Thus the secret of her identity was locked safer with every sigh of her sick lungs.

Porto Bello was good, but there ought to be more, and Morgan found it in Maracaibo. He sent a fire-ship into the harbour, crewed with logs dressed in caps, and when the Spanish galleons approached to arrest the impudent buccaneers, they found themselves capturing an explosion. This was fine, but not enough, and when the port was drunk dry, the Welshman stood on an empty cask and shouted out in the direction of Panama. Away they sailed to smash that city also, fairest of Spain's children. Songs were pouring from guitars now, and he, Morgan, wrote the words in deeds and the melodies in gems, but in the Cup of Gold he was vanquished by a woman. Juanita saw it happen; a marvel. His love was none other than La Santa Roja, a fable from her childhood which had not aged. Nor had she, and this was astoundingly strange.

An answer came in the feast in the ruin, when Morgan returned from his affair to kiss his favourite followers. Five were selected; barber, sailmaker, cook, carpenter, navigator. Yet it was not a kiss; rather it was a secret told to lips, a surer way of entrusting it than against an ear. La Santa Roja had gained the secret of immortality and given it to Morgan. Now he was passing it to his friends. One sentence of ineffable worth, for so long as it was remembered without flaw the body would not die. A mantra of gorgeous tone, simple but profound. Of his crew, these five alone were immune to death; all would see centuries wilt away like weeks. Morgan tapped his nose. His mistress stole it from a squonk, who took it from a man on an island, who had it from a magician. Repeat the chant once a day for eternal life.

His explanation was obscure, but she followed his instructions. It worked, but there were unforeseen consequences. The human mind is large but not bottomless; there are a finite number of memories it can carry. This number is enormous, inexhaustible in a normal lifespan, but for an immortal there comes a time when the brain is saturated with experience and each new event or notion pushes out something old. It is impossible to choose what is to be discarded; the process is automatic. Trivial or treasured memories are equally likely to be jettisoned. All are ballast cast out to keep an identity afloat in the present. When full, the mind starts to leak, to overflow from every point of its circumference. This process may not be regretted because the lost reminiscence has no value outside the skull. It is annulled.

Mortals can live with each other, even in misery, but the prospect of sharing forever is abhorrent. Morgan and his converts experienced an overwhelming urge to divide. Panama was the last adventure. They sailed for Jamaica, a fine place to say farewell. Juanita stood on the deck on a mound of salted meat; as it shrank in the sun, the men joked that she was feeding her ankles. But her view of the horizon was excellent. What was this thrashing toward them? A dozen horses! She shouted for Morgan, who raised his spyglass and lowered it again, but not before running it under his nose. The telescope had an odour: stars and coffee. The first steed crashed against the side of the ship, went under, drowned. With a carbine, the Welshman ended such suffering. Bridles surfaced in the red wake, and the rovers netted these.

Morgan said: "These are the Horse Latitudes. The Spanish transport animals between the islands, but if their ships are trapped in a period of calm, by weed or eels, they push them overboard to save the price of feeding them. It is a sad ritual."

"I offer half my booty for that saddlebag."

She did not dare open her prize until they reached Port Royal. The book was still inside, undamaged for its ordeal. The warty covering had repelled all water like wax. Jamaica saw little of her money spent. Off she went, on a passenger vessel bound for Italy. She decided to keep in touch with the sailmaker and cook, whose creased, steamy friendship she quite enjoyed. Naples held her for a week, then north to Venice. But it was too noisy; she wished to ponder on magic. Into Carniola and a quiet village called Smarje. Here she read and began to understand the obtuse shapes and language of the grimoire. And time passed quickly, for years were expendable and there was no need to hold them back. The deeper she delved into the text, the more she felt that a puzzle was being solved, that a riddle was being undressed.

Already she was several lifetimes beyond her ordained span. It was a cool morning when her mind finally reached the point of saturation. A delicious breeze played the leaves outside the window of her house, and she suddenly realised she had forgotten the name of these trees. Smarje was sheltered by them from the dust which whipped from the factories of Maribor to the north and the vapours from the mercury pits of Idrija to the west. But what were they? Cedars? No, it was hopeless; the name had gone. Her brain was full and any new experience, such as noting the way the leaves rustled, pushed out something already there to make room, in this case the type of tree the foliage belonged to. Forgetting facts no longer meant diluting them, but utterly losing them, so they might only be relearned with still more loss.

Information now used her skull as an alley rather than a jug. Care must be taken with fresh events, to prevent the mundane present shoving precious nuggets of the past into the void. Routine was thus desirable, a quiet existence until her studies were complete. She wrote to her two best friends, sailmaker and cook, and was about to sign her name on the letters when she realised she did not know what it was. The very act of dipping quill in ink, and enjoying the rainbow caught in the droplet on the tip of the nib, had ejected the word of her identity! A fundamental truth had spilled and smashed. But her confidence was intact; she chose a nickname, recalling what the men had whispered about the meat and her feet. Omophagia Ankles she became, and it seemed right, familiar, older than Jamaica, an echo in her ears.

When her friends wrote back, she hoped to read her genuine name on the envelopes as part of her address; it would be returned. But she was frustrated. They had also forgotten it, employing her nickname instead. Worse: they signed themselves with pseudonyms also, having undergone an identical amnesia, and the surprise of this revelation knocked the same knowledge out of her. So the sailmaker was Thanatology Spleen, the cook Muscovado Lashes, words taken from personal episodes, to her as well as to them. She had no idea what they had been called afloat. Only Morgan, the stubborn soak, refused to evacuate from her consciousness. Her mind liked this not, nor that immortality should be responsible for the doom of facts, and she almost deluded herself that the traumas of Panama had charred away their names for them.

The others presumed this. 'Tology was fond of her, but also of the carpenter, who was now Lanolin Brows. And 'Vado liked her friendship in tandem with that of the barber, reformed as Spermaceti Whiskers. As for 'Lin, he thought mostly of 'Ceti and 'Tology, whereas 'Ceti matched his affection for 'Lin with heartiness for 'Vado. Each of the five immortal crewmen knew two others, a different pair. This was interesting. Wheels span in her mind. She forgot the taste of parsley, the sparkle of wine, the smell of telescopes. Slow, slow! There was a profound significance, a complex pattern, to this arrangement. Work it out rigorously. Able to flirt with geometrical shapes until they confessed their sines, she saw an emotional polygon strung above lands. It had firmed for centuries as the love of its angles grew stale.

It was high summer in the modern age and she had finally completed her book. She slammed it and stretched. Then excited cries from outside prompted her to investigate. The streets of Smarje were thronged with a mob of children and adults even younger. A travelling fair was in town, bright wagons and stalls gathered in a circle in the square. Fat men in gaudy costumes were selling balloons, offering prizes for games, frying pancakes in honey. She strolled the tents. On the edge of the carnival, where the crowd was thinnest, she encountered a carriage with a strange creature yoked to the axle. A sign announced: *Billy Barnett's Circus Of Cruelty!* And

448

she gasped, for the horns of the beast swivelled and a low moan issued from a metal throat, summoning a man from behind a flap who dryly listened to her exclamation.

"Rutilicus Azelfafage! A load of bull."

"It is a machine, my good fellow, which rose out of the sea on the coast of Maryland. I was strolling on the shore when it came out, rusty and damaged, as if it had walked the bed of the Atlantic from Europe to America! The skeleton of a dwarf was transfixed on the horns. I cleaned it up and employed it for a mule."

"And you, I assume, are Billy Barnett?"

"None other. Come inside and view the show. I have hired thespians to adopt the roles of famous rascals from the past. Yes, walk this way! The light is dim, but your eyes will quickly adjust. Mind the step! The man who stands before you is Caligula, drunk on gore. And this is Nero, fiddling with himself while rum burns; in tune, ham! Shrink from Attila the Hun, stifled in ambition and fur, both diseased! This recess houses corrupt officials and sadistic slavers. Behold Señor Alonzo and Captain Guzmán! And here is Oswald, the winking troubadour, a vampire who sucks notes not necks. Who else? Ah yes, the Wilson Twins, from a Hyperborean glacier: Snoo, Brian and William."

"Twins? But there are three of them!"

Billy shuddered. "That is precisely what makes them so wicked. Let us hurry past to another display."

"The smell of gunpowder and ship is extreme."

"You are now in the section which contains the buccaneers. Look at Black Grippo and Roche Braziliano arguing over dice! Here are Alexander Exquemelin, Francois l'Olonnais and Bartolomeo Portugues. What is Coeur de Gris saying to Edward Mansveldt? Stylish limes and hats! Gape at the beauty of Charlotte Gallon, more lethal than a cutlass! These are cheap actors, unable to match the archetypes. Here is an adept: Henry Morgan, his high boots stained with grog."

She stood before the figure, who winked.

Laughter convulsed her. "Ah, such a perfect place to hide! To play oneself! Nobody may suspect that."

He bowed, while Billy rubbed his chin thoughtfully. It was her old master for sure, looking even more romantic than under Panama suns, but with a tinge of gloom in his dashing, eyes lowered, pocket bulging with air, not gold. So she spoke first.

"You should call me 'Phagia Ankles now."

"So I will. Do you know what it is to fall on poor times, my loyal navigator? I buried my treasure in a Welsh village, under a black stone bridge, planning to dig it up for my retirement. But I forgot the exact location of the cursed place! Penniless I wandered, until I met my fine accomplice, Mister Barnett, whose business was in shreds. There were no more hides to trade; squonks had become extinct. Together we invented a new profession, touring the world as a circus. The authorities searched for me everywhere but here, for my disguise was too natural to fail. As myself I am secure and do not have to pay for my crimes. We make enough money to survive, but it is hard."

Juanita grimaced. "You have forgotten things? Then both our brains are full and we will turn mortal."

"I do not comprehend you. Provided we repeat the mantra once a day there is nothing to fear. I have passed the gift to others since I last saw you. I kissed Billy here, for I was lonely. You may do the same now your monkeybreath has cleared up."

"A chapter in a grimoire provided the cure. Knickers stitched from banana skins killed the bacteria."

"Knickers? We were at sea too long, 'Phagia! What is this book you mention? Do you believe in magic?"

She took his hand. "I must show you."

As they walked back along the corridor to the outside, a figure in rags jumped up at them from a trapdoor and mumbled a cascade of flowery curses. Billy snatched its rotting collar in one giant hand, dealt it a tremendous blow on the chin with the other and bundled it down into the darkness from whence it came, sliding the bolt on the trap and scowling at the absurdity of the situation.

"A few of these thespians are regular brats. I purchased them at a discount from the Theatre de l'Orotund. There is too little room to use all of them at once, so I keep the most unconvincing ones in storage in the basement, just in case something happens to the proper exhibits. He was Humberto von Gibbon, a man who committed crimes against literature. He tried to grope my pistol once."

"I knew the real fool. The likeness is superb."

They walked on and emerged from the wagon, squinting in the Smarje noon. Billy sat on the steps and yawned as Morgan and Juanita sauntered back to her abode. He would wait here to greet more customers. His bull copied his yawn, and before she was out of earshot, he called: "You had a name for my beast. What was it?"

She clutched her head. "I do not remember!"

Morgan followed her into her house and sat at the wide table while she stood at his shoulder and opened the grimoire before him. He pouted at the peculiar words and symbols.

"This is quite meaningless to me, 'Phagia!"

"Let me share my ideas with you. Numerous factors have been fusing in my mind these past three hundred years. Do you know a bald ghoul who is called Xelucha Dowson Laocoön?"

"Not unless I toasted him anonymously."

"That is unlikely. He is a sort of archfiend who roams space, time and fiction looking for recruits to his criminal society. It was almost certain he would eventually try to enlist a handful of buccaneers. That is what he did in Panama. We did not spy him because we were completely drunk on sherry after months of enforced sobriety. But the story begins elsewhere, in Asturias, when the chief of the Cadiz clan played a trick on a poet, drifting him out to sea on a floating island, prevented from rescue by ancient flying lizards."

"I shall listen better without my hat."

"This book is the most powerful grimoire of Ugolino Cadiz. And the middle chapter concerns the secret of immortality, the words which must be chanted daily to preserve the flesh from decay. The poet was trapped in a castle which contained a machine that spoke the mantra for him, so eternal life was part of his punishment. It was somehow passed from him to La Santa Roja in Pennsylvania, probably by an agency which wept, for it was moist with tears, not spit, when she offered it to you. Then you presented it to us. Immortals feel uncomfortable in close proximity, so when you stood in the middle of the crowd and dispensed drink, the five crewmen kissed by you moved to the edges of the gathering, as far apart from each other as they might be."

"Yes, I wondered why you all fell out."

"Five equally spaced nodes on the circumference of a circle, which is what we were at that moment, form the points of a pentagon. When the sherry lulled us to sleep, Laocoön arrived on the scene, scouting for a brace of buccaneers. He did not care to blunder into the mass of dozing men, in case he woke us, so he skirted the rim, choosing the five outer villains. The way he works is by using a symbolic stick and carrot. The stick always comes first. He slipped a coconut under the skull of 'Ceti Whiskers, so that the barber confused the nut with comfort. He pushed a puppet of himself in the leg of 'Tology Spleen, to lead the sailmaker's knee astray. He hired a group of Indians to butcher vegetables in front of 'Vado Lashes, the squeamish cook. Then he carved his triple initials on the teak helmet of 'Lin Brows."

"These sticks are rather obscure, lad."

"The intention is to niggle and itch, rather than to menace. Later in our lifetimes he planned to return with the carrot, which might be a cancellation of the stick. But our spans are no longer normal, and this has thrown his plans into chaos. Doubtless he is ranging the centuries, astounded at our persistence. But I believe we have finally reached the rear of our immortality and that he will soon appear. I have a personal reason for hoping to foil him, and if you will help me, I shall aid you in turn to recover your treasure.”

Morgan chuckled. “How can immortality have an end? You squander my time with logical contradictions.”

“Three centuries of experience is the limit of a human brain. Full to the brim of our heads, we must now leak memories. One of those leaks will eventually be the mantra which keeps us alive. We shall forget it, allowing death to claim its debt.”

“I see what you mean. This is ironic.”

“Laocoön knows we are almost at that stage. He has wandered to the future to witness our demise and now has come back a little to persuade us into his cabal. He will certainly offer us salvation, the removal of a batch of unwanted memories to increase space for the mantra. He might use surgery to cut out part of the brain which holds trivial nostalgia. That is probably what I would do.”

“A carrot indeed! But what was your stick?”

“That is where he made his biggest error. The first time he met me was not in Panama. When I was a child I applied to join his society and he struck me by turning me down. Thus in Panama, when he thought he was giving me a stick, by sabotaging my octant, he was really finishing the process and letting me bite the carrot. Does this make sense? The order of his tactics was reversed and drove me against his plans, not up with them. So I am immune to his intrigues. And when he comes soon to dangle another carrot, I shall refuse it because I have already eaten one. How this will ruin his subtle design!”

“But we are safe from forgetting that mantra, for it is written in your volume. It may be relearned.”

“True, but one day we shall also forget how to read. However, this is not important. I suspect Laocoön's visit to the five eternal crewmen will be the unusual event that pushes out their memories of the mantra. A bald ghoul with three capes is a new experience which takes up a vast amount of room in the brain. He will materialise and they will lose the secret. Then they will be aware that this act of forgetting reduces all their lifespans to one day, for the chant must be uttered each morning. At this point, Laocoön will announce his offer of surgery, or something similar, and we will accept through fear of death. The old rovers, your men, will be lost to themselves, hollow puppets of a noxious sage. I do not wish to let this happen, sir."

"I agree, 'Phagia. But what will you try?"

"By preceding Laocoön, I can kill the men before he has the chance to save them. None of us have met since 1671. My arrival will be almost as startling as the ghoul's. They will forget the chant, but there will be no offer of a reprieve. The following day, death will come for them, in the most convenient form. The hungry barber will starve, the needled sailmaker will be impaled, the cook will boil, the carpenter suffocate. And I too will succumb, but I do not know how. You will survive because you are a Welshman and too slow to learn new ideas. You will forget how to forget and thus exist forever!"

"I have hung many of my followers at sea, but this smells rank. To betray the vanquishers of Panama!"

"No, to redeem them. Alive in Laocoön's clutches, they would be as placid as zombies. Dead, as ghosts, we can still use them. A fresh crew for one last adventure! A band of phantoms sailing to Wales to look for your lost gold. Our best exploit!"

"This touches my heart, 'Phagia, but ghosts are notoriously fickle entities, like wisps of heated rum. How shall we organise them, control them? Such a party may fade away."

"Look at this chapter in the grimoire. It shows how to raise souls to obey your bidding. A particular symbol needs to be created, a shape. But it already exists. In Panama, the five immortals formed a pentagon. Something in the symmetry of that design has remained with us. Consider the towns we have chosen for our retirements. Here is a list I drew up. When these figures are applied to an atlas, they create a huge pentagon which stretches over many states."

"That is geometry, my boy, not magic."

"Each town is exactly 111 miles from the next one on the chart, at an angle of 72°. But consider the inner lines between the nodes. We have the emotional links critical to perform the spell in question. The five eternal crewmen kept in touch only with two others. Drawing these links and erasing the pentagon leaves us with a pentangle, a star of will and force, a symbol to raise spirits."

Morgan nodded and regarded her charts:

Spermaceti Whiskers	.....	Pirano	.....	45°31N 13°33E
Thanatology Spleen	.....	Wolkenstein	.....	46°33N 11°46E
Muscovado Lashes	.....	Trostberg	.....	48°02N 12°33E
Lanolin Brows	.....	Linopolis	.....	47°56N 15°02E
Omophagia Ankles	.....	Smarje	.....	46°15N 15°34E

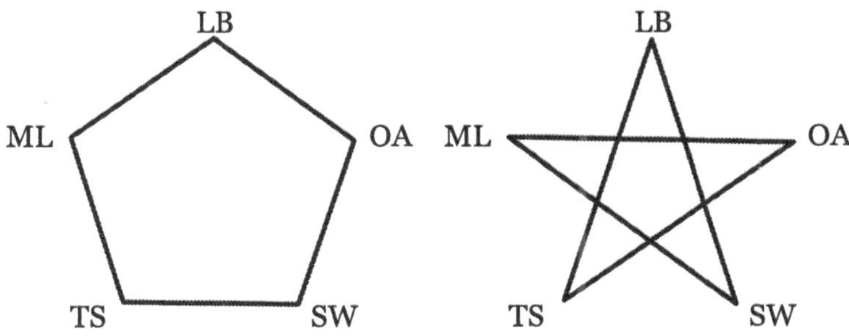

He fanned himself with his hat. "I have underrated you, 'Phagia. I thought you were merely a genius, but this is far beyond cleverness. So I salute the length of your nose."

"Take this book and travel to the centre of the pentangle. It is a point in the wild Kärnten mountains of Austria. The precise location is 46°53N 13°50E. Stand there and intone the spell. Then the five phantoms will rush from the five corners to meet you, arriving at the same time. We shall be all yours to command."

"Very good. Will I require anything else?"

"Human sacrifice. The more potent the individual, the better. That shall be left to your discretion."

"A ship! We need a ship to rove to Wales."

"The crew have already provided one. The finest vessel a buccaneer could want. 'Ceti's bones will be for the flag, and 'Tology's coffin as a sail, and 'Vado's pot for a hull, and 'Lin's armour for a figurehead, and also my octant as the rudder."

"You said your octant was sabotaged!"

"The main gamble we must take. Mayhap it will steer us not to your trove but elsewhere. A risk, sir!"

"Before we set sail, I wish to treat you all to a meal. As ghosts, your tastes will be insubstantial and cheap. There is a restaurant down in Sardinia, owned by a man called Giovanni and his cat. It caters just for pirates and serves a tasty spaghetti and goblin dish. The walls are coloured with turmeric and tears."

"I accept. But now I must be on my way to visit the crewmen. It is fortunate that I have an excuse to do so, for it would be impolite just to turn up unannounced. The surprise factor will still be large enough. 'Ceti wrote to 'Vado asking for a coconut. 'Tology wrote to 'Lin asking for a mirror. So 'Lin will visit 'Ceti and encounter 'Vado, passing the mirror to him. I must visit 'Vado and pick it up, and then transport it to 'Tology, the only two I desire to see. Both 'Ceti and 'Lin will have left their images in the mirror, for it is a camera, not a glass, and I can surprise those as effectively as the flesh men. They will die and I shall return here to do likewise."

"Give me the book and let me be off."

Morgan escorted her out of the house and back to the carnival. The wagon of Billy Barnett was surrounded by people stretching and sighing, but these were not customers. The actors were having a break for lunch. The novelty of the spectacle, with murderers and despots and pogromists standing in little groups chewing sandwiches or smoking cigarettes, was such that it spilled out a dozen older memories. She clutched the elbow of her master and licked her lips.

"I cannot recall the mantra!"

Morgan opened the grimoire and showed her the words. She relearned them and gasped with relief. They pushed through the mob, brushing past a motley gathering of minor scoundrels. Then she noted a figure sitting in the dust, picking at the dirty hems of his capes. Billy was berating him for poor acting, for an inadequate leer. She stepped near and began to grind her teeth. They gazed up.

"Xelucha Dowson Laocoön! The noxious sage!"

Billy groaned. "That is who he is supposed to be! But he is rather more balderdash than bald, and fool instead of ghoul. Look at the twist of his jaw. Hardly an evil smirk!"

She studied the thespian. For a brief moment his eyes sparked with fear and he raised his hand to wipe a drop of sweat from his cheek. She noticed the thumb, the faded scar.

With a shriek, she threw herself on him, pinning him to the ground and shouting to Morgan for assistance. He knelt by her side and rotated the man over and over, so that he became wrapped up tight in his capes, like the congealed filling of an antique pancake. Billy frowned, amazed at this development, wondering aloud whether even a bad actor should be punished quite so sternly as this.

"No, he is real! He truly is Laocoön!"

The ghoul thrashed and cursed, exhausting himself in his sartorial restraints. Finally he gave up and answered: "Yes, I am he. What better disguise to adopt than as myself?"

"Not you as well!" Morgan was disgruntled.

"Naturally, for I am at least as crafty as you. I

hastened to this point in time to discover how you planned to hinder me, and then I went back to preempt your scheme. In the Theatre de l'Orotund, I found a man who was a criminal against drama, and I persuaded him to join my cabal. He is my first and only recruit. I dressed him up as me and sent him to visit the immortal crewmen on the flying machine. So he has a headstart on you and will meet them first. They will become my zombies before you are able to raise them as ghosts!"

Morgan cried: "You will never be able to catch him, 'Phagia! Nor I attain the Kärnten peaks so fast."

"A shame. He would make a good sacrifice."

The ghoul blinked at her. "But there is no point in conducting the ceremony now. Your men will not die and their souls will be trapped for me in reduced minds. Eternal, dull rogues! Marionettes who may dance to my will. I must steal your glory."

A smooth voice announced: "I am able to overtake the other Laocoön and visit the crewmen before him!"

Morgan, Billy and the ghoul turned to stare at the speaker. It was the pirate queen, Charlotte Gallon, her hair tied in bunches, dark eyes glowing, more lovely than all the moonlight in a sea of wine, and not a drop or shimmer less intoxicating.

"That is a lie! You are just an actor!"

"No, I am also real. In fact, every rogue here is the genuine one. It certainly is the best way of avoiding the authorities. And all of us are immortal, albeit temporarily."

"How many people did you kiss, sir?"

Morgan blushed. "The Welsh get lonely, not from being on their own but without constant reassurance."

Charlotte added: "No man will beat a flying machine in a race, but the roads will fall in love with me, like all other things, and help me along. And I can imitate 'Phagia."

"Yes, it is odd how you resemble the navigator even though you are a ravishing female and he is not."

"I may not start without the right cup of tea."

Billy pointed at a tent closer to the hub of the town. "That stall specialises in perfect beverages."

Morgan lifted Laocoön onto his shoulder and grunted. "I shall take this ghoul and the grimoire to Austria, hack him open at the designated place and recite the incantation."

"Wait! I am not a sacrifice. I am a sage!"

But the buccaneer laughed as he strolled with his prize toward the horizon, and his captive was forced to chuckle also, for Morgan stuffed the magic book into his trousers and tickled him with his free hand. As they moved away, Laocoön's giggles became sobs, increasingly weaker and desperate, until they merged with the general hum of the planet, itself tickled by the solar wind. And now Charlotte had purchased her tea, had sipped it, and was hurrying off in a different direction, leaving Billy and the navigator joyously stupefied and eager for tranquillity. But it was not to be, for as they continued to pass through the assembled evil personalities, she stopped short at a couple who were gnawing chocolate and cheese, the man garbed in a waistcoat of pale sequins, the woman in skirts only recently straightened.

"Father! Mother! How can you be here?"

They blinked twice at her, shook their heads and returned to their snack. She was no longer familiar.

Billy explained: "These two come from a part of the exhibition you did not enter. They are Federico and Marina Zanahoria, a trespasser and an adulteress. Rather insignificant criminals really, but they caused a fair quota of pain to each other."

"No, they are my family! Watch close!"

She pulled off her hat and her hair tumbled out, having taken over three centuries to grow back to its childhood length. Then Federico and Marina clapped their hands and embraced her. "Yes, it is us. The horrid Ugolino remade us in a green jar."

"I have many doubts. I am too happy! You might be

actors! Prove to me you are real! What is my name?"

"It is Juanita, of course. Our daughter."

"Ah, relearning that fact has made me forget the mantra again! And Morgan has taken the book! It must be time for me to die. My destiny is here. But how will I expire? How?"

Suddenly there was a sound of stamping feet from within the wagon. Then the steam bull, now nameless, issued a terrible roar and pawed the dust into a cloud. The whole contraption shuddered. Billy was aghast as it rolled forward, drawn by the automaton. It accelerated and turned to bear down on them, dozens of faces peeping from tiny windows. They were all familiar and mutated. From a hatch at the rear, a stream of pistols and blunderbusses tumbled out, the triggers stiff and bored, as if each weapon had been married for years.

"The reserves have broken from storage! Damn those Cadizites! Weak performers every one. They always seemed disinterested when miming acts of torture, so I never used them."

Juanita was fixed to the spot, unable to move as the bull ploughed into her, knocking her down. The wagon rumbled on and the sweet but icy voice of Ugolino floated back to her. He was trying to blow kisses from the open doorway, but with the jolting motion his aim was inaccurate. A window at the top of the wagon sprang open and the head of Humberto von Gibbon emerged, his jowls crimson.

"Help! I am being abducted yet again!"

The last thing the navigator understood was that the iron entrails of the bull were missing and that the ground was hot and damp. Then she died. But the world did not fold into blackness. Her ghost slipped from her skeleton, rejoicing to be free, the marks of the restraining sinews still visible on her arms, but fading as she blew toward a meeting with Morgan, a reunion of her comrades on a barren mountain, over the corpse of a ghoul, and then away, trailing in their captain's wake, to collect the parts for a new ship, including her octant, and off to Wales to dig for gold, but not before a brief diversion to a restaurant in Sardinia, to a celebration where healths do not need to be drunk, but where a cat speaks and a cook grumbles in a kitchen of charcoal ovens at rogues who are bright blue with lewd tattoos.